TWINKLE

To Haward

many happy returns

David Silverman

DAVID SILVERMAN

TWINKLE

Copyright © 2009 David Silverman

The moral right of the author has been asserted.

Apart from any fair dealing for the purposes of research or private study, or criticism or review, as permitted under the Copyright, Designs and Patents Act 1988, this publication may only be reproduced, stored or transmitted, in any form or by any means, with the prior permission in writing of the publishers, or in the case of reprographic reproduction in accordance with the terms of licences issued by the Copyright Licensing Agency. Enquiries concerning reproduction outside those terms should be sent to the publishers.

Matador
9 De Montfort Mews
Leicester LE1 7FW, UK
Tel: (+44) 116 255 9311 / 9312
Email: books@troubador.co.uk
Web: www.troubador.co.uk/matador

ISBN 978 1848760 257

British Library Cataloguing in Publication Data.
A catalogue record for this book is available from the British Library.

Typeset in 11pt Stempel Garamond by Troubador Publishing Ltd, Leicester, UK
Printed in the UK by TJ International Ltd, Padstow, Cornwall

Matador is an imprint of Troubador Publishing Ltd

*To Carolyn,
for the apostrophes and a life.*

CHAPTER ONE

Andy's new beginning

It was one of those bleak Januarys that gets inside your coat and clings to the lining. The newspapers were claiming that the weather men were exercising their calculators in readiness for record snowfalls.

A hired car crept tentatively up the street leaving a snail's trail in the ground frost. It stopped in the middle of the road. There were few spaces available for parking and the driver surveyed each space considering his ability to manage manoeuvering the unfamiliar car into a small space. It was a long time since he had driven a right hand drive and he struggled to twist his unwilling muscles into the appropriate position to back into a space. He went further along the street searching for a bigger gap.

A tall man struggled out of the economy car door. Frosty air stung his bald pate and his kind intelligent face. Here was a man of whom you could ask directions.

He locked the car and walked gingerly back down the slope. Outside number 27 he looked up at the windows where the curtains were drawn. He checked the time on his wristwatch. Irritated, his tongue clicked and he opened the gate. As he was letting himself in the front door a woman appeared. A hard faced woman with dissipated eyes.

'Can I help you?' she asked.

'I'm Andy's father.'

Those intemperate eyes took him in for an instant and lost interest. 'I haven't seen him for days. Weeks,' she added without emphasis and closed the door.

With a shake of the head he climbed the stairs and let himself in the first floor flat, almost losing his footing again on the pile of mail. In the gloom, he peered at the floor and stepped carefully amongst the mess to avoid slipping. He found his way to the front of the building, and opened the living room curtains. It was an eye-catching room painted orange or terra cotta with brown upholstery and the heavy curtains were in squares filled with designs created by an extinct South American civilisation.

The bedroom was in total darkness and smelled of body odour and general neglect. He flicked the light switch but nothing happened. By the twilight from the hall he was able to negotiate his way to the window, separate the bedroom curtains and open a casement to let fresh air in.

On the bed, hidden beneath the duvet was an anonymous lump. 'Andrew! Are you awake?'

There was a reply but it was muffled by the bedclothes. Mr Avecore ripped the duvet from the bed, encountering a short resistance as the man in the bed clutched the last portion in his hand. A second yank freed it completely and revealed a tall thin man dressed in boxer shorts. He had a month's growth of red beard and a significant amount of body hair.

'What did you say?'

'Fuck off,' said Andrew and hid his head beneath his pillow.

Mr Avecore sat in the one uncluttered chair and considered the situation for a few seconds. Fighting against the outside gloom there were posters radiating sunshine into the room, voluptuous nudes stark against white walls.

The older man, an academic, had spent a lifetime at loggerheads with his fellow colleagues' opinions. He found that they were cocooned, contained and restricted by one thing or another. Religion, politics, the tendency to want to belong, some hidden sexual hang up. Sometimes, with age, and way too late they hatched out of this repressive shell.

His pedantic opinion was troubled by nudes in a bedroom. He saw it as an unnecessary prompt, a reminder of what bedrooms were for. He watched his wife getting ready for bed and he was inspired. Knew all that was possible. Nude paintings in bedchambers were the prerogative of bordellos and somehow tainted his ideas about the mores of lovemaking.

The man in the bed remained hidden under the pillow. The older man got up and left the room. He searched around the kitchen for a suitable receptacle and found a large casserole pot. He filled it with water and returned to where his son was laying. Once again he summoned his muscles into an unfamiliar position. Gauging what was required to throw the contents most effectively, he let fly.

He was pleased with the perfect arc of liquid that hovered momentarily above its target and soaked it from just below the knee with the largest volume of water splashing around the shoulders and neck.

There was a gasp of shock, 'You bastard.'

The two men glared at each other for a time until the older man went to fetch a towel and threw it at his prone son. 'Here you are, arsehole.'

He resumed his seat and waited. Sullenly, the younger man dried the damper patches, occasionally looking up. 'How much longer are you going to carry on like this?'

'You don't understand. I…'

'If you give me any kind of excuse, I'm fetching another jug of water.'

'Come off it, dad.'

'No come off it dads either. It's been five months. Grow up for fuck sake.'

'Make me a cup of coffee.'

'The electricity's been cut off. There's a pile of bills out there. Why don't you pay monthly?'

'We do. Out of Karen's account. It must be empty.'

Dry now, the younger man got off the bed and started scratching himself. 'Charming,' said his father. 'You stink as well as itch. You look like a scene from an Orwell novel.'

'I feel like Bleak House.'

'You're a self-indulgent arsehole. A selfish little shit. Your grandparents are worried sick. Is it too much trouble for you to contact them once in a while.'

'Lay off, will you.'

'No. This is the first time in your life that I've given you a lecture and you're going to listen. I've been far too lenient and look where it's got you.'

'I'm going to have a shower.'

'A shave wouldn't go amiss.'

* * *

3

He watched as his son ate his food, revelling in the austerity of their surroundings. Recalling long overlooked memories and atmospheres. This unctuous café with its oily fare, its lubrication aiding the noxious fry up in its descent down the gullet. It amazed him how we English could enjoy this horrible muck. He had eaten on the plane or he would have joined his son for breakfast.

Their fellow diners, like their ketchupped grub, were appropriately dashed and splattered with paint and plaster, reading their Suns and Daily Mirror. His parents took the Daily Mirror and he remembered when King George VI died its red heading was replaced with black and gold for the subsequent Coronation.

This is where he emanated from, basic, humble origins. His childhood had been stark, artless but education had rescued him, given him a life. He did not dwell on the rigours of the past, did not wear the hair shirt of holy poverty. Going without provided an underpinning and he did not forget his upbringing. He had a friend, who, slightly older, had been permanently tainted by the war and post war austerity.

A decrepit woman, old before her time was served by her indulgent daughter, a plump, oafish girl dressed in a short skirt and thigh length boots. No sooner were they comfortable when a solitary man of Mediterranean origin, smart, in a grey suit, began chatting her up.

'What would you prefer, the tirade or the sermon?' asked his father.

'Not today thank you,' Andy took another mouthful and concentrated on his plate, cutting up the next bite.

'Life's too short.'

'Platitudes, now is it.'

'Can't help the truth. The truth can be cliché.'

'You trying to make me throw up while I'm eating?'

It was time to pull back, so Avecore turned his attention to the conversation on the next table.

'I'm going to marry a Jewish bloke,' the plump girl explained. 'They're nice and I like dark men.'

Avecore loved these genial confirmations of his optimism. He loved the melting pot, loved the mix. It was a shame that society set up invisible boundaries.

Even Andrew had stopped eating, eavesdropping the response.

'I'm dark,' the grey suit pointed out.

'You're not Jewish though.'

This was something the smart man could not deny. Andrew smiled and nodded his approval of what was being said. Avecore was pleased that in this respect his son was a chip off the old block.

What was the root of this wallowing in self pity? It was certainly not his mother but there had been signs in the final years of his grandfather. Could genes jump a generation, no reason why not. The more he learned the more he understood that anything was possible.

'You have the opportunity to start again. This time you can get it right.'

'Nobody can replace Karen. She was one in a million.'

'Now who's doing platitudes,' said Avecore. 'That means there are a approximately 60 women out there.'

'30,' Andy corrected him. 'I bet they've been snapped up long ago. The good ones always are.'

'This time you can get it right. You know what to say. You know what they want to hear. You know how to make them happy.'

'If you're unpleasant to a woman, she's disappointed. If you're nice to her, she'll find a way to be disappointed. I always ask, where would you prefer to eat and get the, you choose. So, I choose and later I find out that's not what they wanted. Why bother?'

Avecore sat silently. The smart man in the grey suit settled his bill and wished the girl and her mother a nice day. Then he had second thoughts and gave her his telephone number in case she changed her mind.

'I notice you're not contradicting me.'

* * *

Andy felt a twinge of sympathy for the man in the grey suit. He had the balls to chat to the girl, more than he would dare and he had to leave empty handed. The fat girl should be grateful anyone takes an interest.

'What are you doing in London?'
'I came specially,' said his father. 'To get you out of bed.'
'Mum here?'
'No. You'll have to do your own washing and cleaning.'
'You mean, you're not going to help?'

They sat in the tidied kitchen, drinking coffee using boiled water cooked in a saucepan on the gas stove. The room was lit by candles and Mr Avecore watched while his son opened the mail. He had the bin open by his chair and most of the letters required the fleetest of glances before being torn and dispensed with.

Before beginning, Andrew had separated the franked envelopes and the more personal envelopes with stamps. It was the second on the pile of stamped letters that he read properly. Having finished he passed it across the table.

St Bryans Comprehensive School, Glebe Road, Wyford

Dear Andrew,

I only just heard of your sad loss and I wish to offer my sincere condolences.

I understand you have taken time off and I wish to offer you the chance of a fresh start for your return to work.

I am the headmistress of the above school and a post has come open for the Head of the English Department. I immediately thought of you.

If you are interested in the post, please contact me at the earliest opportunity.

Yours sincerely, Betsy March.

CHAPTER TWO

Bedrock

To outsiders Jinny's life was seated on bedrock.

What is that strange smell, she wondered? Smells of dirty boys. She must talk to the twins. There is no point in leaving it any longer, no matter what Angus says.

They both have their offers. What if one of them gets the three A's required and the other does not? He will be heartbroken, poor little mite. Best to have it out now. She is probably worrying over nothing, they should both get straight A's, the sweethearts but it is best to be prepared. Better to be safe than sorry. Alex applies himself so much more than James but James is more dogged. It was odd that she thought of Alex as the elder brother, there was no justification for it. There had been an emergency in the neighbouring cubicle and in the confusion the boys were not tagged properly. Alex, being the less self-assured, had become the spokesman for the two. If James were to succeed and Alex to fail, she knew he would not cope with the disappointment as well as his brother. Anyway she was going to go against Angus' advice and talk it through with them.

Mind you, they will do that sulky act of theirs and no good will come of it. Sometimes you would think they were eleven year olds. I do not know what we could have done to bring up such immature children.

Margery says that all children's defects are the fault of the parents but she would say that wouldn't she, not having children of her own. Poor Margery, she is such a sweetheart really.

She adjusted her body slightly to get more comfortable. What is that strange smell? For the life of her she could not place it.

Margery, poor soul, overlooked again and she so had her heart set on the job. After all, for her teaching was a vocation. If

only she were brighter. She was bright but not bright enough.
It says that life would signify
A thwarted purposing

The new head of the English department would be starting tomorrow. This is another of Betsy's proteges. I do not know how she has the temerity. It is so disloyal of her. When the school was in trouble we all rallied round and how has Margery been rewarded? An outsider brought in over her head. The plain truth about Betsy is that she is not as clever as she thinks she is.

She sighed.

So many of her fellow teachers are so sweet. Although, most of them can not see the wood for the trees. So many of them have an inflated view of their own abilities and would all prefer to be teaching at the Grammar. I do not think so. None of them are bright enough. She would have taught there herself if it had not been for the twins. It would not have been fair to them to have their mother in school. It would have been uncomfortable.

Talking of uncomfortable, she shifted again. It is nearly over. What is that strange odour?

Her friend, Marcia, refers to it as the exercise of three grunts. Once when he is done, once when he says goodnight and grumble and grunt. She has got such a dirty laugh has Marcia, she is such a sweetheart and everyone thinks she is so funny.

I cannot think what it means, 'grumble and grunt', could it be men in general? Angus grumbles, especially after work, his food is too hot, too cold, too dry, whatever. What does he expect if he comes home at all hours. Then he is on about the traffic, the bad drivers, especially the women drivers. He should take a look at himself occasionally. When I ask about his day all I get are grunts. That must be it! Grumble and grunt. He works that hard though, the darling. You should not be so harsh, Jinny Parish. We have both worked hard and made many sacrifices to get where Angus is today.

Phew, he is finishing. I am glad he put on a thing, save me clearing up that sticky mess. Only trouble is, it takes so much longer.

Grunt.

Gosh, he is going to suffocate me one of these days, 'Angus you're hurting me.'

'Sorry.'

She wriggled out from under him and watched as he wrapped the condom in a tissue and put it on the night table. 'Give that to me and I'll flush it down the loo.'

She had a pee, put on her night things and switched off the bathroom light. 'We must talk about the twins and their uni offers.'

Angus' steady breathing signalled that there would be no further discussion. Asleep already, how does he do it? She laid awake for hours before getting a wink. There was so much to think about, so many things to organise. She shuffled her chores for the following day into a sensible order, checked and re-checked that she had forgotten nothing. Only then did she allow herself to relax. Angus works so hard he is exhausted, poor darling. He will work himself into an early grave if he is not careful.

She said a short prayer. She wanted nothing for herself but asked for good health and well-being of her family. Finishing with a thank you for the privilege of being born English and for the safety and health of the Royal Family.

No outsider can know what goes on behind closed doors and it is human nature to colour the possibilities. When discussing the Parish's, acquaintances rarely got further than 'Jinny is so nice'. Was there any more depth to find? This question did not arise among the Rotarians wives, the church congregation, her fellow staff members at St Bryans or amongst her immediate family. Most, wittingly or unwittingly, took advantage of her niceness and she was glad to let it happen.

Jinny dreamed of her childhood holidays at Camber Sands, playing hide and seek amongst the dunes. She awoke happy and refreshed with sand between her toes. Angus' tennis club had all weather courts, sanded to maintain the pile and he returned with his trainers filled with the stuff, which then got into the carpet. She would tell Lena to give the bedroom a thorough hoovering.

She ran Angus' bath, gave him a prod which elicited that third grunt missing from the night before and went downstairs to get breakfast. Charlotte's picture, sitting on the occasional table, had toppled over. She made it upright, drew the curtains and gave Bobby a pat. He loped along behind her into the kitchen, she was so grateful he did not bark, she did so dislike barky dogs.

Charlotte was Jinny's elder sister by five years. Charlotte had all the brains, all the talent, all the looks and three children. Jinny had begged Angus for a third baby but he refused outright. He had been one of three and proclaimed that inevitably one of three gets overlooked. His psychology training had confirmed his personal experience and he remained adamant.

Charlotte had been her parents' favourite. Her mother had wanted a boy and Jinny was a disappointment. Jinny devoted her life to winning them over and this was how she developed her niceness. They had died two years before within thirteen weeks of each other. Now she would never succeed. To add insult to injury, her mother not cold in her grave, Charlotte deserted her husband and ran away to California. She did not go alone, she went with Doctor Phillips, notorious for fondling the breasts of his female patients. Her estranged husband Joe settled in Morocco and the children commuted.

Angus was wrong about three children and one missing out, her nephew and nieces were absolute sweethearts.

Jinny was marooned. Having lost her parents, her sister, her nieces and nephew, her feelings for her husband and sons intensified. This exaggerated love irritated the recipients so they banded together in a male union and kept her at arms' length. At mealtimes they took sides against her because she was the only woman. Criticising her dainty attitudes, laughing at her ill informed ideas about sport and generally mocking her lack of macho. This mockery provided a riposte and shield to her cloying.

Between her father and mother's deaths, Angus' career took off. He left the house at dawn and returned later and later in the evening. Now, he was barely involved in bringing up the boys and the boys needed their father. Without him they were getting out of control.

She took Angus his tea to drink in the bath. He did so like tea in the bath and a slice of wholemeal toast with marmalade, Scotland's finest. He was standing before the mirror, dressed and shaving, 'I've got an eight thirty, give the bath a rinse will you.'

'Have you changed your aftershave?'

'No,' he glanced at her quizzically. 'Why would I?'

'There was a funny smell on you last night.'

'Funny smell?' he asked. 'What funny smell?'

'Like unwashed little boys.'

'I know what that was,' he said. 'After tennis at lunchtime I put on Mitch Murray's shirt by mistake. We were wearing the same colour. You know how he smothers himself in Aqua Velva.'

'I brought you some tea and toast.'

'Thanks darling, you have it. Must rush. Bath, don't forget.'

As if she would.

At university, Jinny had her heart set on a doctor. She wheedled her way into the circles frequented by the medical faculty and despite warnings, dated Angus Parish. He had a bad reputation. He was a letch and got drunk far too often. Angus was failing and drinking softened the pain. One night he got blotto, relieved Jinny of her virginity and got her pregnant. This gave Angus the excuse he needed to save face, he switched from medicine to a psychology degree. Once again Jinny had failed her parents, causing them unnecessary humiliation.

Her parents did not come to the registry office nor to the dinner Angus' parents laid on at the 'Live and Let Live'. They were only reconciled when the twins were born. Mother had got the boys she had always wanted. Then Charlotte scooped her again with Truman. What a name to saddle a child with, Truman. Charlotte shrugged it off, it was all Joe's idea. Truman proved to be an easily lovable child and became his grandma's favourite. The wedding album rarely surfaced. It was stuck at the back of a drawer beneath the leather bound cutlery boxes inherited from her parents. In the photographs taken by Angus' brother Hamish, Jinny, naturally tall and slim, looked podgy and bloated. Even tubbier after the stodgy fodder at the 'Live and Let Live'. Haggis! Revolting muck! Angus' family were ex-pat Scots. This was why the golden retriever is called 'Bobby', after Greyfriars Bobby or Bobby Moore, she could never remember which. The story changed with the seasons. Jinny was sometimes wistful about the way things had turned out and Charlotte got the doctor.

CHAPTER THREE

Andy's first day

Andy Avecore was troubled by the conception of truth and perceived truth.

A quiet child, it took a long time for him to find his voice. When he gained the confidence to speak the flood gates opened. Small for his age, his red hair came complete with a fiery temper. Working himself into a frenzy, he fought the underdog's corner, stood up to bullies and championed the fat and weedy. His nose was bloodied and his eyes were blackened but he kept coming back for more.

As an adolescent, more cautious and less dented, he fretted for the miners, black emancipation, female equality, gay rights. When he entered the sixth form his father explained the non-sexual facts of life and he calmed down.

Now at thirty five, widowed, his blue eyes and freckled face were a closed book. He had no vision of his future and the shutters had come down on his past.

Andy was cavalier. A necessary gene had jumped ship and been omitted from his DNA. He had a problem with rules and was suspicious of authority. His arrogance believed that rules were a shield for the prosaic and incompetent to hide behind. He detested the institutionalised and surmounted obstacles of the system by flagrant acts of disrespect.

Karen's death had stunned him. Kicked his complacency into touch. For the first time he had come face to face with real life and he had taken to his bed. Sulked. Life had done the dirty on him and he had done nothing to deserve it. Why should he have all the lousy luck?

His father's intervention had helped. He had got out of bed but his cavalier attitude persisted. What did it matter? What did anything matter? His disregard had spilled over to include his own well being. Having little interest in his own welfare enabled him to see the self-protection of others with clarity. He got a wicked enjoyment teasing their fears. Now that he was back in the action, life was too short to waste cowering in a corner.

Children were what he really cared about. He loved children and wanted the best for the children in his care. Why harness them with blind rules and a robotic system? Life and the world it inhabited was full of promise and wonder but the powers that be were not interested in wide horizons.

His kind nature attracted his pupils but it was the troubled students with whom he made most headway. Experience had provided him with intuition. Just a few seconds conversation with a child could uncover a multitude of revelations. His antennae sensed progeny of single parents and divorcees, younger siblings and broken homes. Forewarned, he proceeded with care, his second guessing gave the child in question a bat squeak of promise that he might be a kindred spirit and that gave them confidence in him and his advice.

Astute, Betsy March saw Andrew as a maverick. He would be the catalyst she required to break the shackles of attitude with which her staff were constrained. Even if he did not manage that he would at least shake things up a little.

* * *

The gradient of the slip road from the motorway led up to an elevated roundabout. He took the exit signposted Wyford and the town appeared in the valley below. The town was demarked by a network of functional civil engineering and was unremarkable save for its relative safety in the event of nuclear attack.

Nuclear clouds were predicted to pass over the town. This was in keeping with the town's personality, when the character cloud floated over the town there was no fall out.

It had a football team that yoyo'd in and out of the premiership. It had a town centre that was impossible to distinguish from any other town centre and on Saturday nights it was overrun by foul-mouthed adolescents who thought a life would materialise from the neck of a lager bottle.

The town elders were prone to boast to anyone who would listen that the town was special. They claimed, quite correctly, that Wyford did not possess a red light district. The secular elements conceded this fact but had grave doubts of the townswomen's virtue. There was precedent as the fictional town of Plumber's Park was reputed to be a suburb of Wyford.

St Bryans, a fallen catholic school, had risen again after opening its doors to all creeds and colour. It was located in a suburb north of the town and was hemmed in by motorways travelling to all points of the compass. Activity in the playgrounds was accompanied by a cacophony of traffic and a fog of fumes which wafted into the senses.

Betsy March, the headmistress, was in her late forties, well-preserved and showed few signs of ageing. A pointed face required little make up. There was no visible flagging in her figure and she possessed a pair of shapely legs. In the Colindale common room, the men had fancied her, but the women disliked her unreservedly. Her twee personality irked the female staff but with legs and bum of such distinction men overlooked minor personality defects.

Andy should have been interviewed by various factions of the school. Students, governors and members of the English Department but the ambitious Betsy had cut corners to get him. The previous head of the English Department suffered a mild heart attack and had taken early retirement on medical advice. She used the pressing nature of finding a replacement to cut these corners.

She was smiling her winning smile, dressed in a dark blue suit that showed off her blonde hair. Both severe, but both beautifully cut.

Andy did not understand why he was being headhunted. Flattered to be considered he was scarcely bothered if he got the job or not, sure in his own mind that he was not suitable material to be reviving a failing school. Unaccountably, Betsy was dead set on him taking the post.

Betsy had left Colindale to take on the regeneration of St Bryans. In three years she had not only turned the school around but the GCSE results were creditably close to the prestigious Grammar where parents way beyond the catchments would sell their souls for a place for their children. Now the under privileged St Bryans was close on their heels. At his interview she had shown him the print outs, massaged his ego and claimed success with old values and discipline. An evaluator being kind to Andy, whose dress could best be described as careless, would class him as a free spirit.

Betsy was turning on the charm and he let her. Andy had an ego which enjoyed being massaged. If he was part of a scheme she was devising, so what? What was that to him? He had been at Colindale far too long, his all pervading laziness prevented him from changing. This was his chance to change with the minimum of effort.

He could not help seeking a reason for her keenness, 'Have results been slipping?'

'No,' she exclaimed, her smile vanished. 'That's not why you're here.' She came out from behind her desk and sat on a corner. He tried to sneak a look up her skirt but she was too practised at concealment.

Andy had known many men who turned charm on and off with the flick of a switch. He had learned not to trust charming men. Betsy was the only woman he had encountered with this ability. She was shrewd and it had got her where she wanted to be but he suspected a sub-text. Perhaps he should forget her manipulative tendencies and take her at her word.

'This school has too many cobwebs in corners that are too high to reach,' she put her hand on his leg. 'We need a breath of fresh air.'

'Me?' he thought, preoccupied with her hand. It had been a long time.

* * *

Here it was his first day and despite his supposed indifference, he was curiously nervous. Maybe he did give a shit. A perfect example of perceived truth. He stood at the common room window which commanded a view of the playgrounds, playing fields and swimming pool. Sainsbury, Tesco, Eddie Stobart and James Irlam hurtling back and forth. The window had been designed as a sentry post and a duty teacher spent break time surveying the view with a walkie talkie giving advance notice of trouble to those on duty below.

He had forgotten how that outspoken woman, Jinny Parish, looked. It had been a matter of weeks but the image in his head had faded. She did not have one of those standard pretty faces that adorn the covers of magazines. It was its singularity, its unique quirk that attracted him strongly. It was this quality that kept him returning for more. He needed to memorise her features and relished the fact that her special components eluded him. Each time he refreshed his memory it was like getting a fix.

There was a boy in the pool, doggedly gliding from end to end, his speed as steady as a metronome. Andy wondered what pleasure people got out of boring repetition. Probably from the ability to do something well. There were plenty of pleasurable pursuits which took relatively little effort to do well.

A hand tugged at his sleeve. He had met Margery Shaw knowing that he had been brought in over her head. She carried her disappointment well and he took an instant liking to her. She could have been Jinny's elder sister. Slim, bony with a crop of short hair so wiry and obstinate it had a life of his own. Her face fluctuated between confidence and girlish innocence. A youngest daughter, she had been responsible for her father until he died. Marriage had been out of the question and now it was too late. Teaching had given her a life and she loved it.

'We're all here,' she said.

He was not so sure about Marcia Dore. At their first meeting she had given him a sidelong look and complained, 'that all policemen are looking younger than ever these days.' A large soft woman, her podgy face purposely sardonic, she sat amongst generous folds of expensive silk with her Popeye arms folded across her chest mumbling asides. She reminded Andy of WC Fields' mother.

'Nice to see you again.'

'Nice seeing you too,' she replied and then sotto voce. 'Officer.'

The NQT, Barrie Fairbrother, a cloddish lad with a ruddy agricultural face and Farmer Giles suit, shook his hand with a weaker grip than the women. His voice croaked and crackled, 'Nice to meet ya,' he said with bizarre bonhomie. Andy had to resist the temptation to add the 'mate' for him.

Gillian Finn, the other NQT, boasted a mop of unlikely black hair beneath which was a startled pert face with a ring in its nose and eyebrow. They shared a courteous smile.

'Our part timer, Jinny, is running late,' Marcia explained, her voice rich with sarcasm. 'She's a mainstay of our team.'

'I must go,' said Margery. 'We'll meet properly later.' She smiled awkwardly and dashed off.

'Me too,' said Marcia and winked. 'Behind the bike sheds.' Andy decided he might be getting paranoid, this woman simply fancied herself as a comedienne. She might very well be related to WC Fields.

Preventing Barrie from leaving, he asked, 'Got a minute?' He pulled the lad into a quiet corner and sat him down. Before speaking he made sure nobody would overhear. The lad's face was stricken with horror. 'It's not my job to intimidate you. I'm only here to help. I've seen your results and you obviously know your job. What I want is for you to understand that and stop looking at me like I'm going to eat you. Deal?'

'Deal,' the lad gasped.

'If you have any problems, come to me first. Understood?'

Barrie nodded and raised what might be a smile. A smile that generally comes after the stomach rejects twelve pints and a curry.

He watched the cloddish lad lumber away and cross paths with Margery who was returning with a woman on her arm. Andy knew the woman already. Some mixed up fantasy about this woman had forced his decision to take the job. As they approached he flushed with guilt and his insides sank with futility.

* * *

Jinny looked at him with distaste and shook hands as though he had just emerged from the toilet without washing.

Who gives a shit, he thought, but he did give a shit.

There had been a handful of faces down the years. Susan, child model, who had taken against him because Adrian convinced her he had a dirty mind. Long black hair and the face of an angel that had adorned the cover of knitting patterns. She had ended up a spinster. Sandra, who he did not have the nerve to approach and waited for hours behind the curtains to watch for her to walk past the house with her fair hair tied up in tangles and her hips bulging in yellow shorts. She was unaware that he existed and ended up the same way as Susan. Carol who went out with all his friends but not him. Karen, who he had seen with a wimp at the bus station. Then again with his friend Martin in a nightclub and finally in the King & Queen. That face he had married.

Here was yet another face. He wanted to brush his lips across her neck and drink in the smell of her. There was little chance of that as he seemed to repel her. History, in Andy's life, appeared to repeat itself. He had taken the job for nothing.

Andy's teaching methods were simple. He used his unflagging energy to give a bravura performance. He had learned quickly what drew favour with children and how they would attempt to draw him out. It was not dissimilar to stand-up comedy. He had to learn the correct responses to hecklers and keep his audience entertained. A dash of football and handfuls of enthusiasm, just enough passion to be human and fun and careful not to be patronising. It came easy to him.

Betsy and he had agreed that his appointment should not disrupt the students taking GCSE's. The existing staff would continue these classes for this term and next year they could start afresh. Andy would take all the pastoral care off their hands and teach as many Year 7 to 10 classes as possible. Betsy had spent the Easter holidays revising the timetable.

Andy pushed open the door and was met by a sea of expectant faces belonging to 10D. D stood for Dore. Part of Betsy's approach was against streaming. If a child was struggling this should not be obvious to their fellow students. Children were transferred from class to class but only when disruption or conflict was occurring.

He put his case on the desk and stood in front of the class staring back at them. Classrooms at St Bryans were spartan. Unplastered walls painted mushroom with schoolwork blue tacked to all available space above desktop level. Andy had stopped seeing these collages for some years now and he sought amongst the sea of faces for the class butt. There were two or three candidates and he selected one.

'The girl with the spectacles and bunches,' he pointed and she pointed, at herself.

'Me?' she asked.

'What's your name?'

'Octavia, sir. Octavia Jewell.'

'Hello Octavia,' he smiled. Christ, parents could be cruel. Fancy calling this near-sighted child, Octavia. Not that many names suited the class juggins. 'Who taught you last term?'

'Mr Facey, sir.'

'Thank you. Who can tell me about your last homework? You in the red jumper.'

'We had to…'

'What's your name?'

'Sorry. Michael O'Sullivan,' said the boy scratching his temple nervously.

'OK Michael, you were saying.'

'We had to write a magazine article about somebody we admired.'

'In a 100 words or less,' a boy called out. Andy could see him out of the corner of his eye. A scowling child with poor eyes and potato skin.

'Who did you choose, Michael?'

'The Pope, sir.'

'The Pope? I'd be interested to read that. Who did you choose? The girl in the corner. What's your name?'

'Safia Begum, sir,' she whispered.

'Who is your hero, Safia?'

'It's a heroine, sir,' she smiled nervously.

'A heroine,' he smiled back. 'That put me in my place. Come on, Safia.'

'Victoria Beckham.'

'Right then, we'll go around the class and each of you call out your name and your choice of hero…or heroine,' he nodded towards Safia. 'Start here and go up and down the rows and not too fast.'

Andy concentrated on the names and faces trying to remember as many as possible. There was the usual sprinkling of footballers, pop stars, one for the queen and four had chosen the Pontiff. Two girls had chosen unlikely subjects and two boys had not done the homework at all, claiming they were off sick.

'What's your name again?'

A plain dumpy girl with her tie outside her jumper put her index finger on her chest.

'Yes, you.'

'Tracey, sir. Tracey Emberton.'

'Who did you write about, Tracey?'

'Robert Falcon Scott, sir.'

'Well done, Tracey. You get the prize for the most interesting choice. Why did you choose him?'

'I saw his statue, up London.'

'OK, Tracey would you read it out to the class.'

This suggestion brought a clamour of amusement, and Tracey blanched. Andy waved for quiet, 'Come on Tracey. You can do it.'

Accepting the applause, Tracey made her way uncertainly to the front of the class. She read her piece perfectly well while the class sat quietly.

There are strict rules about touching students about which Andy was not cavalier but instinctively he put his arm around her shoulder and made a friend for life. 'That's very good. I'm impressed. Thanks.' He gestured for her to go back to her seat and she sat glowing red for the remainder of the lesson. 'Anybody else heard of Robert Falcon Scott?'

The smattering of children put up their hands.

'Tracey, where did you do your research?'

'An encyclopaedia for some of it and Google.'

'Cheat,' said the potato boy whose name was John Watson.

'Hey, hey. Who's cheating? Tracey did her research and reworked the information into 100 words.'

Before he really got going the bell rang. That was how it normally was for him. Always leave them wanting more. He set a homework, the whole class were to do research and prepare an article on Robert Falcon Scott of no more than 50 words.

CHAPTER FOUR

Jinny Parish

By marrying Angus, Jinny had transferred from 'old money' the Pemberton Estate to 'new money', a 70's built double fronted carriage drive facing the Houndstooth Road on the Epsom Wood side.

Jinny was a proud woman and took great pains to keep the house in perfect order with everything in its proper place. The boys had become so unruly and destructive the dining room had to be kept locked and they were only allowed in the sitting room with supervision.

Angus was rarely home during the week. There was a television in the kitchen but the boys seldom watched it with her. Her daily diet of UK Drama, History and Discovery conflicted with their twin obsessions, sport and soap. She was wistful that this obsession with soap did not extend to the bathroom, and tide marks on necks were a habitual feature of dinner time discussion. The boys had inherited their grandfather's custom of bathing on Fridays.

Unlike Alex' and James' necks the house was spotless and white. Each room had a framed picture and each picture had been agonised over. They had to have a Constable in the dining room but which one? They had visited every furniture store in the town until Angus lost patience, and so they ordered a copy of The Hay Wain via the internet. The reproduction was of poor quality and the colours had melded. The Lowry in the lounge was an equally distressing exercise.

'You're the art lover,' Angus proclaimed.

She did not relish the responsibility. She had fallen in love with a study of cats in green and orange for the kitchen. It was the kitchen after all and it was her domain but she lost her nerve and bought a Turner. An orangey brown seascape that matched the birds eye maple.

Angus, a self-confessed Philistine, observed, 'The bloke who painted that had very poor eyesight.'

She was livid with him and toyed with taking it back to the shop. This period of flux ended, the painting blurred into the routine and Angus was forgiven.

They had bought the house from an elderly widow whose solace was the garden. She had visited the Ephussi and returned to Wyford with a landscape design. Around the patio she created a Spanish grotto, more grotty than grotto, blotched with a decade of failed pomegranate trees and another decade of failed orange trees. She had settled for a stringy syringa. In the furthermost corner was the Florentine garden. Two armless, bare-chested ladies cast in concrete, a patchy arbour and spouting seraphim fountain. The Provencal garden had been trampled under re-enactments of the final of the 1966 World Cup. Alex and James taking it in turns to be Geoff Hurst.

Angus and the boys never tired of watching re-runs of this momentous event. At the end of each showing the boys danced round the room with their arms aloft and Angus grew misty eyed. It all happened before Angus was born.

The Japanese garden was to the front of the house in the arc of the carriage drive. There was a miniature maple, a pond and a bench for meditation. The bench surrounded by perfectly hoed marble chippings and ophlopogon. The chippings were liberally spotted with cat shit and the pond empty. Originally, the pond was filled with koi carp, but not for long despite a warning sign to keep off in four languages. It might as well have been in double dutch for all the cats cared.

Jinny relaxed, soaking in the corner bath hoping to rid herself of another headache brought on by lack of sleep. The doctor had recommended decaffeinated coffee but she was still up half the night. It took her an age to fall asleep and having dropped off, she would wake up refreshed. Checking the time, she had been asleep for barely an hour. All night she lay counting off the church clock chimes. There was so much to think about.

When she became a published novelist and was invited onto Desert Island discs, her luxury would be a bath and an endless supply of hot water. Her book would be Pride and Prejudice. Her eight records? Jerusalem, God Save the Queen, Summer Holiday, any of the Beatles, and a Gilbert & Sullivan, probably something from Yeoman of the Guard. How many was that? She would choose something for the boys and something for Angus, probably Scotland the Brave.

With the boardroom battle and its accompanying backbiting that was current at the office, Angus needed to be brave. That awful American McAlinney having muscled his way in, without an invitation. Then there was the boys and their pending exams. Their wedding anniversary was just days away and nothing had been arranged. She had missed meeting Margery today to sort out the New York trip. McAlinney, *villain, viper, damn'd without redemption.*

Soothing as the fragrant water was, she was now indignant. Angus' fellow board members were not being loyal to him. *Dogs easily won to fawn on any man.* It was the same as poor Margery, they were trying to bring in someone over his head. It was not fair, after all that Angus had done for the company. She knew he might be considered too young for such a senior post. She had told him as much but Angus was adamant that American companies are not impressed by age, they promoted on results.

Still there was that awful McAlinney man, obnoxious little upstart. How could anybody fall for his unctuous charm, *villain, viper,* he was revolting. Will he be damned? Will justice be done? Angus is confident that he will win the vote but he is not as Machiavellian as this McAlinney. She had been uneasy about that man from the off. She had warned Angus about him. It's lucky she is there for him, Angus can be so innocent at times. He is too trusting. She has a much better nose for types like McAlinney.

Instantly, at their first meeting the man had been so Uriah Heap, his handshake left her coated with a sort of ectoplasm. Recollection of his cloying palms caused her to shudder violently. The water level close to the rim, torrents of soapy liquid spilled over the edge and swamped the floor

Wouldn't it be wonderful if Angus got the CEO hat for their anniversary. They could celebrate the two things together. Their 17th year although they claimed it was the 18th for appearances' sake. In those seventeen years Jinny had achieved total compliance. A twinge of panic for Angus' future caused overwhelming waves of fear to ripple through her, she had to sit up and clutch her knees until the spasm passed.

She closed her eyes and prayed for Angus' success taking care with the wording not to appear venal or to be seeking help for mercenary gain. Hard work and clean living deserved its just reward. She murmured 'Amen' out loud and realised she had forgot to include her children or the Royal Family in her entreaty. She closed her eyes again and was more diligent than usual on their behalf.

Old man Risdon would stick up for Angus. Where had this McAlinney come from? New York had not sent him and according to Angus the Americans did not like him very much. He never fails to bring his double first in economics into the conversation. Horrible man. If it comes to a vote from the shareholders Angus' was bound to get it if Americans always reward success. Profits had tripled since he became head of Marketing. Mind you Angus is only thiry eight and CEO is a very responsible position for a relatively young man.

Where should they go for their anniversary? Somewhere special to give the boys a treat. An experience they will not forget. The Copse, where else, Angus has an account there. It is a shame Wyford only has the one exclusive restaurant. The boys will be impressed and they will be the envy of all their schoolmates. I'll discuss that with Angus tonight. Just over a week to their anniversary and The Copse is booked for weeks ahead, he will have to use his influence to get a table.

Her bathwater had cooled, despite a top up of hot it did not soothe her disquiet. The water had lost its magic and her headache was as bad as ever.

* * *

CHAPTER FIVE

School meets Andy

A Government survey in the 80's reported that St Bryans was perfectly structured to succeed. The state and design of the building would provide the children with a suitable environment for self-respect. So many failing schools have unsatisfactory working circumstances. The grounds were impressive and included a swimming pool donated by an ex-pupil.

Nobody could explain why St Bryans failed. Plenty of fingers were pointed, plenty of staff were sacked, governors stood down but in truth everybody was bewildered. Betsy March was offered the post of headmistress and she would only accept the job if the school opened its doors beyond the catholic community.

She chopped more deadwood, interviewed, employed and put in bucket loads of boundless energy. In just three years she turned the school around. Their Ofsted report was exemplary and subsequently their GCSE results almost equalled the Boys' and Girls' Grammars. The publishing of the results had engendered public interest. A coterie of councillors, the local rag with a photographer and local MP Cochille Dore, a cousin of Marcia's husband, turned up on the school's doorstep. Dore and Betsy had their picture taken together while he was annoyingly patronising. Betsy March was incensed. It would not be for very much longer that she was going to accept being second string to the Grammars.

Jinny, Marcia and Margery had survived the first cull and made up 50% of the English Department. Young Barrie Fairbrother and Gillian Finn, the NQT's had slotted in well and Kenneth Facey had been brought in as Head of Department. Facey had not been Betsy's first choice, he was old school and had taken his foot off the pedal with just four years left before retirement but he would be suitable for the interim. Fortuitously when Facey had outlived his usefulness stress brought on a mild heart attack and he took the opportunity to take his pension. Now there was a new youthful and vigorous Head of Department.

On the first day of term Jinny was horribly late, Alex had left his homework behind and was halfway to school when he realised. The car park was virtually full when she arrived but thankfully she would not be the last. As she hurried up the stairs she met Margery on the way down, rushing to her first lesson. Physically, similar to herself, Margery had a sunny disposition and Jinny likened her to a cappuccino, frothy with sprinkles on her nose.

'Have you met him?' she asked. 'What's he like?'

Margery shrugged and turned back up the stairs. 'It's too soon to tell,' she admitted. 'He's trying hard to be liked.'

Avecore was standing on the far side of the room by the window. From a distance her first glimpse of him sparked a violent wave of irritation. What did he mean by dressing that way. All the effort the team had made and achieved by setting proper standards. What could be more important than the dress code, teachers should set a proper example.

On closer inspection she was nonplussed. Avecore was dressed in a linen suit and a collarless linen shirt both in neutral colours. Sunlight was streaming through the picture window filling his cropped hair with copper. The sleeves of his jacket were rolled to his elbows and his forearms were thickly coated with the same short lengths of copper wire. The pale skin on his arms and hands was flecked with splatter, he might have been creosoting the shed. At his throat was a cluster of darker red hair trimmed straight by a razor.

Esau was a hairy man.

She had avoided his face thus far and as she raised her eyes to his, she wanted to see approval. The blue eyes that met hers were watching her closely and meeting them full on, her heart sank. There was a smile of welcome, as his hand took her own but the eyes belied the smile.

'This is Jinny Parish,' Margery introduced. 'She's married, twin sons, husband Angus and is the nicest woman in Wyford, no contest.'

An odd disquiet, long in remission, seeped through her system. What had she done to offend?

As always, first day of term flew by in a hub of activity, before she could catch her breath the final bell rang.

Margery came to the door, 'We're going to the pub, want to come along?'

'I want to,' she said. 'But I can't. I've got to pick up the boys.'

'Shame.'

The streets were clogged with collecting parents. By the time she escaped St Bryans she was already ten minutes late. All the streets approaching the Boys' Grammar were equally congested. There were just two streets that allowed access to the school, a coach was hemmed in and was blocking all avenues. Two 4 x 4's were forced to back up and the blockage was cleared.

When Jinny got to their rendezvous point there was no sign of the boys. She rang their mobile.

'Where are you?'

'You were late,' said Alex. 'Tom's mum gave us a lift.'

'Why didn't you ring me?'

'I did,' said Alex. 'You must have been out of signal again.'

'Where are you going?'

'Can we go back to Tom's for a while?'

'Be home by six at the latest.'

'OK.'

'Don't use that expression.'

'Sorry.'

She checked her watch. She could have gone to the pub with the others but it was not worth it now. There was shopping needed, she might as well use the spare time to go into town.

Jinny had lived in Wyford all her life. Spring daffodils on grassy banks, burnished autumn leaves and summer walks along the towpath with kingfishers flashing. She loved the town in all its seasons and had a clear conception of its workings. Geographically it was split into discernible districts. Shopping centre, old money, new money, the proletariat and a multitude of industrial estates. It was a town that boasted everything anybody could wish for. All the major shop chains, a theatre, a leisure complex, a multiplex cinema and a football team. What else was there?

The World Cup and promotion were pending and the town was festooned with bunting. Rallying to the causes, cars, pubs and house windows were decorated with the cross of St George and the green and gold of Wyford Town. She felt a warm glow of belonging. Shop entrances were cluttered with flags for sale and she bought two of each in Woolworth's. It was about time the Parish's joined the fray.

Angus had tickets for two of England's World Cup matches and was obligated to take business people. It was a shame he could not take the boys.

The town was bathed in sunshine and shoppers sported cheerful grins and green and gold shirts and scarves. There was a jolly murmur that resonated with the bustle. In the blink of an eye, the sky darkened and rain pelted, scattering fans to cover.

Without an umbrella Jinny nipped inside the nearest doorway and found herself in a card section of WH Smith. It was soon to be their wedding anniversary and she searched for a card for Angus from her and another from the children. She needed to buy a present for her husband but like most men he was difficult. She went into the book section in search of inspiration. On the travel shelves there were just two books on Scotland, one with Edinburgh Castle on the cover.

The Parish's were Scottish and claimed that their ancestors fought alongside Robert the Bruce at Bannockburn. There was no way to check the provenance of these claims. The twins were ten years old when they made their pilgrimage to Stirling Castle to see the battleground where the family had beaten the English. She was most uncomfortable about the twins gloating over one of England's rare defeats but they were so much younger then. There was no doubt where their allegiances lay now.

Still, she was happy to boast of Angus' ancestry, even claimed it was where he acquired his tenacious spirit. What to buy for their anniversary? A book would be as lame as a sweater. Among the offers on cheap DVD's was a box set of James Bond and Angus was a big fan of Sean Connery. While she was paying she was helped by the World Cup display which included a new edition DVD of 1966 complete with interviews. That would be a nice present from the boys. The rain had proved providential, she had done well for a lost afternoon.

The clock on the till clicked onto five forty five. Where had the time gone? The boys would be home at six wanting their tea and Bobby will be growling for food. Panicking, she ran all the way to the car park, then she did not have enough change for the machine and had to go back downstairs. By the time she got on the road home it was five minutes to six.

CHAPTER SIX

Andy at home

As Andy trudged home up the hill, he vowed that he would never drink again. He had joined the staff members for an after work pint and stayed for three. No way could he drive home and he had used British Rail and the Underground. It had cost a ridiculous sum and on a warm day it was not comfortable travelling in a carriage without air conditioning. It had been a hot May and they were promised the best summer in three decades.

As he reached his gate he found his neighbours working in their front garden. Simon's studious face gave him a reticent smile and Majeshri, his heavily pregnant wife's eyes, screened behind horn-rimmed glasses, were surprised like a cornered deer.

He asked about the baby's progress and she was graceful and dignified about her discomfort. She was looking forward to the birth, anxious to get it over. She had the sweetest smile. He came away feeling revivified, feeling good about himself and good about life. These moments had been rare since Karen died.

Without Karen the flat was devoid of atmosphere. It had lost its magic. His father had warned him that the flat would provide a permanent reminder of his loss and that he would be better off moving on. He did not want to forget.

The light on the answer machine was not flashing. In the wake of Karen's funeral his friends had gathered round. Grateful as he was he was glad when the concern for his well-being petered out. Pete understood, thank heaven for Pete. Without Pete he would have surrendered. Dived deeper into the swirling pit of disappointment. In the few months since she died he had drained his allotted supply of self-pity.

He would sit at his desk for hours at a time, intending to mark homework but daydreaming the evening away instead.

There were photographs of Karen pinned to the wall and he enjoyed conjuring an existence for her in which he was merely a spectator.

Her serious face beneath immovable hair, wearing a pale sweater, navy skirt, perched on one leg like a bird. Hands with delicate girlish fingers. He had kissed those hands and could taste her palms in his mouth with the smell of vanilla soap she liked. Karen tasted like ice cream.

He watched her face hoping magic would bring a smile. How she put his parents at their ease with a joke and that smile. What gave it that matchless quality?

During their twelve years together at least one of their friends was in unrequited love with her. Mooning over her in secret as he was with that Parish woman. What a pathetic bunch we men are. Adam, not a pathetic sod but an arrogant sod, had asked her to sleep with him. She had shyly declined and did not reveal any of that Aladdin's cave of wonders that Andy was privy to.

Suddenly aware that he was hungry he telephoned for pizza. It arrived at the same time as the ground floor tenant. They swapped polite greetings and he funked the chance to confront her about her bank missing two payments in succession. He was not cut out to be a landlord, he left all that to Karen.

Andy did not want the rent money, he wanted the woman out of the building and had been uneasy about her from the off.

He had always relied on his instincts about people whether these misgivings were with foundation or not.

Ms Harrison's pretty features were distorted into a scowl. Thwarted because her first class degree with honours was not treated with sufficient respect by her fellow solicitors. As a result, detesting men had become her lifetime's work. He heard her reeking revenge on manhood, invective directed at her men friends rising up through the floorboards. The specification of the separating floors was sub-standard and Ms Harrison's lovemaking was clearly audible and was in a cavewoman mode. Foreplay consisted of wrestling and verbal abuse, mostly scatological. Her guests were put through a test of fire.

Karen, a building surveyor, had suffered similar benevolence. She complained that she was not taken seriously, dismissed as a pretty little thing, an insignificant but decorative addition to the staff. Her disenchantment widened when she kept finding deals that were not pursued by the management.

'Do it yourself,' he suggested. 'Go to a bank and sod them. What've you got to lose.'

Nothing as it turned out, although Timmons & Bryant were not amused. Once they got wind of Karen's successes, they had the temerity to claim a share. A solicitor's letter put paid to that notion.

Andy was amazed at how quickly you could make serious money in the property business. It took just a few months for their bank balance to reach sufficient funds to buy a house in Karen's favourite neighbourhood. She let her contacts know of her wishes and they spread the word.

A property came on the market in one of her favoured streets and she had viewed it the same morning. That evening when Andy returned from school they drove over for a second look and the 'For Sale' sign was gone.

'I smell a rat,' said Karen. 'There's some fiddle going on here.'

They knocked at the neighbours doors and got the telephone number of the owners. An old lady had died and her niece had inherited. One call on the mobile and a visit with the niece, having left a 10% deposit, they departed as new purchasers of 27 Waller Street.

According to Karen this was not an uncommon occurrence. Solicitors charged with responsibility of empty properties, often left vacant by the death of the elderly, line up a developer and a tame estate agent. They sell off the property at a below market value give it a coat of paint and sell it on at a more realistic value and split the profit three ways.

Number 27 was a very large detached house and Karen decided they could create two flats to help pay the mortgage. As it was a temporary measure they did a cheap conversion and skimped on the soundproofing.

Having acquired a nest, Karen was insistent that she was going to lay an egg. Andy had not been keen. He had been equally craven about getting married. Responsibility was not high on his list of priorities. He had been wrong about marriage, it had worked out way better than he expected. Children though, that was a different kettle of fish. His ploy with marriage was delay, not so easy a ploy with making babies. Just his luck, first time out, bingo.

Typical, his friend Pete had spent his single life sweating profusely over his one night stands and possible paternity. He married Eve and announced, 'I'm a Jaffa. All those years of worry for nothing. My sperm count is almost nothing.'

Karen did not have an easy time, suffering lengthy bouts of sickness. She discovered that walking reduced the nausea. It was on one of these rambles that Karen was knocked down and killed.

Ms Harrison offered no commiseration either by word or card. On the day of the funeral, he dressed in black, eyes and hair red, she gave him the merest glance of suggested condolence.

After his father's visit, Simon rousted him out and they went to the local. Ms Harrison was already there with a friend, three or four drinks ahead. Two smartly dressed men tried to pick them up. Ms Harrison, dismissed their advances, forthright and loudly. She confined men's usefulness to suppliers of seed, fast becoming redundant as bedfellows. All men are good for, she concluded, is snoring and farting.

Later that evening, while preparing for the following day's work, prior to going to bed, there was a knock at the door. He found Ms Harrison at the door, rocking gently from a bottle and a half of red. Her pretext for calling was short lived and she made a pass. He rebuffed her offer with a polite thank you.

He could not help wondering what had induced this man-hater to humiliate herself like that. He did not dwell on the conundrum for long but some days it occurred to him that if he could hear the comings and goings downstairs, she could hear what travelled in the opposite direction.

Her contract allowed for a three month default, after that he would let the solicitors handle the matter. He hated confrontation and preferred they deal with the situation. He ate an unsatisfying meal, supplementing his pizza with a salad and sat in the dark listening to the night until it was time for bed. He dreamed of Karen, eight months pregnant and she was stood on a ledge thirty storeys up. He tried and tried to rescue her but nothing worked. Some strange woman kept criticising his failures.

* * *

Since Karen had been killed he had struggled to get back into circulation. He had never been much good at mingling or making the kind of conversation that appealed to women. His friends understood this failing and introduced him to females trying to ease his way. There was no common ground and he became disheartened. Not only was he inept but too set in his ways.

A fellow teacher, Gordon, encouraged him to join a matchmaking agency, he filled out a questionnaire but the computer failed to find a match. On leaving university he tried for a job with a conglomerate and had to take an isometric test, that computer also failed him.

Gordon thrived on the assignations provided by the agency. During a Christmas holiday he slept with thirty six women he had previously met by arrangement. The women were done by appointment at twelve, four and eight pm.

Andy agreed to meet anybody prepared to meet him. These trysts grew shorter and shorter. Early on, he booked a table for dinner, that was cut to coffee and by the end, he met at a suitable distance from their intended destination. More often than not, the rendezvous was over by the time they reached the venue. Those that he did see for a second time assumed a permanence that scared the hell out of him and exacerbated his misery.

Out and about, he saw plenty of fanciable women but did not have the guile or nerve. He was strongly attracted to West Indians and Asians. The agency, for whatever reason, had no West Indians or Asians and he was unable to meet with any woman he liked, white, black or brown. He could not get used to hurting these women's feelings and was glad to put the experience behind him.

It was strange that he was so unskilful in the pursuit of womenfolk because all of his close friends were 'bird' men. Gordon, his oldest friend, Harry and Pete. Harry was a split personality. In the company of men he had a soul but in the presence of a woman, the soul departed. There was not a single word of his chat up rhetoric that was not an embarrassment but the women bought it. Harry was not too fussy either. If it moved and did not have a penis that was fine with him.

Pete was a different story. Pete could not help it. He turned it on every second of the waking day. It was second nature, first nature even and he was no longer aware of what he was doing. Andy would watch waitresses fall in love with him during the soup and starter and Pete would not even notice they were there. Since his marriage and his heart by-pass at just thirty five, he had lost interest and was more than happy to go home to his wife. Pete was not much to look at but he had the knack. Andy, for whatever reason, did not.

Speculating on what was wrong provided many hours of self doubt as frustrating as his sex life. Comparing his own sexuality to his friends caused further doubts. When it came to attitudes, opinions and ideas, he welcomed the fact that he was different from the others. That this manifestation could be lumped together with his sexuality did not penetrate his reasoning. Trying to emulate his contemporaries macho and libido left him floundering.

During these critical years of discovery he had received snippets of advice that stuck in his mind but added to the confusion.

Having attended an all boys' school he was unused to and terrified in the company of girls. At around fourteen years of age his friend Laurie had introduced him to his girlfriend. She was an ordinary sort of girl but Andy could not speak. Could not get a word out because his heart was in his mouth.

He had taken a summer job after his first year in the sixth and been assigned to a man named Edwin Yim. Yim, a married man, claimed that variety was the spice of life and was screwing the boss' PA. The PA was flirtatious with an owlish face and wine breath.

Older but not much wiser, at university new obstacles to sleeping around had presented themselves. The prospect of bed excited but in the event, he was bored. Once the sex was over he wanted them gone. If the conversation had not palled he always managed to attribute his dissatisfaction to the other party. Confronted with a tattoo, body piercing or cellulite his libido flagged. In sex, as in all of his pursuits, he did not see the point of accepting second best. He could convince himself that anything was a turn off. It secretly discomforted him that his friends not only did not seem to care, they did not seem to notice such minor details.

'As long as they stay awake,' said Pete.

Once again he floundered. Was he wrong to be so dogmatic? Did they understand and he did not, that it is impossible to attain perfection? That a sexual Shangri-La was a myth and he was deluding himself.

Then came Karen and he realised that for him women are a place of worship and that sex is not about self-gratification. What he had learned about himself was that he wanted to be macho in the eyes of his friends, be one of the lads. The truth was, he was not the sleeping around type.

Karen had his friends sorted in no time. She explained them to him and all his floundering subsided.

Andy's father had taught him self-awareness, self-criticism and objectivity. Awareness grew into a sense of justice and fair play allowed him to berate his own arrogance. Here you are Avecore, with these supposed standards and taking a job on the unlikely premise that you get into a married woman's knickers. Not only married but married with children. Do not give me all that bollocks that he probably does not deserve her. You do not even like her that much.

When it comes to the crunch you will not go through with it. You will funk it the same as you always have and not for honourable reasons but some stupid irrational quirk of your own. Which is a mild form of the self-gratification you deplore in others.

He enjoyed the fantasy of his possible relationship with Jinny. This way he could edit out the obstacles and keep a foot in reality. Not confronting her with his secret yearning kept his optimism alive and was the real reason behind his inability to make a move. If he did and was rejected the fantasy was over. Hope, which had been in short supply recently, would take another body blow.

He needed corroboration. Karen was no longer there to be his sounding board. To listen to his endlessly repetitive angst. He had become accustomed to sharing. I must tell Karen that. I must ask Karen that. But there was no Karen. He did not know where she kept the tinfoil or anything else for that matter. Every task he set out to do involved opening and shutting numerous cupboards. Asking had been a constant impulse for twelve years.

The habit of waking up every morning and sleepily reaching for her, he would worship. Take his morning prayers inhaling her intoxicating body, wondering on the beauty of her curvature. Now his sleepy arm, finding nothing, disappointment was repeated day after day.

Eye witnesses had stated that the car had jumped a red light and the girl driving the car was exasperated and complained of being kept waiting. They claimed she approached the Police when they arrived and said, 'Could we get this over with, I'm in a hurry.' None of this was in the Police report.

A woman was dead, that was in their findings. A woman worth ten of the driver. There was a small insert in the local newspaper. They got the location right, they noted that she was pregnant but they spelled the name wrong, Karen Anchor.

The driver was not severely punished. She was breathalysed and found to be a milligram under the conviction limit. So that made it all right. The Police told him that nobody could be sure that she had jumped the traffic light. They had done a site study of the witnesses' viewpoints and none of these were satisfactory. Andy did not mind that much, he never understood the eye for an eye mentality before he was a victim. He would have preferred to have Karen back, whatever shape she was in.

CHAPTER SEVEN

Alex and James - The twins

Jinny knocked persistently at Alex' bedroom door but received no answer. She decided he must be in the bathroom. Determined to see through her intention she opened the door and called, 'Alex, are you in here?' Because her parents had not respected her privacy, since the boys had been in long trousers Jinny had made a point of giving them their space.

One Christmas, she had been given a diary and with her love of English she enjoyed this daily routine of recording her thoughts and deeds, until she suspected that someone was reading the entries. She set a trap, her father never entered her room for any reason, that left her mother or Charlotte as the only available culprits. It was her mother. Jinny felt burglarised, but she had lost her faith in adults long before.

Being a small family, weddings were rare. Charlotte had been to two, one as bridesmaid. Glad to be old enough to be going to her first wedding, where Charlotte was once again a bridesmaid, Jinny was envious not to be chosen. She had drunk far too much lemonade before dinner. By the time it was served her stomach had swelled from a surfeit of bubbles and she had no appetite. Sad, she sought comfort from a sympathetic source. Her father placed his hand on her tummy and thought hard, 'Yes, I can feel roast beef, Yorkshire pudding, quite a few garden peas and yes, a roast potato. Happy my angel?'

'Yes, father,' she lied, adding one more to her list of disappointments.

She was ready to talk to the boys and she was not to be discouraged. She rapped on the bathroom door, 'What are you doing in there?'

'What d'you think I'm doing?'

She waited at the door, listening, for a few minutes hoping for an appearance. She was doing the same at James' door when he opened it and caught her standing there.

Cheeks burning with shame she said weakly, 'I need to discuss something important with you and Alex.'

'So,' said James without interest, the familiar sulky boredom darkened his eyes.

She was ready to broach the subject of their A level results and decided to break with tradition. The prospect of a one to one almost caused her to resist but the words were out before she knew it. 'I'll speak to Alex later. Have you got a minute?'

James was surprised, followed her into the room, struggling to remember what crime he was being accused of this time. It must be serious to prompt this out of character behaviour.

Inspired, she sat on his bed and motioned for him to sit beside her. Wary, he did not immediately obey, still wondering what subject would have so much import for his dyed in the wool mother to carry on like this.

'We need to discuss something important.' She saw his eyes lighten, perplexed as to why they had grown so dark? By now, James had gauged this was a pep talk and not a bollocking. 'Are you ready for the exams?'

James' brighter eyes were inscrutable but he had not shrugged with his usual resignation nor had his body sagged with 'Oh no not that again'.

'Yes,' he said, his eyes directly on her own. This was a James she had not seen before his passive face masking his true thoughts. How like Angus he was. She had not noticed any similarity before.

'What if Alex were to get the three A's and you don't? Have you thought about that?'

James threw off the residual of his pose as the silly son and Jinny was made still more uneasy by this unexpected transformation. He was revealing a person of maturity and self-assurance, certainly more assurance than she currently possessed. She was clearly relinquishing the balance of power. He was not exactly laughing at her, nor was he contemptuous but mildly condescending. 'I won't be as disappointed as you,' he said.

She had no inkling of James' intention to fail. He was counting on Alex getting three A's as he intended getting three B's. That way he could shake himself free of his idiot brother.

She wanted to talk some more but it was clear that he did not. He continued filling his case in readiness for tomorrow's school and she waited awkwardly for a minute or two, then went downstairs.

Jinny made coffee and miserably contemplated the error of her ways. The person she had just been talking to was a complete stranger. How could that be? Should she have dealt with the boys individually. She thought it was fair to always include them equally. Had this collective behaviour harmed them? Had she damaged her relationship with them. Could things be different from here on? She must start right away and do everything she could to put things right.

CHAPTER EIGHT

An exchange - Jinny's view - Andy's view

It took three days for Andy to call a meeting of the English department and he purposely chose Jinny's day off. On the Friday, Margery brought her up to date.

'I didn't want to like him,' she confessed. 'But I can't help myself.'

'You do?'

'He was very complimentary about all of us.'

'Buying our loyalty,' Jinny suggested. *'None can usurp this height.'*

'I don't think so,' Margery was firm. 'He wears his heart on his sleeve.'

'You think.'

'There was just one complaint, he feels the curriculum is boring.'

'Boring! Goodness me, how could it possibly be boring. Charlotte Bronte, Jane Austen, George Eliot…'

'That was his point. The boys are falling behind and the curriculum is mostly feminine. He feels the boys need something meaty.'

'This is the thin edge of the wedge…'

'He suggested a book club. That way we might get the students reading, even if it is only…'

'Harry Potter.'

'Female author.'

'Tolkien?'

'That was Marcia's suggestion. He isn't keen on fairies. Conan Doyle, HG Wells, Steinbeck…'

'Of Mice and Men was a choice but we agreed to omit it.'

'Grapes of Wrath, he said.'

'Thin edge of the wedge.'

'Maybe. There are a lot of women authors in the course. He said his father had warned him about women authors.'

'His father said what?'

'Never read women or Russians, soporific he said.'

'Very amusing.'

'He was laughing.'

Jinny felt herself getting red in the face. The foundation of English literature had been laid by Shakespeare and women writers. She had heard academics claim that Middlemarch is the finest novel ever written. That is the trouble with bringing in outsiders, they have to make their mark. No matter how well the system is working they have to add their two pennyworth. She must see Betsy at the earliest opportunity.

'Anyway, that's what he said. He doesn't want to interfere with our course work so he suggested a book club. He reckons that you light a spark anyway you can.'

'Thin edge of the wedge,' Jinny muttered again.

'By the way, he'd like to see you when you've got a minute.'

'Book club!' she exclaimed. 'Haven't we got enough on our plates.'

Avecore's office was empty when she knocked. She gave her Head of Department less respect than the twins and marched straight in. The office was furnished and fitted with a telephone and a radio. He had not as yet personalised it. There were no photographs of a wife and children. Her family would have taken pride of place. How curious that there were no personals, just a half dozen novels on the top shelf. She had to stand on tiptoe to read the spines. Decline and Fall, Coming up for Air, Sound and the Fury, The Wax Boom and Hangover Square.

Americans! His father might have warned him about women authors. Well, her father had warned her about Americans. A botched civilisation. What kind of society was it where you can not walk the streets in safety.

She did not hear his approach and for the second time in as many days she was caught snooping. He wore the same odd disapproval as at their first meeting.

'Looking at your choice of reading,' she said.

'I bet you don't approve,' he said. The words could have been offensive but the way he said it made it otherwise.

'Not really.'
'Not even Evelyn Waugh?'
She shook her head.
'His father wanted him to be a girl apparently, that's why he was named Evelyn.'
'I didn't know that.'
'Please sit down,' said Andy. He sat opposite on the corner of the desk, towering over her.
He is trying to dominate me, she thought. As if.
'We had a meeting yesterday. I didn't realise it was your day off.' Nervously, he played with his nose, feigning an itch.
'Margery put me in the picture.'
'Good! I wanted to say some things to you face to face. Often new people come in and make changes that seem like they are throwing their weight around. If that is the case I wish to apologise because it is not my intention. Equally, when you are on the inside of the situation you don't always see the problems...'
'We have had a great deal of success...' she spoke insistently
'If any,' he added hastily. 'If any. There is just one teeny weeny, miniscule problem. Not problem, tendency.'
His tone was making her comfortable and she felt at ease. Sensing this sudden security she pinched herself. She was being sucked into his web. She must concentrate, remain on alert. Make her point.
'The boys' results are lagging behind the girls'. You agree or disagree?'
'Agree,' her eyes left his as he rolled up his sleeves, revealing that forest of red hair that covered his forearms. She involuntarily squeezed her thighs together.
'I can't give a cast iron reason for this deficiency but I noticed a lack of male writers.'
'Shakespeare was a man.'
'A man yes but gay I believe. Anyway most kids learn Shakespeare with a peg on their nose.'
The shock of his words took Jinny's breath away. How dare he...
He put up a hand to forestall her. 'You'll have to forgive my language sometimes, I enjoy being frivolous. Much of what I

would say to you in private I would not dream of repeating to the students. Why I asked you here,' the giveaway itch on his nose flared up again. 'A book club.'

She waited expectantly without speaking.

'Would you help me with it?'

'You and me?' she was stupefied.

'Yes,' he laughed. 'Don't be so shocked.'

Why would he ask her when they were at loggerheads on almost every subject? She thought he disliked her. Despite that, she was flattered and agreed to it at once.

Later she convinced herself that she was doing it to keep an eye on him. She would make sure that the book club remained in bounds.

* * *

He found her standing on tiptoe, wearing a cashmere sweater which had ridden up baring her midriff, a dogtooth skirt with a two inch slit at the hem baring thigh and her legs stretched to their limit. It may have been the uniqueness of the moment but he had rarely seen anything so beautiful and his heart did another flip flop with guilt following behind.

'Sorry,' he apologised for nothing in particular.

'Checking your choice of literature.'

'Do you approve?'

'Not especially. I understand you don't like Tolkien but I prefer his writing to anything you have on that shelf. You should learn to enjoy fantasy.'

'Sorry but I don't believe in fairies.'

'You don't know what you're missing.'

'I prefer human beings. I don't get this obsession with fairies.'

'It's hardly an obsession.'

'While I was university, during the holidays I got a job working in a picture framers. The owner used to buy up second hand books and put the illustrations in a frame to sell. He couldn't get enough fairy books, used to travel all round the country.'

'So?'

'You like quoting,' he said, 'John Osborne lumped sentimentality together with violence and inhumanity.'

'Did he,' she said. 'I don't think The Hobbit is sentimental. I think it's imaginative and enriching. I imagine he had the United States in mind.'

'Ireland.'

'What university did you go to?'

'Please sit down,' he placed the chair for her and she sat. He wanted to plonk his face in her hair. He leaned just close enough to take in the smell of her shampoo and sat on the edge of the desk. He immediately regretted this pose but felt foolish about changing position so capriciously.

He spilled out his prepared patter watching her face carefully for any sign of censure. They were so diametrically opposed he would need to win her over as slowly and gently as possible. She had been relaxing and then something rocked the boat.

'We've had a lot of success...' she interrupted. 'There are documented reasons for this difference between boys and girls.'

'Of course there are. I'm not pointing the finger at anybody. The curriculum has a lack of male writers.'

'Shakespeare.'

'The boys need some modern day masculinity. Not a load of men prancing round in dresses and tights. They need something to identify with. Something they can relate to.'

He had to stifle a laugh at the frown of horror that greeted this statement. 'You must me forgive me,' he pleaded. 'I like being frivolous. I would not dream of saying such a thing to the students.' He was rather pleased with this speech. It was not often that he could lie so convincingly.

'Why I asked you here. The book club. Would you help me with it?' It looked for a moment that his scheme was going to falter. 'I could do it alone but if you feel an inclination to help.' His question had her baffled, then confusion was replaced with a smile. She was flattered to be asked. He had to resist rubbing his hands together. He would get her alone after school hours, invite her for a drink. Get her up a dark alley.

'You and me?' she confirmed.

You bet. 'Yes,' he said.

* * *

CHAPTER NINE

Life at school

The old world schoolmaster who had come to Mrs Parish's rescue while Andy was waiting for his interview turned out to be Mr Mason, the art master, who had a reputation as a Lothario. Still vigorous at sixty, he used sharp methods to flirt with Jinny. He laid himself at her feet, feigning ignorance, pretending to know nothing about poetry and literature, feeding her ego.

She recommends various poets and he does his study. Whether he reads the books or not Andy could not decide, he might look the synopses up on the internet or know the subject perfectly well in the first place. He reciprocated these tutorials expounding knowledgeably on many topics. He had a wide scope of interests and played jazz loudly in his office.

Mason, rangy, with a full head of oyster coloured hair and matching beard was an unusually urbane character for the wilds of Wyford. He had taught at several demanding establishments. St Bryans could not previously claim such elevated company but it was improving in leaps and bounds.

It was lunchtime and the sun streamed through the observation window filling the common room with a comfortable warmth. Those not on duty and non-smokers sat reading or marking, relaxed by the buoyant atmosphere and the optimistic weather. It was quiet and the unremitting screech and chatter of children seemed to be drowsily distant. There was an occasional crackle of newspaper, a muffled burp or a teeth edging squeak of a bottom adjusting position on leather upholstery. Those assembled honoured an unspoken rule to maintain this oasis of peace and quiet. Andy likened it to a gentleman's club or an exclusive reading room or library in some select edifice.

Sat opposite Jinny, he pretended to read a book. She was sitting cross legged hidden behind The Times. Careful not to be caught he studied closely the curve of her right upper leg and wondered how and where the black line it shadowed onto her left leg terminated.

Suddenly, almost catching him out, she folded the newspaper into her lap and scanned the room. Immediately behind her was the person she sought. She tapped him on the shoulder. 'Did you read this review?' Jinny asked in a stage whisper and offered Mason a section of The Times. 'Isn't he one of your favourite artists.'

'The new exhibition at the Royal Academy.'

'The reviewer does not seem very impressed.'

Mason perched his glasses on his significant nose and read quickly. He handed back the paper and shrugged, 'Modigliani is one of those artists that people like or dislike.'

'Some people don't have a soul,' Andy intervened, feeling oddly foolish for doing so. Jinny looked at him with a quizzical expression which he interpreted as a rebuke. He should not have been eavesdropping nor should he have spoken up.

'Did you read this?' Mason peered over his spectacles.

'Unfortunately,' said Andy, self conscious that their conversation was disturbing the reverie.

'What did you make of it?' he asked getting out of his chair and sitting next to Jinny.

Gaining confidence from Mason's conduct, Andy continued, 'Bland is the last word I would use to describe Modigliani. The world seems to have forgotten that art is about colour. The critic's a devotee of Robert Hughes. I've read reviews of his on Modigliani in The Guardian. Perhaps he's an anti-semite or gay.'

'Or both.'

'I would guess that because Robert Hughes is such a big deal when he speaks out, his minions follow his lead.'

'You think that critics stick together?'

'There's safety in consensus. Anyway when you come down to it, being a critic is just a job. Three of my university friends went into journalism and all three write on subjects they know little about.'

'What university was that?' Jinny asked.

Mason handed back the newspaper to Jinny. 'Modigliani is one of the greatest colourists in the history of art. His canvasses vibrate.'

'Bollocks to Robert Hughes.'

'It seems odd to single out Modigliani for criticism and praise Andy Warhol and Jasper Johns.'

'What is odder is to condemn Modigliani's nudes as bland and go into raptures over Freud's. I know which women I'd rather be with.'

Jinny resented being excluded by these two men, they were bonding or whatever it is that men do.

Then a soldier, full of strange oaths

Why do all men resort to profanity? They do it for effect and it is so childish.

With spectacle on nose and pouch on side

You never hear Angus using those words, not even with the boys. Nor do her boys use such language in front of her, they have more respect. Mason's always playing that horrible noise too loudly. Men never grow up.

Last scene of all, that ends this strange eventful history, is second childishness

'You might be able to help me,' said Andy. 'Why is it so many critics these days are preoccupied with cerebral content?'

'I hear the word cerebral and I run a mile,' said Mason. 'It's an unassailable shield to hide behind. It's that word you used earlier, soul. It can't be taught. You're born with it or you're not. Why you can't enjoy things simply for what they are is baffling. It's some sort of justification to give a subject substance by finding a cerebral slant. Do you know about jazz?'

'My father is a fan.'

'Have you heard of John Coltrane?' Andy nodded. 'I personally don't care for Coltrane. I find his music barren but the opposition often play the cerebral ticket.'

'It's an exclusive club.'

'Yes, I suppose it is,' Mason did that switch with his spectacles. 'Duke Ellington said, too much talk stinks up the place.'

Jinny watched them talking together for a while then slipped away assuming she was unnoticed.

'Could you answer me another question?' Andy lowered his voice to a murmur.

'Sure,' he caught on to the intimacy of Andy's question and leaning forward replaced his spectacles so he could see his inquisitor more clearly.

'Get anywhere with her?'

Mason peered imperiously over the top of his spectacles without speaking and Andy was positive that he had gone too far and was going to get a ticking off. 'Why, do you fancy her?'

'Yes.'

'You're barking up the wrong tree there. I haven't had so much as a sniff. I just enjoy keeping my hand in.'

'What's your hit rate?'

'A couple of years ago it was one in fifteen or sixteen, now it's one in thirty two and slipping.'

'You should get a dog.'

'So I've heard,' said Mason. 'I can't figure her out. I can't decide if she's disinterested in sex or what.'

'What's her husband like?'

'The whiz kid,' Mason stroked his beard. 'I haven't really met him.'

'I wasn't going to take this job until I saw her.'

'Really,' Mason pursed his lips, ducked his head and peered over the top of his glasses. 'I can't think of a better reason to take a job. I wish all the luck in your endeavour. Now I have a favour to ask of you.'

'Anything.'

'Keep me posted.'

Andy had made a wanted friend. His next hurdle was an unwanted friend.

Some weeks later Mason acquired a cocker spaniel, what else and his hit rate plummeted back to one in fifteen.

* * *

Gillian Finn, the NQT known as Mickey, turned up on the second Monday of the summer term having had a makeover. It had taken forty eight hours for her to make the transition from post punk to English rose.

Mickey was a product of an academic system that is functioning well. Primary teaching of English in our schools is excellent and its encouragement of book reading is first class. The majority of children transferring to secondary school enjoy reading books but within a year or two, peer pressure will change that. Reading is not fashionable, not cool and is demonised by teenage children. Learning is for creepy kids, wet kids, being a swot is not cool. It is a peculiarity about Britain that academic prowess is demonised whereas in Europe it is lionised.

Most English teachers can recall that special case of a pupil that makes it all worthwhile. In her day Mickey was that child.

She adopted an extreme image to survive amongst her peer group. Dyed her hair a variety of colours, gelled it a variety of shapes, shaved various bits and for one short stage she shaved it all. The next phase was piercing. Ears, eyebrows, nose, belly button, lower lip and tongue and her wardrobe was almost entirely black.

Mickey knew early on that teaching would be her vocation. She wanted to be an English teacher. To retain a plausible public face amongst her friends she hid behind the eccentric image and got to where she wanted while maintaining her street cred.

When Andy arrived, she saw it was time to give up the remnants of her extreme appearance and be herself. His entrance, dressed in that non-conformist fashion, attracted her attention in several ways.

Mickey's parents owned a picture painted by a man named Norman Rockwell. As soon as she attained the conception of boys, the boy in the picture became the hero of her nightly fantasies. Despite the light hearted portrait of the subject she liked his freshness and adored his red hair and freckles.

Andy Avecore was that boy, all grown up. He exuded a clean cut air, even though his forearms and nose were generously scattered with fleck. His hands were the biggest turn on. He worked them in a singularly attractive and sensitive way. He touched things with respect and she sensed those hands would touch her in the way she dreamed of. Boys in her limited experience had not touched her with respect. Not even those in the 'steady' relationships. She had made bad choices, got too drunk or spent the night with boys whose selfishness astounded her. Virtually all of her sexual recollection left her feeling dirty and disappointed.

Her best friend, Sally, had her drink spiked with rohypnol and while unconscious was raped in the back of a van. She woke up in an alley with her knickers full of blood.

This outrage provided more anger and more disappointment. What were men all about? They might as well have sex with a blow-up doll for all the intimacy that takes place. She had been taught by Rabelais that eroticism is life but she had yet to experience any.

Sex in films and on television invariably reaches a climactic conclusion but this was not her experience. To her the sex portrayed by the arts is a phoney. Mickey was sure that in sex scenes, actors are playing out some mythological perfection experienced by one in a million. From her naïve vantage point, hope promised that to achieve a proper relationship love must be involved.

In literature sex is dealt with more realistically, like the beginning of the *Sword of Honour* when Crouchback's parents have a hard time on their honeymoon and Guy's attempts to sleep with his ex-wife are baulked. Not every man is James Bond and not every woman is Pussy Galore.

* * *

Andy sat in his office studying the set tutorials required for NQT training when Betsy March's PA appeared at the door and summoned him urgently. Matching Mrs Tapper's fast pace through the corridors, he entered Betsy's office short of breath.

'Is everybody in this school asthmatic?' she asked.

Andy coughed twice and said, 'It's that woman. Is she an Olympic standard walker?'

'Mrs Tapper, I don't think so.'

'You wanted me?'

'Are you a football fan?'

'Pardon.'

'Football,' she asked. 'Would you like to go to a football match? There's a free dinner involved.'

'The school team?'

'Wyford Town, this Saturday. We've been invited into the directors' box and our seats will be empty. Would you like to use them?'

Andy said, 'Yes, that would be nice,' but immediately

regretted accepting the offer. Think of an excuse, remember an important engagement but for some reason his brain remained blank. 'Who's got the other seat?'

'My daughter's fiance, Jeremy, you'll like him.'

Andy doubted it.

'It's a big match,' she explained. 'If Wyford win they're assured of a play off place. You'll enjoy it.'

Andy doubted that too.

To alleviate the pressure on his fellow teachers Andy volunteered to supervise NQT training. He had chosen Thursday evenings and there would be eight tutorials on subjects ranging from class management to coping with children with special needs.

He had been waiting for some time before his NQT's arrived and they turned up en masse having been directed to the wrong room. He opened his manual and began his preamble when his mind began wandering. His instruction to the group was half-hearted due to a preoccupation with finding an excuse to get out of Saturday's football.

At the end of the lesson, which despite his absent-minded delivery, they claimed to enjoy, he was invited to join them for a drink. He repeated his error of earlier, responded positively to be affable and immediately regretted his decision. Now he would be expected to go with them every Thursday.

They had chosen one of those new pubs with Moon in the title that had cropped up in the High Street. This was the most popular because you could park in the access road behind. Andy was the senior customer by a handful of years.

A screen showed a football game and there was a cluster of craning necks stood in an arc around it. They made their way through the twilight to dark recess and gave him the place of honour in the corner. When Andy's eyes acclimatised to the dim light he saw they occupied the mock up of a boat with himself at the helm.

There was only ten to twelve years difference in their ages but it was a significant chasm. They chattered on merrily and more merrily after one or two drinks. Large glasses of Merlot put rosy spots on either side of Barrie's ruddy face and he became more expansive than Andy had ever seen him.

'I have,' he claimed, his moribund face darkening to claret, 'Danced with Emma Bunton at my cousin's wedding.'

'Not cheek to cheek, surely. Isn't she tiny?'

'She is a bit but what does that matter.'

'Girls are all the same size on the dance floor.'

'And in bed.'

It was time for Andy to leave but trapped in the corner his escape was daunting. He spent a few minutes turning over excuses for Saturday but none rang true. With a resigned breath he gulped down the last of his pint. 'I have to go.'

He stopped for a pee and coming out of the toilet he encountered Mickey getting into her jacket. 'You off?' he asked.

'Yes, I've got essays to mark.' She had a local timbre to her whimsical voice and her face was not quite pretty. He was glad to see the piercing gone but he was positive there would be a tattoo secreted somewhere. She actively worked on being more sophisticated than her companions, did not laugh like a drain at every comment and avoided slang or phrases that the other student teachers enjoyed repeating over and over, 'I'm not bothered' or 'no worries'.

'Can I give you a lift?' he asked.

'That would be nice,' she said with a hint of satisfaction. 'If it's not out of your way.'

For the third time that afternoon Andy regretted an assignation. What had got into him? He was out of practice at avoiding awkward situations. He had a suspicion that this girl had planned this accidental happening.

'I live on the Pemberton Estate.'

'Where?'

'I'll direct you.'

He let her into the passenger's seat and closed the door. Having been with young people he was feeling curiously patriarchal.

'They're ever so young, aren't they,' she explained.

'Which way?' he asked, resisting the impulse to point out that she was too.

'Right at the lights and straight over the roundabout. They can be so embarrassing.'

'They're a nice bunch of kids,' he said purposely patronising.

'But kids nevertheless.' He glanced down and saw the extent of her white legs. Her skirt seemed to be exceptionally high and her legs exceptionally beguiling. Again he had to resist pointing out that she was one of them.

They pulled up alongside a smart detached house with a full size flag of St George on a flagpole in the front garden.

'Would you like to meet the family?'

'Thanks but I've got to get home.'

'Where's home?' she asked pleasantly.

'Up London,' he mocked the local accent.

'You're a bit of a mystery aren't you. Do you do it on purpose?'

'No,' he said. 'But there are things in my life I don't like to talk about.'

'Are you married?'

'Now you sound like the kids.'

'I suppose I do,' she said, bypassing his snipe and putting her hand firmly on his leg. The unexpected familiarity of her touch caused him to recoil like a teenager. 'Are you?'

'I was.'

'Divorced?'

'That's the area I don't want to get into.'

Her hand remained on his leg, she studied his face for a time, leaned across and kissed him. 'Goodnight,' she said and opened the car. Before closing it she leaned in, 'Thanks for the lift.'

'Anytime,' he said. 'For what it's worth. I'm a widower.'

She shut the door and he drove away. From his rear view mirror he saw she stood and watched him disappear from view.

He made his way through a maze of streets before he found a place he recognised. While he waited at the lights he could still feel her lips branding his face. Hanging around and happening to be in doorway, that was no accident. Mickey Finn fancied him. The prospect did not excite him at all.

It was not appropriate for senior staff to sleep with the young and innocent. He knew of some teachers who were having affairs with their students. One of the senior spokesman on the school system had married a sixth former. It did not do his career any harm even when the teaching union were up against him.

She was a nice enough kid and she may be way younger than he but she came out of that encounter with more poise than he had.

As he drove through the night he reassessed his prospects with Jinny Parish. Realistically he had no chance. Why not have a tryst with Mickey? It did not have to be serious. It did not sit right in his mind. It was ridiculous but even contemplating an affair felt as though he were betraying his objective.

'You get nuttier every day,' he told himself.

CHAPTER TEN

Andy goes to football

In her three years in Wyford Betsy March had become an ardent fan of the football team. It provided her with welcome relief from the unremitting pressure of the role of headmistress.

In some respects Andy was stubbornly old fashioned and was uncomfortable listening to women pontificate on football. Betsy March was no shrinking violet and she spoke out assertively.

The Wyford Town dining room was bright and cheerful as were the assembled guests, the majority spurred on by the free wine supplied by the sponsors. Dress code was being observed, jackets and ties, blazers with club badges and Andy in his linen suit and granny shirt caused Betsy slight embarrassment. Unconventionality was all right at school but this was a place of worship.

Andy had a chequered football history. His father lost interest in football and so his uncles, Edward and Robert, had stepped into the breech. While he was very young he had been lifted over the turnstiles and watched the game seated on an uncle's lap. They took turns, sharing halves. Later, his father financed a season ticket for him but he himself only went to matches over the Xmas and Easter holidays. It was a family tradition to go to the Boxing Day morning game but other than that his father restricted his sporadic watching to the television.

Saturdays were a ritual. Driving across London to Highbury with his uncles and cousins in the back of a van. Some weeks it was a trip down soccer's memory lane, Tapscott and Lishman, Forbes and Barnes, Goring and Hess and other great players of their childhood. Some weeks the topic would be the insufficiencies of the current management. Some weeks it was the utter waste of space that is Tottenham Hotspur or Uncle Ed spitting vitriol at the cynicism of Italian soccer and Uncle Bob, who always drove, nodding agreement.

They would park, walk the streets of Highbury amongst the red and white, past the noisy street vendors selling programmes, hats and scarves, past the hot dog stands and the stench of smoky onions.

Through the turnstiles and the cold lower reaches of the stadium which had never experienced sunlight, up the stairs where a steward was silhouetted against the sky. At the top of the stairs was a burst of colour. The red bucket seats, the red and white bunting and the vivid green of the pitch, the white faced clock in the North Stand. His heart soared. Not even an iron grey sky on a freezing cold day could prevent this elevation in his chest.

The players emerged in a blaze of colour accompanied by a cheer that exuded optimism. As the afternoon wore on elevation subsided to enervation and Andy watched his team play out a game in the classical Italian style.

Both his uncles were strong stocky men with saturnine and craggy faces that were clumsily uncomfortable when sporting a smile.

Uncle Ed, was a shadowy character, leading a solitary life running a dubious building business from an ivory tower, coincidentally in a back street of Wyford. Financial success gave him the wherewithal to expand his ego almost as much as neat whiskey was expanding his nose and liver. He was adept on the pontificating front, spouting dogma and brooking no contradiction.

On the plus side, country music, Dad's Army and Arsenal football team, on his black list, jazz, Spike Milligan and Spurs.

Uncle Bob was more conventional. He owned a string of card shops in which he installed his sons as managers. Without warning he sold the shops from under them and moved to Spain. There he developed a melanoma and died. Early on Andy noticed both Robert and Edward had thought his father was a man to be respected but as they got richer they began to refer to him as a bit swank.

Uncle Bob had died a couple of years back and Andy's father, lecturing in Melbourne, was unable to attend the funeral.

Andy had represented the family and prepared a few words, Uncle Ed solemnly shook his hand but before Andy could recite his prepared speech, Ed got in before him, 'We won the double.'

Andy guessed that Uncle Bob had died a happy man.

Andy believed that football has replaced religion as the opium of the people. Whereas church was a place to congregate to meet like minded people it has been usurped by soccer stadiums. Whether it provides the same sense of belonging Andy did not know. All those years of travelling to Highbury he enjoyed the trips there and back but was never at home inside the stadium. He had not belonged.

Jeremy, Betsy's son in law, led the way to their seats and Andy was captivated by the colour all over again. Green, red and white filled his heart with expectation.

Jeremy took the aisle seat and sitting next to Andy was a kid with that sickly look that clever 'boy' children seem to be saddled with. These children are plentiful on Junior Mastermind. The boy was fully grown with a substantial shadow on his upper lip. Andy estimated his age at around eighteen, an age by which the boy should have grown out of this sickly stage.

'Are you at university?' Andy asked, flattering the boy to boost his confidence.

'I'm taking my A levels soon,' nausea mounted between the boy's nose and mouth. There was a semblance of a smile but his eyes remained inanimate. 'I've got an offer from Oxford.'

Rich kid, Andy decided, studied hard because his parents leaned on him and would be heavily into play stations.

The arrival of the players was greeted by a deafening roar and put an end to their conversation. The boy stood to greet his team, checking his mobile and texting. Within ten minutes of the start all Andy's hope of a spectacle were dissipated. Wyford expended a lot of effort playing a route one system, their defenders, mostly of the clogger variety, running the opposition down by any means. Southampton tried hard to play an attractive game but Wyford would not let them. Attempts to make a swift break were prevented by a nudge here, a trip there, stopping play and allowing Wyford's defence to regroup. This is a method perfected over the years by Liverpool and Arsenal.

Bored, his attention wandered to his immediate neighbours. There was an anachronistic man with the last vestige of flyaway hair who regularly called, 'Well played, sir.'

A hunched over accountant type sitting amongst his four children kept standing to berate one of Wyford's forward players, turning a frustrated glance in all directions hoping someone would share his disenchantment. 'Why does he bother,' thought Andy.

The usual referee attacker was two seats away, separated from Andy by the nauseated boy. Any decision given against Wyford met with a torrent of abuse.

The sickly boy, seemingly as bored with the football as Andy was giving far more attention to his mobile telephone than the match. His video game was not going well and the boy kept clicking his tongue in frustration. Curious as to why, Andy tried to catch a glimpse of the game. He pretended to stretch and saw on the screen a half naked woman dressed in a slip which she lifted from behind to expose her backside. The silky material slipped from her grasp, she re-gathered and repeated the mishandling. Each time she failed to keep hold of the material she bent further over, each revelation showing more of the nether region. Just as the full exposure was imminent the screen went black and returned to the beginning, hence the tutting.

Wyford went in at half time, two up, one scored by the hunched man's bete noir just before half time. The accountant was now grudgingly contrite. 'I know he's got potential but with a bit more effort he'd score a lot more goals.'

The sickly boy disappeared giving Andy a clear view of the referee basher. He was expensively dressed in a black ski jacket, mohair slacks, probably Armani, and black beetle crushers, probably Barker. He held court and his audience went up an impressive number of rows.

A swarthy man, well turned out with a beard that needed attention twice a day. His eyes revealed what resided beneath his immaculate veneer. Menacing dark eyes that promised ferocity and a smug self-satisfied air that showed he was aware of his own strength.

'I can't imagine why anyone would travel to watch this lot,' his voice more strident than necessary. 'What a shower.'

For a moment, Andy could not follow the point of this boomed statement until he swivelled and saw two men in red and white scarves sitting a few rows back.

'Sad,' he continued louder still.

The two men knew they were being taunted but pretended to concentrate on their programme notes. Releasing the stress on his neck, Andy turned away.

'I reckon the manager would be justified in asking for their wages back. Pitiful. I wish just for once the visiting team would give us a game.'

'Why don't you grow up?' called a voice behind.

'Why can't you take your beating like a man?'

'Beating is right. Week after week we get crunched by cloggers like your lot. Cloggers on and off the field.'

'Who you calling a clogger?'

'You,' said the voice. 'Prat.'

Out of nowhere three burly policeman barged past and charged up the stairs and the two men in red and white were roughly removed from their places They tried to make their case but the policemen were not having it. They were manhandled toward the exit and Andy followed them down the stairs.

He chased the departing group, caught them at the turnstiles and tapped the nearest of the policeman on the shoulder. 'These men were not at fault.'

The policeman turned to face him, grim and indefatigable, 'What?'

'These men were not at fault, they were provoked.'

The two men stared at him forlornly.

'Do you want to see the rest of the game,' the policeman asked unpleasantly.

Not particularly, Andy thought but he could see the copper was in no mood for humour. 'What's that got to do with anything? These men were provoked.'

'If you want to see the rest of the match, sir, I suggest you go back to your seat. Now!' He glared at Andy and waited for his instruction to be obeyed. As Andy moved away, the policeman spun around, renewed his hold of the innocent supporter with renewed vigour and and hurried him away.

Back in his seat next to the small beer Jeremy, the

provocateur, was still holding court. 'I got out my car and as he rolled his window down I let him have one. Caught him right in the eye. Any sign of trouble you've got to get in first. That's the secret.'

The unpleasant man stopped to relieve his son of one of his cups and begged Andy's pardon as they shuffled along the row with polystyrene cups and bags of crisps. The sickly youths were a pair, twins, one with less frightened eyes.

Larry March appeared at Jeremy's side, 'I heard there has been some trouble. You all right?'

'We're fine,' said Jeremy.

'Who's that man?' Andy asked.

'Him, he's married to one of your fellow teachers, that's Angus Parish. His wife's Jinny.'

'Is he now,' thought Andy, the crime of adultery suddenly seeming less of a mortal sin.

CHAPTER ELEVEN

Opinions and book club

Smoke escaped through the partly open door to 'coughers corner' and billowed erotically across the shafts of sunlight streaming through the gap in the curtains. Countless specks of dust and hair floated indomitably upwards in the glint. Newspapers rustled but nobody spoke. It was too hot for conversation. Margery, Marcia and Jinny sat mute. Andy bet with himself on which of them would hold out the longest without speaking.

He had become disenchanted with reading in recent months. He had not read a novel or newspaper in over a year prior to joining St Bryans. Since his arrival, when he had no homework to mark or a child's file to review, he had taken to picking up whatever was lying around.

A sardonic article in The Times caught his attention because it poked fun at left wing liberals and what the writer referred to as 'the intelligentsia'. Andy wondered how a journalist from The Times staff, even an aspiring journalist, might separate himself in the eyes of his readers from the intelligentsia. It said that the aforementioned muddy thinkers had the wrong idea about the proliferation of St George flags that had appeared on the populations' motor vehicles or hanging from their windows in anticipation of the World Cup. No matter what spin the muddy thinkers plied us with, the truth was plain and simple, patriotism. From the arrogant tone of the article Andy surmised that the journalist was the only person on earth who had nailed down the facts.

The warmth, the diffused sunlight and silent reading caused him to recall a train trip he had made with Karen from Florence to Venice. The journey had been addled with stops and starts and they had been kept waiting in Bologna Station for over an hour. Andy had finished his book and had been forced to read The Independent from cover to cover. He read page after page of guff that he would not have usually bothered with. He was staggered to discover how snide the attitudes of the contributors were and this had sown the seed of his dissatisfaction with newspapers.

The paper had proved useful in one respect. Using the broadsheet as cover he adjusted the pages to spy on the woman sitting opposite. She was exotically beautiful and he tried to guess her country of origin.

Her hair was jet black and was wrapped in a silk scarf with a mottled pattern which matched her blouse. This was a chemise traditionally worn by European peasants in a bleached cotton with beautifully darned patterns made more effective by their brevity. What captivated were her grey eyes. Breathtakingly grey. Her face was beautiful but those eyes elevated her to the realms of the Italian gods.

She had the undeniable look of a gypsy. Exotic, mysterious, she sat stoically patient at each break in the journey, sporadically reading from a tiny volume open in her lap. The script of this book was too small to read from his side of the carriage.

Italian? French? Rumanian? Which country could be the provenance of such a stunning work of female art?

During a long stopover at Bologna Station a young woman took the spare seat next to the gypsy. This woman made meticulous preparation for her comfort on the last stage of the train's journey and once settled thumbed through a glossy magazine. Whatever the magazine contained attracted the gypsy woman's interest and the two women struck up a conversation. They were both American.

Andy could not recall a more bitter disappointment.

It was his first trip to Venice and when they emerged from the train station to get the water bus all his disappointment was forgotten. What a spectacular place. Everywhere you looked, Venice had grey eyes.

Andy would have liked to contact the journalist and offer him an alternative reason for the flags. Marketing. So many shops had England flags for sale, a large number of them being sold by the till. This possibility had been overlooked by the man from The Times and was not included in his reasoning.

In his bet on the three witches, it was Marcia who was eliminated and broke the magical silence. The falseness of her studiedly jolly voice bringing a wave of irritation.

'I'm actually looking forward to the World Cup,' she pretended. 'The trouble is, once it starts, there's no escape. It isn't long before you want to get as far away from it all as is humanly possible. It takes over your life, everybody's life. It is all pervading, like World War Two. I get this constant urge to go underground and avoid the blitz.'

'The moon would be the only safe place. I doubt that they broadcast there.'

'Last year's cricket was exciting,' said Margery. 'The players look so smart dressed in their whites.'

'Wasn't it,' Jinny agreed enthusiastically. 'If you would have told me that I would ever have had any interest in cricket, I would have laughed in your face.'

'Will the football be as good as the cricket?' asked Margery.

'If we win, I suppose so,' supposed Marcia. 'Can we win?'

'Of course we'll win,' said Jinny. 'We're the best team.'

'I'm not so sure about that,' Marcia doubted.

'I was reading an article in The Times that said we have a very good chance,' said Jinny. 'Apparently, we have all the right ammunition.'

'Is it a war?' asked Margery. 'It seems to me that all sporting adjectives are somewhat savage. Attack! Ammunition! Strike!'

'I told you,' said Marcia. 'World War Two.'

'Andy, do you think we're going to win?'

'If it says so in The Times,' said Andy. 'It must be true.'

'Who remembers The Whiteoaks of Jalna?' asked Jinny.

'Mazo de la Roche.'

'I loved those books when I was young. I wonder if they're still in print?'

When he got home that evening Andy put on a CD. Music wafted through the rooms, breaking the silence, for the first time in a long time.

* * *

During the day prior to the first book club, Andy suffered a dose of cold feet. What if he and Jinny turned up that afternoon and nobody showed. This notion caused a shiver of fear and embarrassment. How triumphant might Jinny be? He was definitely losing the battle to win her over and he had nobody but himself to blame.

Jinny's optimism expected a turnout of around twenty maybe twenty five students. They arrived to find the room bursting at the seams. There were so many children they were sitting two to a desk and standing against the walls. It had taken a large portion of the allotted time to organise the room into some sort of order.

'What is the point of reading?' Andy asked the room.

'To learn, sir.'

'To learn. I saw an interview with a very famous French actress named Jeanne Moreau and she said she learned about life from reading books. All of you can do the same. What else.'

'Places and people and that.'

'Anything else?' Andy sat on the edge of the desk one leg dangling. 'Come on. What about you, Davis, why do you read?'

'Escapism?'

'Can you put that more simply?'

'Pleasure.'

'Well done, Davis. Pleasure. It's supposed to be fun and if we learn something on the way, all well and good.'

Andy was bursting with enthusiasm. Coming into the room and seeing so many children had filled his chest with optimism. He could see the surprise on Jinny's face and knew that she was equally chuffed.

'Something I want you to do for me. It's not a difficult thing but you'd be amazed how few people do this little thing. Anybody from my classes going to help out?'

'Think, sir.'

'Thank you, Safia. Hands up who thinks England will win the World Cup?'

Orderly hands flapped in the air, Jinny was so involved she almost raised her own hand.

'You in the green sweater. What's your name?'

'Jennifer Cowan, sir.'

'OK Jennifer, are they or aren't they?'

'Yes sir, they are.'
'Why do you think that?'
'The newspapers and telly say we will.'
'We're the best, sir.'
'Fair enough, who agrees with Jennifer, put up your hands. Hold it a minute. It's going to be easier to have the disbelievers. No disbelievers? Fine. I'm the only person in this room who knows that England will not win the World Cup. In fact I'll say they won't come anywhere near winning.'
'What if you're wrong, sir.'
'What if they win, sir.'
'I'll do a forfeit.'
'Kiss Mrs Parish, sir.'
'That's not a forfeit. Can't you do better than that?'
'Eat your hat.'
'Run naked across the playground.'
'There's something to think about, a forfeit. But and it's a big but, what if I'm right? Then I'll be the only person in this room who thought differently but I'll still be right. That's what I want you to do. Think differently. When you read a book don't just let it wash over you. Think about what the writer is saying. Whether you're for or against it, make your own decisions. Don't take the writer's word for it. Do not be afraid to be different and to think differently. Almost any topic has spin. Who knows what spin is?'
'What bowlers do in cricket?'
'Changing stuff.'

The resonance of the occasion jogged Jinny's memory. Reverend Bingham with his white hair and whiskers, stood elevated in the pulpit. The pulpit was carved wood, highly polished like the top of the Reverend's head. That was a different sort of resonance. Reverence and resonance. Reverend Bingham had a deep bass voice that he raised vigorously from the depths of his bowels and the words emerged like a tummy rumble. Virtue, he growled, virtue. Virtue was a big word in Reverend Bingham's sermons. He was a passionate man Reverend Bingham and especially passionate about virtue. As a child she had no idea what virtue meant.

'Propaganda.'
'Who said that?'

'Andrews,' Jinny told him.
'Andrews, where are you?'
'Here, sir.'
'Do you watch Robin Hood on TV?'
'Sometimes.'
'In Robin Hood, King Richard the Lionheart, is supposed to be a great hero. Historians will tell you this is complete crap. Prince John, the baddie, was actually a decent man. There are plenty more stories like that. Don't accept everything you're told. On this basis I want you read about subjects personal to yourselves and get a new spin.'

A hubbub created by waiting parents, anxious to collect their offspring, caused the meeting to close. Still a queue formed to ask for recommendations for reading matter. Several disgruntled parents removed their children from the waiting throng . Andy, sensing the disenchantment spoiling the moment, called for quiet and made himself available for lunchtime the following day. Jinny, carried by the excitement, agreed to join him.

School life is a constant contrast of activity and suspension before the next brisk commotion. Andy sourced energy from these agitations like a bicycle dynamo reviving its light system. The more feverish the lesson, the better it went.

The tumult of the occasion had propelled Jinny into an unfamiliar intoxication. If she drank excessively or smoked dope she would recognise a high. Shell-shocked, the two teachers sat in that lull after the storm, each caught up in their own thoughts, too euphoric to break the spell.

She wanted to say something nice but perversity prevented her. Was she afraid that if she was complimentary, she might give him some misguided encouragement. If she was afraid, why was she afraid? She must review her regard for Betsy March. She was not such a fool after all. The energy this man brought to the classroom was exhilarating. Exhilarating and something else. She struggled to pluck this elusive ephemera from the charged atmosphere that remained in the wake of the book club. It hovered, tantalisingly fluttering around her but remained at arm's length.

 Andy's emotions were being utilised to feed his ego and provide vindication. His father had discouraged his intention to teach but he seriously believed he had a vocation. It was the sole action of his existence that could be justified as resolute. All his other life decisions had been a consensus of vacillations, even his pending marriage to Karen had taunted his fickle backbone.

Andrew shook his head, 'Wow. That was really something.'

'It's what makes it all worthwhile,' Jinny agreed.

The forfeit suggested was, you'll have to kiss Mrs Parish and his response, that is not a forfeit. He had said it. Was it a thing of the moment or was it a Freudian slip. Could he like her? He did not show any sign that he did. Did she want him to like her? She wanted everyone to like her.

Sexy, that was the word she was searching for. Reverend Bingham had been sexy in his virtuous way and Andrew was sexy. Now, as an adult she had a clear understanding of virtue. Pity some of the students did not share her understanding. With the word sexy she was less sure of her ground. When she was growing up it applied to the opposite gender but recently the word had achieved a more flexible usage. Today it might describe anything. Was Angus sexy? She had never thought of him in that way. If she was totally honest, she could not recollect ever having felt sexy. Sometimes while watching films, violence stirred her in a curiously pleasant way but sex was something they did on Friday nights , birthdays and their anniversary.

They shared eye contact for some seconds, her face shining with innocent pleasure like a teenager. Andy saw that this was a perfect opportunity for him to make an advance but a craven spirit blocked his way. Excuses swarmed his brain, her innocence, his lechery, her existing marriage, his expired marriage, he was not ready yet, too short a mourning period, her children and most important of all, possible rebuff.

CHAPTER TWELVE

Anniversary dinner

The Copse was a purpose built prestigious hotel that did not choose to be wedded to the negative kudos associated with the name of Wyford and gave its address as Cordwainers Cross, the village at its rear entrance.

There were two restaurants, the Arboretum, which specialised in carved meats and cost an arm and a leg and the Spinney, which served a buffet and boasted a four week waiting list.

Their anniversary had been the previous Thursday, the table was booked, the twins were dressed and ready but Angus was held up at the office and they had to postpone. Re-arranging at short notice took a lot out of Jinny, both in energy and humiliation, but she was determined to make her belated anniversary evening memorable.

The table was booked for eight and at seven thirty, the boys were dressed in their suits and getting fidgety. There was no sign of Angus and his mobile was switched off.

As angry as Jinny could manage, she was livid. This was the second time he had done this. Some things are more important than work. What is the point of success if you cannot share the spoils with your family?

The boys went into the lounge to watch Eastenders while Jinny retried his mobile. It was on the answer phone service so she tried the office. Angus' secretary, Geraldine, who preferred to be called his PA, was not there but a pleasant voice picked up the phone. 'They left over an hour ago.'

'Do you know where he went?'

'I'll check his diary,' said the voice. 'The last entry for today says 'anniversary dinner at The Copse'.'

'Thank you.'

'Congratulations, Mrs Parish. Enjoy your meal.'

She thanked him again, wondering if they would ever get to dinner and toyed with dialling 999. She joined the twins and checked her watch every thirty seconds. Too keyed up to watch television, unable to sit still for a second, she tidied the already spotless kitchen and circled the telephone. She adjusted the display of anniversary cards, realigning them carefully, savouring the acknowledgments from friends and family. Her trembling fingers could not cope and like dominoes the cards toppled to the floor. Sighing heavily, she packed them together and began again.

As she put them back on the shelf she re-read some of the dedications. Those from Alex and James were beautifully written and the thoughtful wording helped settle her nerves. She sought out those sent by her nieces and nephew. The sentiment expressed on Truman's card was so sweet it made her weepy. She was so fond of him, he was such a darling boy.

At seven fifty it rang, 'Where are you?' he demanded.

'Waiting for you,' she struggled to keep her temper.

'I'm here, waiting for you. We agreed to meet at the hotel.'

'No we didn't.'

'We'll talk about this later,' he hung up.

'We're meeting daddy there.'

'Let us watch this 'til the end,' whined Alex.

'It's almost finished,' said James.

'We're late,' she said.

'What difference will five minutes make?'

Jinny was in no mood to have her evening spoiled and she switched off the television. This uncharacteristic action, not her normal compliant self, alienated both the boys.

The waiting staff at The Copse were extremely well-trained. Smart, efficient, discreet, dressed in trim dark suits with gleaming white shirts and blouses that glowed in the subdued lighting. They provided a high standard of service that impressed but the clientele preferred lager to wine.

Being late they were made to wait in line. Not used to being kept waiting, caused Angus to get petulant. The boys, set on revenge, spent the time jostling each other like ten year olds. Their silly behaviour was being upstaged by a teenage girl in the party before them. She and her mother squabbled vehemently, their argument culminating in the daughter stamping her foot. The mother attempted to pacify the girl, took her arm and lectured her directly in her ear. The girl twisted free and gave Angus a severe bump. The parents apologised profusely and the twins giggled.

'This girl is a pain,' said Angus.

'Girls mature faster than boys,' Jinny replied.

Angus did not bother to answer, so much of what his wife said did not warrant a response.

The party in front were escorted away to a table and the floor manager approached Angus and spoke confidentially, 'There is a table coming available in the corner. I would appreciate it if you let the party behind have that one. You won't have to wait much longer.'

'We booked and we have been kept waiting…'Angus began angrily, blotches spotting his grim countenance but Jinny stepped in.

'Of course,' she said and indicated for Angus to look behind.

A lady in a wheelchair smiled up at him, 'Of course,' he echoed. 'Will you two grow up.' The boys stopped wrestling and stood aside to let the wheelchair through.

Their table was close to some sort of celebration, four tables had been pushed together and were liberally covered with empty bottles. Two waiters shuffled past carrying trays of beer and lager bottles .

'Can I get you a glass, sir.'

'No thanks all the same, I prefer to drink like a man. Bring me a straw.'

Their waitress tried to take their drink order but they could not make themselves heard above the guffaws and howls of laughter. Angus was peeved by the adjacent festivity. 'Could we get another table?' he asked. 'In a quieter part of the room.'

'I'll try, sir,' she promised. 'But we are particularly full tonight.'

Angus was now in a mood and the boys continued playing up. Jinny asked them nicely to behave like adults. As usual, Angus took their side and the three of them begin ganging up on her. They were a team, all with the same colouring and the same temperament.

She so wanted it to be a family evening and she tried to make conversation. 'That man Andrew Avecore, says that...'

'Who?'

'Andrew Avecore, the new Head of Department...'

'Oh him,' Angus scarcely tried to conceal his irritation.

Angus was sitting opposite Alex whose foot was wobbling at a rapid rate and he checked under the table for the source of the shaking.

'He was saying that England...'

'Must we talk shop,' Angus complained, his fierce eyes glaring at the revellers.

Their drinks arrived, Alex leaned forward to slurp a mouthful of cola, sitting back with his foot jiggling at a faster rate, the glassware and ice on the table tinkled nervously.

'For goodness sake, Alex,' Angus scolded. 'Stop fidgeting.'

Alex slumped deeper into his chair and sulked. Jinny panicking that the evening was going to be a complete disaster, made the boys swap seats. She would put up with Alex' constant footwork. Pouting, the boys swapped places, and as he flopped into his new chair James jarred the table and spilled the drinks. This caused general cheers and merriment on the neighbouring tables.

'Now look what you've done,' Angus snarled at her. 'Can't you let well alone?'

'Please, Angus...' downcast and hurt she prayed he would leave it there.

'You have to interfere.'

Staff appeared instantly, armed with towels and swiftly cleared away. Alex and James siding with their father, wore 'isn't she sad' expressions. They went to choose their hors d'oeuvres, leaving her alone, her body quivering with shame and disappointment. She breathed deeply trying to collect herself. When they returned she used her desperation ploy, 'How are you getting to the match on Sunday?'

Peace at last. Wyford had won their way to the play-off final and the three of them were going to Cardiff. They happily discussed their travel arrangements and what paraphernalia they should take. They wanted a banner flag to wave at the match but had no time to get to the Club Shop.

'You'll have plenty of time on Saturday.'

'They will have sold out, long before then.'

Jinny, already chairing a parents' meeting to finalise the New York trip after school on Tuesday and a book club on Wednesday, was delegated.

Jinny decided that the evening had been a success after all. The meal had been excellent, the boys, their stomachs full seemed to have enjoyed it. Angus, having eaten heartily and with the adjacent celebration petered out, was patently in a happier mood.

'I've got a surprise for you boys,' he announced with a mischievous glint. Angus loved to tease his children and force them into guessing games.

'What?' the twins asked in unison.

'Uncle Jock has got you jobs for the summer. Guess where.'

'Glebe Road.'

'Nothing to do with football.'

'I can't guess.'

'Me neither,' said James, well practiced with his father's games. 'Give us a clue.'

'Virginia Woolf.'

'Who?'

'Shows how much they look at your mother's bookshelves,' Angus was enjoying himself. 'I'll give you another clue. As You Like It.'

'As we like what?'

'As You Like It, the play, by Shakespeare. The first line.'

'Orlando?' Jinny was confused.

'Orlando,' Angus laughed in triumph.

'Orlando, Florida.'

'Disneyworld!'

'Your uncle Jock has arranged it for you.'

Jinny was at a loss also. Jock? Who did he know? He had recently returned from America but that was a holiday.

'Disneyworld.'

'Disneyworld!'

'They need some well-spoken English boys, preferably twins, to help for the summer.'

'Really!'

'Accommodation's included and you get paid.'

'When?'

'The World Cup final is July 9th and the flights are booked for the 10th. It's a six week contract, so you'll be back on the bank holiday Monday. You'll have the whole summer there. It's good timing. Your mother will be on her trip to New York.'

'You might have consulted me,' said Jinny.

'What, they'll be getting the best of everything. The day after England are crowned World Champions they'll be off to Disneyworld for the chance of a lifetime.'

'They'll be away for their A level results.'

'So what. You have to find the downside of everything.'

Jinny was about to defend herself when the waitress appeared at her side. About to decline the offer of further drinks she looked up into the face of Betsy March. 'Hello, I thought you were a waitress.'

'Yes, it wasn't the most sensible choice of outfit but I've not been here before.'

Betsy was with her husband, Larry and another man. With the light behind him she could not discern his face. He was dressed smartly in a black mohair suit with a dark shirt and a striped silk tie, stripes gleaming weirdly in the muted lighting. They exchanged greetings and well wishes and the man stepped forward to be introduced.

'This is Jinny's new boss, Andrew Avecore, this is Jinny's family. Angus, James and Alex.'

Andy shook hands as each was introduced.

'We were talking about you earlier,' said Angus.

Jinny placed her hand over her husband's hand but he quickly withdrew it.

'I'm sure you'll get over it,' said Andrew in an unpleasant tone.

'Having enticed Andrew to Wyford,' said Betsy. 'I felt we owed him a dinner.'

'It's very nice here.'

'Very swish,' Betsy confirmed. 'Is this a special occasion?'

'It's our wedding anniversary.'

'How many years?'

'Eighteen.'

'Congratulations.'

How well black looked with his red hair. She was not gifted

at intuition but while Andrew was watching Angus and Betsy talking she saw disapproval in his dark blue eyes. He seemed to know Angus and sensed he did not like him. How could that possibly be the case?

'We must be going, there's a taxi waiting.'

'Nice meeting you.'

'See you in school tomorrow.'

Jinny declined dessert but the twins returned with their plates piled high and Angus disappeared to make a phone call.

'I sat next to that man from your school,' said Alex, his mouth full of pie. 'At the football.'

'Don't talk with your mouth full.'

When they got home, the boys went straight to bed and Jinny took a leisurely bath to make herself ready for Angus. He was checking his e-mails before coming to bed. Tastefully perfumed and powdered, she lay naked amongst the clean sheets and awaited his arrival.

Andrew looked quite handsome in a suit. He looked very respectable, dressed properly. Why can't he dress that way all the time and stop trying to make an impression. He is too old to be a rebel. Why is it men never grow up? Why are they all pigheaded like Lear?

Fools by heavenly compulsion

Why is this the case? She searched through her beloved Shakespeare for a solution but there was none. She sensed some misogyny in his writings, but did not condemn her hero. These attitudes were based on the mores of the times. Basically people are the way they are and have been down the centuries. With a few minor adjustments, Shakespeare is equally applicable in the 21st century as it was in the 16th and 17th.

She awoke at four am, feeling cold and the bed empty. She put on her robe and went to investigate. In the lounge, snow was hissing loudly on the television set and Angus lay slumped, head back, snoring. Drool slid from the corner of his mouth, down his chin, creating a wet patch on his shirt.

CHAPTER THIRTEEN

First lesson

Wyford had won their play-off final. Their success had lifted the spirits of the school to an unprecedented level. The classrooms and corridors buzzed and vibrated. There was an air of expectancy because the victorious team was returning to circle the town in an open-topped bus. Nobody was going to get a detention and be kept behind to miss the celebrations.

It had been a smoothly efficient day and Andy was also feeling good. He had answered all his telephone messages and there was no outstanding homework to mark. He entered the classroom and in the expectant faces awaiting his arrival he sensed some energy. He opened his brief case and got out the 'Scott of the Antarctic' articles he had set the class. He dumped the paperwork on the desk and turned to face the students. 'What can I say? I'm gob smacked.'

He picked up the homework, called the names and passed them along the rows of desks. 'Michael O'Sullivan. Excellent work. Daisy Winter. Good stuff. Safia Begum. Excellent work. What I'd like to do today is show you something I found on the net and get your views. Tracey and Michael give me a hand.'

Together they taped to the blackboard a sheet of paper Andy had written out the night before.

SCOTT WAS BEATEN TO THE SOUTH POLE BY THE NORWEGIAN EXPLORER ROALD AMUNDSEN BUT HIS STIRRING DIARY RECOVERED FROM THE POLE 6 MONTHS LATER AND THEN PUBLISHED LARGELY ECLIPSED ADMUNDSENS ACHIEVEMENT IN THE ENGLISH SPEAKING WORLD. 38 WORDS.

'This was published recently in a newspaper. Now then, with what you've learned about your subject what is this article telling you and what is being omitted.'

'Jerry.'

'His full name. It could be any Scott.'

'Good one but such is his fame that as you read on you know which Scott.'

'Only because I have the knowledge to know which Scott, sir.'

'Absolutely. What else? What is being left unsaid? Tracey.'

'That Scott failed but even though he lost the race he's remembered better than Amundsen.'

'Well done, Tracey. Why is this the case? Tim.'

'His diary, sir. Oates going out into the snow to die was extremely brave and the way he faced his own death.'

'Somebody paraphrase Tim. Daisy.'

'It's a good story.'

'Yes, what else is it?'

'A tearjerker.'

'Who said that?'

'Johnson, sir.'

'Philip, exactly, a tearjerker. Gets you right in the...' he rammed his stomach with a clenched fist. 'What the film critics call visceral. What do you we call this kind of manipulation nowadays? Philip.'

'Spin, sir.'

'Spin. Isn't it clever how we can encapsulate two men's lives into 38 words. How would you feel if your life was cut down to 38 words. Yes, Malika.'

'Why the English speaking world, sir?'

'In what way, sorry.'

'Why the English speaking world. There are more people speaking other languages than English.'

'Why do the English speakers have all the power? Good question. At that time, before World War One, England ruled the World. Within the next decade or so they lost the job to the United States.'

'That doesn't explain why the other languages don't get a hearing.'

'Too bloody right, Khan. Who can explain why English has become the dominant language of the World when the majority speak Spanish. Nobody.'

'Television.'

'Scott came before television but you're not far off.'

'Hollywood.'

'Was that you Philip?'

'Yes, sir.'

'You're going well, today. Hollywood. Technology was getting a massive foothold and films could be transported around the world easily. Silent films could be understood everywhere, even in the darkest jungles of Africa. Hollywood made countless billions from silent films. When talkies came along they still had all the power. Most of the world's talent gravitated there. Jasmine.'

'Why'd they put up a statue to a failure?'

'I can't really answer that but what I will say is search around London and see what statues there are. Quite a lot of them have been forgotten or were not that big a deal in the first place. Abraham Lincoln's statue is in Parliament Square and to me his connection with Britain is paper thin. They were of the moment.'

'He was a hero, sir.'

'Who was, Tracey?'

'Scott, sir.'

'He was indeed. Let's try and equate this with our own lives. Who can you think of that was once a hero and is now discredited?'

'Geri Halliwell.'

'Anybody else, more political.'

'Blunkett.'

'George Best.'

'Hardly political, Jerry, but interesting. Who has a view on George Best?'

'Michael.'

'Britain's greatest ever footballer.'

'John.'

'A piss artist, sir.'

Andy waited for the laughter to die down, 'Thank you, John. You put that very succinctly. Malika.'

'He was given every chance, sir and he didn't take proper care of himself. I can't feel sorry for him.'

'Anybody else? Safia.'

'I agree with Malika, sir. He got a new kidney and he wasted it. There are lots of more deserving people.'

'Shut up Begum,' said Michael. 'He was the greatest footballer this country's ever seen. He should have a statue.'

'Thanks, Michael but let someone else get a chance to speak. Let's take a vote. Who agrees with Safia and who agrees with Michael?'

The vote was almost entirely split between the boys and the girls, except for one or two dissenters. 'Sabrina, why did you vote with the boys?'

'George Best was Irish, sir and so am I.'

'What about you, Philip.'

'George Best played for Manchester United. I'm a gooner.'

'I see, valid stuff. How many of you went to the match Saturday?' His question induced a vibrant show of hands. 'Did you read the match report in the papers the following morning. Jasmine?'

'Yes, sir.'

'Did the newspaper report the match the way you saw it?'

'No, sir. There wasn't much of a report in my paper but it went on and on about some kid I'd never heard of.'

'He's going to be in the World Cup squad, idiot.'

'Was there a particular incident in the match that wasn't in the article?'

'We won but our paper said we were lucky.'

'Kept on about if we get promoted we'll come straight back down again.'

'So what have we established. The reporters had different issues to you. Saw things differently. Had different concerns.'

'I'll say he did, sir. He was at the wrong game.'

'They weren't Wyford supporters.'

'That's right, they weren't Wyford supporters. They were supposed to be impartial. Hands up those who thought the reports were fair.' He waited a moment but no one raised a hand. 'Those who thought the reports were unfair? Right, that's what you call a majority. On that basis, how would you feel if your life was condensed into 50 words? 50 words of part misinformation. It's up to you to do something to prevent that happening.'

He went to the board and wrote in large letters KNOW YOUR SUBJECT.

'Too many people have opinions based on little information. Too many people don't read books and therefore get their information from the newspapers and we've established how slipshod they can be.'

He pointed to the board, 'Know your subject. I cannot stress this any stronger. If you really care about anything do not rely on one source. Don't be satisfied with this information just because it meets with your own prejudices. That person providing the information might share your bias and be researching just enough to enforce those biases.'

The bell rang but the class waited for him to give permission to go.

'You can all make your mark. Every one of you. It's up to you and the effort you are prepared to put into it. Don't always believe what you read. Research and decide for yourself. Don't let other people put words in your mouth. Thanks for a good lesson. Hop it.'

'Bye, sir.'

The classroom emptied in a flash and he removed the taped article from the board.

Scott was a comparatively young man when he died and they crammed his entire life into 50 words. They crammed Karen's life into 24 words. Car, killed, name, location of the accident. That she was pregnant that was newsworthy but they spelled her name wrong, Karen Anchor. Indifferent incompetents.

* * *

The one evening Jinny was available to join the others for a drink nobody else was free. Even Margery, who was always available, was going on a church outing to 'Phantom of the Opera'.

Angus had taken the day off work to take the twins to Wyford's away leg in the first round of the Division One play-offs. It was an evening kick off and their opponents' ground was three hours travelling time, so they had set off straight after lunch. She did not expect them home before midnight.

At Wyford Grammar, sixth form teaching for A levels was over. In the remaining period before the exams students were free to revise wherever they chose. As far as she was concerned, the boys were wasting a valuable day designated for study and she was unhappy about it. The tickets had been bought in advance without reference to her.

To placate her, they were taking their books along to read on the journey. It was an empty promise. Since children, any attempt to read while in motion had made both boys sick to their stomach.

She did concede that they had been slogging non-stop and a day off might rejuvenate them. They were working ever so hard, the sweet little things.

So, she would have the place to herself. She could do exactly as she pleased. She would not be required to make dinner. She would make a salad, or Welsh Rarebit, or eggs on toast. Curiously, this promised freedom did not cheer her. She felt as empty as the house.

Bobby, equally forlorn, put his chin on her knee and gazed up her with sad brown eyes.

'I'll take you for a walk later,' she promised but in her heart did not feel like doing so. When they had got the dog it was for Angus and the twins and between them they vowed to take proper care of Bobby. When it came to walking time, Angus was never there and the boys were always busy with schoolwork or some other pressing matter. Yet another unwanted responsibility pushed upon her. She did not mind really, Bobby was such a sweet dog.

In truth, this night would be the same as most other nights. Angus had missed supper and as soon as the boys finished theirs they locked themselves in their rooms. Angus rolled up around ten pm, ate a spoiled dinner or made do with cheese and biscuits.

Angus was not taking proper care of himself. She must have a stern word. He must be made to listen. One day he will collapse and it will be too late. Working all hours and not eating properly. It will catch up with in the end. This truth made her feel more depressed.

She ran a bath but the warm water did not spin its usual magic. She could not summon any good thoughts, so she planned the following day.

Composing her shopping list, making her way down the aisles at Tesco which triggered a fond recollection of winter suppers. She was positive there was a tin of Heinz spaghetti in the back of the larder. She would have that tin on toast with a steaming mug of tea, so thick you can stand your spoon in it. Just like daddy used to do.

That reminded her of a firework night when daddy had gone to a lot of trouble. He had been secretly buying fireworks for weeks and hiding them in a tea chest in the garage. On the night, Mummy and Charlotte had the flu and she and daddy had done Guy Fawkes night together. She could still feel the heat from the bonfire on her cheeks and the tingles of pleasure in her tummy from the sparkles and glitters of colour.

She dried herself quickly, hurrying to check, to be sure her memory was not playing tricks on her. As she emptied out the over crowded cupboard, a panic took hold, no such tin seemed to be there. If she took Bobby for a walk before supper she could buy a tin at the corner shop. A can of pilchards toppled over and collapsed several more tins in its wake. There, in a corner was what she had been searching for, unmistakable in its bright yellow coat and red lettering.

Winter Sunday evenings after church. Songs of Praise and the four of them cosy, huddled around the television. Her tummy full of spaghetti, or macaroni cheese. Sometimes daddy would join in with the hymns and the three women would gently complain, laughing, pleading with him to stop and he, feigning to be hurt by their complaints.

As the spaghetti warmed in the pan, the smell it gave off tore at her heart. It was all gone. Angus did not love her as her father loved her. Sitting on daddy's lap in church while he cuddled her to him and played with her pigtails. Her chest warmed with nostalgia.

Angus did not express much affection towards her or the boys. It must be the male genes because the boys were not affectionate either. Is it a male thing? Her father was affectionate in church but much more reserved at home. Maybe it's a thing of the times. It is not macho to show your feelings physically.

With a sigh she served up her meal, sat at the kitchen table with Bobby crumpled at her feet. She opened her new book, one that Marcia had recommended. Marcia's judgement was so reliable. Jinny loved starting new books. In a few brief sentences, being transported to a new world.

The story was about a woman who had a baby and hated the child from the instant it was born. This sour theme distorted the flavour of her food and both left a bad taste in her mouth. What is the world coming to? Women's emancipation was all very well but what is the one irrevocable blessing that women have over men. Maternal instinct. Now this writer, a man of course, wants to deprive a woman of her greatest gift.

She pushed the book and plate away and considered what other gifts God had blessed her with. Children's faces, good, bad and indifferent, paraded across her memory. She felt a strong sense of accomplishment and self worth. Then there had been the book club. Why had that evening been so intoxicating? Is it that man? Does he have something special to offer? She could not fathom the answer to these questions.

Not only was Avecore good looking but he had a softer side. Was it that which attracted the students? Was it that which attracted her? Would children be attracted to his looks the way she was? Children develop so quickly these days, even the boys. It is not good for them, innocence is one of life's wonderful treasures and it is disappearing. It is not healthy to have too much too soon.

The innocent sleep,
Sleep that knits up the ravelled sleeve of care
Was she jealous of him? Could that be possible? Were his outrageous views real or were they a ploy? Was he being different just for the sake of it? Or was he simply stirring the pot?

'He's stirring the pot,' she told herself out loud and felt odd that she was enjoying have her pot stirred.

'My goodness,' she exclaimed. 'I forgot to telephone.'

Jinny had taken to talking out loud quite a lot recently.

It was almost eight o'clock. She turned on the television and switched to Teletext. The match had kicked off fifteen minutes before.

'Damnation!'

They might have called her and told her they had arrived safely. It works both ways this calling business. When they first got their mobiles they called on the least pretext. This was happening less and less of late, only when they wanted something.

They used to go into Wyford shopping together but this had stopped entirely. She remembered vividly how hurt she felt when the boys began to be ashamed to be seen with her. Not wanting to be spotted by their friends going out with their mother.

From their mother's womb
Untimely ripped

At the approach of their school friends they would inextricably put distance between themselves and her. Disappearing on flimsy pretexts to be alone.

It was Marcia who explained what was happening and put her mind at rest. Marcia was such a good friend and quite bright on matters that required common sense. That was something she had to admit about herself. She could not say she was a worldly person. The way the world was she did not care all that much.

Being weary of these worldly bars
Never lacks power to dismiss itself

Julius Caeser for a change, there had been too much Macbeth for one evening.

She flicked back to Teletext and found that Wyford had taken the lead and was glad because the men would be happy.

She touched the wrong button and clicked back to the headlines which struck her as childish and inflammatory. ARSENAL GLORY, TOTTENHAM TRAGEDY. It is only football after all and the grammar is pitiful.

The art of conversation will soon die out.

One afternoon during the Easter break, she, Marcia and Margery had met at Costa for coffee. On the next table, out with their parents and still at an age when this practice is not heinous crime, were a brother and sister. Bored stiff, they sat morosely staring at the dials on their mobiles, swapping texts. Not only will conversation die out but essays will be written in mobile shorthand.

Shkspr, gd 4 u or bd 4 u, discus.

There is so much beauty in language, so much beauty in life and it is passing the children by.

CHAPTER FOURTEEN

Book club

On the first evening of book club proper, Jinny turned into the corridor and could hear a riotous din coming from the classroom. The noise suggested a good turn out. There had been so many requests to join they were separating the club into two evenings. Years 10 to 12 on the first night and the younger children on the second. They had miscalculated the numbers and there were forty students fighting over thirty seats. Jinny attempted to organise the seating but confusion still reigned as Andy arrived.

'Quiet!' he yelled. 'Please. Boys to the windows, girls to the wall. Now! Quietly.'

Girls outnumbered boys two to one but Andy came up with a quick plan. 'Years 11 and 12 take the nearest seat.' Eight spaces remained. 'Year 10, hold up your hands. You lot can sit.' Andrew went among them and picked the largest of those left standing. 'You two sit. The rest of you can sit on the desk top and sit to one side so those seated can see to the front and no squabbling. Davis, why are you always there when there's a problem. I went to school with a boy like you. There's always one.'

'Stop going on, Davis.'

'Yeah, shut up, Davis.'

'Yes, sir. Sir, can I read Lady Chatterley's Lover?'

'You can read anything you wish. I'm sure Mrs Parish has got a copy at home you can borrow.'

'I have not…' Jinny spluttered and caused a lot of raucous amusement.

'Davis, like many books that get a lot of publicity, it is overrated. Compared to the books most of your parents leave lying around the house, the sex bits are quite tame.'

'You've read it then, sir,' Davis was pleased with himself.

'Yes, Davis. I read it. For a friend.'

'Are there any football novels, sir.'

'Sure. None of them are up to much. Fever Pitch is probably the best. Do you know that one?'

'No, sir.'

'See me after,' said Andy. 'I'll have remembered the author's name by then. Anybody else?'

'Gibbs, what about you? What are you interested in?'

'Palaeontology, sir.'

'There is a very good book to read for you. Mrs Parish?'

'The Lost World by Arthur Conan Doyle.'

'Anybody know what Conan Doyle is more famous for? Malika.'

'Sherlock Holmes, sir.'

'Exactly. Conan Doyle was an enthusiast like Gibbs. He was also interested in boxing and the occult. All his books are a compelling read. Malika what are you interested in?'

'Boys, sir,' offered Davis.

'A very worthy topic. There's a book called the Catcher in the Rye that's about an interesting boy. What I want you to do is decide what kind of subject you want to read about. It doesn't matter how shite the subject. Find Mrs Parish or myself and we'll give you a reading list. Next meeting will be next week in this room. Then we will find out how you got on. Anyone who knows what they would like to read about already. Form a queue and we'll give you a list now. Remember, no request is too silly.'

Jinny took up a position behind the desk, she had the chair while he remained standing. Her ears and face were burning with shame. How could he use language like that? As soon as the children had dispersed she would tell him she did not want any part of his book club.

'Yes, Jessica.'

'Are there any books about being black?'

'Sure there are. There are a lot of black writers. Black Boy by Richard Wright might be hard to get a copy of from the library.'

'Anything else?'

'Black Like Me by a man named Griffiths. I've got a copy of that, also a book called Nigger. I'll bring them in for you tomorrow.'

'Thanks, sir. Thanks a lot. How come you're interested in coloured people?'

'I'm interested in everybody. Why, shouldn't I be?'

'I don't know, sir.'

'You try and find the Richard Wright book, OK.'

'Yes, sir.'

Jinny got caught up in the children's enthusiasm and got a kick out of giving ideas to these eager readers. Jinny felt upbeat and had lost the momentum of her displeasure.

When the last of the children had left she packed away her papers and said, 'That went well.'

'It did didn't it. Let's not count our chickens though. They've still to read the bloody things.'

'The majority will,' Jinny said sincerely. 'I'm sure of it.'

'You know as well as I do that at least half of those girls were here because they fancy me.'

Jinny's ruddy complexion returned, 'You conceited...'

'You don't approve of me, do you?'

'Not much. Your language doesn't set a good example. I'm not sure I want to be associated with that sort of language and if you don't stop using such words I think I might leave you to run the book club by yourself.'

'I couldn't give a fuck what you think.'

'I don't think that's called for.'

'You're absolutely right, it was childish. I did it for effect.'

'Why?'

'To loosen up your tight arse.' He grabbed his case, turned out the lights and left her sitting in the twilight. She sat there frozen for several seconds taking in what had happened. He reappeared in the doorway. 'I'll see you tomorrow then?'

'Fuck off,' she replied and clapped her hand over her recalcitrant mouth. She could hear his laughter to the end of the corridor and then he was gone. She remained in the dim room, her face crimson with embarrassment.

CHAPTER FIFTEEN

Pastoral care

It was funny how lessons were giving a buzz again. Prompted by the success of the book club, his adrenalin had surged and he felt a trickle of optimism that had eluded him in recent months. He had always looked to children for the key to hope. Adults were hard to penetrate they were so steeped in their own doctrine

When Andy returned to his office there were two boys waiting outside and they had been waiting some time. So protracted was their wait, they had had time to fall out and were ignoring each other completely. One of the boys had been pointed out to him early on, Edward Holmes, the school's number one reprobate. Holmes had dull eyes set in a potato head covered with rusty iron filings of hair welded at a multitude of angles. Beetroot coloured ears at ninety degrees to his temples and a red nose more plasticine than plastic. He boasted two facial expressions, nasty and about to be nasty. While he waited he passed the time flaying his leg at imaginary stones.

Andy had not seen the second boy before. Heavy set with sturdy legs and arms he evoked a sensitivity that his build denied. He had a round anachronistic face you might see on a Greek statue, topped with a clutch of black hair brushed sideways. This boy's eyes possessed self-assurance beyond his age and Andy wondered if he might have worn long trousers too early in life.

Upon his arrival the unknown boy, leaning indifferently against his door, gave Andy an amused glance. His companion simply scowled.

'Who are you two?'

'He's Holmes,' the self-assured boy spoke on their behalf. 'I'm Watson.'

'What's he on about?' Holmes asked. 'He's Morrissey.'

Morrissey handed him the note from Margery explaining his misdemeanour. By the time he had unravelled Holmes' crumpled missive it was almost illegible.

Andy unlocked the door to his office and ushered them in. They slouched opposite him, Holmes legs and arms in all directions trying to fill as much space as possible, Morrissey, hands firmly planted in his pockets, kept up his supercilious masquerade.

Through the partition Mason's music was clearly audible.

'You're the new teacher ain't you, sir. The one who talks about football. I'm a gooner, meself, sort of thing. They're the greatest team in the world, ain't they sir.'

'If you say so.'

'Are you a gooner, sir?' Holmes tone was provocative, almost threatening.

'Why are you two here?'

'I'm here because nobody understands me,' said Morrissey, self-mocking and he waved his chin in Holmes direction. 'He's here because he's a fucking moron.'

'You're lookin' to get your teef smashed in and your brains spilled all over the playground.'

'Make sure you clear up after you Holmes, you can use all the spare brains you can get.'

'Arsehole. Which team do you support, sir? What about you arsehole, you a gooner? Is everybody deaf? I'm talking here and nobody's listening. I might as well not be here. I might as well go.'

'Do us both a favour, Holmes. Sit down and be quiet.'

'Hey, smartass, mister super cool. He thinks he's Teary Henry. You know what a gooner is don't yer?'

'It's a synonym for wanker or tosser.'

'No it's not, it means…'

'All you gooners are the fucking same. You're like Catholics, some time in the conversation you've got to let it slip, let the other person know what you are. You've all got your heads up your arse, hence the teams name and I wish the whole lot of you would shrivel up and die.'

'Did you hear what he said, sir. I'm a caflick anorl. You gonna let him get away with that? He's got no right insulting my religion.'

'I'm a caflick anorl,' the self-assured boy mimicked. 'Born one but wouldn't be seen dead in church or Highbury.'

'It's the Emirates now, ain't it. Smartass. Sir, how about it. You gonna let him talk like that, sort of thing?'

'It was a bit excessive but let's leave Arsenal football team for another time.'

Holmes sulked, re-spread his limbs, lacking the dramatic effect he intended, he readjusted. Turned his face to the wall, crossed both legs and arms and grumbled in a monotone to express his dissatisfaction.

'I'll try again shall I. What have you boys been up to?'

Morrissey shrugged, 'Doesn't it say in the note.' Holmes twisted his head in two 180 degree arcs to notify he was still sulking.

'Are we going to sit and listen to Louis Armstrong or are you going to explain why you've been sent to see me?'

'It isn't Louis Armstrong.'

This time the boy's self-assurance was unsettling. His eyes were bright, the dark irises glittering. Of course, Andy had been showing off his knowledge of music but what if he was wrong. Louis Armstrong had many imitators and what it what they heard was one of them. It might not be Louis Armstrong playing the trumpet that boomed out of the next room.

* * *

Andy had written to Holmes' and Morrissey's parents and had not received a reply. He had a telephone number for Holmes but no contact number for Morrissey, simply an address. Holmes lived on the Houndstooth Road, four doors down from the Parish's.

Morrissey was brought up by a single mother who had disappeared shortly before the boy graduated to secondary school. He had been accepted as a charity case but had proved to be a recalcitrant student. His file referred to foster care but recently he had been taken in by family.

He called the Holmes family and tried to arrange an interview. They blankly refused to come to the school, so he agreed to visit them at home. He agreed to a Friday simply because it was the opening match in the World Cup. How better to avoid it.

Andy sneaked a look at the Parish's house which was a simple double fronted house like those that infant children draw. There was a strange arrangement in the front garden, a park bench beside a pond surrounded by cat litter daubed with faeces. The Holmes' house was quadruple fronted with a trio of silver Mercedes on the drive. A female ragamuffin with dull eyes, opened the door to him, hopping from one foot to the other, 'What d'you want?'

'I'm Mr Avecore, from St Bryans.'

'You don't look like a parson.'

'St Bryans school. I'm here to see Mr and Mrs Holmes.'

'Mum,' she screeched, 'It's for you.'

She showed him into an office, hidden behind a cloakroom, adjacent to the front door. The house was curiously serene, there was a distant murmer of a television and he could clearly hear the ragamuffin using the toilet.

Along one wall of the office were a series of heavy duty leather horse collars hanging on large wooden pegs and the room smelled of dubbin. There was a desk with a computer and an untidy pile of invoices. Shelves were filled with box files dated in a childish script. There was a glass cabinet with a dozen or more silver cups, a John Grisham novel and an aerial view of Highbury Stadium. An occasional table had DVDs precariously balanced on top of it. James Bond, Titanic, Four Weddings and the complete Carry On series. There were pictures on the wall of pigs indulging in procreation and members of the Arsenal team portrayed in cartoon form on cigarette cards.

It was a full ten minutes before anyone appeared. 'I'm sorry, my husband is watching the football,' said Mrs Holmes. She was a wizened woman, old before her time with those familiar dull eyes.

'It doesn't start for forty minutes.'

'It is the World Cup, you know.' She said as though it explained everything. Her costume was Primark with various accessories in Burberry check. Her accent was London estuary with clear echoes of dissipation. Her nose was a network of burst capillaries and her breath three fingers of Smithson Square.

'I've never been happy with the school.' She got in first, not interested in Andy's reason for being there. 'We never oughta a sent young Edward. They've never done right by our boy. We fought about takin' him away several times but just didn't get around to it. Anyway, there's little point in him getting GCSE's cos' when he leaves school he'll come into the business.'

'I'm here about the bullying.'

'I'm sure our Eddie is provoked. There's lots who are jealous of us round 'ere. Exclude him, I'm not bovvered.'

'I'm sorry but you leave me no option,' Andy got up to leave. 'It's more serious than exclusion this time.'

Mrs Holmes shrugged.

'Mrs March will be writing to you explaining your rights.'

'If she must.'

During his wait and the subsequent interview with Mrs Holmes, there had been no sign of Kevin or his father. As he was shown to the door, a shabby man with an old lag's round shoulders and a grapefruit in his pocket loped down the hall towards them. There must have been a commercial break and he was taking advantage, entering the toilet his daughter had vacated. The look he gave Andy left him thinking there was a distinct possibility that he was invisible.

He saw Mr Holmes some months later at a fete in Bedford Park, taking part in some sort of horse show. Whatever the competition involved Mr Holmes' carthorse was declared the winner and he was presented with a silver cup and several £20 notes. Mr Holmes extracted the grapefruit from his side pocket in full view of the spectators. He unwound this bankroll, added the winnings to the wad, rewound it tight and put it back in his side pocket.

Rabbits Rise is a council estate middling to west of Wyford. It is built on streets travelling in straight lines only deviating for the curtilage of Bedford Park and the grounds of Jezzard College.

The principal thoroughfare would be called Main Street in the United States. Here it is called Pratt Street after some luminary in the Wyford Highways Department.

Saint Bartimaeus church was built in an era of misguided optimism and is way too large to accommodate the estate's pious. It looms over Pratt Street like a Tate Modern and worshippers resonate hollowly every Sunday in hymn and prayer, huddling together to keep warm. On the forecourt is the temperature chart for the bell tower restoration and a black spot notice numbering the yearly road deaths. This signpost was swathed in flowers commemorating a recent smash.

On the next corner, heading north from the church, was an unkempt end of terrace house in an over generous plot. The gardens to the front side and rear were a junk yard of rusting bric-a-brac. The house itself was as decrepit as Mr Holmes and as neglected as Mr Holmes' children.

In the surrounding houses World Cup fever developed a temperature. There was an expectant hum, undoglike yelps, elongated groans and groups of children kicking a ball at a variety of goals. A sub-station, two piles of coats, a bus shelter, a flank wall. As they played, they called the names of their Gods, Apollo, Beckham, Mars, Lampard. A roar of approval. A roar of delight. A roar of dawn.

The windows of the corner house were wide open and music blared, filling the street. Andy rattled the letter box but no one answered. He waited for a break in the recording and rattled harder. Someone inside turned the sound down and a shadow peered at him through the front room curtains. The front door was opened by a stocky man with a full head of greying hair and a thick well-trimmed beard. He was dressed in khaki shirt and jeans and seemed to be tilting slightly as one shoulder was higher than the other. There was a set of goggles hanging around his neck.

'Mr Morrissey?'

'Who's asking?'

'Andy Avecore, from St Bryans. I wrote I was coming.'

'Dick isn't here.' The stocky man had vibrant eyes.

'I came to see his parents.'

'That'll take some doing,' he stood aside. 'I'm called Erwin. I'm Dick's grandfather. Come on in.'

The hallway was choc a bloc with rusty iron. Reinforcement rods, weightlifting weights, cog wheels. Some of this metal had been welded into recognisable articles. A rusty cockerel created from steel plate and a collage of nails, screws, nuts, bolts forming a nude man.

Through the open door of the front room he saw further stacks of raw material supplemented with books, records and video tapes stacked indiscriminately. Haphazard shelves supported on bricks housed framed photographs, musical instruments and a collection of stuffed birds in glass domes.

Andy was led out back through what was a living room and studio. More records and books and welding equipment. The man circled the clutter and continued onto a kitchen. This room was relatively clean and all the wall space was accounted for. Photographs, pots, pans, a Cezanne print, Chinese lanterns, a wooden parrot, several types of ivy in terra cotta pots, glass pickling jars and an Italian calendar.

'Tea or coffee?'

'White coffee, no sugar, please,' said Andy. 'Where is Richard?'

'It's his theatre night,' said Erwin, filling a kettle and lifting the lid off a cafetiere and adding several spoonfuls off coffee. 'Hope you like it strong.'

'Fine. What does Richard do on theatre night?'

'He's learning stage management and general theatre mechanics.'

'Not acting.'

'No, no. he wants to write. He's really talented. Haven't you read anything he's written?'

'I had no idea,' Andrew apologised.

'Don't go getting hurt on me,' he poured boiling water into the cafetiere. 'What's he done?'

'Nothing too sinister. He put some drawing pins on the ceiling during an English lesson.'

'Hardly worth a house call,' Erwin replaced the lid and put the cafetiere on the table. He poured milk into a jug, set a pair of cups and saucers and placed a spoon in each saucer. He sat down opposite and lit up a cigarette. 'Dick's mother had a drug problem, she's long gone and probably dead, Dick's father, my son, is a selfish little shit and the last I heard he was living in Germany.'

'You brought Dick up?'

'Somebody had to. The family that were fostering were nice people but I couldn't leave the boy with them. He'd have died of boredom.' He squashed down the lever and poured two cups of jet black liquid. Andy added milk but Erwin drank his without.

'I know this record,' said Andy. 'My father is a jazz fan. Mercy, Mercy, Mercy.'

'That's right. So, what Dick did wasn't too sinister. Why're you here?' Erwin was having fun with him and a step ahead all of the way.

Smiling broadly Andy said, 'Well. It is obvious that Dick's attainment level at school is well short of his ability.'

'Really,' Erwin mocked.

'It doesn't matter much, then?'

'Your school can take a flying fuck,' said Erwin without emphasis. 'He was written off in his first term. Written off, sport, studies, even the drama club wouldn't take him. I'm sure he had problems and took it out on the wrong people at the wrong time. Without a mother or father what do you expect. Despite the encouragement your lot gave him, none, he has come through it. He's a level-headed and talented lad.'

'I know,' said Andy.

'You're lot down there are churning them out. Nice little boys and girls that do as they're told and make as few waves as possible. My Dick thinks for himself, therefore he's a bad influence. The last thing your lot and the government for that matter, want is people than can think for themselves. They're a nuisance, they do make waves.'

'So,' said Andy. 'Why aren't you watching the football?'

'I haven't got a fucking television.'

* * *

'I hear Holmes has left us for good,' said Margery. 'Good work.'

'It was nothing I did,' admitted Andy. 'I couldn't say his parents were indifferent, they did not care that much.'

'They're a *Blott on the Landscape*, that family. Him and those carthorses of his. Occasionally he stables them in the back garden, which is entirely illegal. The police have been brought in, petitions got up but they're oblivious. They just stick two fingers up to the world, that sort.' Jinny only stopped to draw breath.

'What about Richard Morrissey?' asked Margery.

'Talented lad,' offered Mason. 'A lot more to that boy than meets the eye. He hides it all behind that rebellious streak.'

'Usual story for the most part, parents gone, mother could even be dead. Drugs. Brought up by his grandfather, Erwin, who's a sculptor of sorts.'

'Erwin Morrissey,' said Mason. 'I don't think I've heard of him.'

'He works for the railways and welds sculptures out of the waste iron. Lots of cogs and iron rods, the occasional bit of velocipede.'

'Handle bar moustaches?' said Jinny.

There was an awed silence, Jinny had made a funny.

'My goodness, Virginia,' Marcia was patronising. 'I do the jokes.'

'He was an interesting bloke. Claimed that we're churning out robots. That there's a government conspiracy to prevent the growing populace thinking for themselves.'

'Well,' Mason adjusted his spectacles and jutted out his chin. 'I had a lady friend who decided to retire early and fill the time she took up sitting on committees. They found out this woman was clever, I mean seriously clever and she was promoted up the ranks. Eventually she was asked to head a committee to prepare a white paper for the government. This white paper was published you can get a copy at any Stationery Office. The committee came to four conclusions and two of them were omitted from the publication. The two omissions were that the obsession with brand names should be discouraged and that children should be encouraged to think for themselves. So there you are. Mr Morrissey may have a point.'

'I don't believe a word of it,' said Jinny getting red in the face. 'I'm sick of all these conspiracy theories. People are even accusing the Queen of having Princess Diana assassinated. People are too too sick making at times. I encourage my students to think and that's all there is to it.'

'I'm sure you do,' said Mason apologetically, startled by the effect his story had had on his friend. 'I'm sorry you've taken my story so much to heart.'

'And that's what it is,' said Jinny, still angry, she got up to leave. 'Just a story.'

'You mustn't tease her,' said Marcia.

'I assure you, nothing was further from my mind,' Mason opened his hands in bewilderment.

'I was reading an article quite recently which explained that censorship isn't always purposeful. It is just that people who get into institutional positions often have an internalised opinion.'

'Like our Virginia, you mean,' said Marcia.

'She is a patriot, pure and simple,' said Margery. 'There's nothing wrong with that.'

'However quaint,' added Marcia. 'You men can be so cruel.'

'I think you're being very cruel,' said Margery. 'She means well and she is a so very nice.'

CHAPTER SIXTEEN

Parish party

Parish family gatherings are set in concrete. Tradition is not to be treated lightly, it is paramount. To miss one of these assemblies requires a doctor's note or a death certificate. The family patriarchy took turns in hosting these occasions. Christmas, Hogmanay, Burns Night are shared amongst the elderly sisters who no longer owned up to birthdays. Other significant anniversaries are the responsibility of those celebrating.

The Parish's are unbendingly loyal to their Scottish heritage. The décor in the houses of the elderly aunts had been purchased from the bankrupt stock of a failed brewery. Walls geometrically sectioned into rectangles with dark-stained strips of oak with tartan cloth infill above the dado and more dark-stain below the dado. The tartan displayed a variety of plaques, sporting trophies including the stuffed heads of reindeer, an arsenal of rusty weapons and assorted shields decorated with implausible heraldry.

Aunt Annie, as the senior of the sisters, had the family set of bagpipes pinned above the mantle piece. The tartan of the windbag clashed fiercely with its cloth panel.

To accommodate the assemblage required pushing two dining tables together, one end uncomfortably crushed into a corner. The women were seated strategically to allow free access to the kitchen. Jinny had the worst seat, backing on to the kitchen door and opposite Aunt Flora who was conveniently hemmed in.

Aunt Flora was Jinny's least favourite of Angus' relatives. She died her mop hair auburn and painted the fingernails of her claw-like hands vivid red with matching lipstick. She continually boasted that she was the personification of good taste and owned more shoes than Imelda Marcos. Jinny, though she would never admit it to Angus, thought of her as the *scarlet woman and her sins were as scarlet*, with lipstick on her teeth.

As they grew older the three sisters and the lone surviving brother grew more alike but Flora seemed to be the most characteristically pronounced of the surviving Parish's. This might have been because she was the youngest sibling and the baby of the family.

Those not involved in cooking and serving, placed at the upper end of the table, were raucous. They were playing a traditional Parish game of I am cleverer and I know better than you. Most often the men argued about sport, sometimes the topics were quite esoteric, biology or philosophy but tonight it was cinema.

Thwarted, Jinny helped with the dishes but longed to join the affray. Sometimes she tried but could not make herself heard. A fact would arise that the throng was not certain of and Jinny gave the answer but nobody was listening. The fun for the Parish's was the argument and scoring points against each other. Outsiders were supposed to remain spectators. Resigned, Jinny collected more plates and returned to the kitchen.

The Parish women dismissed Jinny as a snob and as far as they were concerned she admitted it. The family had a bizarre code of conduct, its rule book laid down by the acclaimed dead and propagated by Aunt Flora and her sister Annie. This weird etiquette forbade the stacking of dinner plates even though they were heading for the dishwasher or wearing open toed shoes to formal occasions. The flipside of these proprieties was equally singular.

Inaudible at the table and unwelcome in the kitchen Jinny often hid in the bathroom with a book or played Monopoly with the children. Her absence was rarely noted. Tonight, Angus had got home late and in the hurry she had left her book on the dressing table. The children were in a bedroom pressing buttons epileptically on play stations. Jinny watched the screen for a few minutes but had no wish to join in. She had such a headache. In the bathroom she found some Sinutab, then sneaked into the television room and closed the door after her.

She wanted to think of something that was nice for a change. She wanted to remember the book club evening and how good it made her feel but she could not summon the mood. She could not shake off her exasperation with Angus' family which held on to her disposition with an unshakeable grip.

Sitting in the dark, with her eyes closed, she listened to the distant, unremitting clamour from the dining room. Where did they get their energy? Massaging her temples with her fingers, she found a smudge of gravy on her arm and dabbed it clean with a tissue.

A vision of a forearm smothered in red hair and freckles triggered an unfamiliar tingle. She wriggled in her seat to alleviate this unwelcome manifestation. Avecore was a closed book. Even Margery, who got to know all there was to know, had nothing to tell. He had been married but was not any longer and the circumstances were shrouded in mystery. Margery had tried to pump Betsy but she was not forthcoming. Andrew is a very private man and I must respect his wishes, was all she would say. What is it that could be so confidential? Murder? Adultery?

Who would not make her husband a cuckold.

She would not for one What was she thinking? Why was this Avecore man so...? So what exactly? Sexy? She must not do this anymore. It's not...

The door opened and a rickety shadow occupied the glare framed by the doorway. 'Why are you hiding in here in the dark?' asked Uncle Scott Craig, Flora's husband, then switched on the light.

'I've got a terrible headache,' Jinny covered her eyes with her hands and peeped through her fingers.

'I'll get you some pills,' said Scott in his avuncular burr, his ruddy face whisky flushed.

'I've just taken something.'

'Good, good. Do you mind if I join you?' He asked, fiddling with the dimmer switch.

'Not at all,' she lied.

Uncle Scott subdued the light to a satisfactory level and slumped heavily next to her on the sofa. Unsteadily placing his filled glass on the arm, he shimmied upright and put his horny hand on her knee, 'You're sure you're all right?'

'I'll be fine,' she told him confidently, hoping he would go and leave her alone. His unsolicited hand remained where it was causing her more distress.

'We outsiders must stick together,' his tipsy hand grasped her knee more firmly. She wanted to get up or pull her leg away but was frozen rigid. Fortunately his glass was toppling over.

'Watch out, your drink.'

He needed both hands to save the glass and she took her chance, swung her legs away and crossed them.

'That was a close shave,' he swallowed a generous mouthful and patted his stomach. 'Better in here, than on the carpet. Good scotch this. Can I get you one?' She shook her head and he waved his glass in a mock toast. 'To scotch and to myself. The only genuine scotch, or should I say 'Scottish'. To the only genuine scotch in this house.'

'I don't understand…'

He emptied the glass and giving Jinny further cause for discomfort shifted closer. He leaned in and whispered, scotch fumes filled her nostrils. 'Tinkers, the lot of them. Irish maybe, Scottish, never. The clues are there for all to see. No self-respecting Scot wants England to do well at sport, especially football. Your husband's nostalgia for 1966 is odd don't you think. He wasn't even born in 1966. The only way you'll get a Scot to discuss 1966 is to point out in what way the Sassenachs cheated…'

'They did not,' Jinny was indignant.

'That dog of yours, Bobby, named after Bobby Moore…'

'Greyfriars Bobby…'

'Suit yourself. You know best, anyone with legs as shapely as yours, always knows best,' he gobbled at the glass unaware that it was empty, lay back and imperceptibly rocked.

Jinny was both angry and curious, Uncle Scott's feigned indifference made her angrier. She wanted to know more about the Parish history but wanted to punish him for his outrageous accusations. England never cheat. It is all the other countries.

'You know the old crook died on top of his mistress,' Scott giggled. 'The great Jock Parish, a tinker from Galway Bay. Shanklin Road more like.'

Scott shook his head to clear it, lay it gently on the linen antimakassar and turned to her. His eyes were serious and bloodstained. 'He got the name Jock because he couldn't say Jack properly. He was a fully paid up spiv. You know, teddy boy, with the Tony Curtis haircut smothered in Brylcream. You have no idea what I'm talking about, do you.'

'Some of it,' she pretended.

'Made his money black market racketeering during the war and was arrested. The old lady even spent a couple of nights in Holloway and had a good time, said the place was full of characters. After he died, she invented this Scottish baloney.'

Jinny was so absorbed she had not noticed his hand was back on her knee, edging up her skirt. Startled, she jumped to her feet, her elbow accidentally giving Uncle Scott a solid bump on the jaw.

'I must be getting back,' she said.

Uncle Scott rubbed his chin and claimed forlornly, 'We outsiders should stick together.'

CHAPTER SEVENTEEN

Leaving party

Andy had almost given up on Jinny when she made a late entrance, looking more elegant and slimmer than he had ever seen her. She was wearing a tobacco brown string cardigan over a milk chocolate shirt and a skirt decorated with a tableau in a darker chocolate. Her face was dabbed with powder and her mouth painted lightly with cerise lipstick. Her eyes were untouched and for Andy the powder and paint were equally unnecessary.

She looked so beautiful he felt a strong pang of desire. Andy knew that when it came to appearances he was a fascist. He could not disassociate the person from their anatomy. Mind you this tyrannical attitude only applied to women. As he talked to a variety of the guests present his eyes followed her jealously around the room.

Jinny was out to make an impression. She liked to wear good clothes, dine in smart restaurants with smart people and make intelligent conversation. In Wyford, smart people were few and far between. Angus' business dinners, especially executives visiting from the States rarely rivalled her and Angus' IQ. These visitors, both the men and the women, had sizable egos and they tended to be condescending but it was all on the surface.

Her diet of intelligent conversation outside of school had been meagre of late. In fact it had almost disappeared completely. She was looking forward to this leaving party.

Jinny had made the effort to dress well because she thought the Cat & Fiddle Inn to be a smart venture, despite being in Moor End which is the lesser half of Millworth.

The Inn is over 300 years old and a Grade 2 listed building, structure and publicans in a well advanced state of decay. The conserved windows and pumps leak cold draughts. Winter and summer the customers blow hot and cold. The restaurant had been booked by St Bryans for Kenneth Facey's farewell party.

Marcia plumped herself in the seat between Andy and Margery. He had to shift his chair to continue their interrupted conversation. 'What had he done?'

'That was what was so infuriating. I had no idea what he was up to until one of the pupils pointed it out after the lesson.'

'Who are we talking about?' this time Marcia's intrusion was less physical.

'Richard Morrissey.'

'A dark horse,' said Marcia over-dramatically.

'I agree,' said Andy. 'Margery thinks he's the devil's son in law.'

'What did he do?'

'During my lesson, without me noticing, he smothered the ceiling above his seat with drawing pins.'

'Not the crime of the century,' Marcia, dressed in silk, swished and crackled in her chair. Marcia's husband, William Gonabit, foreign correspondent to the Daily Post often returned from Bonn or Strasbourg with a size eighteen in cadeau packaging.

Jinny appeared in front of the big woman's chair, her outfit held up well alongside Marcia's silk.

'Have my seat,' Andy stood up.

'I'm fine,' Jinny protested. Andy grabbed her around the waist and guided her into his chair, his arm delightfully brushed her breast.

'I felt his intention was to purposely humiliate me, I can't let that go unpunished.'

Mason arrived with a tall athletic man with a 1950 haircut, careworn face lined like an underground map. Gracefully, the man leaned down and kissed each of the women in turn.

'Kenneth.'

'How are you?'

'It's certainly more inventive than the horseplay we get nowadays. Hello Kenneth, we're ruing the demise of horseplay.'

At that point Mickey Finn made her entrance. There was a gasp from the women and men's head's turned to see what the fuss was about. She wore a low cut black dress and the hem terminated twelve inches above the knee. Her hitherto unseen breasts were unblemished parchment white, her legs a shade too stalwart for so short a skirt, but few of the men present, not being fascistic, noted the fact.

Jinny, as surprised as the men by the volume of this exposed chest, found herself embarrassed by the girl's exposure. She hid her discomfort by condemning the lascivious looks on the faces of these mature teachers. Dirty old men.

Mickey's transformation, though she would not admit it, gave her serious disquiet. She had a rival for the new Head of Department. She darted a glance to see Andrew's reaction. He, like her, was embarrassed by what he saw, so his attention was pointedly elsewhere.

Andy thought he knew something that neither Jinny, nor anyone else present knew, that this display was for him.

'It is all too personal nowadays,' Margery complained. 'Horseplay.'

'Are you married, miss?' Marcia mimicked

'What team do you support, sir?' Andy joined in.

'All so predictable. Easier to handle though, I must admit.'

'A lost art,' Facey fetched two chairs and the two men joined them while Andy remained standing. 'Several students I was at school with were extremely witty. We were in the middle of a history lesson and one of the class was ill and threw up. Quick as a flash a boy named Khurt, said, 'sick man of Europe'.'

'Wit is a thing of the past. Inside school and out,' Marcia was prudishly nostalgic.

'You're right. It died out with toilet humour,' said Margery.

'The pooh fetish,' said Jinny. 'And the demise of sophistication. *Praising what is lost makes the remembrance dear.*'

'Unfortunately all does not always end well,' said Marcia.

'I was at school with witty lads,' Mason momentarily dropped his urbanity and was wistful. 'I often wonder what became of them. Jinny, I don't think it's fair that Andy hasn't got a seat. Sit on his lap.'

Andy, who had been savouring the sensation of softness that had recently brushed his arm, felt his face redden. Mason took her hand and pulled her up. Nobody listened to Andy's feeble pretence at protesting.

'I would have volunteered,' said Marcia. 'But I took pity on his knees.'

'David Frantzeskou was amusing,' Mason continued. 'We had a master who had tried to make a life in the US and one of the jobs he'd tried was selling dance lessons over the telephone. He told us of a call where the client wouldn't take the bait, he tried every wrinkle he had been taught and finally the potential customer owned up to having one leg. He described how humiliated he felt and Frantzeskou suggested, you should have invited him to a hop.'

Mason, finishing his story, gave Andy an amused wink. He felt his cheeks blushing hard.

'How awful,' said Jinny, trying to pretend she was not bothered by the situation.

"Hop', that's a word that's been lost to the world.'

Andy felt her soft thighs on his legs and wondered at how light she was. He adjusted his body allowing her the opportunity to snuggle in to him and to his surprise she took it.

'Comfortable?'

'Yes,' she smiled, intimately. 'Thanks.'

Her perfume and its undercurrent of femininity teased his nose. She began fidgeting, rocking slightly back and forth. While contemplating touching her neck with his nose, a waiter appeared and they were summoned to eat. She jumped up instantly and hurried away. Every time he thought he was getting somewhere his hopes were dashed.

* * *

Jinny sat on the toilet with her head in her hands. She could not recall the last time she felt so ashamed. What was she thinking of? She is a happily married woman. Her recent behaviour was alien to anything she had done before. Maybe it was fashionable to jump in and out of bed with other men but bed-hopping was not for her.

Why was she attracted to this man? He's got a good brain but not a first class brain. How sweet he was to give up his seat.

Dreamily she imagined another chance of sitting in his lap. Never before had she experienced the excitement that ebbed and flowed inside her. Her panties were soaking.

In the past few months lovemaking with Angus had been a problem because she could not summon any fluid in her front bottom. He claimed that it did not matter, said that it made each occasion just like the first time. She shuddered involuntarily, not wanting to remember a suggestion he had made. It was unspeakable. *The unspeakable in pursuit of the uneatable.* Angus had wanted her to allow him to do some hideously unthinkable things and she would not hear of it. How could he be so disgusting? All men are bestial.

During the time she had wanted a third child and her fluid was plentiful, he had first made this lewd suggestion. His excuse being that it was a sort of family planning. She retched and had to twist herself quickly to lift the seat. She retched again fiercely but nothing emerged. She cupped her head in her hands and decided that all men are the same. Hoping beyond hope that this may not be the case.

Again a thought she did not want to recollect hovered in the stratospheres of her brain. Kneeling on the cold tiles her body chilled and nauseous, this elusive thought caused her to flush a bright crimson. It danced in and out and of her shame and she decided once and for all that she was going to stop any further deliberations about Mr Andrew Avecore.

Standing in front of the mirror, she dried her face and reapplied her make up. She was composed, she was her normal self, all would be well from here on. Why are you attracted to a man to whom you are diametrically opposed. Marcia calls him a free spirit but some of his views are pure anarchy even treasonous. She had never met such an unpatriotic person in her life before.

Sitting in his lap, feeling the warmth of his body next to hers. Did he have an erection? She needed to know but could not find one. He is not attracted to you, Jinny Parish and that is just as well in the circumstances.

'Jinny Parish,' she told the image in the mirror. 'You're becoming a sex maniac.'

She re-checked her make up and could feel a headache

coming on. Should she take a couple of paracetamol just to be on the safe side. No, just don't drink anymore, Jinny Parish, that should do the trick.

She re-entered the dining room, saw Andy laughing at what Marcia had said and instantly sensed seeping in her underclothes.

* * *

There had been some sort of table plan and Andy had checked his placing which was between Mason and Mickey Finn on the other table from Jinny. She was placed between Marcia and the guest of honour.

Jinny's disappearance gave him pause, he hovered around the bar pretending to order a fresh drink. He had wanted to switch cards but worried that he would be caught out and make his intentions obvious. He waited too long because Marcia beckoned him over, 'You're sitting with us.'

She pointed to a space between her and Kenneth.

'It seems appropriate that the new king meets the old king.'

'God save the Head of Department,' Kenneth smiled at him shyly. He looked a lot like WH Auden with the scribble of lines on his craggy face and was probably sick of having it pointed out.

'It's very nice of you to say so but I think it's a shame to share your farewell party with a stranger.'

'I like to meet new people,' said Kenneth, pulling a chair out for him and patting it.

'This seat was allocated to our least favourite person,' Marcia confessed.

'Who's that?' Andy asked innocently, knowing full well who they meant.

'Mrs Knowall,' said Marcia, with a cruel edge to her voice. 'She's got a good brain but not a first class brain.'

'Curious what a fervent flag waver she is,' said Facey.

'Jinny, short for Virginia,' Marcia returned to her normal sardonic persona. 'It could easily be short for Jingo.'

'Odd isn't it,' said Facey. 'Have you noticed how new immigrants are overtly patriotic?'

'Perhaps she has a skeleton in her cupboard.'

'I thought you were friends,' said Andy, purposely mixing it.

Marcia's roly poly features glared at him, 'Any more of that sort of talk and I'll send you to the headmistress.'

'I'm sorry, miss. Are you married, miss?' Andy mocked.

Marcia's soft features softened, 'I'll forgive you just this once.'

'I had no idea you had a problem with her.'

'All that niceness irritates me beyond endurance and if that isn't bad enough the point scoring. I wasn't asked to wash and clean the entire school with the tip of my tongue but I did it anyway.'

'Please, please, please, may I mark your homework for a decade,' said Facey

'Kiss Betsy March's backside for a week, just for you.' Marcia tilted her head and fluttered her eyelids.

Andy could not help laughing but felt extremely guilty enjoying the ridiculing of his 'dream girl'. The truth of their mockery made him feel more guilty. Out of the corner of his eye saw the subject of their damming take the seat beside Mason and next to Mickey Finn.

'I always found her elaborate confessions cringingly embarrassing,' Facey admitted. 'Having her wonderful husband's business success thrown in my face was definitely worse. I think Jinny sees teaching as women's work.'

'Aberdeen Angus,' said Marcia. 'Mind you he's got three hands not three stomachs. Perhaps that should be free hands.'

'Angus? That's's Jinny's husband?' Andy acted innocent.

'Yes,' said Facey. 'How could anyone so overtly English marry a Scot?'

'He got her up the duff,' said Marcia with relish.

'I didn't know that,' Andy continued his act.

'And the quotes,' Kenneth raised his eyebrows to the heavens. 'She has the most amazing capacity to digest and retain information.'

'Like an actor. She once confided to me that she believed the world would be a better place if they culled the low IQ. I'm sure she would also like to cull the unattractive. That's me for the gas ovens.'

'Marcia tells me you've started a book club,' Kenneth topped up their wine glasses.

'Yes, it's going OK,' said Andy and waved his drink. 'Here's to it.'

Andy missed the subsequent savaging of Jinny, preoccupied with sums. The boys were over seventeen and it was their 18th anniversary. If she was pregnant they were quick off the mark. For such a fastidious lady she was playing fast and loose with the truth on this occasion.

He could not rationalise the woman he knew with sex out of wedlock but was glad to know of such a prospect. She was not the straight laced goody goody she claimed to be.

* * *

CHAPTER EIGHTEEN

Andy at the weekend

When Andy woke on Saturday he dared not look at the time. It looked dark outside and therefore early. Too early. He could hear the dove that owned the space to the side of the house. Wa ooo wa, wa ooo wa incessantly and all year round. This dove or wood pigeon did not migrate.

For Andy the weekends had become interminable. On Friday nights he headed home and planned the best of intentions. He would go to the cinema, or visit a museum, or walk down the embankment, or go to cricket with a book, or anything to get out of the flat.

He had done some of these things on his own but could not help feeling self-conscious. He felt conspicuous being alone. When he was married and was doing things by himself he did not feel the least conspicuous. Even though the circumstances were none of his own doing, he could not help feeling he was included among the sad and pathetic. He was at his most uncomfortable eating alone.

Being the last bastion of 'men only' seedy pubs were the safest and the most anonymous of venues. The pitfall with this system is that seedy pubs attract a seedy clientele. If not seedy, certainly quirky, eccentric or idiosyncratic. At first, he got some fun hearing the singular views of these cranks but this indulgence soon palled. He soon exhausted all the accessible pubs and had to travel further afield. It amazed him the number of people who still believed that England ruled the World and whose answer to every international problem was for our navy to send a gunboat.

There had been an elderly man with a bulbous nose in the Prince of Wales with whom he had struck up a conversation. They had been talking interestingly about politics and football.

The older man had an unusual slant on these subjects and then, apropos of nothing much, the man announced, 'Johnny Cash, musical perfection.'

A sentimental song, sung by a gravelly voice, groaned through a series of crackles and gently pervaded the room. Perplexed that his audience was inconclusive he continued proudly, 'Country and Western, it's the finest music there is.'

Andy smiled apologetically and asked, 'Is it?' What made him uneasy was the finality of the man's statement. It brooked no disagreement. He did not want to humiliate the old man by expressing his true feelings and continued smiling apologetically, hoping the *music* would stop.

His friends had been exemplary. He was not sure that he would have been as generous of spirit if the shoe had been on another foot. Despite their kindness he felt out of place being the only single. He preferred that to the matchmaking and he preferred being on his own to both of those.

His weekends had become a mundane routine. Shopping in the High Street, again purchasing goods for several healthy meals most of which developed penicillin and ended up in the dustbin along with the empty boxes that were delivered by the local pizza, Indian and Chinese.

He could not concentrate for long periods. He would cook supper, choose a DVD and by the time he was finished eating he was bored with the film. If he persevered his eyes would grow heavy and he would drop off to sleep. If he was in a livelier mood he would switch off the film and channel hop, constantly optimistic that something would grab his attention. To date, nothing had for very long and certainly not to a conclusion.

He sneaked a look at the clock, seven-forty. He groaned because he had counted on it being at least nine am. More reason to feel sorry for himself. England were opening their World Cup challenge later today and that was another discouragement to be out and about.

His travels further afield searching for anonymous pubs had reduced him to watching football. More and more women are going to live football but as yet not many are prepared to watch matches through a fog of smoke. No doubt when smoking bans become mandatory their numbers will increase.

Deciding that Hampstead pubs would have more enlightened drinkers, he had gone to the North Star on the Finchley Road. It was a prematurely dark night. Persistent rain, an insistent wind, the street filled with puddles and the café windows blurred with steam. People struggled to control their umbrellas and to avoid the splashing of passing cars. He pushed open the pub door and it was heaving with spectators of an FA cup game. A musty odour of damp rose off the coats of the imbibers and fused with the clouds of cigarette smoke.

The match was a half an hour old and the room was in complete harmony, braying like donkeys in unison at the events appearing to them on a giant overhead screen.

Andy bought a beer and found one of the few remaining seats. Its vantage was poor for a direct view of the screen but he was able to follow the match via a reflection in an upper window.

It was a poor game and he scanned the faces of the engrossed fans. Their body actions were synchronised with the tempo of the match. He decided someone might write a paper on the automatic choreography of sports' fans. A close shot and the spectator half stood in their seat, a brutal tackle and up they bounced with a finger pointing, a goal and the arm erect, the fist clenched. They would have made Adolph proud. Like pre-war Germany the crowd was united in hate. Hate for United.

Their behaviour was how he imagined the audience that gathered around the guillotine. It was a shame that knitting had gone out of fashion.

He left his drink unfinished and went back out into the filthy night.

Against his better judgement he accepted advice to meet with a counsellor who specialised in bereavement. She admitted to him that he was proving a difficult subject. She claimed that those who were in good relationships generally found it easier to get back in the fray. Divorcees or those that had been in bad relationships expected the worst and were more apprehensive.

Andy saw these prospects completely juxtaposed. If someone had been in a bad relationship and if they were a tad more discriminating they could not fail to get a better one. Good relationships were much harder to emulate. He felt that life's luck invariably balances out and he had had his turn of good fortune.

While he was considering all this, he dropped off again and woke at ten-thirty. Too lazy to get out of bed and open the curtains, he switched on the light and stared about him. Dust cobwebs swayed gently about the ceiling, the sunshine had bleached a section of the wall and there was a tidemark arcing behind the wardrobe. He must redecorate, that would be something to keep him occupied. He would have to move the furniture first. This would be awkward with help. Without the prospect of help he was able to sideline another scheme and wallow in his ennui.

He used the last of his milk to make coffee and toyed with a walk to the newsagents to fetch a paper and buy some bits and pieces. He did his weekly clearance of fungus from the refrigerator and checked the freezer for supplies. The cupboard was bare.

He dressed and set off for the High Street and only made it to the bottom of the road before he realised he had no money nor cards with which to pay. Muttering a host of expletives and generally berating himself he trudged back up the hill.

The High Street was busy, families out doing their Saturday shop. Elderly children who have suborned their parents as matriarchs directed their mothers and fathers, here and there, warned them to be more careful when crossing the road, chided them for buying the wrong bread and bore their name, Octavia, with as much dignity as such a travesty would allow.

Hearing frustrated parents summon offspring named, Octavia, Quentin and Freddie was slightly less risible than the dog owners in the park summoning their equally recalcitrant dogs. A smartly dressed matron in her Barbour and green wellies yelling 'Sybil' in a posh voice was definitely more comic.

He knew he had bought too much because the plastic bags were cutting into his fingers. He had bought less on his last shop and over half of that was consigned to the dustbin. It was too late now.

He frittered away the hours through the afternoon. Marked some homework, wrote a summary of statements taken over a fight at a bus stop and read through a few UCAS applications. Betsy had asked him to consider a NPQ8 qualification and he read most of the blurb before he binned it. Over lunch he half watched Poland play Ecuador and by half six he was already feeling soporific. Careful to avoid the build-up he prepared dinner and put it on a low light in the oven. Within twenty minutes of the kick off he was fast asleep. He awoke as the hoo ha for the Trinidad versus Sweden match began shortly after nine pm. His dinner had dried out somewhat but was just edible. He finished and cleared away, began watching the half time summary hoping to see England's goal scored earlier. Fed up waiting. he switched off the television and went to bed. Another Saturday carefully negotiated. Sunday was more of the same only the teams were different.

CHAPTER NINETEEN

Mickey Finn

Gillian Finn, known as 'Mickey' to the pupils but never as 'Gill' to anyone, was not one to wallow in self pity but she was sorely disappointed. She was practised in keeping her thoughts to herself, not a malcontent but naturally reticent. She aspired to an ideal that existed on the page but nowhere else in her experience. Gillian was frustrated, her life moving along a long dark tunnel with no sign of daylight.

Just like Jinny, she was born and raised in Wyford on the Pemberton estate. They had attended different schools and their lives had few parallels.

Gillian's parents were civil servants who had met in the department of Agriculture and Fisheries and were united by their mutual partiality to socialism. They shared few cross words with their daughter, encouraged her enthusiasms and understood her need for camouflage.

Teachers with a modicum of psychology assumed Gillian's outlandish dress to be a mask to conceal a lack of self-confidence. This was not the case. Gillian was a secret swot and maintained the respect of her friends by stretching the rules and dressing to extremes.

Now she was an adult but still had to disguise her love for unfashionable pursuits. Her friends were disinterested in all that she was interested in and as time wore on she was reciprocating.

Weekends began on Friday night in the 'Sussex' or the 'Oddfellows' getting pissed out of their heads, or doing drugs, dropping an E, that left them wasted. Hung over from alcohol or ill-tempered until the chemicals dispersed, the weekends frittered away.

There were other sorts of Friday nights. When a contestant

was going to get chucked out of the Big Brother room. They took turns, congregating with beer and pizza and made a party of it.

The worst addiction, more toxic than drink or drugs was Play Station and X Boxes. Hours were spent frenetically pressing buttons. Gillian found their occasional nights at the cinema to see a film with special effects was simply a Play Station in the making.

The most futile of these pursuits was drinking. Her friends, male or female, drank far too much. They claimed to like booze but they only did it because it was fashionable. She read in her parents' Guardian with a smile that the Government claimed to be winning the war on drugs. Drugs, for the time being were passé but they were out there and easily available.

Four of them would share a litre bottle of vodka before going out clubbing, just to get in the mood. The liquor numbed her brain but none of her friends showed any ill effects from a mere quarter of a litre.

One afternoon, during the Easter break, she had been thoroughly bored while wandering through the market, half-looking at the stalls, when she had an awakening. 'There's got to be more to life than this?'

She had the vague intention of searching for some Paul Weller or a Joe Strummer she had not previously encountered. Instead she bought a three CD compilation of Billie Holiday and walked hurriedly home. She fetched her car and drove over to Sidware.

Wyford had no second hand bookshops. She had tried surfing the internet but she preferred to browse and had to travel to St Aubyns or to Sidware for what she wanted.

The Sidware bookshop was run by a kindly grey-haired lady and her uncertain son. Gillian would inquire after Edith Wharton, Dodie Smith and Radclyffe Hall. Those kindly eyes would glow and flicker and she would disappear out the back. Gillian waited expectantly, her heart beating fast with hope and often the grey-haired lady would return with dusty treasure.

Gillian knew the root of her problems. She was a home bird. Her biggest mistake was doing her PGCE Diploma at the local college. Her parents encouraged her to go away to study, warned her she would regret it but had not listened. In truth, she was afraid to go and leave the umbrella of their protection.

On the afternoon of her renewal she decided she must throw off everything that was dragging her down and begin again. If she wanted a life she must go out and get one. Forget her previous mistakes and begin anew. Her breast soared with expectation.

On the first day of the new term she was introduced to the new Head of Department. He was Darcy Fitzwilliam, Heathcliff and Corporal Tullidge rolled into one. He was the type of person she aspired to be, not the least bit Wyford and had a way of talking that fizzed with possibilities. He had expressive hands with slim wrists and glittering hairs like golden threads.

* * *

Sitting in the cinema alone, in the dark, Gillian luxuriated in the shadows. She pulled the peak of her cap further over her eyes and furtively looked about her.

She had scoured the pages of Time Out and The Guide, this was her third trip *abroad*. It was her original plan to go to the theatre on her own but she expected to feel conspicuous. Anyway there would be less likelihood of meeting a sophisticated young man. She started with more familiar territory and chose the less ambitious venue, cinema.

She had pushed the boat out, bought sophisticated clothes she had seen advertised in The Guardian magazine. She borrowed her mother's silk scarves and pashminas. Hoping she looked elegant she hung around in the cinema lobby sipping tonic. So far there had been no approaches. Attractive men were invariably taken, either with a woman or a gay companion.

She had seen a much vaunted French film that she barely understood. At least it got her thinking but she had no one to share her puzzlement with. Her second outing was spoiled when the man sitting next to her put his hand on her thigh. She sat there, frozen, unwilling to make a scene. Her only impulse was a reluctance to draw attention to herself.

She remained frozen as his hand moved slowly up to her pantie line. Suddenly desperate, she twisted her hip free of his prying fingers and came face to face with the man. He was an elderly gentleman, smartly dressed in a blazer with a military badge on the breast pocket who reminded her of Mr Mason, the art master. She took his thick wrist, put it back in his lap and spent the remainder of the film feeling a mixture of pride and dread of a repeat performance.

Later, in the safety of her locked car, she fumed at the outrage. There she had been, acting out a scene from *Separate Tables* and incapable of carrying out retribution. She should have whacked him in the balls but she made do with fuming.

Enjoyment of solitary visits to the cinema stemmed from her childhood. The first time she was allowed to go on her own she was supposed to meet Pauline Jay at the doors but Pauline did not show up. So Gillian had gone inside by herself, armed with a lollipop and a packet of fruit gums. The film was so enthralling the fruit gums remained unopened.

M & M's had replaced fruit gums and she kept them deep in her jacket pocket so that the rustling paper did not interfere with the audience. She sucked off the sugar coating, then the chocolate before chewing the peanut to a paste. This way the packet lasted the entire performance.

This highly praised film was a disappointment. The leading man was unattractive, both in appearance and as a person. The synopsis in the magazines was entirely misleading and she felt no sympathy for the main character whatsoever. He was a waster who did not get all he deserved but ended up living well on the proceeds of his wife's talent. Mickey could find no artistic merit in the film at all.

Outside, it was not quite dark and the pavements were busy with people enjoying the warm night. The lights on Hampstead station were shining brightly and its very name conjured a multitude of images. She lacked the courage to roam the back streets alone. She might find the house where Gordon Comstock resided behind that aspidistra or the Millers' place where the Belseys loved to visit.

She stopped to look in a café window and dreamed of a time when it would be commonplace for her to frequent such a place. Inside, women were at their ease, eating and drinking alone. She felt reluctant to go in because the women looked rich and self-assured.

A few yards ahead, a toothless old lady, hunched over like a pigeon was gobbling and pecking at pedestrians. Most were giving her a wide berth but she snatched at them with her claws. Dreading her attention Gillian fixed her gaze through the window. It did not do the trick. She felt the old woman's fingernails scratching at her sleeve. Once again, frozen to the spot, panic rushed through her body.

A man appeared and guided the old woman away.

Her heart skipped a beat, Andrew was wearing a denim shirt and jeans, red hair bursting out of the collar and below the cuffs of his half-rolled sleeves. 'What are you doing here, alone?' he demanded.

'I've been to the pictures.'

'I know, I was sitting behind you,' he said, smiling broadly. 'I'm surprised you could see with that hat.'

She liked the idea that he was making fun of her and tried to reply in kind. 'Why didn't you come over?'

'You looked like you wanted to be alone.'

'I did.'

'You eaten?'

'No,' she lied.

'Come on, I'll buy you supper.' He crooked his arm and waggled it and she took hold of his bicep. He squeezed her hand into his side and the warmth of contact caused her heart to skip another beat. Now she would find out all about him, although she must be just as careful not to appear as though she was prying.

'Did you like the film?'

'Not really,' she answered cautiously, not wanting to give herself away.

'Crap wasn't it,' he said and she envied his confidence.

He pushed open the door of a Greek restaurant and guided her inside. He chose a corner table and handed her a menu but the fare remained a blur. She chided herself to concentrate on what she was saying. She must choose her words carefully, not sound young and silly. She must keep her guard up. She was certain that someone as sophisticated as Andrew would be put off by gaucherie. Little did she know how correct she was.

'So, what are you doing here?'

'It's a long story.' Mickey could not stop taking in the decoration.

She thought it was the highest art. Floor and walls simulated a Mediterranean villa, decked out with oil paintings and authentic looking pottery. This off the peg décor thrilled her to the marrow.

The waiter came to take their order and stood pencil poised. 'You chosen?' he asked.

'I don't speak Greek.'

'Are you vegetarian?' he asked and she shook her head. 'Two moussakas, two glasses of red wine and a bottle of water. Do you prefer still or sparkling?'

'Still,' she answered.

'And a mixed salad. Thanks. You were saying.'

'I had this thing. Not a vision exactly but an enlightening.'

'Religious?'

'Are you going to stop teasing me?' she demanded, her plain face coming to life. For an instant he thought she might be pretty. So many Wyford women are plainer than they need to be. She lacked self-confidence, hiding behind those ridiculous clothes that do not look that good on the beanpoles that model them. And as for that silly hat.

'Sorry,' he apologised. 'I can't help myself. I'm not very good with women and it's my idea of flirting.'

'You're flirting with me?'

'No. Anyway, you were saying. Enlightenment,' he held up his wine and they tapped glasses as though the word were a toast.

She was fascinated with the sculptural way his hands held the glass and the perfection of his fingers. 'It sounds so pathetic in my head. My life is so boring. Pathetic or what.'

'How so, boring?'

'My friends are all into the same things and none of these things are the least bit uplifting. Drinking, smoking, the occasional coke line, dropping an 'e', Play Stations…,' she hesitated at sex. Should she be talking to this man about sex? 'They all like the same music, same TV, none of them read and none of them go to the theatre except to see Billy Elliot, or Evita, or Phantom of the Opera. The very mention of Shakespeare causes instant slumber.'

'I agree with them on that one,' her shocked face made him laugh out loud. He leaned forward to confide a secret. He looked to see who might be listening. 'Shakespeare bores me stiff,' he whispered.

'You're kidding me.'

'Am I?'

'I can't tell with you whether you're serious or not.'

'Good,' he sat back and allowed their food to be served. Uninhibitedly, he studied her face which was prettier then he realised. When she blushed blood red he felt a twinge of pleasant emotion.

'So much Shakespeare is propaganda. Othello, for instance, could never have been a Brit. To be such a berk, not only did he have to be foreign…' He took an over generous forkful of food, some of it spilling down his shirt. 'Bollocks,' he complained and sucked up the miscreant food.

Not the least motherly, Gillian had to stifle an impulse to wet her serviette and wipe his shirt clean.

'He had to be black and that makes his folly believable to audiences who were racists even back then. Merchant of Venice, need I go on.'

'No, I prefer that you didn't.'

'So, what is your plan?'

'I'm starting with seeing films I fancy that will never come to Wyford. I've got no one to go with so I'll go on my own. I'll join the RSC mailing list and then I'm going to find Prince Charming and live happily ever after. In the meantime…' She shrugged.

'Is it nice?' he pointed to her plate.

'Lovely,' she said.

'Was it always the case, this antipathy with your friends? When you were at school, for instance.'

'I always loved books and English. That's why I became an extremist, as cover. I had hair in vivid colours, spikes for a time, then I had my Goth phase which included the piercing.'

'Tattoos?'

'No,' she shook her head sadly. 'Somehow I never fancied one. Never had the bottle. My body is very white without a single blemish.'

It was her turn to tease but she resisted adding, 'You can check if you like.' They were flirting but because of the gap between their ages he was being correct. She was unsure that remark would be too obvious, whether it would be going too far. She felt so very different from the night in the car when she kissed him. Less sure of herself, her confidence was wavering. That evening she had been on her home ground and this was his territory.

Why was she sure that this bloke was able to make love to her in the way she fantasised about. In the way she had read about. Those hands did not look selfish, they look tantalising, as though they touched with care. She needed to create the opening so that he would invite her back to his place.

'How come you're still at home?'

'That's pathetic too.'

'Now it's your turn to stop,' he said firmly. 'Nothing you're saying is pathetic. Nowhere near.'

'OK. I like it at home,' she said, gaining assurance. 'My parents are OK about almost everything. You wouldn't believe it to look at them.'

'What do they do?'

'Civil Servants. They love telling people how they met in Ag and Fish. They're quite sweet really.'

For the first time since they met, Andy felt ill at ease. He was always uncomfortable when women talked this way, or men for that matter, talking about family using adjectives like 'sweet'. It was worse when Americans used the word, 'cute' but only just. His parents were not the least bit saccharine and he was grateful for it. Jinny refers to her family in those cloying adjectives, 'fond', 'darlings', especially when she had her 'nice' hat on. What was he thinking of, having designs on that woman. It was a waste of time and energy.

Perhaps this girl would be willing, she had a body without blemish apparently and as far as he could make out, a mind with few blemishes.

'I should move out and get a life.'

'There are plenty of ways of pissing your life away but living at home isn't necessarily one of them.'

'What do you suggest?' she asked. Whoops! She had relaxed too much, if only she could take that back. Now he was going to be her favourite uncle. Damn it.

'I'm not giving you advice, cheeky bitch. You know what you want. It's got to be out there somewhere.'

'I'm not so sure.'

He folded his cutlery neatly across his empty plate and drank the last of his wine. 'Sometimes I'm envious of those who just want to be married and have two kids, play bridge and tennis, go to football every other Saturday and never miss an episode of Casualty. Some days I think they've got it made, other days, I'm not so sure.'

He paid the bill and she took his arm as they made their way to where she had parked the car. She wracked her brains for a gambit but all her words rang false. She was sure she was going to get a kiss goodnight, and while she was thanking him for supper she leaned forward but he stepped away. 'We might do this again sometime. You know, sit in separate parts of the cinema. Goodnight.'

He was gone in a flash but had he meant it about doing it again? She drove home, winding through London's varying shadows and lights. It created a cosy atmosphere in the cabin of the car just like the one in the cinema. She reflected on the evening and realised that her intention to find out more about Andrew had failed miserably. He had found a good deal about her but she knew little more about him than that brief word after the NQT session.

* * *

In the common room, Gillian overheard a conversation where Andy mentioned he liked reading the plays of Joe Orton but had never seen an actual performance. She spotted a production of Funeral Games at the Square Hall, took a chance and ordered two tickets for a Saturday matinee. To her delight, Andrew was happy to go and even agreed to pick her up.

He allowed too much time and was way early. Mrs Finn offered him tea, he and Mr Finn made small talk, while they waited for Gillian to finish getting ready.

'You're a civil servant,' said Andy.

'Not for much longer, thank Christ,' said Mr Finn vehemently and added with glee. 'I'm taking early retirement.'

'You sound disenchanted,' Andy was surprised to hear such passion from this grey man. He appeared to be the perfect product for his profession. Perhaps he was a chameleon or like a dog had taken on the persona of his master.

'Funny how life takes its natural course. I was young and full of hope, entered into a career that would help my country. Age proves that life and the system repeats again and again. We go round and round in the same circles and nothing changes. Anyway, you don't want to hear my aches and pains.'

'Its exactly the same in the school system. Plenty of directives, plenty of talk, nothing much changes.' said Andy. 'Tell me, what's wrong with life in government?'

'There are so many talented youngsters coming out of university. They have initiative, they are intuitive and have fresh ideas and no one listens to a word they say. The system allows the most emasculated to rise to the top and they maintain the status quo. Once they get to the top all they do is kiss the tail of their Secretary of State or chase their own tail.'

'I've heard that before. My father-in-law is a management consultant and he has advised several government departments including the Home Office. He says the police are only interested in promotion.'

'Father-in-law?' Mrs Finn fetched a small table and placed a mug of tea on a coaster.

'My wife was killed,' Andy explained. 'Knocked down on a pedestrian crossing.'

'I'm so sorry,' Mrs Finn was shocked. 'When did it happen?'

'Early last year.'

'I'm so so sorry.'

He put the mug to his lips when Gillian entered. He caught a glimpse of her dress and choked, almost spilling the entire contents. The low cut black dress she had worn to the farewell party had been revealing but this red number might be described as a T-shirt.

* * *

If she wanted make a dynamic entrance, the Square Hall was not the place. It turned out to be a gay theatre. Andy nipped into the Gents and a policeman stood either side of him at the urinals. Back in the auditorium which is served by one exit, he and Gillian were seated at the far side. To access their seat required walking across the stage and disrupting the row to take their place against the wall.

The lights dimmed and the bed that formed the centre piece of the play was wheeled onto the stage with the leading man under the blankets. The policemen he had seen in the toilet were part of the chorus. No expense had been spared in hiring a supporting cast even though they doubled as scene changers.

The production had been camped up with musical interludes. It was excruciatingly bad and Gillian sat flushing wave after wave of embarrassment. Andrew sat quietly heightening her anguish, she wriggled with pain and stifled a groan which emerged as a squeak.

She felt his mouth against her ear and he whispered, 'I think you need oiling.'

'I'm so sorry,' she repeated her mother's words.

'Let's go,' he stood up and grasped her hand. 'Come on.'

'We can't, not right across the stage.'

'The way you look the audience will think you're part of the production. Thirty seconds and it will be over. Come on,' he pulled her up and dragged her along. 'Excuse me, excuse me.' As they made their way out, Andy almost collided with a prancing policeman in a tutu.

An angry man in a comic doorman's costume shouted after them, 'You ignorant rabble.'

Gillian flushed redder than ever but Andy only laughed. 'What are we going to do?' she asked.

'Did you know your face is as red as that dress. I can't quite see where the dress ends and you start.'

Tears formed in her eyes, streamed down her face and her voice trembled, 'I so wanted it to be good.'

'I was only joking,' his face fearful of having hurt her, she fell on to his chest, immediately not the least upset. 'It's a shame. It really doesn't matter all that much. Not enough to cry about. We can do something else. What would you like to do?'

* * *

She lay awake unable to sleep, her head spinning with all that they had done that afternoon and evening. She hardly ever ventured 'up London' and today she had seen so much. They had walked along The Embankment and stopped to watch the budgie show, had a coffee at the NFT and sat outside on a bench, people watching. She had wanted to go inside Tate Modern but he would not. He promised to make a scene and she had given in.

'The only reason to go to Tate Modern is to use the toilet.'

'It's the most visited art museum in the World.'

'It has very good toilet facilities.'

'Is there anything you like that you're supposed to like? You're an 'againster' aren't you?'

Andy was focussing on all the passing men getting an eyeful of his companion, wondering where they might hide and save her reputation. 'Let's sit on the wall,' he suggested, relieved when she put her jacket across her lap. 'What's an againster?'

Gillian was feeling well again, her confidence was high and she had decided there was nothing to lose, she should be herself. She felt feisty, 'An oppositer, a noncomformist, contrary Mary, misfit, crank, miserable git.'

Andy snapped out of his preoccupation with Gillian's celebrity. 'Who's a miserable git?'

'You are.'

'Just because I don't want to visit the Tate Modern. Excuse me, the Tat Modern. I'll have you know, my girl, I have been round the World twice. There's nothing I haven't seen, including your knickers.'

'You can be really horrible sometimes,' she feigned a sulk, turning away from him.

Fucking hell, he thought, I'm regressing, I'm turning back into a teenager.

'I just wanted to look good for you.'

'Next time be a little less sensational,' he said. 'I'm having trouble coping with the notoriety.'

'I look sensational?' she turned back looking very pleased with herself. 'Honestly?'

A myriad of quips careered around his head. It was like having too much time to play a tennis shot and changing your mind a hundred times. There had been enough jokes, it was time to say something nice to the girl. She deserved him being nice, she was a sweet kid and not the least bit vain. 'Sensational,' he repeated.

CHPTER TWENTY

Revelations

After six weeks in the job Andy had sussed the customs and pecking order that segregated the common room. Each of the main departments seconded a corner but the more esoteric subjects such as religious studies or sciences did not inhabit the common room at all. They had hideaways.

Those that did attend were split into four definite factions. The most predominant of these were the moaners and these could be found in all four corners of the room and were the most vociferous. The second group were the whisperers, those who were afraid to put their nose above the parapet and obviously the more craven amongst this group belonged in the first group. The third faction were the stoics. These hardy individuals got on with the job, let each day take care of itself and dreamed longingly of early retirement. The last group were the dissidents.

Alan Angelou had been a whisperer, he had spent the six years of his tenure amongst the Humanities, using his common room time to mark his Geography homework or leafing his way through the Daily Mail and clicking his tongue. Andy had marked him down as a secret grizzler but recently he had come out of the closet. His wry sense of humour was welcomed in foreign parts of the common room's geography.

This lunchtime the women were absent. There was to be a summer fete including a jumble sale and the female staff were sorting the donations. The men sat together, ignoring the usual apartheid and fondly discussed the foibles of their absent friends.

'I made a grave mistake recently,' Angelou explained. 'My wife had a difficult situation to deal with concerning our son and babysitting for our grandson. We discussed it and agreed how we would proceed. Later that evening I heard Ros on the telephone telling him the complete opposite to what we agreed. She upset him for no good reason and I confronted her about it. Here's where I made my grave error. I was reasonable, in fact the personification of reasonable. I don't understand why you did that, especially when we agreed and whatever and whatever. She didn't speak to me for two days. I'll not be doing that again. In future I'll stick to abuse. Tell her she's a stupid fucking cow and in half an hour it will all be forgotten.'

'I can describe marriage in simple terms,' said Mason.

'Are you married?'

'Of course,' he replied. 'Forty years, therefore I know of what I speak.'

'I'm amazed.'

'When you marry, a man's rating in his wife's estimation is ten out of ten. During the course of their marriage it decreases in increments to one out of ten. The moment the gentleman in question passes on to the next world, his score rockets back up to eleven out of ten.'

* * *

The summer fete was a week away and some of the staff had been volunteered to prepare the stalls in readiness. Flint, the assistant caretaker had elected himself supervisor and flitted from group to group to check on progress. Margery and Marcia were sorting through the jumble for items suitable for sale and putting the unwanted rubbish in black sacks.

'Coping, ladies,' he entwined his fingers in mock prayer.

'Yes, thank you,' Marcia spoke peremptorily, not disguising her contempt.

'Would you like another pair of hands?'

'Jinny Parish is expected,' said Marcia. 'Thanks all the same.'

'I'll leave you to it, shall I?'

'I think that's best,' said Marcia, following his progress further down the hall. 'Fuck off, you unctuous wanker.'

'Marcia!' Margery could conceal the mirth she truly felt. 'He is though, isn't he.'

'Undeniably. God knows why I agreed to this. Every year it's the same, boring, boring, boring.' Marcia complained. 'Isn't there any gossip?'

'What d'you mean, boring. Look at this,' Margery held up a pair of red lace panties.

'How does a thing like this turn men on?' Marcia took them gingerly between thumb and forefinger. 'Perhaps he wipes his nose with it, anything's possible where men are concerned. One of my ex-boyfriends got arrested for stealing knickers off washing lines. He didn't like this frilly kind. He liked voluminous flannelly things middle aged ladies wear.'

Jinny crashed through the doors at the far end of the hall, 'Sorry I'm late.'

'Another victim here for the slaughter,' said Marcia.

'I don't mind volunteering,' said Jinny. 'It's not such a big sacrifice and we raise a lot of money.'

'Haven't you got any juicy gossip?' asked Marcia. 'Now that Hugo Mason is slowing down, I don't know what this school is coming to.'

'The caretaker's guinea pig had triplets. I don't think she's married.'

'That's pretty funny for you, Margery.'

Jinny hung up her coat and put on a pair of rubber gloves, 'How's it going?'

'Badly,' Marcia handed her the red lace panties. 'Except for these.'

Jinny dropped the panties into a sack as though they had burned her fingers.

'There is some gossip, well, sort of gossip, about Andrew,' Margery confessed. 'What do I do with these?' She held up an oversize pair of cami knickers.

Marcia glanced up, 'I'll look up my old boyfriend's telephone number. Humphrey Ingram, care of Dartmoor.'

'Humphrey,' said Margery. 'You're not serious?'

'Very charming boy, Humphrey, had a mass of black hair. I expect he's bald by now.'

'What gossip about Andrew?' asked Jinny.

'Yes, what about Andrew.'

'It's not gossip exactly. He was out with Gillian...'

'Miss Finn. What kind of nickname is Mickey for a girl. Typical that these young troglodytes chose Mickey. If they were the least bit literate she would be called Huckleberry.'

'Andrew was out with Gillian?' Jinny wanted to know why and how but was too guilty to ask.

'Apparently,' said Margery. 'He told her he's a widower.'

'He's a dark horse that one,' said Marcia, folding a cardigan neatly and then dropping it. 'Bother. In my opinion that's some sort of fairy tale. He's far too young to be a widower. Speaking of fairy tales, he's probably gay and wants it kept under wraps.'

'What makes you think he's gay?' asked Jinny, trying to sound unconcerned but inexplicably hoping it was not true.

'The way he dresses. Those effeminate hands of his. They should be cast in bronze they are so beautiful.'

'Aren't they,' said Jinny relieved to hide behind the consensus.

'I think he's very attractive,' Margery was suddenly on uncertain ground and hesitated. She opted for, 'generally.'

'Steady now, Margery,' Marcia folded her beefy arms and pretended to study her friend with intensity. 'Does your mother know about this?'

Margery laughed and sorted the clothing with renewed vigour, hoping that her red face did not show.

'Why all the secrecy,' Marcia demanded. 'Tell me that.'

Jinny felt enough time had elapsed to hide her need to know asked, 'What else did Gillian have to tell?'

'Not very much, after the NQT session, he went to The Man in the Moon for a drink and he gave Gillian a lift home.'

Jinny, relieved that there was nothing more to Andy's liaison with Gillian. Widowed, it must be true. Who would invent such a lie? While she sorted clothes she mused as to how she might find out more about him. Where he went to school and university, where he grew up, who his wife was, anything.

'Has anyone looked in his file?' Jinny asked.

'You seem to be taking an inordinate interest in this young man,' said Marcia intuitively. 'Should Angus be anxious.'

Jinny's insides quivered violently. She had gone too far and it must stop now. Like Margery she covered her embarrassment with a laugh that rang false to her own ears. 'I just like gossip,' she said. 'Don't we all?'

His file was in the cabinet in Mrs Tapper's office. She could not think of a legitimate reason to ask to review it. She would have to sneak a look. While they finished sorting she struggled to work out a plan. Betsy March was away on some junket but there was still Mrs Tapper to contend with. She protected her territory vigorously. With her boss away she would be extra vigilant and the headmistress' office even more impenetrable than usual. How might she create a diversion? Set off the fire alarm. She did not have the nerve. With Betsy away Mrs Tapper would not work late but she would lock up. Did someone here have a key? The question was who? She could not ask the question for fear of giving the game away completely. She had let her guard down once already and must be more careful in future.

'What are you two up to this evening?' Jinny asked innocently.

'We're invited to dinner with Charles' editor. So I've got an extremely exciting evening of shop talk.'

This was typical of Marcia, to be mocking her husband. It was all part of her pretence of being blasé. Jinny slightly envied her lifestyle on the fringes of celebrity. There had been offers of television work but so far these had not panned out.

Charles was a nice man but it was true that he did talk shop a lot. Inevitably the evening would focus on him and his name-dropping. He is quite a bright man but not totally convincing. He and Angus were always at loggerheads and Angus would fume all the way home in the car. 'Bloody dilettante, he ought to find out what life is like in the real world. Patronising me like I'm a naughty schoolboy. People like him don't know they're born. Until you've experienced commerce you aren't qualified to comment. If he was working in the States they would eat him up for breakfast.' And so and so on.

'I'm almost tempted to stay and sort the entire school,' said Marcia. 'It might prove to be less boring than Charles' editor and his stuck up wife.'

There would be a few other people for dinner but unlike Charles, Marcia did not name drop. She is a nice woman is Marcia.

Her desperate need to see Andy's file flared up again and she excused herself to go to the toilet but headed for the office to check if the coast was clear.

'She's got the hots for that man,' said Marcia as soon as she was gone.

'Surely not,' said Margery, genuinely shocked.

'It seems all the female staff in the English department have got the hots for him.'

'You too?'

'Except me, I have to save my hots for my menopausal vapours.' Marcia sat back and folded her arms, 'I can't blame the woman, married to that yob.'

Out of loyalty to her friend, Margery who did not like Angus, did not respond. Nor did she feel inclined to defend her friend's husband. She did feel a pang of jealousy that Jinny might have a fancy for Andrew, it intruded into her mild hope.

'It would be ironic wouldn't it, all you women lusting after the man and he being gay. It would be George Michael all over again.'

Jinny, her head craned at a ridiculous angle, walked past Mrs Tapper's door. She was sat at her desk busily typing. Disappointed, Jinny carried on past.

'Jinny,' a distant female voice called. 'Jinny.'

She stopped to see Mrs Tapper emerge from the office, 'Jinny, the very person. Could you do me a favour?'

'Of course,' said Jinny, following her into her room. 'Whatever.'

'I need to find Flint,' said Mrs Tapper. Jinny noticed that she did not use 'mister' when referring to the assistant caretaker. 'I can't leave the office unattended.'

'He's in the hall,' said Jinny, her eyes hungrily ogling the filing cabinets. 'Sorting jumble.'

'I know it's an awful cheek but you couldn't fetch him for me,' she pleaded. 'I need him to run an errand.'

'I could watch the office for you.'

'I'm expecting Mrs March to call,' she turned her head to one side like a dog begging for scraps. 'I know it's an awful cheek.'

Jinny tried to find another way to get the woman to go herself with the filing cabinet tantalisingly available. All the way back to he hall she tried to figure out a bargain but she surmised that Mrs Tapper was equally ignorant of commerce.

* * *

CHAPTER TWENTY-ONE

Andy invites Gillian to dinner

She turned the car off the main road and finding an unexpected steep climb, struggled with the gear stick. It made a hideous screech before engaging. Bouncing a couple of times, then lurching, she regained control. Judging that number 27 would be at the top end of the street she almost overran the house. She paused, took a deep breath and calmed herself before stuttering into a parking space. She locked the car carefully, rechecked and entered the gate.

It was a cloudless evening. Dusk was falling, casting charred shadows. Painted with black the house could have featured in a Sherlock Holmes story. There was a wisteria like a hand shading the eyes of the bay window. The front garden was thick with bushes that had not been kept in check. The pathway had become so narrow she had to take care not to graze the sleeve of her new jacket.

She had complained to Andrew that Wyford did not have a cinema that showed foreign films . She had missed so many films that she would like to have seen. Andrew had some of them on DVD and offered to lend them to her. Fortunately her parents did not have a DVD player and he had invited her to watch them at his place.

They had been out several times but her fantasy was yet to be realised. Apart from that first night in the car there had been no intimacy and that occasion had been her doing. He was not patronising her but was acting like her favourite uncle. She still knew nothing about him except what he had confided to her parents and that his own father was a teacher. She did not know where he grew up, where he had gone to school nor what university he attended or what degree he had got. Not that they were ever short of conversation. Their afternoons and evenings together flashed by. He had taken her to haunts she had never heard of and restaurants in the most unlikely places. Some of the food was not much to write home about but if Andrew liked the atmosphere of a restaurant for him the food was secondary.

She had learned a lot about him in general ways. He slopped his dinner down his front, his shirt was forever coming out of his trousers and he sometimes had toothpaste around his mouth or shaving soap in his ear. For the moment she found all this endearing.

He hated pretension, hypocrisy and injustice and liked things that were exciting or unpredictable. She did not have to work hard to keep on his right side but she could not shift his avuncular attitude towards her.

He had told her which bell to ring but she could not recall the instructions and neither bell was labelled. She closed her eyes and pressed. Almost instantly the door was thrown open by a hard faced woman dressed for the office, 'What do you want?' she demanded roughly.

'Andrew,' she recoiled.

'Try the other button,' the woman spoke rudely.

Her face flared. Why had she closed her eyes? Now she had no idea which button she had pressed. Finger poised, she hesitated and then took the plunge. Still the wrong bell. Hastily she pressed the other one and a voice called, 'Come on up.'

The hard faced woman stood at the door to her flat glaring. She could feel her eyes watching her climb the stairs and then Andrew appeared on the landing, crouching to see down.

'Giving tutorials, now?' the woman snarled.

Gillian's face flamed all the darker at the obvious reference to her youth. She managed a sickly smile and handed him a bottle of wine. He put the bottle on the hall table and relieved her of her jacket. The flat was spilling over with treasure. There was so much to look at and a fragrant smell of cooking filled the rooms.

'Don't mind that miserable bag.' He kissed her, took her hand and sat her in a dark red sofa. 'You look great.'

Her head was spinning. Things to look at everywhere in her eye line, the taste and feel of his lips on her mouth, she was glad to be sitting and able to collect herself. Why had he kissed her like that? Out of the blue.

There were prints, books, pottery, records, DVD's, plants, a glass sculpture of an elephant, photographs. She got up to look closer. Which was Karen? She saw immediately who it was. A pretty woman, hair falling across her face and a natural smile. Her eyes sparkled as though the cameraman had used one of those special lenses that create exaggerated twinkles. For some inexplicable reason the face reminded her of someone. Gillian screwed her eyes and tried viewing the picture from different angles but the resemblance eluded her. She put her hand over the top part of the picture blocking out the hair and saw at once, it was Mrs Parish. It was not the hair that had suppressed the identity it was the twinkle.

'That's Karen just after we met,' he held out a full glass. 'She's not so happy in subsequent photos.'

'Why do you do that?'

'What?'

'Take the piss out of yourself.'

'Habit.'

'Why did you kiss me?'

'Habit.'

'I give up.' She turned sulkily away and picked up a picture of Andrew as a boy. It was a standard school snap, he with missing teeth and juvenile hair.

'I'm sorry,' he apologised. She pretended to study the photograph closely and let him stew.

'I don't know why I did it,' he said. 'It just seemed right at the time.'

She turned to him and said angrily, 'Am I staying the night or not? I bought new underwear specially.'

'I'm not sure that's such a good idea.'

'It's only sex, it's not marriage. I'm not going to go out and commit suicide after.'

'You might,' he said. 'When it comes to sex I'm a fabulous letdown.'

They solemnly stared at each other until she broke down first, giggling she told him, 'You're impossible.'

'That as well.'

'Can you ever be serious?'

He scratched an area above his ear and she saw some shaving soap secreted on the side of his jaw. 'Not often,' he decided.

She put down her drink, stood in front of him and wiped the soap from his neck. It took a time for him to make up his mind but he pressed his mouth to hers. Her feelings pitched acutely and promised a prospect that did not materialise.

'I'll put the dinner on a low light.'

It was just as he said it would be, a letdown. It was all of her own doing. Her body was exactly where she had dreamed of being but her head was somewhere else. He smelled so nice and masculine, soap and cologne subtle against her nose. He was putting her needs first but her head churned with irrelevancies. Spectres, Mrs Parish and Tommy True haunted her, teasing and frustrating like one of those nightmares where you are trying to complete some task and you are continually distracted by side issues. Now the dream was tormenting her while she was awake.

His hands were encouraging her to relax but her brain was in overdrive. Gentle fingers coaxing but her body was lacklustre.

Why were all the terms used by men for female genitalia so unflattering? The pet word her mother used to describe the vagina's inner workings made her skin crawl. Evelyn Waugh had written *'narrow loins'* and John Banville *'ripening fruit'* neither of those inspired respect. There was a poem she had read in one of those self publishing magazines.

A rainbow haloed moon
In a Rebeccan sea of skin...
Some have chosen and chosen well
The irrevocable token.

He stopped, leaned on one arm and brushed the hair from her face and smiled. 'This was your idea.'

'I'm sorry. It's the moment I've fantasised for weeks and...'

'Fantasies are rarely realised, didn't you know that?'

'I've never come this close before.'

'You weren't even close to coming.'

'How d'you know?'

'I don't know, I just know. Your heart wasn't in it. A man can tell,' he kissed her softly and his hair fell on her face. He brushed it away with the palm of his hand. 'Some of the differences between men and women couldn't be more polarised. It takes all a woman's concentration to climax and all a man's concentration not to. You hungry?'

'Can we stay like this for a while longer?' she asked. 'Touch me some more.'

He threw back the duvet, kissed her breasts and belly, tracing her body with his free hand. 'You're blonde,' he said. 'Why on earth do you dye your hair black.'

'It gives me an image, sort of sinister. Anyway, I like it this way.'

'You should be yourself,' he said. 'That way you are more likely to get what you want.'

'What are you doing now?'

'Checking for blemishes.'

* * *

Jinny walked the dog passed the Finn house at nine o'clock and saw the car was gone and the bedroom lights off. For two hours she fretted and using the dog as an excuse, went out to check again. All the lights in the house were out and Gillian's car was still not there.

Having exercised Bobby for twice his normal allowance, he collapsed into his basket when they got back to the house . On Sunday morning Bobby, the family's morning alarm was sound asleep and Jinny did not have the heart to wake him. She poured all the milk down the sink, told Angus that it had gone off and that she was hurrying to the corner shop. The Finn's house was a short diversion and the car had still not returned.

* * *

Eating dinner in large armchairs, they had watched a romantic film called, L'Equipier. Dinner was a sort of stew cooked in an iron pot, duck sausages in lentils. They soaked up the gravy with thick chunks of fresh black bread and for dessert he had bought a rhubarb tart. They finished her wine and started another bottle. There was no way either of them were in a fit state to drive to Wyford. She prepared to stay the night. This time she would concentrate.

She lay naked waiting for him, the duvet cover felt cool and invigorating against her body. She had drunk more than she was used to but was not the least light-headed. The dinner had petrified her because cooked pulses gave her shocking bouts of wind. She had waited expectantly for the worst but nothing had happened, not a sign of indigestion, nor a sign of an aftermath.

He got in beside her but was not wearing a condom. They embraced and he kissed her tenderly while his fingers shaped her bottom, 'Some people can't make love without emotion being involved.'

'I really care for you,' she stroked his face and wiggled her backside wanting him to continue the fondling.

'When Karen was having sex for my sake I could tell. You can tell. I never liked these sacrifices, it made me feel cheated.'

'I wasn't doing it for your sake. I wanted to.'

'For some of us making love is making love but one partner getting their rocks off isn't making love is it?'

'I want to,' she said and he kissed her again. Slowly and leisurely their mouths touched and their tongues probed. He pulled away and caressed her face.

'Sometimes the chemistry doesn't happen. It's nobody's fault, it's nothing to be ashamed of, it's just one of things that prove your instincts are above the animal kingdom.'

'I want you to,' she pleaded.

'Not tonight,' he said. 'Next time.'

Next time! There would be a next time. She could feel his body against her, his arm across her thigh, his breathing almost inaudible. She could not sleep because she was hot. She assumed this excessive heat was desire but it was simply a reaction to too much red wine.

To date, sex had left Gillian frustrated and fearful, certain there was something lacking in her libido. She had read the magazines, she had read novels, old and new and when it came to sex she expected a balance of modern and old fashioned. So far sex had left her filled with self-disgust and a strong sense of having been violated.

There was no meetings of minds and bodies, just meeting of anatomy. No synchronisation of any kind, a few minutes clutching, thrusting and just as *Lara* complained, ending in a sticky mess. After sex, there was no bonding, only embarrassment and the obvious boredom of her partner, anxious to get back to his Play Station or his mates.

She expected the male to take the lead in these encounters because she did not have the temperament to make the moves that Cosmo recommended. Was it her outlandish appearance that gave these boys a fallacious expectation? As a result she attracted the wrong sort of man. Was it that her ideal world exemplified in novels was remote from reality.

Sex is greatly overrated by the poets.

She did not confide her true feelings to her friends for fear of ridicule. It was for fear of ridicule that she concealed most of her thoughts and feelings. So she had lied and told Hilary, Sally and Debby that sex was a trip to heaven and back. None of the boys came back for more and that omission was easy to pass off as boys being boys. She maintained the façade but her heart sank with recollections of humiliation and self-loathing.

She had bided her time and studied what boys might be more sophisticated and experienced. Those who might have outgrown the furtive, self-fulfilling stage. She tried talking to her mother but she, like her euphemism for the vagina, was bogged down in a bygone era. People no longer talked of sex in reverential whispers the way her mother did, they flaunted it, even if it was embellished with a pack of lies. She told her mother that love and sex was no longer a Barbara Cartland novel.

Gillian could not decide whether it was bravura, but Sally and Debby claimed they liked it rough or from behind and scoffed at any notion of tenderness. Both revelled in violent films and the more prolonged and explicit the violence the better.

Hilary was more enigmatic, cleverer than Gillian. Most days they walked to school together or if it was raining got the bus. It took the length of the bus journey for Hilary to do a quick revision and get 80% or 90% while Gillain read and re-read and read again to get 70%.

They would congregate in a bedroom and share their experiences. Hilary, although she joined in with the rest, generally gave off the notion that she was above it all. There was a mocking air about her, implying that she knew the facts and her friends were young and inexperienced.

Gillian tried to draw her friend out, to get her to reveal this secret knowledge. She composed questions, like 'What do you want out of life?' Hoping Hilary would drop her guard and confess but she could not find the right moment or summon the appropriate mood for confiding. There was always the fear that she herself would be exposed as a pathetic wimp.

It was Hilary who set her up with Tommy True. She thought they were an item but that was not the case. Tommy was a couple of years older, claimed to have lived with a girl for a year and pretended to an urbanity. Unlike most boys he noticed things. Like you were wearing new clothes or had dyed your hair a new colour. Things that girls noticed about each other but boys rarely did. Gillian thought he was a phoney but because of Hilary's protracted involvement with him she pretended to like him. She did not fancy him in the least and ignored his false compliments.

'He's frightened of you,' Hilary told her. 'You're so unapproachable.'

Having this unlikely power over a man caused her to re-evaluate her attitude toward him. Still she did not find much to attract her but he had lived with a girl, he must have some experience.

Tommy was the ageless type. A mop of unruly fair hair, a pleasant face and an ability to chat to females. There was a hardness in his eyes that gave her reservation but he had been talking about her with Hilary and she was flattered. Next time he began courting her she responded and counted on his experience improving on her limitations. He did in a way she had not dreamed possible.

Gillian did not want to remember those things right at this moment.

She listened for Andrew's breathing, like a mother afraid that her child was dead. There was a bright moon and a shard of light flickered through the curtains. She was just able to see his sleeping face.

Squalid memories were trying to sneak back, which she struggled to stave off. Gingerly she placed her hand in his chest hair and let it slip through her fingers. Gaining nerve she let her hand slip to his stomach, pausing for a reaction, let it continue down into his pubic hair. Her fingers traced the angles at the top of his legs then she pushed uncertainly at his dormant penis. In his sleep, he brushed her hand away, turned over and pulled the duvet tight around him.

She caressed herself, contemplating masturbation, wishing for sleep. Tommy and the Council flat block where he lived, creeping quietly past his drunken mother, who was snoring loudly and calling plaintively for a lost cause.

'Gillian!'

She came awake with a start, Andrew was asleep still facing the other way. She was alone, unprotected.

'We must be quick before my mum wakes up.'

She had dressed specially for the occasion, black skirt without tights. He took her from behind and congratulated her on being so tight. He came in a matter of seconds and as he pulled away he left the condom behind, splashing her with sperm. To her unremitting disgust he had penetrated her anus.

She had washed and washed and washed but the revulsion lingered. Hilary asked her how it was and she had smiled knowingly and said, 'Great.' Why had she done that, Hilary was not fooled and she was even more disgusted with herself for lying.

At the best of times, Gillian's periods were irregular and she spent five agonising weeks positive she was pregnant. The relief she felt when her period started had been the most graphic emotion of her life and as yet remained unsurpassed and that included this night.

When she awoke he was sitting on the bed playing with her new knickers, 'Nice.' She snatched them from him. 'Do you want any breakfast?' She disappeared under the duvet to dress.

Sitting silently either side of the kitchen table, each reading a section of the Sunday papers. 'There's a review in here about Edith Wharton's biography. I can't find any of her books for love nor money.'

'There's some out there,' he nodded.

She got up and went to the bookshelves. 'How come you've got so many books?'

'My parents have emigrated. That's the non-fiction section you're looking in, fictions by the window.'

She found copies of *Valley of Decision* and *the Age of Innocence*. 'Can I borrow these?'

'Keep them.'
'Thanks,' she stared at him waiting for him to notice.
'What?' he asked, without looking up.
'You're so fucking smart aren't you,' she flared. 'Know it all. You're not the least bit vulnerable.'
He looked at her for a long time before speaking, 'Now I'm afraid you're showing your age. Of course I'm vulnerable. That's why I pitch my sights on easy targets.'
'Like me, you mean?'
'Like you. I'm thirty seven and you're twenty years old. How much easier does it get? First time I laid eyes on you. Hard on the outside and as soft as mush on the inside. Who do you think you were fooling?'
'What makes you so bloody sure of yourself?'
'Because I was exactly the same.'

* * *

It was a typical weekday evening, Angus was late home and the twins were at their extra tuition class. Jinny had shared a snack meal with Bobby and had intended to finish her new book but this silly infatuation intervened. It was driving her to extremes that she could not control. She wanted to find out Andrew's history. Was it possible to send an e-mail inquiry without detection? If she pretended to be somebody else, somebody anonymous or Gillian Finn, what answer might she get? Inexperienced in Machiavellian manipulation she could not decide what form this e-mail should take. First step was to find a suitably anonymous computer to use. As the boys were out she let herself into Alex' room and turned on his laptop. She had no idea what his password was but it would be more guessable than James'.

Wyford FC, did not get her in with or without spaces, nor did Alexander or Parish. She looked round the walls for inspiration. Why women allow themselves to be photographed in such undignified poses. Why did men find these hard faced women attractive? What was titillating about a woman squatting at the bottom of a pole.

She typed in the word 'knickers' and again the screen told her the password was incorrect. She changed it to 'knockers' and the screen fired into life, her son's predictability causing her to cringe. She scrolled slowly through the headings, resting for a moment to decide if she might open one or two files to check on her son's safety. You never knew these days, paedophiles and other deviants being so astute. Obviously girls were more vulnerable than boys but you could not be too sure. Her finger hovered over the mouse, her conscience pricking. However bland or otherwise the contents of these files may be, it was the same intrusion as her mother reading her private diary.

Her mobile rang, causing her to jump, it slipped out of her grasp and bounced on the keyboard. Picking it up off the floor, she said, 'Hello.'

A naked man appeared on the screen lying on his back, his hips imperceptibly thrusting his penis skywards. A woman's hand began caressing the erection and the man thrust higher. Then the woman began licking round the top.

'Jinny, is that you?'

'Who's calling?'

Jinny watched, stunned, as the woman administered fellatio. The film cut quickly, bobbing in rhythm to a series of women carrying out fellatio on a variety of men.

'Jinny, are you there?'

'Sorry.'

One extraordinary hard faced demi-monde consumed an extraordinary sized penis.

'Jinny, are you all right?'

'Sorry, Margery. Can I call you back in a few minutes?'

Jinny sat through the entire show until the screen went blank, then, she followed suit. She could not decide what was more wretched, the participants in this debauchery or her son for being a voyeur.

She pressed file and the icon listed four files. 1. Plate. 2. History-WWI 3. History-Lloyd George 4. Triangle. She clicked on 4 and another film began with another three protagonists, a woman and two men. She sat open-mouthed as these persons carried out their dull cavorting which ended with the usual anti-climax.

Not a day was going by when her ideal world was not rocked to its foundations. Who inhabited this mysterious underworld?

What kind of people participated in this sort of decadence? How would these films warp the minds of her children? Angus must talk to the twins immediately and get these laptops blocked. There is no way that she could talk to the boys about such things. This is his responsibility. Going to football does not constitute pastoral care and he has been extremely remiss in that department. This is his chance to make amends.

She was so agitated she rang Angus' mobile but it was switched off. She rang Alex and he cut her off. Now she was livid. How dare he, the little pervert. Her hand clamped her mouth. What had got into her? She rang Margery back but the line was engaged. This was not her day.

She made a cup of hot sweet tea and felt better. Images of naked men and women flickered in and out of her head. Needing a distraction, she opened the newspaper and began reading reviews. There was a revival of a play called, *The Anniversary* and she tried to recall a good moment from their evening at The Copse.

Instead of others, she remembered herself being naked, waiting for Angus to come to bed. She did enjoy lying without clothes in crisp fresh sheets. It gave her a sense of freedom but she was unsure of how attractive she was in the altogether.

At one of Angus' work junkets in a Park Lane Hotel there had been a tombola and she had won a weekend at a health spa. Seeing other women naked was a revelation. So many blondes and redheads with black body hair, so much cellulite and so many dewlaps, neck and tummy. She marvelled at the nerve of some of these women, allowing themselves to be seen in public.

Ever since then, she had taken very good care of herself. She used Angus' cycling machine more than he did. He was getting a bit of a tummy if the truth be told. Something else she must speak to him about.

Laying in bed naked waiting for Angus to check his e-mails. He had been a long time checking e-mails the night of their anniversary.

She went to the study and nervously contemplated turning on his computer. In fact it was *their* computer but she never used it. She only needed a computer for work and preferred to use her school laptop. Did she know his internet password? Would she need it?

She turned on the machine and waited while it loaded. She went into Microsoft Works and pressed the mouse at file. There were the headings, 1. Frank Risdon 2. Alec Shingler 3.Triangle 4. Plate.

She pressed the redial buttons on her telephone and Margery answered. 'Hello, it's me, Jinny.'

'I've just been speaking to Gill.'

'Gillian Finn?'

'Yes, I've quite a lot to tell you.'

'I've got quite a lot to tell you too, are you in?'

'Yes, come over. I'll put the kettle on.'

'I'm on my way.'

She let the dog out into the garden to relieve himself, Bobby would have to go without his walk until tomorrow.

Margery lived in North Wyford, in the house she inherited from her parents. Wyford is spotted with lollipop shaped developments fed by a single street. This one is located on far side of Rabbits Rise where the Morrissey's live and Jinny had to pass their house on her way.

Tea was laid when she arrived, teapot in a knitted coat and generous slices of Manor Cake. Margery still dressed in her school clothes.

'What did you want to see me about?' she asked.

'You first,' said Jinny unable to contain her need to know. She was like a man waiting for the final score in a non-televised football match. 'What did Gill have to tell?'

'She spent the night at Andrew's flat,' said Margery.

Jinny felt her insides sink straight into her shoes. She had felt the same panic before. As a new mother, out shopping and the twins disappeared. They turned up in the arms of smiling policemen.

Margery sounded unsure. 'They had too much wine and neither was safe to drive. She slept in the spare room.'

'Very sensible,' said Jinny without conviction.

'They watched a film and he made dinner,' Margery continued. 'Cassoulet.'

'He sounds too good to be true. Isn't there anything he doesn't do?'

'He does live on his own,' Margery justified. 'I'm sure he can't live on takeaways and he's got to eat something. I don't think she liked it all that much.'

'What else did she have to say?'

He lives in a flat in Hornsey or Muswell Hill. It's full of books and pictures. She saw a picture of his dead wife…' Margery hesitated.

'What?' Jinny wanted to know everything. Nothing was to be withheld.

'I'm not sure about this,' Margery studied her face curiously. 'Uhm.'

'Come on,' she demanded, getting impatient. 'You can tell me.'

'She said that his wife's face reminded her of you.'

'Me!'

'Yes.'

'Really,' Jinny had to fight to repress her glee. 'How odd.' To cover her feelings she took a piece of cake she did not really want and chewed it thoroughly. An image of Gillian in bed, in her underwear or not as the case may be, did little to help her digestion. Could she believe that she spent the night and nothing happened. 'It's nice that she confides in you.'

'Why is it do you think?'

'Does she have problems with her mother?'

'Quite the opposite, but her mother doesn't know Andrew does she.'

'I sometimes wish I had a daughter,' Jinny would not normally have said anything so indiscreet to Margery who had no children but her manic infatuation was scrambling her brain. 'Don't you regret not having children?' She asked kindly.

'Of course,' said Margery, shrugging. 'But I had no choice. Someone had to stay and look after mother and father while they were alive and I was the youngest. It is the way of things.'

'Do you like living here?'

'I've got some wonderful neighbours. They're very kind and then there's St Bartimaeus. I've got so many friends there.'

'Why don't you marry? You're still young enough and you look really good for your age.'

'I don't have much experience of men and I don't feel inclined to start.'

'You've got a point. More of a point than you could ever imagine.'

Jinny told of her findings on the computers and Margery

listened, horrified. What on earth was she doing intruding in her son's private laptop?

As Jinny delicately described the two porn films she realised that Margery was even less worldly than she and barely able to advise her. Despite this, they chatted until late. Margery, unable to stifle a yawn, checked the time. They had no idea how late it had got, the football had ended over two hours before. Apologising profusely for keeping Margery up, Jinny made a hurried exit.

She fired herself up ready for the men's return but immediately he got through the door Angus demanded to know whether she had collected his suit from the dry cleaners.

'What suit?' she asked, bewildered.

'I left you a note,' he replied.

'Where?'

It was where he had left it, on the notice board.

'I'm sorry, I didn't think to check. What was the point of a note? By the time I got home from work it would have been too late anyway. Why didn't you telephone?'

'I can't rely on you for anything. I'm tired. I'm going to bed.'

Instead of having the upper hand and facing him over the pornography, she had ended up on the back foot, lost her courage and there would be no confrontation.

CHAPTER TWENTY-TWO

Margery finds a lump

It was one of those lovely May afternoons that suggested summer. Optimism was in the air, pervading the whole school and joyous yells of children floated around the building.

Andy sat in his office staring out of the window. Across a clear blue backdrop, traffic hurtled back and forth on the M1, the swimming boy stroked steadfastly back and forth and a football game between Year 7's moved around the field like a scrum.

Everything on his desk had been dealt with and he could have gone home if he wanted but for some reason home did not beckon him. It was not an evening for being cooped up in a flat. Nor did he fancy an evening of drinking at the pub. He sometimes enjoyed the banter of his fellow teachers but he only really went in case she joined them but she seldom did. The handful of evenings she had made her brief visits the party had been segregated. Boys together, girls together. As far as he could tell there were no affairs going on between any of his fellow workmates. Even Hugh Mason was having a lean spell.

He had opted out two days before and gone home early. Sod's law sprung into action and that night she had gone for a drink. Even then, apparently, she had not stayed long. How was he going to get to see her socially, free of the shackles of school? He could not work in front of an audience because he was uncomfortable with spectators having an inkling of his true intentions. No more excuses, he must start some inroads into a relationship.

Why did he so love lost causes? They had little in common. Did he really believe the moment she fell for him and they kissed, she would turn into some perfect woman. Transform into a metaphorical handsome prince or princess.

He did have an outside chance. What he had seen of Angus at the football and in that restaurant was enough fuel to keep his hopes up. Her husband was an arsehole and her kids were none too clever. You never truly knew what goes on behind closed doors but he suspected it was not a bed of roses. Could she be desperate for affection? That he could give her in shitloads. Put your mind to it, Andy my boy and think what you can do for her. You could try the Mason approach, express an interest in her interests. You might have burned your boats there. A sudden about turn will probably create suspicion.

Her face appeared before him and his mind's eye dwelt on each feature longingly. Her soft mouth, in repose, opening slightly, not to speak but to welcome him.

Knock that off, you prat.

There was a soft knock at the door and he swivelled his chair and leaned forward to open it. Margery's doe eyes smiled apologetically, 'I know it's late. Are you busy?'

'Yes,' he joked. 'Overwhelmed. Come in.'

She stepped half way through the door but did not close it. Shielded from whoever was outside she whispered, 'Have a word with Liam, he's got a problem.'

'What problem?'

Margery stepped further in but still did not close the door fully. 'Cold feet,' she mouthed. 'He's on the America trip but wants to cancel.'

'OK, I'll see him.'

Liam Donnellan was bullying fodder. Not because he was a swot, not because he was overweight or possessed any other physical idiosyncrasy. Medium height, slim, with a pleasant face there was an air about him that provoked the impulse to clout him across the head. To knock some sense into him. His fellow pupils were not inhibited when it came to following this impulse. Andy knew that those who are bullied made themselves scarce. He had spied Liam skulking around the dustbin enclosure hiding out with other victims.

As a student he held his own. There was no evidence of a problematical home life. Andy prided himself, maybe falsely, that he could discern a child from a single parent home within the first few sentences of any conversation. On several occasions Andy had attempted to draw Liam out, as he did with all his pupils, but Liam remained tight shut.

Liam sat across from him, avoiding his eye and not speaking. 'What's up?' Andy asked and got the usual shrug for an answer. 'Say something, Liam, even if it's only drop dead.'

'I don't want to go,' his voice was surprisingly big. 'That's all there is to it.'

'You wanted to go once upon a time,' said Andy. 'Your parents have paid haven't they?'

'So,' he said. 'It's only money.'

Andy tried to catch the boy's eye but his practiced head eluded him. 'I tell you what I reckon is going on here and you tell me if I'm wrong.' He paused but there was no response. 'When the chance came up you thought going to America was a great idea and you talked your parents into paying the deposit. What does your dad do?'

'He works in a factory up London.'

'Your mum?'

'She lives under the motorway in a caravan, with her hairdresser.'

Single parent. He had got this one wrong. He cast his mind back to being seventeen, going away to university and being utterly miserable. 'Going to America seemed like a good idea at some time or other and then today because the trip is getting nearer it's becoming real and the thought of leaving home for a week didn't seem such a good idea. You got a twinge in your stomach.'

Liam's head was bowed still lower and just as Andy was going to continue just to break the silence, he said, 'I won't have anybody to talk to.'

'None of your friends going?'

'I don't have many friends.'

It was a shame he was not going on the trip, he could keep an eye on this poor kid. A flash of inspiration sprung into his mind but it must wait. He must deal with Liam first and then find time to think.

'You won't make friends locking yourself in your bedroom or hiding behind the dustbins.'

This was the first time Liam sat upright and his startled eyes came alive. 'How did you know?'

'I want you to sleep on this decision of yours. Try and think positively. Will you do that for me? We'll talk about this again tomorrow.' Andy made a mental note to give the boy some responsible task.

Liam shrugged.

'Hold your head up,' said Andy, lifting his chin. 'Look the world in the eye. You can do it.'

He watched the boy slouch his way down the corridor and turn to see if he was being watched. He then stood erect, head held high but as he turned right towards the stair his body slumped.

Margery appeared, 'How did it go?'

'Not too great.'

'His mother ran off with the milkman.'

'Hairdresser, he said.'

'Oh, really.'

'Better getting your split ends taken care of than free milk.'

Andy opened the door of his office and ushered her in. She must have sensed danger because her ears pricked and her doe eyes were alert.

'What are you afraid of?' he asked.

Reluctantly she entered his office and he closed the door but waited for her approval. 'Should I leave the door slightly ajar?'

'Why?' she asked unconvincingly.

'Do you see all men as potential rapists?'

'Don't be silly,' she said, getting more uncomfortable. 'I'm not used to men. I just don't know how to behave with them.'

'Naturally will do.'

Margery could not relax and did not know where to look. Her doe eyes flitted, desperately searching for inspiration and her hands worried together in her lap.

'I feel like talking,' he said. 'Do you feel like talking? Not here though.'

'Where?' she asked hastily, relieved to be escaping.

'Where do you suggest? Not a pub. I'm sick of pubs.'

Her anxious eyes rotated, 'I did a Sunday roast but my aunt cancelled at the last minute. She's got some bug. That reminds me I must call her. There's lots left over. Do you like beef?'

'You're inviting me to your place?'

'Stop it, you. If you don't behave I'll withdraw the offer.'

Margery lived in a semi-detached, orange roof tiles, white render and plain windows. There had been no man living there for two decades and the exterior showed signs of fatigue. The front garden was crazily paved, nettles, dandelions and moss had replaced the mortar in the cracks.

Inside was spotless but similarly toil worn. Picture rail retained with watercolours depicting Castle Combe, Malvern, Ledbury and all points west. Carpet tending to threadbare, furniture waiting for the summons to the V & A and curtains from a bygone age. The sideboard was a pictorial history of family in black and white. Groups of smiling children in ill-fitting swimming costumes, shoulder to shoulder on the beach, wedded couples standing in a pool of confetti, carrying silver horseshoes, ladies in hats with netting over foreheads and erect non-commissioned soldiers with berets and forage caps. Toothless smiling children with nondescript faces posing for the school photographer.

Above the sideboard, pinned to the wall, was a wax crucifix with a church flier for Easter services taped alongside.

'I'll peel some potatoes.'

'I'll help.'

Margery opened the larder and found just two wizened King Edwards in the wire tray.

'I'll nip up to the shops,' said Andy.

He returned with a bag of spuds, a bottle of wine and bunch of chrysanthemums. He opened the bag, helped himself to a knife and began peeling.

'You always do the right thing, don't you.'

'I was very well trained.'

'Your wife?'

'My wife.'

'What was she like?'

Andy decided to open the wine, concentrating on the corkscrew, he wondered how to answer or whether to bother. 'I don't like talking about it.'

'Sorry.'

'That's all right, you couldn't know,' he poured out two generous glasses. 'What about you? How long have you been living alone?'

'Mother died two-and-a-half years ago.'

'Why don't you get married?'

'I told you,' said Margery firmly. 'I'm not comfortable with men.'

'Find a same sex partner.'

'I don't think so.'

'Seriously, you shouldn't be alone.'

'I have the church.'

'Margery, that's bollocks and you know it. You can get used to men. Why don't you have an affair with Hugo Mason, I bet he's very skilled with virgins.'

She was holding a glass to her lips and her face went the colour of the wine.

'I'm sorry,' he laughed. 'I was only teasing. Did I go too far?'

'Yes,' she said tearfully. He took her glass from her, placed her arms around his waist and pulled her to him.

'I'm sorry, truly sorry,' said Andy. 'Just squeeze a bit and you'll feel better.'

They stood stock still, embracing for a minute or two.

'How do I smell?'

'What do you mean?'

'How do I smell, different, pleasant, unpleasant?'

'Let me go.'

'No, not until you answer.'

'Nice,' she said. 'You smell nice. Now let me go.'

'Just one more minute. Relax. Isn't it good to be close to another person, feeling the warmth of their body against your own?'

'Yes.'

'Now, about getting married.'

'It's too late for all that.'

'What are you talking about now?'

She wrestled free and escaped behind the table. 'I'm too old for that sort of thing.'

'No you're not.'

'I'm old and unattractive.'

'No you're not. Your fears are the same as young Liam's. Unfounded.'

'Let's stop this, *please*.'

After dinner, Andy reminded Margery to ring her sick aunt

and while she telephoned he did the washing up. He was on his best behaviour, he wanted something.

She returned to the kitchen and did the 'you shouldn't have' bit and told him that her aunt was none too well. He listened politely waiting for the moment when he could raise the topic he was there for but she did it for him. 'I might have to cancel America.'

'You are going to stay behind with Liam?'

'My aunt is very elderly, over ninety, she's quite unwell and can't cope. I feel very guilty going away and leaving her.'

'You do?' he sounded as sympathetic as he dare.

Kismet.

'I feel so guilty. If I don't go I'll be letting Jinny down and if I do I'll be leaving my aunt in the lurch.'

'Difficult.'

'Then there's finding a replacement at this late stage. You wouldn't go would you?'

'I don't know…' he feigned uncertainty. 'I suppose I could.'

'Please think about it,' said Margery slightly preoccupied. 'Jinny would be happy to have you along.'

'OK,' said Andy. 'I'll do it. It's not as if I have a lot on. Just one thing I will make all the rearrangements, talk to Betsy and so on. Can we keep it quiet for a while, just in case.'

'Just in case of what?'

'Just in case,' he finished the last of his wine. 'I'd better not drink anymore.'

'Coffee?'

'Yes please, then I'd best be making tracks.'

They made coffee and he guided her back to her seat, purposely using the excuse to touch her platonically. They sat silently staring at their drinks, each preoccupied.

Had Karen changed him? Of course she had. He had taken everything to heart until she taught him to laugh.

'Why don't you like talking about your wife?'

He checked out those doe eyes and knew whatever he said would get back. 'It's hard to describe a dead wife without making it sound like a eulogy.'

'What did she look like?'

'Dark hair, pretty face.'

'Slim?'

'No, not so very, she envied slim women but she did not know how beautiful she was, or how clever she was. You women have a tendency to underestimate yourselves.'

Margery, being lumped together with the world of women, felt contentment for the first time in a long time. She liked the feel of his hands on her person and it was true what he said, they made her feel warm. They made her feel safe.

'You were saying about…'

'Karen, was a positive person, always smiling. I know it sounds corny but every morning she got out of bed rejoicing that she was alive. Our neighbours cat liked to sleep on our window and she would sing to the bloody thing.'

'What did she sing?'

'Gobbledegook, waving her arms about.'

'Has any of it rubbed off on you?'

'I don't know, that's for others to say.'

After her bath that night Margery dried herself in front of the full length mirror in the spare bedroom. Her breasts were small, her hips narrow and her legs gangly. No man would look at her twice. Mason who flirted with all the female staff had not flirted with her. She had been kissed. John Cox, who had a mop of hair and freckles. It was Christmas Eve, in the balcony of the church used by the choir. He had held up a sprig of mistletoe and slobbered on her mouth. The experience left her unimpressed and in fear of having sinned the mortal sin of all mortal sins. Committing a sexual act on consecrated ground.

Confident that she was dry, she let the towel slip to the floor and checked her figure from either profile. She tested her breasts for their suppleness and found a lump. She tested the unfamiliar knot with her fingers but it would not disappear. The other breast was empty. This was a punishment for her lewd conduct. Cavorting about naked at her age.

* * *

Voices bounced around her but she did not hear what they were saying. What was she to do?

Jinny had the floor, 'Girls mature earlier than boys.'

'So.'

'Girls are much more able at assimilating literature.'

'This is the trouble. Assimilating is not digesting.'

'The problem we have with Years 7, 8 and to some extent 9 is that around eleven to thirteen they present problems because they are making a transition. Girls cope much better with this evolution.'

'I still don't see the relevance of what you're saying.'

'It sounds like a broadcast on behalf of the women's party.'

'If you take Judy Blume she interests both sides of the transition. Some of her books deal with pre-elevens and some with post-twelves and this helps girls to understand the crossover.'

'Jinny you aren't listening.'

'I think the problem here is that as much as you think you understand what boys think and how they operate, you aren't a male and you never will be and you can't know how males think.'

'Judy Blume's writing is unisex.'

'Judy Blume was not a help to me,' Barrie was not going to let her browbeat him. 'Boys have other needs than understanding. They have pressures that women are oblivious to. How can you have any concept of emasculation when you don't have a dick?'

'I don't appreciate that sort of language…'

'That's because you're a woman.'

'I didn't want my boys reading graphic sex and I put them onto science fiction.'

'I didn't know that emasculation was a conspiracy.'

'Harry Potter is emotionally suitable for this age group. JK Rowling understands eleven year olds and their interaction. She deals with this age group cleverly and with great insight. Its not all wands and wizards. She understands what they need, what kind of enmity occurs between that age group and anyway they are rattling good yarns.'

'All the writers you mention are women. Boys don't always like women writers because women write from a female perspective.'

'There's no getting through to some people.'

'I've always found boys more straight forward than girls,' said Marcia. 'If they want to play football they get several other boys and start kicking. Girls are totally different. They skip together but they're saying to each other 'you're my friend, I'll play with you' and then tomorrow they have another friend and they ignore the first friend completely. Little girls are bitches.'

'Marcia! That's so untrue.'

'Always have been. Always will be.'

'I find that boys withhold the truth. Now there are new pressures so their secrets are multiplying. Its no longer the sole role of a man to be a breadwinner. He has to be partly mister mum, be sensitive and share the household duties. This boy probably grew up in a household where this was not necessarily the norm.'

'It'll do them good.'

'Jinny, please get off your soapbox.'

'Margery,' said Jinny. 'You're on my side.'

'Excuse me.'

'Are you all right?'

'I'm fine.'

'You're ever so quiet.'

'You do get some revelations in the exam papers. Paul Cosgrove's essay for the mocks for instance. The composition title was 'The day that changed my life' and Paul obviously thought that the papers would be marked by complete strangers. His essay was not particularly well written. It was the about the day his dad left home and was as poignant as any novel. It made me feel sad.'

'I must go,' Jinny stood up. 'I've got to collect my boys.'

'It is late,' said Andy. 'I think we'll call it a day. Thanks everyone for coming.'

'Jinny, have you got a minute?' Margery asked.

'Of course.'

Marcia caught Andy's eye and smiled, 'I just love saying things just so she can contradict me.'

'What's her problem?' Andy asked.

'Her husband's always working. I think she brought the twins up without any help. Goodness me, they were little monsters. She spends a great amount of her time alone.'

'What kind of bloke is he?'

'Arrogant pig,' Marcia's plasticine features screwed up in pain. 'Full of himself but then he's got tangible proof of how clever he is sitting in the bank.'

'What does she do with all this free time?'

'She reads a lot and has a remarkable capacity to remember things as written. She has almost all Shakespeare's plays committed to memory and often quotes...'

'I've noticed.'

'The joke is that when it comes to emasculation she's a fine one to talk. She is your classic doormat.'

* * *

Margery wanted privacy so led Jinny away from the Common Room to her form room and closed the door.

'I cannot believe how implacable those people are,' Jinny was indignant and searched through her handbag for her mobile. She quickly checked for messages and looked up to see tears streaming down Margery's face. 'What on earth's the matter?' She clutched her friend to her and for the second time in twenty four hours Margery had tripled her close encounters with another party.

'I found a lump in my breast,' she breathed.

'What have you done about it?'

'Nothing. I only found it last night.'

Jinny released her and pressed buttons on her mobile. 'Alex. It's mum, you'll have to walk home today…I'm sorry but something important has come up…I'm sorry but that's hard luck. Oh and by the way you can get your own supper…No not a take away? Can't you try to cook something healthy for once in your life?…There's some money under the bread bin…Bye bye darling.' She rang off and immediately redialled. 'Hello, I'd like the number of the switchboard at Wyford General hospital…Yes put me straight through…Good afternoon. Is Doctor Adams available. If not can I speak to somebody on his staff…My name is Jinny Parish, Angus' wife…Thank you…'

Jinny put her arm around Margery's shoulders and gave her a squeeze. 'Yes…The doctor will be free in a few minutes…Is there a direct line?…I'll call back.'

Jinny used a tissue to wipe Margery's face and helped her on with her coat. 'Let's go.'

'Where?'

'To the doctor.'

Jinny drove her to the hospital and waited with her. She was seen, not by Doctor Adams but another doctor in the oncology department. They took a blood test, an x-ray and made an appointment for the results. It was after nine pm and they went to a café for a bite of food. Margery ordered a plate of pasta but barely ate and Jinny prattled on.

'You must come and stay the night.'

'No, no, I couldn't impose.'

'I insist,' Jinny was adamant. 'We'll nip back to your place and fetch your nightie and a change of undies.'

'I couldn't possibly.'

'No arguments.'

'Thank you,' said Margery. 'You are ever so sweet. Thank you, for everything. I couldn't have done it without you.'

'What are friends for?'

CHAPTER TWENTY-THREE

Angus gets the job

Jinny could not get onto the driveway nor could she park on the street immediately outside. She knew the Willis' were away and parked over their drive.

'What's going on?' Margery asked.

'Football, I suppose,' Jinny sighed. 'Angus said he might have a few friends over. I'd no idea it would be this many.'

It was a warm night, the sky was still clear. The house lights shone brightly and happy voices tumbled out of the open windows.

'It sounds like they won,' Jinny opened the front door and let Margery go before her and be swamped by idolaters like paparazzi greeting celebrities.

'She's here,' a man yelled over his shoulder and the news was passed down the line. 'She's here. She's here. She's here.'

Bewildered, the two women were surrounded by smiling faces. 'Let me through,' said a jovial New York accent. 'Coming through.'

The paparazzi stepped aside, forming a cavalcade and through the opening appeared a stocky man, dressed in a white shirt and dark trousers, carrying a tray on which was balanced a bottle of champagne and champagne glass. Solemnly, the man handed the tray to a woman in the crowd. He filled a glass and handed it to Jinny. 'Another glass, please.' He poured a second glass and handed it to Margery. 'Would the guest of honour please come forward.'

Angus, foggy-eyed and unsteady on his feet, made his way tentatively toward them while the idolaters clapped him on. He bowed slightly, providing enough action to spill some of his champagne. Liquid splattered softly onto his shoes and dribbled onto the carpet.

'Toast.'

'Speech.'

Angus raised his glass, 'I give you my wife, Virginia Godalming Parish formerly Virginia Godalming Bull. A lover of Shakespeare and I quote, *Now all the youth of England are on fire…*'

'We are the champions.'

'Two nil, two nil, two nil.'

'*We are victorious…*'

'Happy and glorious.'

'I toast my wife, a queen and her husband, the man who is *every inch a king*. The new CEO of Anglo Saxon (UK) limited, Angus McDonald Parish. *For England and Saint George.*'

'England and Saint Angus.'

Amidst the ensuing uproar, Jinny was hugged and kissed and Margery tried as best she could to cope with the flood of well-wishers and hand-shakers but yearned to escape. Frantically, she sought refuge but could not decide which was the toilet door.

Jinny dragged her reluctant husband into the study and closed the door behind them. He clasped her to him, 'Darling,' he began biting her neck and spilling champagne down her dress. She struggled to break free but he was too strong. She adopted the defiant tactic the children had used when they were little and stood stock still, frozen. It took some moments for Angus to take in her coolness. He stepped back, head wobbling like an Indian waiter, and asked sharply, 'What's got into you? Where the hell have you been?'

'Margery and I have been at the hospital all evening. You switched your mobile off again. You're doing that a lot lately.'

'We were watching the match. I didn't want to be disturbed. What were you doing at the hospital, another of your darling pupils try to top themselves.'

'Margery has a lump in her breast.'

Angus nodded, faking sobriety and took a mouthful of champagne, swayed gently, he said, 'Oh.'

'I couldn't leave her by herself, so I invited her to stay here.'

'Absolutely,' said Angus, waving his glass. 'Least you could do.'

'We can't stay here. Not with all this going on,' said Jinny. 'I'll pack a few things and stay with her tonight.'

'Sure,' said Angus. 'Don't you worry about a thing. I'll take care of it. Aren't you proud of me?'

'Of course, darling. What I don't understand is how come it happened today? Without any warning.'

'It happened last week, Stateside. Gottlieb, the man with the tray, flew in to make the announcement to the board. He supports England, you know. Got English relatives. They live in Sidware.'

'You enjoy the party,' she kissed him on the cheek. 'I'll be back in the morning.'

'You should have seen McAlinney's face,' said Angus but Jinny was gone.

Jinny lay in a twin bed pretending to sleep. She suspected Margery was also awake but was in no mood to talk. Mixed humour was pulling her in opposite directions.

The spirit of the sad house weighed down upon her. Everywhere your eye alighted was signposted with melancholy memories of departed souls. Could it be more lonely to live in a sepulchre, alone and unloved.

How lucky she was to have a family and what a family. Her husband, only thirty eight and CEO Europe in a global organisation. Two sons destined for Oxford and its associated tickets to paradise.

Poor Margery.

Beggar that I am, I am poor even in thanks.

How we take our good fortune for granted. We moan and groan about every little setback but rarely are we grateful for the good things. Margery is a good person, she deserves better than this.

'Andy said I should get married,' Margery's voice startled her, it sounded like a stranger. 'Who would have me?'

'Any man in his right senses. Not that there are many of those. Any man would want someone as sweet and kind as you.'

This mutual admiration society fell into troubled sleep. Jinny berating herself for jeopardising her marriage with her insane infatuation. She said a short prayer that was more a bargain than an invocation. In a promise to give up her foolishness and eliminate Andrew Avecore from her thoughts and deeds she asked for God to make Margery well and safe. Her family could wait for another time to receive his blessing.

Margery speculated on what future, if any, she might expect.

CHAPTER TWENTY-FOUR

Pastoral Care

Andy sat in his office marking essays, waiting for Richard Morrissey to keep his appointment. He would give him until he had completed the pile and maybe join the others in the pub. He was sick of beer and wine kept him up in the night with the sweats. He enjoyed the company but although out of sorts with alcohol, could not resist emptying whatever glass he had in front of him.

He opened Daisy Winter's exercise book and her neat handwriting filled the pages. He read slowly at first and then began skipping, clocking in at intervals, getting the gist of what she had to say. He gave her a B and wrote some words of encouragement. Octavia Jewell turned out to be a surprise package. He had fallen into the trap that he so often railed against and taken against her because she was fat. Octavia had a genuine personality and a startling turn of phrase. He enjoyed her piece and found that he had read all of it without skipping a word, gave her an 'A' and resisted making a comment. Octavia did not need to be patronised.

There was a knock at the door, 'Come in.'

Richard was suitably late to keep his street cred' and his eyes were without their usual hostility. Andy nodded at a chair and the boy sat down. For no reason he continued marking, interested to see what effect it had. Then it occurred to him that his action might be translated as tit for tat and he closed the pile of books and turned to face his guest. 'You came,' he said.

Richard made a gesture with his head that was a cross between a shrug and a yes. Andy had noticed that often children who were reluctant to talk were keen on writing. Once they did start talking it was hard to stem the tide. 'My…' he croaked and cleared his throat. 'My grandad says you're…' Again he coughed. 'OK.'

'Thanks. Say hello to him for me.'

'He said you should drop in for a drink sometime.'

'I will,' Andy breathed deeply. 'So, what about you? You going to make something of yourself?'

The boy shrugged.

'You aren't going to get three A's but you might get one and that could carry the day. Did you send out a UCAS form? Did you get any university offers?'

'They made us,' he sniffed. 'The old bag is dead keen to get as many university placements as she can. It makes the school look good.'

'I suppose it does,' said Andy. 'Offers?'

'Nottingham three B's and York.'

'Harry Enfield went to York.'

'So they told me. What you want me to do?'

'Take some private coaching for your English.'

'I can't pay for anything.'

'Sorry, there won't be anything to pay. Private is the wrong word, extra coaching.'

'With you?'

'Mrs Parish.'

'Sorry,' said Richard, sitting up and coming to life like a switched on computer. 'She's got her head up her arse.'

'What about Miss Finn?'

'Tasty,' he said. 'OK, I'll give it a go.'

'You haven't got long, so no pissing about.'

'Sure,' he shrugged.

'I'll have to ask Miss Finn if she'll do it and I'll let you know.'

'Sure,' he said. 'That it?'

'Yes, that's it. Anything bothering you.?'

He shrugged, 'Only the bloody football. That's all they talk about. You can't get them interested in anything worthwhile. If it was up to these morons the theatre would die.'

Andy sat back in his chair without answering, it was his turn to shrug.

'Why are they still banging on about 1966. It happened before they were born.'

'It happened before I was born,' Andy offered.

'It's pathetic.'

'Your grandad around tonight?'

'Sure.'

'I'll run you home.'

Andy followed Richard along the path and into the house. 'Grandad,' he yelled. 'You've got a visitor.'

Andy went out back and found Erwin and two other men playing cards. The table was strewn with bottles, ashtrays and mugs of tea. 'How'd it go?' he asked.

'He's agreed to cramming and I'll speak to one of the staff.'

'Good,' he nodded. 'Tea, or something stronger?'

'Tea.'

'This is Richard's teacher, Andy. Neil and Rob. Sit down, sit down. Do you play cards?'

'What're you playing?'

'German whist. If you play we can switch to auction or solo.'

'Deal me in.'

'I do a lot of schools,' said Neil a dark haired man of about forty with a moustache and careful eyes, He was practised at making small talk and checked closely the reaction to what he was saying, wary he might upset his listener. 'We have nearly 200 on our books. It seems to me that morale is very low.'

'What is it you do?'

'Service and repair photocopiers.'

'Ah!' said Andy. 'Photocopiers. Don't take this personally but in any school, the photocopier is the focal point of discontent. Not necessarily because of the school but more because of the photocopier.'

'He's sorted you out, Neil my lad,' said Rob, a world weary man who moved his head like a tortoise and spoke words in a chewed ruminative agony. Sentences spoken like severe back pain. 'Doing photocopying is the worst punishment known to teaching staff. It's bad enough being stuck with doing fifty copies in triplicate but then the machine jams or that little service man starts flashing and your heart sinks to your boots. Private schools employ someone especially to do photocopying.'

'That's because you bloody schoolteachers do so much copying,' Neil defended some unspecified cause. 'You put too much pressure on the machinery. Machines, like men, can only take so much.'

'Keep your Mrs out of this.' Rob swallowed hard and surveyed the horizon.

Richard joined them, peeped under a dishcloth that revealed a pile of sandwiches, took one and sat at the table eating.

'You think Mrs Parish has got her head up her arse?' Andy asked.

'Too right,' Richard mumbled. 'She gets this snippy look when she starts banging on, quoting Shakespeare. Always letting you know how clever she is.'

'We all live in our ivory tower,' Andy pointed to his temple. 'And it is a very small world.'

'Too right,' repeated Rob.

'We all remain in our comfort zones,' said Erwin, putting a mug of steaming tea in Andy's corner. 'We mix with like minded people which only consolidates our views.'

'It's not easy to accept contradictions.' Andy got up and removed his jacket. 'None of us are very good at accepting truth, especially someone else's.'

'How does this apply to Mrs Parish?' Richard asked.

'It's a matter of self worth,' Andy sipped his tea. 'She feels a constant need to prove herself.'

'It's invariably the sad cases that get off on how clever they are,' said Erwin.

'Auction whist,' said Erwin, adeptly mixing the cards. 'Twelve cards dealt, clubs are trumps. eleven cards, diamonds, ten hearts, nine spades, eight no trumps and seven misere. The same from six down to one and then back up again. Dealer can't bid the exact number of remaining tricks. Man with the most points wins. You want to play, Dick?'

'Maybe later,' said Dick, glancing at Andy. 'I've got some work to do.'

'Cut for deal,' said Erwin. 'Highest card.'

Neil cut a jack and picked up the pack gave it a last shuffle and dealt quickly.

'It's funny when someone's showing off or bragging about themselves, we end up embarrassed for them, but they rarely do.'

'Avoiding the truth about oneself is a universal pursuit,' said Neil, picking up his cards and arranging them immaculately.

'That's why you should go to university, Dick,' said Rob. 'You need reining in.'

Each player made his bid and Erwin noted it on his pad alongside his initial and Andy being alongside Neil led a card. Andy loved the way the players talked while their focus was entirely on the cards.

'Mostly it's the way we're brought up.'

'Parental influence.'

Cards flashed across the table and Andy had to concentrate hard. Tricks were counted and scores registered. When it was Andy's turn to deal he placed the cards carefully.

'The newspapers we read.'

'We read our newspapers like we choose our friends. That way we hear and read what we want to hear and read.'

'To verify our biases.'

'To create our biases.'

'Mrs Parish has never come into contact with a seriously clever person. If she had she would be more circumspect.'

'You think so? I don't. That type never learn.'

Andy was winning. After each hand Erwin called the score and as Andy opened up a lead his tone became more pointed. There was a sudden change of atmosphere and Andy miscalled several hands in a row. They were ganging up on him.

'Bastards,' he thought.

'We all have a driving force,' said Rob and added ironically. 'Mine is money and success. What motivates you, Andy?'

'I'm on a crusade to eradicate bullshit. What about you Erwin?'

'I'm that character from Catcher in the Rye.'

'Holden Caulfield.'

'Yeah, him. I'm him as a grown up,' said Erwin, proudly.

Andy picked up his cards and swiftly put them in order. Four trumps including the ace. They were not going to get him this time.

* * *

Jinny stepped out of Holborn Station into bright sunlight. She turned left along Kingsway, the buildings loomed over her, ahead the sky was a vivid blue with vapour trails scratched by high flying aircraft.

She felt a weird release, like playing truant. The call had come early that morning, Marcia had to be relieved halfway through the day trip and she was to meet the coach at the north end of Waterloo Bridge. She had allowed too much time and was an hour and a half early for her rendezvous.

She continued toward Bush House without realising it was Bush House. Her experience of London was limited outside of the immediate environs of Drury Lane. She had not been to the RSC as often as she would have liked. If Angus was not moaning about the uncomfortable seats, how over long the plays were, he was finding elaborate excuses not to go. The majority of her London theatre visits had been confined to school outings. These days it was hard to get any subscribers from amongst the students for Shakespeare. Plenty for the Lion King, Mary Poppins and Chitty Chitty Bang Bang.

It has to be said that Wyford has a perfectly good theatre of its own but they never do Shakespeare. Her BBC production videos of Macbeth and Lear were perfectly fine.

She thought it best to make sure of where she was to meet Mason but turned the wrong way down Aldwych towards Fleet Street. A rowdy group of boys dressed in red football shirts, yelling 'England, England,' charged across the road against the traffic causing a taxi to brake violently and ran into a pub opposite the High Court.

She turned into The Strand, mesmerised by the scale and bustle. Passing between King's College and St Mary-Le-Strand she found what she was looking for exactly as Mason described it.

He had suggested, if she was early, she should visit the Courtauld gallery. He had also suggested a unique way of viewing the exhibits. 'Don't read the names on the plaques. They inevitably prejudice your opinion of the painting. Stand in the middle of each salon and view one exhibit at a time and see what has an effect on you.'

She did not often get the chance for window shopping or to see the river from Waterloo Bridge and it was such a beautiful day. She stopped on the north end of the bridge and looked about her. The skyline was very impressive, the wheel, the Savoy Hotel, the Festival Hall. Charing Cross station was too modern, so was that Gherkin thing. Feeling the heat she turned back intending to see inside the church she had passed but it was a day for beauty rather than sobriety.

She went through the narrow entrance way, bought a ticket and mounted the stairs into the gallery. 'The Courtauld is one of London's most unpublicised treasures.' Now she could decide for herself.

She did as she was instructed and stood in the middle of each room and pivoted round on the spot. Some of what she saw was familiar but she could not be sure that she could identify one solitary exhibit.

It was in the last salon that she experienced a reaction. She was tired, her feet hurt and she was dying for a cup of tea. She saw out of the corner of her eye that there was an explicit portrait of a nude and her initial impulse was to turn her back on it. Something, she could not discern what, lingered. Keeping her discipline she applied the method Mason suggested and stopped at a loosely brush stroked head of a woman. It was the first of the gallery's collection to intrigue her. How could the artist dash off, in what appeared to be a few brush strokes, a finished article of such vivacity.

Finally she confronted the nude. The colours, by comparison to everything that went before, were modest. The body glowed with such vibrancy she could feel their effect inside her.

She wanted to be a prude about the candid nature of the work but the power of the colours held her attention. It was then she realised that she was revitalised. The ache and pinch in her feet had vanished. Her throat was no longer dry.

She checked her watch, she was nearly ten minutes late for her rendezvous. 'My goodness,' she said out loud. 'That's amazing.'

The other spectators in the room thought she was referring to Modigliani but Jinny meant the time. It was startling to have been so engrossed. Without checking the plaques she ran down the stairs and rushed out into the street.

As late as she was, there was no sign of them. Had she missed them? No, they would not leave without her. At the approach of each coach she felt sure it was them but it was not. As she was getting anxious, standing on tiptoe, the coach pulled up alongside. The door opened and Mason helped her on board,

'Sorry we're so late. You know how it is.'

He let her sit by the window and the coach pulled away and slipped down into the old tramway tunnel. 'How was The Wheel?'

'Just like the North Circular,' said Mason. 'Impossibly slow.'

The coach turned off Rosebery Avenue by Finsbury Town Hall and stopped in a side street that comprised a single building. They filed through the entrance and were met by their guide, a woman of similar age as Jinny with a large face and eyebrows pencilled on in a perfect semi circle. Jinny was having a geometric day.

The guide gave a brief history of the Registrar General of Births, Marriages and Deaths. Founded in 1780 something by Thomas somebody. Jinny could not concentrate. This was her chance to check the provenance of the Parish family. For some reason this idea made her very nervous. What harm could it do? Somehow the need to know seemed disloyal.

The guide explained the system and the children quickly got involved. Mason disappeared for a smoke and the two women were left waiting. They exchanged a shy smile, 'Wouldn't you like to try?'

Jinny shrugged, 'Why not. My name is Parish, with one 'R'. Angus Parish.'

'Don't you want to find your family?'

'My husband's family are more interesting. He's a Scot.'

'Scottish records are held in Scotland,' said the guide. 'We can trace them on the computer.'

'Angus was born in Hertfordshire.'

They found his birth certificate and that of his father but the trail ended there. No trace of his grandfather anywhere in the United Kingdom. 'There is a new theory that names like Parish come about when there is no family name or for whatever reason the person registering wants to hide their true name. Searching for an alternative they see the word 'parish' on some document or on the wall and choose it for their own. Child of this parish or London as in London Borough of. In this area there were quite a few Clark's as in Clerkenwell.'

Back out in the sunshine, nothing seemed to matter. Her heart was light and the sun was shining behind her eyes. They were late and there was a crowd awaiting their return. Having been kept, the crowd of parents was irritable and in a hurry. Mason and she tried to get the children to clear up their own mess on the coach and barely half obeyed. As Jinny stepped carefully off the coach a mother thrust a package in her hand. It was a brown paper bag filled with a banana skin and orange peel.

'Have you got Daisy's mobile?' asked a tetchy voice.

'Sorry.'

'Have you got Daisy's mobile telephone?' Mrs Winter's patience was exhausted. 'It was confiscated.'

'I'll fetch it,' said Jinny.

She hurried to the office. This was the perfect cover to go nosing in the filing cabinets. Neither Betsy or Mrs Tapper was there but the filing cabinet was locked. She searched the drawers and found Daisy's mobile. It had a postit with her name stuck to the dial. Nothing though that looked like a key to the cabinet. About to give up she opened a box of paper clips and found what she was looking for. Her heart pounding in her ears like silent thunder she released the lock and opened the drawer. Avecore should have been at the front but it was the last wallet. When she opened the file all she found was a piece of notepaper on which was written Andrew's address and telephone number. Shaking with nerves she fumbled the file back in its place and struggled to relock the cabinet. Pocketing the mobile, she ran back down the corridor.

CHAPTER TWENTY-FIVE

Margery's party

Margery had kept the date of her test results from Jinny. Her summons to the consultant had arrived in the post on Saturday and her appointment set for the coming Friday. She was hoping this lack of urgency was a good sign but if the news was bad she wanted to face it alone. Margery was not practiced at lying and when Jinny asked about the Doctor's response, she had pretended that she had heard nothing as yet. Jinny got indignant about the delay.

'That's disgraceful,' biting her bottom lip. 'Would you like me to call and find out what's happening?'

'Let's give them one more day,' Margery, unable to contain her guilt, blushed.

Her feelings while she sat in the waiting room were not what she expected. To be without one of her breasts would settle the issue of marriage once and for all. Somehow she was pleased to be dispensing with this dilemma. If she was dying, so be it, it was God's will and she must accept the situation. She had hardly slept since she found the lump, not wanting to waste a second of the time left to her. She was doing her chores at speed trying to cram in as much as she could.

Now her future was just the other side of the door none of it seemed to matter that much. On her way in she crossed paths with a young woman getting out of the lift. The woman was sobbing uncontrollably and a nurse had come to her aid, put her arm around her and said calmly, 'Let it all out.' What was to become of that woman? Was she ill or was it a relative? No matter which of these possibilities applied to that poor girl, her devastation was clearly greater than her own. She felt ashamed. The moment she found the lump all thoughts of her sick Aunt were supplanted by her own well-being. Finding this true side of herself had been hard to reconcile.

The Oncologist was a kindly man with brown eyes and a rubbery face. Like the nurse, he was experienced in dealing with distress and he put her out of her torment immediately. 'A cyst,' he rummaged amongst his papers. 'Benign. I'm surprised you hadn't noticed it before now.'

Instead of relief, Margery felt embarrassed that the Doctor might be thinking she did not wash herself regularly.

Returning home on the bus, the colours were more vivid, the landscape more beautiful and she had to resist an impulse to hug her fellow passengers or kiss the bus driver.

The following weekend, England were to play Portugal so Margery invited the female staff for a buffet supper, 'Nothing too involved you understand. Quiche, sausage rolls and other bits and pieces.'

She wanted to celebrate a new beginning. She did have a future and decided it was not going to be confined to a meagre possibility. The reprieve had given her the impetus to start over. She might get married. She would take Andrew's advice and start talking to Charles Mason. Nothing suggestive, not even flirting but just enough to let him know she was out there and that she was a woman, even if she was not a particularly sought after variety.

Jinny had been wonderful as usual. When she told her the good news, she was genuinely pleased and gave her a hug. Guilt for the lies she told resurrected itself and she felt a strong desire to make amends.

'I'm going to have a party to sort of celebrate, but I'd rather you didn't tell anyone about the scare,' said Margery. Part of her was feeling like an impostor.

'We'll bring desserts,' said Jinny, wanting to help.

'That would be nice,' Margery was uncertain, feeling that her idea of a party would no longer be her own.

* * *

The weekend after her interview with the Oncologist Margery stuck to her usual routine. Saturday she shopped at Asda and Sunday she went to church but these familiar habits left her dissatisfied.

Her reprieve had opened a gate in her psyche which she could not grasp. What passed through this gate was a mysterious energy that bubbled around the heart.

As the days passed the energy did not subside and the wellbeing that followed in its wake, fermented nicely. Margery was permanently on a low light, simmering.

In the subsequent days she found that she was purposely deviating from her routine. She experimented with her diet. Spent longer evenings at the pub and drank more than was good for her. Thought bad thoughts about some of the staff and skipped her rosary, nor did she confess her minor transgressions to Father Finnegan.

Her Aunt had needed minor surgery and she was taking care of her convalescence. She visited every day, saw to it that she had everything she needed. Arranged for a nurse to look in on her during the morning. It was best that she had dropped out of the America trip. She should be with her Aunt while she needed her.

It was Wednesday and the church's bridge evening had been cancelled because of the football. Margery did not want to be alone. Cooking for Saturday's buffet was in the freezer and with the food her guests had promised there was going to be a lot left over. She would do a few salads on the day.

Nobody was going to the pub and she sat in her classroom, essay papers spread across her desk, bored. The familiar walls provided no inspiration and the empty school was hollowly quiet.

Along the corridor, a door slammed and two sets of echoing footsteps clattered along the floor. Two men were arguing.

'Just a minute you,' said Ben, the caretaker.

'Don't talk to me like that,' said Flint, his assistant.

'I asked you three days ago to clear the crap out of the swimming pool and you still haven't done it.'

'You're always getting me to do the unsavoury jobs.'

'Don't be an arsehole,' said Ben, nodding to Margery as they rushed past her door. 'Who cleaned out the girls bog? Who cleaned out the pool last month when all that crap from the hornbeams was in it? I did. You don't do any bloody thing without moaning.'

Another door slammed and they were gone. Entertainment

was over for the night. She might as well go home. She had left her coat in the Common Room. She pulled the papers together into a neat pile and put them in a folder. On her way upstairs she could hear the caretakers still arguing.

The curtains and blinds to the Common Room were half-closed to reduce the effect of the sun providing an eerie twilight. Not wishing to linger she snatched her coat and hurried to the door. Her attention was arrested by a regular tapping sound and she stopped to trace its whereabouts. In the English Corner two armchairs had been pushed together and the tapping was coming from behind them. Was there a couple copulating over there? Should she go and leave them to it? Gingerly, she stood on tiptoe but could see nothing. Holding her breath, slowly she moved toward the regular sound. Andrew laid sprawled across the two armchairs, his mouth open, knocking a biro against his upper and lower teeth.

'What are you doing here?' she asked.

'Hiding,' he answered matter of fact.

'From what?'

'Disease. A plague is afoot, it is infecting the entire population. Bubonic football.'

'Ben and Flint are having a row outside.'

'There's a shock. That Flint is a pain in the bum. I don't know why anybody puts up with him. Want a drink?'

'At the pub?'

'No. In my office. Cup of tea. I'm not doing pubs for the moment.'

He stirred her drink and spilled some into the saucer as he handed it to her. Then made a bigger mess trying to clear up the little mess. Then made more mess topping up the half empty cup.

'It's all arranged,' he said.

'The America trip?'

'Yes,' he said. 'You OK with it?'

'Why shouldn't I be? Is Jinny?'

'I haven't told her yet. I want to save that titbit of information until next week. Thursday or Friday. You don't mind do you?'

'No. She won't be surprised that I'm not going.'

'She won't.'

'I had a bit of a scare.'

'You never said.'

She liked the way he was about these matters. He did not turn on a tap full of saccharine. Without any histrionics, he genuinely wanted to know what the problem was. It gave her a platform to confess her innermost feelings without shame. She did not feel that she was being a bore or seeking sympathy.

'Now, after it all, I feel odd.'

'A release?'

'Yes,' she said uncertainly. 'I can't get a hold of what it is exactly.'

'How did it all start?'

She admitted everything without fear of humiliation, including the circumstances of how she came to find the lump. He laughed so easily when she told him that she laughed along with him and was swelled by the intimacy their laughter brought. Temporarily, they were soul mates and her new words helped her rescue dormant knowledge.

'I feel more than just getting a reprieve. More than having hope renewed. I don't sound trite do I?' He shook his head. 'Like the slate has been wiped clean and I can start afresh.'

'You've lost your fear.'

'Not lost it but as though it was a stain I found it lying on the floor and I've trodden it into the carpet.'

He started giggling, 'That's a good one. It must be like getting old suddenly. Don't take me wrong. When most people reach a certain age they've got nothing to lose and they stop caring. Caring is not the right word either. I don't mean they don't dress themselves properly, which some of them do, but they stand up to authority, hiding behind the respect that goes with age. You've been lucky. You've lost that fear while there's still time.'

'Have I?'

'Just don't sink back into the old routine. Live a little. There's nothing to be afraid of.'

'I'm having a party on Saturday for the football grass widows. You can come if you like.'

'I might at that.'

* * *

Andrew sat in a quandary of his own. He was bored by the football but there was no escape. Plenty of pubs were now smoke free zones but unfortunately none he knew of were football free. He had tried playing tennis during matches but you could follow the games progress from the squeals of excitement and groans of disappointment emanating from the surrounding houses. When there was quiet, there was an ominous expectancy. The tension would become too much for some of his fellow players and they would nip into the pavilion for updates.

Perhaps he should go to Margery's party, surprise them all and sit and stare at Jinny's legs.

'What are you doing here?' Margery, feigning surprise, was pleased to see him.

'I brought ice cream,' he held up a tub of vanilla.

'The magic password,' she said, standing aside to let him by and adjusted his clothing. 'Your collar's twisted.'

He had noticed recently how she found excuses to touch him.

Once he had enrolled on a writing course at the City Lit and tried to befriend some of his fellow students. After class the men went to the pub and a small clique of the women to the canteen. After a few minutes amongst this second group he cottoned on that they were either gay or in bad marriages. He tried to make conversation but did not get a warm reception and sensed an undertone of hostility. His welcome in Margery's living room was not dissimilar.

'He's brought ice cream,' Margery explained.

'Crawler,' said Marcia.

He searched for Jinny's reaction but she busy nattering to Denise Rodgers, the school Bursar. Jinny was suffering pangs and was talking quickly trying to stave off guilt. She ought to be at home with her family, supporting the England team in their hour of need. She wanted to like football but in truth she found it very repetitive and rather tedious like most sport. She had used her loyalty to Margery as her excuse to join the party but this half truth added to her guilt. Another source of guilt had arrived. He did look nice in his crisp clean clothes. I wonder who does his laundry?

After saying, 'hello,' they lost interest in him and carried on as though he was not there.

He leaned back in the chair and drank in the mixture of perfumes. His eyes flitted from face to face, locks of Marcia's hair were unravelling at the back, mingling with the down on her neck, her skin soft and lustrous. Marcia interrupted the Bursar, to explain how the Assistant Caretaker was at fault. Jinny listened intently, worrying her hair with her forefinger. Denise, her mouth perpetually on the brink of an ironic smile, was stifling a yawn.

Jinny was sat on a foot stool, her legs splayed out at an awkward angle. One leg was in profile to where he sat and starting at the ankle he followed its flowing line all the way up to the hem of her skirt, which was mercifully high. She would only have to adjust her body slightly for any reason and he would get a glimpse of her panties.

Is there anything more beautiful than a woman, he wondered? Being with Gillian naked had been a privilege but he did not fancy her. For whatever reason he could not take his interest to the next stage. Pictures of her flashed in and out of his head. Curves and secrets wherever your eye settled. Fragrant, the smell of her still in his nose. The magical feel of her still taunting his fingers. He could not believe in God but a woman is a wondrous creation. A work of art. One of the best things about women is that you never truly know your subject. There is always more to wonder on and always more to learn.

Amazing, he thought, that such a fantastic thing could sometimes irritate the hell out of you.

Margery handed him a plate of food and sat next to him on the sofa. She gave him an old-fashioned look, snuggled up to him and said, 'I wish I were ten years younger.'

Andy, careful to take a small mouthful of quiche, because Jinny might be watching, chewed before answering. 'There is no gallant response to that statement.'

'You know all the appropriate answers don't you. Bit of a ladies man I'll bet.'

'No,' he said emphatically. 'No, I'm not.'

She leaned close to his ear and whispered, 'I know you're not.'

'How's that clever clogs.'

'Gillian told me everything.'

'She didn't,' he was genuinely worried. Christ knows what women tell each other. What was there to tell? They went out, they went to bed. Not much news there. 'I don't believe you.'

'She told me enough.'

'She's not upset is she?'

'I don't think so,' Margery was flirting and she liked it.

'I can't think of anything worth telling.'

Margery turned to face him, 'I'd say that unrequited love was your thing. Making eyes like a little puppy.'

In unison they turned their heads to where Jinny was sitting. Uncomfortable, she shifted her position and Andy saw a flash of white cotton. Coloured lace underwear was not for him, nor was all that stocking top stuff. He liked the plain white that Karen preferred to wear. A gremlin gnawed at his innards. Was it the glimpse of something secret or that his secret was out.

'How did she know?' He shovelled a larger piece of pie in his mouth, so she would have plenty of time to answer.

'Your wife's picture,' said Margery. Seeing his puzzled look she continued. 'There's a resemblance.'

Andy kept chewing. He had heard people say that divorced men marry the same wife over and over. Often these wives are a reflection of their mothers. No way was Karen like his mother. Or was she. He could not distinguish this resemblance between Karen and Jinny but Gillian had spotted his secret fairly easily. There must be a truth out there that he was unaware of. Perhaps there are more truths out there that he was unaware of. A shiver of fear slithered up his back, Andrew liked to be in control

He gulped his food and said irritably, 'Does everybody know?'

'Your longings are safe with me,' she told him, leaning her back on the sofa confidentially.

Andy felt a flush of warmth for Margery.

'You've no chance,' she teased. 'You're better off with a more mature and experienced woman.'

Andy took another mouthful to delay his answer, 'Mature, I'll give you. Experienced,' he raised his eyebrows. 'I don't think so.'

'You're a cruel cruel man,' she tweaked his nose.

'You're very different,' she told him. 'Too different. You'll not change her.'

'I might thaw her out a bit.'

It was then they discovered that all eyes in the room were upon them. Margery, '*experienced*', blushed deep crimson, Andy gave them his biggest grin.

Marcia, as usual, took it on herself to be spokeswoman. 'What are you doing here? It's not natural. You should be glued to the television screen like all the other morons that make up your gender.'

'Anything we should know about you?' Denise asked, joining in the fun.

He had to check himself, took another fork full of quiche and chewed before responding. They were playing with him and he enjoyed games. He must be careful not to get cocky and bring the wrath of womanhood down upon himself.

'I don't like football,' he confessed. 'I don't like beer much either.'

Marcia feigned an intake of breath, 'Do you read the poetry of Oscar Wilde?'

'I have been known to,' he said. 'Although I once accommodated six women in one afternoon.'

'Six,' Denise played along. 'We're more than impressed.'

'I shouldn't be,' he said quickly, hoping he had not gone too far. 'It's a lie. I dreamed about it once, actually more than once.'

'Nothing of the Noel Coward's about you then?'

'No, sorry.'

He caught Jinny watching him and when their eyes met she turned away. Why had she done that? Some unreliable intuition suggested that she might be guilty and that would be why she averted her eyes. She fancied him? Probably his foolish showing off had embarrassed her. She is so prudish. He kicked himself, why do you do it? You and your big mouth.

'What's wrong with footer?' Margery asked. 'It is not like it matters much. It's not exactly the Iraqi war is it.'

'A lot you know.'

'No,' said Marcia. 'I don't know, that's why I'm asking.'

He put his plate on the table. 'I was at a Kenwood open air concert for the Last night of the Proms. That evening the England football team were playing Germany. ...'

'Is that when we beat Germany five goals to one?' Jinny

asked, looking around for approval as though she had played in midfield alongside Steve Gerrard.

'That's right. The Master of Ceremonies gave out the score and I quote, 'Ladies and Gentlemen, the England football team have beaten the krauts five goals to one'. Krauts! Then we had Land of Hope and Glory and Jerusalem. 90% of that audience had driven to Kenwood in kraut cars. It may not be war but there is a nationalism that goes with football and I don't like it much.'

'It's patriotism not nationalism and it's a bit of harmless fun.'

He knew the voice without looking in her direction. Squirming at his own outburst, he wanted to say, 'If the boot were on the other foot, if Germany had a Kenwood and made remarks about beefeaters and limeys, it would have been reported as the rebirth of the Nazi Party.' He had gone too far already. You silly fool. Why do you allow your passions to take control?

The telephone came to his rescue and sounded horribly loud in the quietened room. Margery went out into the hall to answer.

'I bet that's some irritating husband,' said Denise. 'Phoning to tell us the result. As if we care.'

'Is it over?'

'How should I know?'

'It should have finished by now,' said Jinny. 'Unless they're playing extra time.'

'It all seems like extra time to me.'

Margery returned, her face extremely serious. 'Jinny it's Alex for you, it seems that Angus has had a funny turn.'

'Why didn't he ring on the mobile?'

'I don't know.'

Jinny and Margery went outside together and the room remained silent. Muffled voices, filled with concern, could be heard but few words could be distinguished.

Jinny, frowning, her eyes frightened, said nervously, 'I have to go.'

'Do you want me to come with you?' asked Marcia.

'Thanks awfully but I'll manage. Goodnight everyone.'

'Hope everything's all right.'

'Thank you. I'll call and let you know.' She made it to the front door before turning back. She stood in the doorway a half broken woman and spoke gravely, 'England lost on penalties.'

No call came that night but it was not long before everybody had pieced together Angus' problem.

They plied Margery with questions. She wanted to be forthcoming but she did not have any details. 'Angus had some sort of breakdown.'

'Over the football?'

'My god. Not really.'

'Surely not.'

'Men,' they cried in unison.

'I best get home,' said Marcia. 'My hubby will be sulking for weeks.'

'Thanks Margery, for a lovely evening.'

Andy hung around until everybody had gone but Margery was having none of it. The old-fashioned look this time was the one she reserved for students, 'You're not getting anything out of me.'

'Margery…'

'None of your flirting, Mr Avecore. I can see that little boy butter wouldn't melt smile.'

He took her face in his hands and kissed her softly and lingering on the mouth.

Margery lay in bed unable to sleep. What were Andy's exact words? 'There are only two things that cause men to throw a wobbly. Death or a woman.'

Angus Parish and a woman?

She touched her lips where the kiss had been and smiled. She would not wash or brush her teeth for a week.

CHAPTER TWENTY-SIX

Angus Confesses

Fully dressed, Angus lay on the floor of the en suite, scrunched up in the foetal position. He seemed to be moaning softly but on closer inspection, he was sobbing. Jinny was embarrassed for him and her ears burned. Why? She wondered. Was it having to announce at the party that her husband was not Henry V but King Lear? What was this about? Because England had lost at football and were out of the World Cup? Surely not. Even CEOs must grow up sometime. Then the good fairy that lived inside her saw it clearly. It was the job. His new responsibilities were proving too onerous. Rummaging through the past weeks she had sensed a sea change. It must be the pressure and the inevitable stress that went with it.

'Poor darling,' she said, caressing his hand.

He twisted away. 'I'm sorry,' he gasped. 'I'm so sorry.'

'What's there to be sorry about, darling?' she said. 'You can't help it.'

Angus twisted further into a corner behind the toilet.

'Can I get you a cup of sweet tea?' she asked. 'Run you a nice hot bath?'

Angus put his hands over his ears, 'I'm so sorry.'

There was a rap at the door and Alex' head appeared in the gap. Jinny jumped to her feet and pushed him out. 'Daddy's not feeling well.'

'We only want to help,' Alex moaned.

'Tell me what happened.'

'We were watching the game and daddy started crying.'

'Just like that?'

'Just like that.'

'Was it that bad?'

'It was just like normal. The way it always is.'
'Then what.'
'He came upstairs for a while...' said Alex.
'We could hear him shouting on the telephone,' said James.
'Did he make the call or did the phone ring?'
'Who's going to call when the football's on?' said James.
He is so clever, she thought.
'Then he came back during extra time,' said Alex.
'Then we called you,' said James.
'What made you call me?'
'He kicked in the television screen.'
'He did what?'
'He kicked the TV.'
'Show me.'

They trouped into the lounge where the carpet was sprinkled with broken glass and television screen had a hole in the bottom corner. Bobby stood on all fours watching them, his brown eyes bewildered.

'Did he say anything?'
'That's all I bloody need, or something like that,' said Alex.
'That's all I fucking need...'
'James!'
'I didn't say it, he did.'

Jane wound up her teacher mode and ran upstairs. Angus was almost as she had left him. He was wrapped around the toilet bowl as if they were embracing.

'Angus, pull yourself together,' she spoke as if he were in Year 7. 'It's only a football match.'

He lashed out at her with his nearest leg but missed and cracked his shin on the basin pedestal. This gave his sobbing new impetus.

Jinny should have taken the hint and dropped her school ma'am but grew more pompous. 'Angus what's got into you. That was the last straw. Come out from there and tell me what's the matter. Is it the football? Is it? They'll have to try again next year.'

This speech had the effect that she had been seeking. His body stopped throbbing and he lay quietly, she with baited breath. An arm appeared on the toilet lid, his red and swollen face emerged from under it, there was hate in his eyes. 'The World Cup is every four years, you stupid...stupid...cow.'

She had never heard him use such language toward her before. Her mother, when angry could not bring herself to admonish her in such a way. Ten or eleven years old she had spilled jam on the new carpet and her mother referred to her as a meadow lady. Her father never cursed, ever. He farted a lot. When he sensed an attack coming on he would go to his study and close the door. She and Charlotte would stand outside and stifle giggles.

She grabbed at what she could, shirt, hair and got him upright with his head on his knees. 'Now tell me,' she demanded. 'Get it off your chest, once and for all.'

'I'm so sorry.'

'About the television?'

'I love...I love...'

Jinny's nerve endings triggered alarm in every corner of her body. Never could she remember needing anything quite as much in her life before. She desperately hung on that third word and she desperately needed it to be 'you'. She focussed on his mouth, put her ear as close as she could and when the word emerged it was incomprehensible. It certainly was not 'you' but more of a sound to signify retching.

'Ooh...er.'

'You love ooh-er?'

'I love her.'

'Who?'

'Jez.'

'Jez? Who's Jez.'

'Geraldine.'

'Geraldine! Your secretary. She's called Jez?'

Jezebel more like. Jinny's nerve endings having slipped past alarm, now collapsed. Her insides plummeted, gathered in her bladder and exploded in frenzy. She shoved Angus aside and used the toilet. She dried herself and adjusted her costume right in front of him. She flushed the cistern, washed her hands and left him to it. No more questions for the moment. He was remorseful because he had fallen in love with someone else. What was she to do? She was marooned. When the boys went off to university she would be totally alone. It was her worst nightmare realised.

The boys were in their rooms watching television so she sneaked into the spare room and lay down in the dark. She lay awake, her body aching with misery. She tried to picture them together. Intimate. What could Geraldine offer that she could not? She did not have very large breasts, and she was not especially attractive. Did he sleep with her? Did he sleep with *Jez*, come home and sleep with her? Did he have her on his body when they had intercourse? She needed to be angry, revolted, anything for comfort but her fear was too pervading.

Bobby sniffed her out, pushed his way through the bedroom door and plonked his chin on the duvet. She ruffled his nose but was in no mood to dish out affection.

Margery! That is how she would be. A lonely spinster. She tried to cry but no tears came. The liquid in her system had frozen and her organs shrivelled. She searched amongst her Shakespeare for a reference to accommodate her situation but there were none. She was not Othello. Bugger Andy Avecore and his opinions, the arrogant little so and so.

After all she had done for Angus. Stood by him. Backed him, no matter what. Advised him on every move he had made to the top. Encouraged him. Gave him belief in himself. Made all those sacrifices. Spent all that time alone, waiting for him to come home. His leaving would not make such a difference in that respect

The boys would visit, so she would not be totally alone. She would have all of term time alone. She could visit them at weekends. Weekends, that is the time they would least want her around. She was not going to be one of those sad mothers who had nothing else in their lives and lived through their children.

The fact is Jinny Parish, that will be all you will have in your life.

Would she revert to her maiden name? Jinny Bull. Virginia Bull. It sounded odd to her after all this time.

What would she do for money? There was the trust fund they had set up from the sale of her parents house, but that was for the boys. He would have to pay alimony. She would take him for everything. No she would not. She wanted her life back where it was twenty four hours ago.

You must not give up so easily. If it is Angus you want, then fight for him. Confront this Geraldine. She groaned, had no fight left in her, was on the verge of despair. Who could she talk to? Should she talk to anyone? What if it all blows over? Could it blow over? Who could she ask? Who could she confide in without it becoming common knowledge?

Margery. She would do the right thing. Call her now. No, that would be a mistake. Sleep on it. If only she could sleep. Can this pain get any worse? She groaned out loud, it sounded like a lion's roar. Frightened that the boys had heard she lay fearfully listening out for any sign. The house was silent. Only her heart could be heard drumming. What time could it be?

She got out of bed and looked out of the window into the street. Nobody passed by, not even a car. The streetlight illuminated the bench in the Japanese garden, where the ginger cat lay curled up in a fur ball. Perhaps a stranger would pass by, walking their dog and she could join them and tell them her troubles. She went to the bathroom and washed her face, checking for signs that she was losing her looks, comparing her appeal to Jez's. What has Angus promised this woman? Were they naked together and intimate? What will the boys think? How will they react? She had seen children, products of broken homes. They were easily recognisable amongst her students. The boys were probably past the age where it would do lasting damage. This gave her a first moment of comfort since Angus' declaration.

What is it she has that I do not? What have I done to deserve this? No answer came. No relief came. Still no sleep came. She tried emptying her head of all thoughts. Went through her timetable for tomorrow.

The American trip. She would have to cancel. There was no way she could go now. Avecore would have to go in her place.

His bare arms with all that soft red hair and the same on the back of his delicate hands. How would his hands feel on your breasts? She tried her own for size. She imagined they were dining after a visit to the National Theatre in that lovely restaurant opposite full of theatricals, and then sleeping in the same bed. Lying cuddled up to each other, facing the same way, his arm enfolding her, without his stiff penis jabbing into her back like Angus does. Happy and contented. If only she could be happy again. Would she ever be happy again? Like…

She was awakened by a ringing telephone.

That smell of dirty little boys. That is what it was, Jez the Jezebel. Someone get the telephone. 'Mummy it's for you. Margery, I think.'

'I'm coming.'

'Is dad all right now?'

'I suppose so.'

'He went out early.'

'He's gone?'

'Ages ago.'

'Tell Margery I'm coming.'

She adjusted her clothing, brushed her hair and went to the phone. 'Hello. Margery, yes everything's all right. Pressure of work. I'll tell you more later. I must get the boys to church. Thanks ever so much for calling.'

She had carried that off well, Margery would have suspected nothing. The bedroom was as Angus had left it. He had slept in the bed, the duvet strewn across the floor and the bath had not been rinsed. She began brushing her teeth and then she broke, tears gushed from her eyes and a wail grew in her throat but did not emerge. She must be strong. It was her job to be strong. Especially where the boys were concerned. She redressed hurriedly and went downstairs.

CHAPTER TWENTY-SEVEN

Angus aftermath

It was all too obvious now. That smell of dirty little boys. How easily he had lied about Mitch and his after shave. How many other lies had there been?

Angus was nowhere to be found, nor was there any sort of note. Alex and James were on the their best form, breakfasted and dressed for church. They set off without him and Jinny excused his absence with white lies about his health.

Angus' mobile was switched off and Jinny spent an anxious day waiting for news. Slumped in a chair, petting Bobby's head, vaguely listening to the radio burbling. The boys took it into turns to poke their heads round the door to find out if there was any word.

James was on his way downstairs as the telephone finally rang and he stood at his mother's side while she answered, 'Yes, darling….I'll come right away….Where?….Yes, I know it….OK darling, don't you worry….Yes, right away….Bye, darling.'

'Where is he?' James asked aggressively.

'Not far.'

'I'm coming with you,' he said.

'I don't think that's a good idea,' Jinny was taken aback by his aggression. 'We need a few minutes alone.'

'I'll wait outside,' he stated with finality. In the event both boys accompanied her.

The hotel where Angus was hiding out was situated on reclaimed industrial land beneath the mainline railway. A moderately priced chain with tiny rooms and paper thin walls, Angus was on the top floor, laughingly referred to as the penthouse suite.

Jinny found the room amongst the maze of corridors and fire doors, knocked softly on maple veneer and rattled the blue plastic handle. Not a sound could be heard from inside. She was just about to return to reception when the door flew open and Angus' blurred form moving back into the room fell face forward onto the bed. She could hear a loud and long groan.

She stepped inside, the air smelled strongly of alcohol and beside the bed was a discarded bottle of Johnny Walker. Angus was dressed in a crumpled blue shirt and striped boxer shorts, his jacket and trousers thrown in a corner.

Beige and white walls, beige and white bedspread, beige and white furniture and a pair of beige and white paintings. The room was a void unsettled by the presence of two strangers dressed in colours.

Jinny, unwilling to speak, surveyed the artwork. Were these insipid splurges manufactured by a computer or were individuals paid to purposely produce studied anonymity? Andrew would have plenty to say about these daubings. The sort of vacuity that personifies modern existence. That would be too pompous for Andrew. Fucking crap, that would be a more likely assessment. Fucking crap, that summed up her situation to the letter. She needed to be rescued. She needed a knight in shining armour. Her stomach quivered with a desire to be elsewhere. There was no doubt in her mind as to who she wished to be with. If she was not any sort of a fool, she should leave now and go to him. He would hold her and tell her that all would be well.

Angus groaned pitifully.

She looked at his prone figure and was filled with disgust. His over generous backside and thickening midriff no longer attracted her. She had noticed lately that his breath had become sour, blaming his irregular diet and increased intake of booze. He smelled of dirty little boys.

He let loose a loud explosion of wind and the room was quickly filled with a sulphurous gas. Her husband was a descendant of the devil.

'Sorry,' he muffled an apology into the pillow.

'Put your clothes on,' she said sadly defeated. 'I'm taking you home.'

She had to dress him and guide him like a blind man. She got out her Visa Card to settle his bill and was cut short, 'Mr Parish is one of our regulars. He has an account.'

This final insult barely touched the surface. Her body and soul and heart were empty. Overnight she had plummeted to the lowest of depths and her emotional system emptied by a diuretic.

* * *

Monday at school was an eternity and no message from Angus. After school as she made her way to the offices of Anglo Saxon Limited, the traffic was mercifully light.

Margery had been wonderful. As they chatted during the lunch hour, Jinny could see the concern in her eyes but she had not pressed her for detail. Jinny kept it vague, pretending that pressure of work was to blame. She noticed Andy watching her with a knowing look on his face. What could he know? He could have guessed I suppose. He does not have to be that clever to guess what had happened because men are all the same, bastards.

'Bother,' she said. She had so much on her mind today she had forgotten to stand down from the America trip. She could call Margery later.

Wyford's business district was sited in Under Street, which ran at right angles from the High Street, all the way to the Wyford British Rail station. A clutch of insurance companies took buildings in the 80's but with the recent demise of equity more diverse business had moved in. Anglo Saxon (UK) Limited, founded by Harold J. Tenzer II had been based in the City until 1999. When their President, Harold T. Tenzer III went green, the company was moved to the provinces.

The BBC building at the station end, had been empty since its erection in 1996 and ASL took the complete letting. It was a glass box with seams and the working life of the tenancy was visible for some distance with the only privacy available in the cloakrooms.

Jinny parked the car at the rear and watched a man and a woman arguing at the window. It appeared that the woman, whose manner was hangdog, must have been in the wrong. This pleased Jinny and added to her resolve.

The receptionist offered her a seat but she declined and paced the marble floor, her shoes clacking as she walked in time to her stomach churning. She had been angry all day, now she was here and the confrontation was imminent, she was no longer indignant but nervous.

She pictured herself living in a Lynn Reid Banks novel. In rooms so small they were not even L-shaped. A shoe box in town. When her courage was fired by her indignation she saw herself in the Deep Blue Sea featuring Andrew as her toy boy and Angus visiting her bed-sit regretful of his misdemeanours, begging for her to come back.

'Mrs Parish,' the smarmy receptionist summoned her and continued in a discreet whisper. 'It seems that Geraldine is unavailable until after six today. I'm sorry.'

'Who told you that?' Jinny was firm.

The unctuousness mingled with fear. It seemed the receptionist knew the reason for her visit and was afraid there would be a scene. Her restrained voice croaked, 'She did.'

'You'll call her back and tell her we will need somewhere private and we'll be doing it now.'

'Yes, Mrs Parish.'

She redialled and spoke softly into the intercom. It took some persuading but as she replaced the receiver she said, 'She'll be with you shortly.'

Geraldine ushered her into the boardroom, closed the door after them and gave her a sheepish smile.

Jinny studied the opposition closely. Tall for a woman, she wore a low cut Swiss blouse which revealed modest cleavage. Jez' fearful eyes were fixed on her, awaiting the barrage. Deep blue ringed with overly thick mascara. Her hair was dyed black. This woman could have taken part in one of those pornographic films she had found.

'I've given notice.'

'You have. Why?' Jinny's tummy had quit churning and she felt much cooler, in control.

'I don't like to say.'

'I don't think you can hurt me any more than you already have.'

'Since I broke it off he's been declaring his love for me. To tell you the truth he's become a bit of a pest.'

'Has he now. Your relationship was...?'

'Just sex,' said Geraldine, brazenly. 'You know, a bit of a lark.'

'Just sex,' Jinny felt her temper rising. What was the matter with the man. She had never once denied him sex 'You don't return his love.'

Geraldine laughed, 'Sorry.'

'Why did you pull a face when you mentioned the sex?'

'If you want to know the truth….'

'I do.'

'He's not very good at it, is he?'

Jinny left it there. She sat in the car unable to focus on a topic. He was not leaving her. She was safe. Was she going to pretend it never happened? What could be better about sex? How many other women had he slept with? She needed to talk but who could she trust? Marcia, the most worldly of her friends, would be best but the minute she knew it would be all round the town. What if she already knew? She sagged onto the steering wheel.

'Everybody knows but me,' she muttered, swamped with self-pity. 'It's so obvious. I am a cuckold. Queen of all the cuckolds.'

* * *

The room was deathly quiet apart from the mechanical efficiency of their eating. Knives and forks clinking on crockery, the atmosphere macabre, eyes blinkered stolidly fixed on dinner plates and nobody wanting to be the first to break the silence.

Jinny and the boys were unused to having their father home for dinner and the events of the previous forty eight hours weighed heavily in their minds. The boys had received no explanation and concern was turning to resentment. Neither felt they were given the regard their age deserved. Each was surprised how these unlikely events had rekindled their sibling unity. They had talked late into the night about both parents' failings.

Angus had appeared early as though nothing was awry, his entrance received with stunned silence. He made himself a drink and sat sullenly in front of the television.

Mute, he accepted the call to the dining table.

When Jinny had finished her meal, she gathered her nerve, raised her eyes and faced him. He was sat facing forward, chewing his food thoroughly, tears torrenting down his cheeks.

Jinny knew then her marriage was over. They may stay together until their dotage but trust, respect and love were gone. Maybe she was old-fashioned but she had standards, she had self-respect but if she was going stay with him she would have to forfeit both.

* * *

Angus remained in this detached state for the next two days and Jinny dithered over her decision to quit the America trip. A week away would do her good but she felt guilty leaving the twins to deal with their errant father.

In the event this was not to be the case. So confident was Angus that England would win the World Cup he had bought tickets for the semi-final and the final. He had booked a week off work to accommodate these matches and in the circumstances decided to take up the booking.

'Who are you going with?' Jinny asked suspiciously, talking to her husband's back while he shaved.

'McAlinney.'

'McAlinney! You're joking.'

'No,' said Angus without humour. 'It's best to keep the opposition where you can see them. While the cat's away, etcetera, etcetera.'

'Aren't I included with the mice?'

Since his confession in the en suite, Angus had deftly avoided catching her eye. He snuffed through his nose, turned away from the mirror and looked her up and down. 'You,' he said contemptuously and snuffed again.

The twins could not be trusted to be left alone. Angus spoke to his brother and Jock was able to get their work experience at Disneyworld brought forward a week.

Jinny's choice now was to spend a week at home alone or go through with her school obligation.

She had been tempted to skip book club and arrived late to find a good turnout. Andrew was being teased for predicting England's downfall but he was not playing.

'Did you put a bet on, sir?'

'No.'

'You didn't put your money where your mouth is?'

'You've got no bottle.'

'You could be right,' said Andrew. 'Can we let this drop now? Daisy, what book did you choose? Quiet!'

'To Kill a Mockingbird, sir.'

'Quiet! Please. OK Daisy I want you to tell us what you thought of it. I'm going to let Jinny deal with this. She knows so much more about this book than I do.'

The evening overran again and the club only ended because impatient parents began tapping on the windows. The mournful face Jinny arrived with was now bright with pleasure and she received the thanks of a quartet of happy couples.

'I never dreamed he'd look inside a book just for the fun of it.'

'He actually talks about what he's read.'

'Thank you.'

Andrew sat patiently while Jinny finished. 'You did that on purpose.'

'Did what?'

'Let me take the stage.'

'You did a good job. It was a nice evening.'

'Nice? You're patronising me.'

'You're right and I was trying my very best not to,' he got out the chair and sat on the desk next to her. 'Do you want to talk?'

'Talk about what?' she tried to sound calm but she began trembling. Her hands took on a volatile life of their own and her legs went weak.

'What is it that's troubling you?'

'What business is it of yours?' she wanted to sound angry but she was shaking so violently the stuttered words were barely audible.

Andrew closed the door and squatted beside her, she was now having trouble catching her breath. She let him pull her to her feet but her wobbly legs gave under her and she crumpled to the floor behind the desk. He sat slightly behind her and manoeuvred her limp body inside his own and held her close. She sank into him and he let his nose play soothingly around her ear and neck. Once he was sure that these advances were acceptable he grew bolder.

He cupped her chin and let his fingers trace the shape of her mouth. Having allowed enough time for her to deny him, he put his mouth to hers. As soft as he could manage because of the intensity generating from her trembling frame, he kissed her lingeringly, taunting her like a flitting sable brush, pushing her emotions as far as he dare without losing the moment. Her urgency signified the moment for him and their mouths clamped together so fiercely he thought her neck might break.

She knew nothing of the art of kissing. Her tongue was inept and her head awkward. She wanted to match his efficiency but she was spoiling their synchronisation. He pulled her away and caressed her face before taking it slowly. She allowed him to make the pace and the intensity was resurrected.

'I've got a secret to tell you,' he said.

She pulled away and looked at him intently.

'I've replaced Margery on the America trip.'

CHAPTER TWENTY-EIGHT

US trip begins

Having refereed the various squabbles over seating arrangements and annoying the flight staff, Jinny and Andy were escorted to their places at the rear of the plane where they were to share a two seater. She preferred the aisle seat and he the window. She had forgotten some important item in her travelling case and he watched her straining hips and legs reaching up to the luggage rack.

He was on his guard not to take matters for granted. Sure, they had kissed but that was three days ago and there had been no follow up. No secret glances across a crowded room. She was vulnerable and that was to his advantage. Whatever was going on between her and her husband surely had not been patched up in that short a time. He warned himself again about making assumptions, not to get carried away and hog the conversation. He should start slowly, ease the way and get her to talk. If she were to confess to him about her marriage she might reveal something of herself.

Vulnerability and white panties caused a forgotten longing to flare. It was his turn to be susceptible.

Jinny handed him a book to hold and closed the hatch before collapsing into her seat and securing her seat belt. She peered down the aisle for signs of trouble until satisfied all was quiet, then nestled deep into her chair. Leaning her arm against his, she turned to him in a private and conspiratorial fashion, 'Peace at last.' The intimacy of this action churned his already active breadbasket.

'Is this your first visit to New York?' she asked.

'No. Yours?'

'Angus' HQ is there,' she spoke proudly.

The aeroplane had stopped taxiing and revved engines in preparation for take off. A sudden surge and they were under way. Nightlights appeared below like frosted cobwebs until the plane slipped amongst the clouds, London and its suburbs were behind them. They climbed for a few minutes longer into a purple twilight and then the seat belt sign was switched off.

Were she and Angus reconciled? Her face had recovered from the evening of the book club. Whatever had happened the night of the party had scrubbed the life from her face and darkened her eyes with fear. Today the lustre had returned.

'Why are you looking at me like that?'

Some uncharacteristic impulse told him this was his chance but he bottled it. 'Was I staring? Sorry.'

Jayson appeared at her side, 'Excuse me Mrs Parish, but can Russell and me swap seats?'

'Jimmy,' Andy intervened. 'This is a long flight and you're starting already. If you want to change seats organise it yourself and don't get in the stewardesses' way.'

'OK.'

'I wish they would take more care with their grammar,' she complained.

'Russell and me,' he said. 'You live in a dream world.'

'Why were you staring?'

'I didn't know I was,' he said getting excited. Everything was fine, she was making the play.

'Can I ask you a question?'

'Sure,' he said, his heart thumping.

'Do you think I'm pretty?'

He feigned interest and pretended to study her as if for the first time. 'No,' he shook his head.

Frown lines scarred her face, the lustre momentarily tarnished. He leaned close to her and mumbled, 'I think you're beautiful.'

He had got it right for once in his life. He would never forget the reaction those words elicited. It was one of those mind snaps that stay with you to the grave.

'You're teasing me,' she said, her eyes brimming with moisture.

'No I'm not,' he said sincerely.

She turned away and pretended to read her book. He had generated more reaction than he expected and he knew not to press the point but he did anyway.

'Have I upset you?' She shook her head. Christ, she's on the verge of tears. 'I'm so sorry, I only meant to be nice.'

Jutting her head forward as though chucking the tears back inside her head, she murmured, 'It was…'

'It was what?'

'Nice.'

Jayson reappeared, 'Sally won't let me sit with Russell.'

'Why not?'

'She'll have to sit next to Davis and she doesn't want to.'

'You're sitting with Davis?'

'Yes.'

'I'm not having you leaving Davis out on a limb.'

'But, sir.'

'But me no buts,' said Jinny. 'Sit down and be nice.'

'Yes, miss,' said Jayson sulkily and slouched away.

She tilted her head and rested on the chair back, while he lusted for her elongated neck. He wanted to pepper it with kisses.

Jinny's thoughts, like the aeroplane, were hanging in the air. Angus had said nothing positive about the situation and had given no indication of his future intentions. He had simply withdrawn into a shell. Occasionally, he popped his head out as though nothing were amiss and equally unfathomably he snapped it back. He was not over the woman, she knew that for sure. The two evenings they had spent together watching TV he had sat quietly with tears streaming down his face.

What was their future? Was there a future? She could not bring herself to think beyond those abstractions. If he were to leave what would become of her?

Involuntarily, she turned to the man next to her. Beautiful, he can not truly think I am beautiful. Why did he say such a thing if he did not mean it? More to the point, why did he say it at all? What did he want from her? Sex. You must face it Jinny Parish, men only want sex. That is an area in which her beloved William Shakespeare had failed her. Did he want her to do those things in the pornographic films? Chance would be a fine thing.

She shuddered and he asked, 'Are you cold?'

She shook her head, 'A shadow walked across my grave.'
Angus had never kissed her that way, softly, passionless. Angus was passionate, rough and his whiskers burned. Not that he had kissed her very often either way in recent months. Other than a peck 'hello' or 'goodbye', there was little in the way of tenderness anymore. If she were to be totally truthful there had never been much in the way of foreplay. There was rutting. Making a connection was becoming more and more difficult because she was unable to summon any natural lubricant. Which is also odd because the merest contact with Andrew flooded her underwear.

'Do you have any siblings?' he asked.

'A sister, why do you ask?'

'I was wondering.'

'You?'

'I'm an only child. Isn't it obvious.'

'How would it be obvious?'

She was wistful. Why, he could only guess. Was her sister the favourite? Is that why Jinny played so hard at being nice? Her way of winning influence with her parents.

'She lives in California, so I don't get to see her much. Hardly at all as a matter of fact.'

'Are you meeting in New York?'

'No,' the idea had not occurred to her. 'It would be halfway for both of us.'

'Yes.'

'I never thought.'

Dinner was served and she saw that he hardly ate his food. Was he scared of flying? What food he ate he chewed carefully. That was another characteristic that was opposite to Angus. Angus gobbled his meals and took pills for heartburn. She had told him but he did not listen.

Few love to hear the sins they love to act

No love lost between these sisters. Envy on Jinny's part? Lack of parental love?

'What's she like, your sister?'

'Charlotte. Very clever, gifted. She can do anything she turns her hand to. When she was at home when her children were young and she found she was getting bored to distraction she started sketching to pass the time. You would not believe how good these sketches were. Everybody admires them. My parents were very proud of her.'

But not you though. They probably wanted a boy and you were a disappointment. He stopped himself eating any more of the meal. Plastic food invariably gave him a bad reaction and tonight was not the night for bad reactions.

When he agreed to replace Margery he had changed the flight tickets, but had done nothing about the sleeping arrangements. What everyone had overlooked was that Jinny and Margery were to share a room. He knew enough of campus vacation accommodation to know that all the rooms would be spoken for and that rearrangements would be highly unlikely. If they were to share a room or, more hopefully, share a bed, everything must be in good order.

'...I followed Charlotte into the Girls' Grammar. That wasn't easy. All the teachers remembered her and comparison was inevitable. She wasn't an easy act to follow...'

She was talking more and he travelled with her into her childhood, seeking out her pain. Perhaps she had never known affection. Her husband is a shit, her kids are complacent and her mother does not seem to have cared for her.

She had probably not had a compliment like 'beautiful' in her life. Look at that neck, boy that Modigliani knew a thing or two.

'...My parents wanted Bristol because Charlotte had been there. I chose Edinburgh, in truth it was way too far away...'

'You didn't want to follow in your sister's slipstream again.'

'No. Exactly.'

The way she talks about this Charlotte she should have a double first at Oxford. Bristol? Should I ask why? Better not, you are supposed to keeping your gob shut. Where can I touch her and get away with it?

'...I had a good time. That's where I met Angus. We were married in our second year...'

You were pregnant. Nobody gets married at university unless they have to. Angus is a trapped man.

'...I got pregnant immediately and switched to teacher training.'

Angus is the only man she has ever been with. What had his

affair done to their relationship? There was no inflection when she spoke his name, just that goofy 'isn't he wonderful' thing she does.

She was pregnant so they had to get married. Her first lay and wham. How Angus must hate her guts, especially her uterus. Perhaps that's going a bit far but there must be plenty of resentment and plenty of justification for catching up on his lost youth.

Suddenly the possibilities were endless. All that repression. Mind you Avecore, you are treading on dangerous ground here. You only need to be kind to her and she's going to cling like a barnacle. You had better keep this relationship on a proper footing. There is no way you can marry this woman, you're total opposites. You'll spend your married life in separate rooms and only meet at bedtime.

'St Bryans your first school?'

'Second,' she said. 'I was an NQT near uni'. Angus still had a year of his degree to do. I waddled through.'

I bet you did. You are the type that spends nine months holding your back and eating for two. How can you fancy this woman, just because she is so beautiful. You shallow immature twat. He let the outside of their arms connect and placed his nose close to hers. His feelings were amplified like a teenager on his first encounter.

Dinner was collected and the intimacy was broken for a spell.

What kind of a mother plays a favourite? Being an only child he had no experience of preferential treatment.

'What kind of woman was your mother?'

'She was pretty, had beautiful hair like Margaret Thatcher. She greatly admired her...'

Fucking hell. What am I getting into?

'...I would say mummy was a very strong character. Much stronger than daddy. She was definitely in charge. One thing she did, she did a few times, that I have never understood. Charlotte occasionally offered to take me places and my mother stopped me from going...'

'Dances? With boys?'

'No, I don't think so. Once it was to the pictures to see James Bond. I really loved the Bond films. I had a big crush on Roger Moore.'

'Roger Moore?'
'You're not going to get all superior.'
'About what?'
'James Bond. Everybody loves James Bond.'
'Sure.'
'You're doing it.'
'Doing what?'
'Your superior thing.'
'Sorry. You were saying, about your mum.'
'She stopped me going out. It happened a couple of times but I never got a reason.'

Jealousy, he decided. Mummy wanted Charlotte to herself and she was not going to let Virginia get in on the act. That was what was at the bottom of all of this. Had Jinny done anything wrong to cause her mother's peculiar behaviour, perhaps it was as simple as her being born and spoiling the party.

Blind faith in her parents, total obedience and trowel loads of niceness. Yet her mother still rejected this perfect child? Now, she has nobody. Parents dead, sister emigrated, husband estranged, children, an unknown quantity. You are treading on dangerous ground Andy boy.

'Where did you read English?'
'What makes you think I read English?'
'Didn't you?' she asked. He shook his head. 'What did you read?'
'French.'
'You're teasing me again.'
'Got a two:one, did a PGCE and switched to English. It was easy, I've always read a lot.'

The lights were switched off, the film began and Jinny got inside a blanket. She nodded off and her head slipped sideways onto his shoulder. He slipped his hand under the blanket and found her hand. Their fingers played together, teasing, fingertip to fingertip, fingertip to palm, the barest touch. They kissed and for the first time Jinny experienced true uninhibited passion.

CHAPTER TWENTY-NINE

On campus

One suitcase went missing, Davis'. It turned up on a neighbouring carousel but none of the students owned up to the prank. They were being met at the airport by a university bus and when they emerged from the terminal they were horribly late. Thankfully the driver did not seem to mind.

Following lengthy last minute negotiations, the students were all in their assigned bedrooms. Andy and Jinny stood waiting to sort out their problem. Just as Andy surmised, the late change in personnel had not been considered and nobody had changed the accommodation. Also as Andy predicted, the complete campus was accounted for.

Jinny asked to speak to the Bursar, named Milne, who was a short teddy-bearish man with very little brain.

'If the kids get wind that we're together, we'll never hear the end of it.'

'You are in a completely separate block from the students. We encourage our younger guests to fend for themselves. We have learned that their chaperones tend to inhibit them a tad.'

'Let's give it a look, if we don't like the geography we can move later,' Andy hoped he did not sound overly keen.

Jinny allowed herself to admit to being tired and agreed. With the kids locked away responsibility was over for a few hours.

'If you'd return to the coach, the driver will take care of you.'

They sat together in awkward silence. The driver, strictly obeying the speed limit, meandered at a snail's pace along the winding roadways. He pulled up alongside a manicured hebe bush smothered in white blossoms, behind which was a pair of doors.

'That's one of the executive suites. It belongs to one of our senior members. He's away in Europe. We took the liberty of putting your luggage in the room earlier.' The driver handed Andy a key.

The room was lived in. Apart from two small wardrobes and two doors, one to the kitchenette and one to the bathroom, the walls were completely decked with shelves filled with books. There was a digital clock, a castor oil plant and bright red impatiens in a terracotta pot. Their cases were laid on either side of the solitary bed.

Jinny sat on the bed, her hands resting in her lap, her eyes downcast, as sad as an abandoned car.

'You OK with this?' he asked.

She turned to him. Her face was heart-rending and he dismissed any idea of taking advantage of her distress.

'Make love to me,' she said.

Andy's feelings did a somersault or two. He pulled her up from the bed and embraced her. Mesmerised, she undressed slowly and Andy tried not to stare. She kept her white panties on and tried to get under the duvet but he stopped her, 'Lie down on your face. I'll help you relax.'

He caressed her back, searching out what she liked but nothing stirred. His fingers shaped her shoulders, the small of her back, the sides of her hips but no reaction occurred until he ventured inside her underwear. Teasing as deftly as he could, he moved the elastic top to expose the top of her bum. This stimulated a familiar response and he continued with renewed hope. He traced the line of elastic, slowly travelled up her side to her breasts pausing momentarily before touching them and this elicited another familiar twinge. Patiently, he retraced these steps in preparation for a proper kiss. He leaned over and let their mouths meet, not letting her pressure his own mouth. Her body twisted to enjoy his lips play on hers and his fingers sought new areas to excite her. His fingertips ran across the cotton fabric and as his hand prepared to probe deeper inside, her legs slammed shut on his hand.

'Down there,' she announced with vigour. 'Is dirty.'

* * *

Unable to sleep, her body cradled in his, he wondered whether to give up on this poor woman. Even if he did manage to undo some of the physical damage the polarity of their viewpoints would not be turned around overnight. What right did he have to change her mind? What made his life so special? What they had was physical attraction. Sex, and if tonight was anything to go by, that was proving a forlorn exercise.

This woman and Karen were poles apart.

He had not confronted repression before and could only speculate on how he might deal with it. Dishonesty was another matter, that he had come across before. Jinny's dishonesty was commonplace but he was not so sure of what spawned it.

Jinny's mother was a strange bird. Andy knew of mothers who competed with daughters but these were usually acts of vanity. Mothers not wanting to get old or admit their age. Utilising the proximity of a younger woman to vicariously prolong the fountain of youth, that was understandable. From what Jinny had told him her mother's motives were more sinister. A woman who could usurp one child for the company of the other was new to him. This was a rivalry and behaviour too strange for him to understand. Jinny had mentioned her mother was a midwife. Perhaps this accounted for her singular behaviour.

Andy understood men far better. Men were easier, especially those pathetic fathers who were jealous of successful offspring. This did not apply in Jinny's case.

There was so much that Jinny was leaving out. If she had a shotgun wedding how would an experienced midwife react? She would go one of two ways. Understand her daughters predicament or be humiliated that a daughter of hers could be so stupid. It was not hard to guess what option her mother had taken. She had not attended the wedding nor travelled up to Scotland. Left with her own shame and two babies to cope with on your own would have been hard but would not create repression. That came long before. That was some household.

He wished he could have been a fly on the wall for one day of her childhood. It was rare that he was at a total loss.

What was the source of Jinny's dishonesty? When she speaks of her father there is credibility, but the portrayals of her mother, her husband and her children ring hollow. Why do so many people live a lie? When he is at his most bullish falsehood is the domain of the immature and when he is at his most sensitive he acknowledges that for many the truth is tough to take. It was all very well for him, life had been handed to him on a plate.

Where did the repression emanate from? It would have to be parents, but how did they manage it? A midwife comes face to face with the sordid facts of life on a daily basis. Why pass a fear of blood and gore onto your children?

He now had a multitude of questions to ask her over the next few days. Did she have a difficult labour? Who told her about the birds and the bees? Or was it vultures and scorpions? Are you catholic?

Catholic women have a heavy burden to carry. He was instantly transported to a doctor's waiting room. His mother, spirits and general fear of needles were making him nauseous. She who smelled of powder and soap had her arm around him. He was to have a tetanus booster. The wait, the underlying odour of methylated struggled to take his mind off the inevitable and listened to the conversation of two women in the next room. One must have been the nurse and the patient was explaining that she was catholic and unable to use contraception.

'I daren't be civil to him,' the woman complained. 'I can't go through all that again. Not at my age.'

His mother started coughing violently and he missed the nurse's response. He thought his mother was being discreet and saving him from finding out too much too soon. That evening, laughing merrily, she repeated the snippet of conversation to his father. His father smiled but was not so amused. 'I never realised how hard it must have been for women before contraception.

How natural Karen had been. Their emotion for each other was immediate, so the sex had been easy. He could summon her smell and taste and that first glimpse of her was etched in his brain. Blond hair, green eyes and deadly serious, more make-up than was necessary.

He slipped out from under the sleeping woman. Dawn was breaking outside and watery light was filling the room slowly like a leaking tap. There she was, all that he had fantasised about for the past weeks, exactly how he had dreamed of her, naked in bed with him. He touched her exposed breasts, let his hand cautiously slide down to her bellybutton and paused.

'What a waste,' he muttered, gave a sympathetic thought for poor Angus, hopped out of bed and got in the shower.

* * *

CHAPTER THIRTY

Metropolitan Art Museum

The Summit conference was not what the students expected. They thought their trip to the United States was a holiday and had received a rude shock. There had been complaints. An unending litany of moans and grizzles. They had their hearts set on shopping but on their first day off a tour of the Metropolitan Art Museum had been arranged. Jinny and Andy felt obliged to accept the hospitality. A further tour of Carnegie Hall had also been organised but they excused themselves from that to placate their disgruntled charges.

Their guide was an elderly man with a shock of white hair and more than a hint of a European accent. He introduced himself with a mischievous smile as Janos, 'Hands up who would rather be at the movies.' He did not wait for their response but charged off into the building with a startling amount of vigour. 'These paintings,' he waved his arm in an unspecific direction, 'have magical powers. I am 134 years old but these paintings give off vibrations that give me the energy of a man half my age.'

More like a quarter, Andy and his group of boys struggled to keep pace. The ticket seller had intimated that the forty minute tour would be restricted to approximately half the exhibit. At the pace Janos was setting they would do the complete exhibition, twice.

'Ladies and gentlemen, others?' He looked his party over with the same wicked grin. 'Your tour today is forty minutes and the text is set by the museum. The opinions are all my own and can be disregarded if you choose. Follow me.'

They entered the salon designated to the impressionists and Janos made straight for the Monet. Starting on familiar ground.

'Claude Monet, a view from his hotel at a resort called Saint Adresse near Le Havre in France. The gentleman sitting in the garden is the artist's father.'

'Is Monet a great artist?'

'Monet is one of the greatest artists of all time but his popularity belies his true standing.'

They moved to the next painting, a swathe of greens, blues and orange.

'Paul Cezanne, undoubtedly the greatest artist of his generation. A troubled man, very shy, ridiculed by his neighbours. See, even the French can be crass. Got caught in a rainstorm returning from painting a landscape, caught pneumonia and died. Terrible shame.'

'Was he a great artist?'

Andy hoped that this was not going to be the sole question his boys could manage. Janos did not seem to mind.

'His work is the source of modern art, an accolade he probably would have spurned. Not all progress is for the better.'

'How d'you mean, Mr Janos?'

'We'll get to that later, young man.'

'Edgar Degas, a miserable fellow, an anti-semite but with the delicate touch to kill for. Before I came to New York I worked in London. I heard a countryman of yours measure Degas' worth against Walter Sickert. This is like comparing Britney Spears to Pavarotti.'

They zoomed through the building at a furious pace. Janos knew his public. Their attention span required quantity rather than quality. His information was clipped and pithy with the occasional polemic thrown in. These jibes went over the party's head.

'Jackson Pollock. One of the United States' glittering treasures,' Janos's head motion was clearly theatrical.

'You don't think so?'

'Production line. He should be in the same museum as Henry Ford.'

Inevitably, the boys' tour finished before the girls'. They went to the cafeteria and Janos accepted Andy's offer of coffee. Under instructions not to leave the building under any circumstances, he let the boys go. He had barely sat down when he was called to deal with Davis. He wanted to use his credit card to pay for a can of Coke.

Andy returned to find Jinny and Janos chatting merrily. He was a smooth old rake enchanting her with his stories.

'Fortunately I was circumcised and was able to leave for Israel but I couldn't cope with living a lie or the lifestyle. Also there are a plethora of guides. So,' he shrugged and smiled. 'I went to England. My problems were similar there. I found work as a butcher's assistant. Not so good the salary. Eventually I come here, get work I like. Especially with the children. They are a good audience.'

'Janos worked at The Hermitage.'

'He did,' said Andy who had his doubts. Why would a Czech get a valued Russian job?

'Do you like our wonderful museum?'

'To be honest I'm a little disappointed...'

'Disappointed. That's a shame,' Janos beamed, the glint in his eye sparkling, he winked at Andy. 'What's the problem?'

'There aren't many pictures by English artists in the collection.'

'Ha,' he cried, shaking his head from side to side. 'We got many visitors at The Hermitage. Many many visitors and every so often a group from the United Kingdom. We would pass from salon to salon and as they entered the group would huddle in whispers. These conferences would increase with as the tour progresses. Finally a spokesperson would be appointed and they would take me to one side and ask discreetly, 'Where are the English exhibits?' and early in my career I would be embarrassed but later...' He shrugged.

'What later?'

'I told them straight out, there aren't any. Britain is a great nation, it has given us the telephone and the television. Probably the two worst plagues of the 20th century.'

'It is a curiosity that the least prosaic and the most prosaic countries of the world are separated by twenty miles of water. It's about repression, I'm thinking. What nudes have British artists painted. I can only think of one. Now you have Bacon and Freud. They depict quite clearly how the British see themselves. Ugly.'

From the depths of Jinny's handbag her mobile went off.

'Aha,' said Janos. 'You must excuse me, my next party has

arrived. Very lovely to meet you both, especially the beautiful young lady.' He kissed her hand, bowed and made his way to a group waiting across the foyer.

By the time she had rescued the phone it had stopped ringing, then beeped.

Andy raised his eyebrows, 'He fancies you.'

She ignored him and toyed with the buttons. The old man's mischief had annoyed her. The message was from a network welcoming her to the United States.

Davis and Shaw joined them at their table. 'Where to now?'

'Lunch. What have you bought?'

'Postcards,' Davis and Shaw showed off their purchases. Monet, Matisse and Manet.

'You're not very patriotic boys,' Jinny was plainly peeved. 'Why not buy an English artist.'

'Which were they?'

'Francis Bacon, the head of the Pope and Lucien Freud, the nude woman quite close to it.'

'Those brown paintings.'

'Brown.'

'I prefer paintings with colours.'

Jinny shook her head in exasperation.

'Out of the mouth of babes and…'

She stormed off across the foyer and did not talk to him for over an hour.

CHAPTER THIRTY-ONE

Jinny's birthday

She awoke, laying on her side, foetal shaped and he was moulded into her profile. His legs warm on the inside of hers, his hand across her waist but no prodding erection. There must be something the matter with him.

She reviewed the intimacy of the past nights, a riddle of strange and unfamiliar. Moving carefully so as not to wake him, she shifted the coverlet and exposed the forearm laying across her body. She wanted to touch but resisted, afraid she would wake him. His hand shifted and rested on her lower stomach just above her pubic hair.

It's my birthday!

She needed to check her mobile for messages. Easing out from under his arm she rescued the phone from her bag and shut herself in the bathroom. Sitting naked on the edge of the bath she waited for the SIM card to kick in and the bleeper echoed loudly. It was another text from the local network welcoming her to the United States. No other messages. The twins were in the same time band so she would be hearing from them later. What is the time? She had forgotten to check. In the gloom, Andy was still sleeping, the clock glowed vividly, six fifteen.

Where was Angus today? She had his inventory in the blackberry but she would check later. She sat on her side of the bed and eased her way back in. He stirred but did not wake, she placed her body hoping that his hand would rest where it was before.

Thirty seven years old and she would soon be forty, it did not bear thinking about. How would Angus get his card to the University? He always gave her one of those A4 cards with a sentimental message. He could be sweet when he wanted to be and here she was in bed with a stranger.

She remembered Andrew's gentle hands on her body, his mouth softly on hers. Angus rarely kissed her anymore, not even when they were making love. He was always in a hurry to get inside her and then his head rested in her neck, slobbering.

This would have to stop. Just because Angus had sinned did not mean that she should. She did not believe in an eye for an eye. She had not yet committed adultery. Even though she had wanted to Andrew seemed reluctant to go that far. Was he being gallant or feels he is being unfaithful to his wife's memory. Best to put an end to it now, before anybody gets hurt. Where was it going anyway? She could not focus her mind properly.

Angus had committed adultery. Seemingly without a conscience and how many times? When it comes to sex, men are all the same. Andrew was only the second man she had been with and she had not really been with him. She had thought all men were the same but the two she had experienced were not the least alike. She had offered herself and he had declined. What was the point of all this foreplay? She shivered in agreeable recollection. It was lovely for her but what was he getting out of it. As far as she knew he had not managed an erection. Perhaps he has been rendered impotent by his wife's death. She had read about such things.

Is the matter with him or is it my fault? What am I supposed to do? Angus does not require her to do anything. What is there to do? Should she touch him the way he has been touching her? It that appropriate for a woman? Who could she ask?

Does Andrew really care. If as he says he was attracted to her from the first, why had he been so horrible to her. He is too complicated for you. It isn't necessary to twist life like a corkscrew. Gentle hands. She pressed his hand to her and his fingers twirled her hair. What if his hand moved lower? With the tips of her fingers she traced the shape of his arm. His fingers played more fervently and for a split second she needed his hand to go lower.

Frightened by the changes coming over her, she jumped out of bed, chose a set of clothes and went to the bathroom to dress.

* * *

Andy waited for the door to close before moving. He lay on his back, stretched and snuffed a laugh. His searches were getting warmer but will she ever thaw out? She had touched his arm, that was a step forward. Amazing how selfish women could be. He had fondled her every night and not once had she reciprocated. No emotional involvement? Maybe she thinks its not expected of her. That arm bit was promising.

She felt and smelled good. It was odd to lie beside a woman again with so much softness to digest. Jinny is so innocent that the emotional involvement could be tricky. She is barely able to enjoy sex let alone enjoy sex for the sake of it. Experiencing these new feelings could easily be misinterpreted. Especially now that her husband has been caught with his pants round his ankles. You have no right to play ducks and drakes with her emotions at a time like this. But you are going to anyway aren't you. You are determined to get your way. You will worry about the consequences later. I know you. You could be making a big mistake.

'I'll worry about that tomorrow. Andrew you are a typical man. Live now, pay later.'

If it's going to happen at all it's going to happen today.

* * *

After breakfast, the kids were waiting in the foyer for their long awaited shopping trip. Some were lounging checking or sending text messages, Davis was arguing and some were upsetting staff with boisterous horseplay. Andy returned with their coach driver and his arrival restored order. Jinny joined the slouchers and checked her blackberry once more for messages. Clearly disappointed, she put the phone away in its leather case and resignedly joined her party. They were exiting single file through the doors when the Bursar called her back inside. She was handed an envelope, Andy spied her clutch it to her chest.

She had not been forgotten after all. Withdrawing to a quiet corner she opened it and found a copy of Gainborough's Red Boy. Inside was printed 'Many Happy Returns' and written beneath in capitals was TO A NEW BEGINNING, LOVE - A. Her heart surged with gratitude. How thoughtful of him to find a copy of her favourite painting. Was there a better way to start a new beginning? She so wanted to call him but the children were getting impatient and they had been hanging about long enough. She put the card away and hurried outside to the waiting brats. Andy raised his eyebrows and gave her a querying smile. She smiled back but decided that she would not sleep with him tonight. All that had to stop and right away.

They took the ferry and visited Ellis Island and the Statue of Liberty. Lunch was organised at Pier 45 and Andy was looking forward to sitting in the cafeteria the whole afternoon. He had no obligation to buy presents and was going to drink coffee and read.

The gaps between Jinny checking her mobile grew shorter and shorter but no message came. She checked the power of the signal with the other students who had brought mobiles but did not establish a definite answer. Twice she shut herself in a toilet cubicle, dialled Angus' number but hesitated before pressing the green button. It did not feel right to be ringing so she aborted the call and continued waiting.

She bought Angus and the boys T-shirts with New York logos and a silk scarf for poor Margery. She dialled her home number but there was no answer. She dialled Margery for news but again got no reply. She found Andy sitting in the café alone, three empty cups of coffee uncollected on the table. He was engrossed in his book and had not seen her approaching. She turned on her heel and went upstairs.

She found another café and ordered an unwanted herbal tea and chose a seat in the window overlooking the muddy river. A river as muddied as her brain. When she re-checked the Red Boy was lost in thought and she empathised. A NEW BEGINNING. She was safe. A warm glow replaced her fear. The bleak bed-sit she had seen in the Lucien Freud, the ugly and desolate life portrayed on the canvas frightened her. If Angus was to wipe the slate clean and take her back then she must accept even if was for the boys' sake. She must arrange a separate room as soon as they get back to the campus.

She checked the mobile and her heart plummeted to the bottom of the muddy river outside the glass. Some new beginning, he did not even have the courtesy to call her. He cannot be that busy. It did not make sense.

She brought up Angus' number and pressed the call button. It rang for an interminable number of rings and the messaging service kicked in. About to compose a message she pressed the cut off button instead. She did the same with Alex and James but their phones were switched off. She had spent her life bragging to her friends and acquaintances what a wonderful husband and children she had. Now she was not so sure. A card was nice but a phone call on her birthday was the least they could do. Where had she gone wrong?

Alex had been a difficult infant and the doctors discovered his susceptibility to E numbers. A strict diet had an instantaneous effect and they quickly turned that corner. James' difficult period had come later. When they transferred to the Grammar he got in with the wrong crowd. Vandalism, smoking and drinking and goodness knows what else. They never did get to the bottom of it all. Thankfully that Simmons boy had been expelled and James slowly returned to normal. What had she done that was so wrong? She had given them everything. Body, soul and more significantly, her time. She had devoted every minute she could. Had it been enough? Had her career got in the way?

What had she done to deserve Angus? Their marriage had started on a wrong note but surely they had worked beyond that. Andy's considerate behaviour is simply a difference in temperament. Remembering Andy's hands on her she shivered with pleasure and then was suffused with guilt. No more of that, it is not right, even though she could justify revenge. Revenge is such a base emotion.

A new beginning. There it was and that was it. She would explain this to Andy immediately and get a separate room. He would understand. She gathered her things together and marched downstairs to where Andy was sitting. She could see from the end of the corridor that he was still alone. As she drew nearer he saw her from over the top of his newspaper and gave her a broad smile. She sat down opposite him filled with determination and as she opened her mouth to speak her mobile rang.

Alex!
'Mum.'
'How are you enjoying…'

'Great,' he cut her short. 'I can't talk long, I'm on a break. I forgot to bring my Wyford shirt.'

'What do you want that…'

'Mum.'

'I'll send it to you as soon as I get home.'

'Where are you?'

'New York, with the school trip.'

'I forgot,' he paused for thought. 'Send it on when you get home. Must go. Love you.'

After he rang off, Jinny held the silent phone to her ear, too stunned to move. She tried Angus again but he did not answer.

CHAPTER THIRTY-TWO

Consummation

The kids were full of fun on the evening of Jinny's birthday and they were late getting back to the room. He had watched her all day checking the phone but she had not said anything. It was obvious now that she had not received a call. He could not imagine what was going on in her head. He guessed she had wanted to broach some topic but she had not as yet. Her sadness tainted the atmosphere of the room. While she was in the bathroom, he opened his suitcase and took out a package. As she emerged from the bathroom in her robe he handed it to her.

She stared at the card for an age before unwrapping her present. Her hands were shaking violently and he failed to understand why. Her head dropped slightly and he saw that she was at a loss.

'Should I open it for you?'

When she raised her head, he could not discern if it was disappointment, fear or what? He had hurt her, he could see that but he could not perceive how.

'I thought...' she hesitated and switched her attention to the package. Her trembling fingers struggled with cellotape and tore at the wrapping paper. She inspected the spines of the two books, dropped them on the bed and covered her face with her hands. She was sobbing. Would he ever have any positive effect on this woman he had now reduced to tears. Laughing, he prised her hands apart and pulled her to him. She clasped him so tightly he could not escape. He wanted to kiss her face but they remained locked that way for what seemed an eternity.

'I'm sorry,' he said, only to break the silence. He was not the least sorry.

She lightened her grip and pulled away. She took hold of his hand and twisted it over. She ran her fingers over his arm gently ruffling the hair, pulled his hand to her face and kissed his palm and fingers. He did not make any move to interrupt or hurry the imminent sex. He knew that she was aching for him and he was completely dispassionate, in complete control. This was a chance to take her schooling a step further. Timing was paramount.

* * *

Written on the card in capital letters was HAPPY BIRTHDAY - A. The same lettering as the card she had opened earlier. Angus had forgotten after all.

He strip his sleeve and show his scars
And say, 'These wounds I had on Crispin's day
Old men forget and young men too.

Wrapping paper could not disguise the fact that there were books contained inside, her shaking hands fumbled with the tape. He helped release the contents and she adjusted the spines. Whiteoaks and Jalna by de la Roche. She was stunned. How did he know? A jumble of feelings made her head swim and she feared momentarily that she would lose consciousness. The storm inside continued unabated pushing her into panic, she put her face in her hands to hide her shame and throbbed uncontrollably. He forced her hands apart and she grabbed him around the neck until she collected herself. What had gone before in her life bore no comparison to this moment. Her head would not clear and there was so much to consider, so much to savour. Slowly the maelstrom in her brain subsided. Angus and the boys had forgotten her birthday. This man, who hardly knew her, had remembered. Not only that he knew what she wanted more than anything else in the world.

'I'm sorry,' he said.

What was he sorry for? Where did he get the books from? A longing in her abdomen caught her unawares. Gosh she wanted him inside her. Shock swept over her but the longing remained.

She touched the hair on his arm and the longing intensified. She opened his hand and kissed his palm. He lifted her face and kissed her mouth, teasing her softly. She allowed him to lay her down and ease her out of her housecoat. He wasted no time and pulled her knickers over her knees and over her feet. He kissed her feet and she grew impatient, spreading her legs as wide as she could and lifting her thighs. His mouth ran slowly along the inside of her leg and a feather brushed her clitoris and the sensation it left in its wake was beyond description. They were kissing and more feathers were massaging her down there. Longing was replaced by a weird expectancy. Something was imminent but she had no idea what. The sweetest of tingles loomed inside her promising more. She pictured a firework and the blue touch paper was lit. The massaging teased the sensation relentlessly onward and as she reached the brink her body instinctively tensed to increase and hasten the pleasure. The explosion that followed caused her to clutch her to him to retain her equilibrium.

* * *

She was wearing the white panties he liked. He slipped them off and she uninhibitedly spread and showed what she wanted. Was there anything more glorious than a woman giving herself to you with complete abandon? He would when the time was right. He kissed her feet, teasing her purposely.

'Please,' she cried, the beseeching tone gave him pause. Perhaps he had gone too far, too slowly, not the time to blow it now. Tracing her inner thigh swiftly, he paused before licking the fold of skin amongst her pubic hair, eliciting a cry of pain, clamped his mouth on hers and massaged her slowly.

Anticipation of her impending pleasure registered in their touching lips. She groaned into his mouth and grasped him to her.

He waited patiently while she recovered, expecting to swap smiles. She solemnly touched his face and said, 'I love you.'

Now what had he done?

* * *

Why had she said that? It had slipped out. He was not happy with her declaration and could she blame him? They hardly knew each other. Something prevented her withdrawing the remark but she desperately wanted to make amends with no idea how to do it. She wished he would go to the bathroom and wash his hands.

The offending hand ran down her side and rested on the swell of her hip, causing her to recoil.

'You want me to wash my hand?'

'I'd prefer it,' she admitted.

He got out of bed and went to the bathroom, did as she asked and got back into bed.

'Why don't you ever…?'

He produced a condom from out of nowhere. 'We're going to. Later.'

They lay quietly, his hands cupping her body and she wanting to rid her declaration from his mind changed the subject. 'How did you know about those books?'

'I overheard you talking to Marcia.'

'How did you find them? I've been looking for ever.' She played with his chest hair.

'Internet,' he told her. 'I had them sent over from Canada.'

'That makes sense. Mazo de la Roche is Canadian.'

'Really?'

She looked up from his chest hair, he was laughing at her. It was kindly laughter. 'You mustn't make too much of sex.' He was referring to what she had said. 'All these new…'

'What's new about sex. I've had lots of sex.'

His face betrayed nothing. He knew she was lying. She'd had sex but not like this sex. He cupped her face in his hands and kissed her lying mouth. Within seconds the longing returned and he was immediately aware of it and slipped on his protection. With a minimum of foreplay he entered her eliciting a joyous gasp. Unlike Angus she felt no bulk on top of her, it was as if she were a pool of water and he sailed on her. Smooth, efficient, fitting as perfect as a hand in a glove, without rushing. She wondered at all this action and his magical levitation. His mouth nuzzled her neck and they synchronised, he shifted to her ear, his hand played close to their connection. Then she was lost, connected but separated, totally immersed in what was impending. Another firework appeared in her head. A red ball emerged from the box and disappeared from view. Then another and another. Waves of thrill ballooned inside her. The firework sat momentarily inert with expectancy and a final flash emerged, the red ball shot out of the box, hovered, exploded into a million sparks the length and breadth of her body and gently subsided onto her person. Instead of burning the sparkles tingled.

Cried out, God, God, God, three or four times.

* * *

He lay listening to her soft breathing. Where did this go from here? If you are being frank, nowhere. You're never going to win her over. We will all go back to Wyford and carry on as before. Briefly he pictured a life for them together. He could not get past, he in one room, she in another, meeting at meal and bedtimes.

Now he had proved what he wanted to prove, he had won and now he was bored. They had nothing in common and no future. This prosaic and deluded woman.

He sniffed the fingers he had pretended to wash. Is there a more perfect work of art than a woman? Especially a woman as beautiful as this. He turned on his side and the coverlet slipped to her waist. He watched her in the night light. A rosy nipple, decorated with wrinkles stark against the white of her skin. Her shapely hip undulating to greater secrets below the quilt. Her mouth slightly open and similar wrinkles scratched on her lips. Woman was God's greatest creation. If there were a God. He touched her breast and marvelled at its quiet silky. He took her jaw between his thumb and forefinger tracing its arc until the tips met. She was beautiful but for all she had to offer him in empathy she might as well be a blow up doll.

'Why don't you come?' she asked.

'To be honest with you, I don't know.'

They lay in the dark, each pondering the reason for his omission.

CHAPTER THIRTY-THREE

Back home

It had been a sultry evening with a full moon pending. Darkness had brought an unreliable but welcome breeze and sporadically the net curtains danced coquettishly in the window casting exotic shadows on the wall. Andy lay spread out on the sofa beneath the window unaware of the cavorting above his head. Inside his skull chemicals fermented vivid and frustrating dreams.

Friends for generations, well fed and filled with wine, hypnotised by the shadow puppets, shared a mood of mutuality. No one in the group wanted to break the spell and leave. Andy, purposely intoxicated, was snoring gently.

In respect for their sleeping friend voices were moderated, occasionally a bottle tinkled against glass and music hummed softly from the corners of the room. Chatter rolled easily, the listeners mesmerised watched the tableau flickering on the wall.

Having emerged from his mourning period, referred to by his guests as a 'fug', Andy had cooked a long overdue dinner for his friends. He had cooked his specialty and bought a box of expensive wine.

It was past midnight when steady flow of reminiscence was jogged off track as the front door bell rang.

'Who can that be?' asked Bridget.

'How the fuck should we know?' said Pete tapping his temple with a forefinger and muttering without malice. 'Stupid bitch.'

'A late comer,' as always Martin spoke in well meaning apologies. 'Who's missing?'

'I bet it's Ray,' said Pete with a laugh. 'Only that arse wipe would turn up this late.'

Nobody wanted to move and break the spell. Helen, nearest

the door made the sacrifice, jumped up went down to find out who it was. The party waited expectantly, listening to the muffled voices below.

'It's the riot police,' said Gordon. 'It's late, the music's too loud and we're past our bedtime.'

'Too bloody right.'

Footsteps mounted the stairs and Helen appeared with a woman in tow, 'This is Jinny.'

'Hello, Jinny.'

'Do you belong to Andy?'

'We work together.'

Jinny was regretting her impulsive decision to call. She had memorised Andy's address from his file. Having found the street and the house she was suddenly uncertain that 27 was the right house number. Tentatively she rung the bell and waited, feeling hemmed in by events and the unruly foliage about her. She was about to leave when she heard footsteps on the stairs and the door was opened by an enviously slim and athletic woman with bright button eyes and amused lips, 'Hello.'

'Is Andrew Avecore at home?'

'Yes,' said the woman. 'You are?'

'Jinny Parish.'

'Come on up.'

The room was filled with blurred people staring at her from behind a film of cellophane.

'They work together?' Helen repeated.

'At this time of night?' said Pete. 'Bit late for a teachers' conference.'

'Peter, leave the poor girl alone,' Bridget ordered. 'Don't mind him, have a seat.'

'Have some wine.'

'Andy's had a few too many.'

'I didn't realise Andrew had guests, I'd better go,' said Jinny, rubbing her eyes to help them acclimatise to the dark.

'Don't do that. If he wakes up and finds out we let you go, he'll never forgive us.'

'Please, stay. Have a glass of wine. What do you prefer, red or white?'

'White.'

The man called Peter got out of his armchair to fetch her drink and Helen made her sit down.

'Let me introduce everybody.' Jinny looked vaguely from face to face without hearing the name that went with it. All of the faces were welcoming and wanted to put her at her ease but she could only think of escape. She would finish her glass of wine and leave.

'There now,' said Pete handing her a glass and sitting beside her on the arm. 'How long has this been going on?'

'Peter, stop it.'

Peter was a heavy set man with an owl-like face and a suppressed aura of non-stop energy. 'We need to know these things,' Pete put his arm around Jinny's shoulders. 'I take it you're married.'

'Peter, if you don't stop it, we're leaving.'

'You don't mind do you, Jinny?'

'I do as it happens,' said Jinny. 'This is all very embarrassing. I think I'd rather go if it's all the same to you.'

'No, we'll go. I hate playing strawberry.'

'It's gooseberry not strawberry.'

'I was never much good at games,' Pete admitted. 'C'mon beautiful, take me home.'

'Best we get going to,' said Gordon. 'You coming?'

'I'll stay a little longer,' said Majeshri, Andy's next door neighbour. She had hardly spoken all evening and being addressed out of the blue she looked more like a deer with her deep brown eyes caught in the headlights

'We'll stay for a few minutes,' said Martin, a gentle and fastidious man with a shaven head and caring eyes. The way he deferred to his wife in a fond kindly way, reminded Jinny of her father. She sensed Martin's hands were at a loss and he would be more relaxed if like her father, he smoked a pipe.

Pete's progress down the stairs was loud but Andy did not stir. Majeshri asked, 'Would you prefer coffee, I certainly would. Everybody?'

'Please.'

'Would you like some help?' asked Helen.

'You keep our new guest company,' said Majeshri.

There was an embarrassed silence, awkward smiles turned into shrugs. Jinny wanted to ask about Karen but this was not the

227

moment. The room was full of objects and she struggled to see them in the subdued light.

Helen studied unabashedly, 'Is this your first time here?'

'Yes,' said Jinny coyly.

'Have you known Andy very long?' she asked.

'Just the one term. You?'

'Martin was at school with Andy,' said Helen.

'Has he changed much since his school days?'

'Andy's always hoped for a better world,' said Martin, making an excuse for the world having failed him. 'He sees himself as a crusader. It's the chink in his armour.'

'It's the little boy in him,' Helen qualified.

Majeshri returned with a tray of steaming mugs. 'Sorry but I couldn't find teacups.'

'For all his peculiar views,' said Helen. 'He's the most level-headed man I've ever met.'

'Including me,' asked Martin.

'I'm afraid so, darling.'

'When I met his parents at the funeral you could tell why,' said Majeshri.

'I've known them for twenty years. Andy says they never bug him like other parents.'

'Andy does come right out and say things doesn't he,' said Majeshri. 'Gets things out in the open.'

'He was always somewhat confrontational,' Martin offered, again seeking his wife's approval for speaking. Jinny felt another twinge of envy for the affection this man felt for his wife.

'When I first met him I thought he was arrogant,' said Helen. 'Until I knew him better, all that enthusiasm was hard to take.'

They shared another embarrassed silence. Jinny scanned the room again searching for a picture of Andrew's dead wife.

'I'll show you,' said Helen intuitively. They took their mugs of coffee and Jinny followed Helen through the flat.

The study was in the back addition and was shelved with books, except for an area above a desk and around the windows. There was a poster of Billie Holiday in the gap with photographs taped in the corners. One was of sisters in summer frocks, smiling hugely for the photographer, the younger seated in the lap of the elder who had her arms around the sister's midriff. Both girls were pretty, one conventionally with high cheekbones and perfect teeth, the younger girl had an interesting face, a snub nose spotted with freckles and her uninhibited smile producing strong laugh lines. Jinny looked closer and saw that the eyes were slightly out of alignment.

The second photo was of a teenage girl, dressed in a light blue twin set and a navy skirt on the arm of middle aged man in a suit with a pullover, shirt and tie. The suit jacket was buttoned tightly over his protruding stomach. Both parties wore serious expressions that did not strike Jinny as anyway comic.

There was a third picture of a woman in a white wedding dress. This woman beamed, celebrating with the photographer. Jinny peered closely and saw how beautiful the girl was and envied her unbridled happiness.

'Isn't she pretty.'

'Yes,' Helen agreed and caught Jinny's eye with that knowing grin worrying her mouth. 'Remind you of anyone?' she asked mockingly.

Jinny felt it was not her place to answer as she could not identify a similarity.

'At the time I met Martin he was in love with her,' Helen laughed.

'Really?'

'You couldn't help liking her.' Helen stared at the photos with her and added in a matter of fact tone. 'She was pregnant when she died.'

'Really? Sorry,' said Jinny. 'I must stop saying 'really'.'

'It is probably what caused her death. She was having a lot of morning sickness and found, or got it into her head, that if she walked a lot, she felt better.'

'How did it happen?'

'She was crossing the road and a woman jumped the lights.'

'He doesn't talk about it.'

Helen drank the last of her coffee, 'We best be getting home. Will you be OK?'

'I should probably go to.'

'Don't do that. To my knowledge Andy never got drunk before. That's got to be something to do with you. I also understand now why he is out of his 'fug'.'

'Fug?'

'Mourning for Karen. We've been trying to get him to snap out of it. You must be the reason.'

'You think so?'

'I know so.'

Majeshri had disappeared and Martin was standing, Helen's jacket over his arm, waiting to leave. 'We should go. It was nice meeting you.'

'Nice meeting you to.' She stood frozen to the spot listening to their discreet departure. The front door closed with the merest click and she and Andrew were alone. Still she was unsure about staying.

She knelt beside him, his breathing regular, his troubled face contorting. She kissed his forehead. What was to become of them? Could she give up her family for him? Her conscience claimed the answer was no, but she scarcely believed that herself. More importantly, did he want her?

He was not bad looking but not especially attractive. Those sensitive hands of his, that was what she had come there for. They fired a wanting inside her that was not yet free from shame. She clasped her hand between her legs, pressing, trying to suppress the need.

She felt an urge to impart what she was feeling in some physical way for his benefit but was at a loss. Kissing the forehead of a sleeping child was nice and motherly but what was driving this impulse was not the least maternal.

The few square inches of living room wall left uncovered were painted terracotta. There was a large poster of dancing men, their outlines not completely filled with colour and they were maypolling around a plant pot on a table. She studied it closely but could not find anything to like about it. Nor any of the other artwork.

She peered at the photo collages. Andrew as a boy in football kit, pulling faces and a teenager smiling awkwardly. Studying the pictures so closely she knocked the litter bin over. Clearing up the mess she found an unopened magazine from Cambridge University and the envelope was addressed to Andrew Avecore MA. Cantab.

How strange that he would keep this provenance a secret. How many more secrets were there?

* * *

She sat, legs tucked under and wished hard for him to wake.

What a week it had been. She half-hoped Angus would be at the airport but he was not even waiting at the school, nor had there been any kind of message.

No matter which way Jinny's mind led her it inevitably left her alone on a desert island but with no Man Friday. Along with all the new sensations she had learned recently, fear scythed through her.

As she put the key in the door, she was as nervous as a stranger. What did the house have in store for her? She would rather it kept its secret for another time. She was tired and in no mood for confrontation. She was not even sure Angus was home. His Mercedes was on the driveway, lights were on in bedroom and hallway, the door had not been Chubb locked but these clues signified nothing. Angus had codes of behaviour for others that slipped his own sense of propriety.

Feeling like a burglar she crept inside, dreading what she would find. Angus had animal intelligence. That was a huge factor in his becoming CEO. He had a nose for people's weakness and relished manipulating those weaknesses. Would he smell her guilt? Would he detect her adultery? Did she reek of sin?

Leaving her suitcase in the hall, she tiptoed to the kitchen. Pans, plates and cutlery were strewn everywhere. Rubbish propped up the dustbin lid and piles of newspapers covered the table.

In the lounge she found similar mayhem. What had happened to Lena? The television was on with the mute button activated. She then heard a distant moaning sound coming from the study. She crept to the door and peered in. On the computer screen a couple were copulating at an extraordinary angle. The woman was thrashing about, faking a climax. Angus was sitting in his revolving leather chair, eating from a plate.

Jinny returned to the front door, left the house with her suitcase and closed the door after her. She rang the bell loudly and persistently. She waited patiently but he did not answer the door and Jinny rang the bell again.

'Hold your horses. I'm coming,' he called.

As Angus opened the door he was wiping his hands with a towel. 'Where's your key?'

'I packed it by mistake,' she stepped inside, he made no move to help her with her case.

'Isn't that typical of a woman. In a supermarket queue, the last thing a woman expects is to pay. Get to the front door the last thing you would expect to need is a key.'

That was the end of the matter for the time being. Angus had nothing more to say and disappeared back to the study. Jinny had a long relaxing bath and slept in the spare room.

It was the following evening that matters at home came to a head and via an unexpected source.

Jinny went to school as normal and was careful to avoid Andrew. In a weak moment she had declared love for him and it was obvious he did not return that sentiment. She had humiliated herself. They had sat apart on the return flight.

At home that evening, not sure if Angus was going to join her, she prepared dinner for two but chose a meal that would be equally satisfactory for one, to be eaten over two nights. These solitary preparations made her sad and she struggled not to feel sorry for herself. Less than a month ago everything was normal and now her world was upside down. If it had not been for the night of Margery's party she would not have followed through with her little infatuation. That is all it was. A little infatuation. Isn't it amazing how circumstances can conspire together. Some of the pieces of her rationalising did not fit but she pushed these aside. She could leave Angus. On the known evidence she had right on her side but she would be alone. She could not face being alone.

She stopped what she was doing and gave Bobby a hug and petted him for a few minutes while the vegetables came to the boil.

She washed her hands, dished up her plate and started eating when a delegation crashed through the house like a tidal wave, carrying Angus in its wake.

He ushered the Parish matriarchs into the kitchen and they dismissed him to a far corner of the house. The Gorgons closed in on her, their tentacles flaying and smoke emanating from their nostrils. Jinny, curiously, was not intimidated and continued consuming her meal.

'How can you be so unconcerned?' asked Aunt Sadie.

'I'm doing the talking,' Wendy explained to Sadie fiercely. 'We agreed. Angus is my son.'

Wendy, dressed in Burberry checks, puffed herself up like a set of bagpipes. 'I'm going to be perfectly frank you with you, missie. I've never liked you much. I think you tricked my boy into marriage and significantly bettered yourself. I've noticed the airs and graces you lay claim to but you don't pull the wool over my eyes. Your family might go running off with flotsam and jetsam but the Parish's are a cut above all that. We are a proud family. There has never been a divorce in the Parish clan and there is not going to be one now. Do you understand?'

Jinny, seething inside but afraid to speak, nodded and took another mouthful with exaggerated gentility. She avoided their faces and to keep her temper she studied the three women's hands. Navvies hands, clumsy, inarticulate artisans' hands, ludicrously manicured and polished. Perhaps they were once men who had a sex change or perhaps they were men. Transvestites.

'You think this is a laughing matter? I want you to understand, missie, that this is one of the most serious moments of your miserable life.'

'Ah!' exclaimed Jinny, glad to latch onto a morsel. 'You're right about something, at last. My life is miserable.'

Defiantly she met each of their faces in turn. They were certainly alike. Mops of hair, the texture of the Dulux dog, each dyed in streaks of ludicrous colour. Pinched mouths misshapen with lipstick and nasty eyes filled with venom.

'*Hubble bubble*‘, '*toil*' and '*trouble*'.

'It was my birthday last Thursday,' said Jinny gathering up a further forkful of food and holding it poised at her mouth. 'I did not get a single birthday card from the Parish family, including your darling boy.'

Angus' mother glared at her, that snippy mouth waiting to spit nastiness in her face. 'Have you considered whose fault that might be?'

'I'm not the guilty party,' said Jinny blushing with guilt from the lie on her tongue. 'I'm not the adulterer.'

'None of my boys have ever needed to console themselves elsewhere. You get my meaning. I suggest you look to your laurels, missie. We have told Angus he's to stop seeing this woman. They'll be no more hanky panky. I believe there will be what is known as a reconciliation.'

'There will?' Jinny was no longer taking the matter lightly and lay the fork back on her plate.

'One thing you can be sure of,' said his mother. 'A Parish promise is a promise that will be kept. He knows that if he doesn't, it's his neck that will be broken.'

The witches trouped out in line, stage left. They were like a trio of ponies leaving the circus arena in trained unison. They did not have the tails but their rumps fitted the bill. Angus, *hovering through the fog and filthy air,* appeared sheepishly carrying a dozen red roses. Their reconciliation continued in bed that night but their lovemaking did nothing to deter her need for Andrew.

She lay awake, feeling Angus' naked body warm and safe, his heavy breathing resonating. Like he had promised his mother, she too planned to put an end to her mortal sin before anyone found out about it.

* * *

Choosing a suitable rendezvous for breaking off with Andrew proved a problem. There were dangers to avoid. Where could she make the break and not be seen or even worse, interrupted. Nowhere in school would be safe. None of the pubs in Wyford were suitable, almost all of them were habitués of the staff. They could meet at his flat but she suspected that she might fail to remain vertical. She was at a loss and then she remembered the Premier Hotel.

She left a note in Andrew's pigeon hole and arrived early to check that they could be discreet and remain undisturbed. On her single visit to the Hotel she noticed that the bar was empty. She ordered a gin and tonic to steady her nerves and sussed out quickly why this was the case. Not a hundred yards away you could get a drink for half the price.

On her first visit she had been impressed by the light and airy atmosphere the décor imparted. Now, waiting, seeing the blemishes, the hotel was cheap and seedy. A place tailor made for afternoon trysts.

He arrived dead on time and his puzzled face asked, 'Can I get you another?'

Seeing him, she quaked with a mixture of want and what must be. 'No,' she said and swallowed hard. 'You go ahead.'

'I'm not thirsty,' he said and sat opposite. 'What's up?' He tried to take her hand but she pulled away.

'You know,' she pleaded. 'Don't you?'

'I guessed you were avoiding me for a reason. Had second thoughts. What is it I did?' He was playing for sympathy but she had her duty to do.

'You made it obvious that you don't love me...'

'New sex plays tricks on you. It's the adrenalin.'

'It was nothing to do with sex. I meant what I said.'

'You only think you mean it. It was wonderful but love isn't that simple.'

Did he have a point? Was she wrong about her feelings? What did it matter? It was irrelevant, she had her family to think of and she must put them first. She must put an end to this and it must be now.

'Why did you yell at me like that?' she asked, finding it easy to be indignant.

'I don't want you to run me a bath. I'm a big boy I can run my own bath. I don't want you to be a door mat or a bath mat for that matter. I don't want to be bought with niceness. I like you for what you are.'

This was what she most feared, a scene, but a part of her was flattered by what he said and she hoped he meant it. His eyes were showing more and more hurt and she was enjoying his pain.

'I don't want to see you again. There I've said it,' she said gleefully, proud with herself but the hurt vanished from his eyes and was replaced with an unfamiliar steel.

'Everything OK at home?' His voice was tinged with disappointment.

'What d'you mean?'

'The night of Margery's party your husband threw a wobbly. The way you've been carrying on since. Sorry, that sounds bad. The way you've been since suggests he has a bird on the side...'

Jinny felt like a kettle coming to the boil. Words dashed into her head, words she would not normally speak.

'...When you didn't get a birthday message from him I thought the marriage was over.'

His eyes grew fearful again. He saw that he had gone too far. He must have gleaned this from the expression on her face. 'You arrogant bastard,' she hissed.

'Arrogant, yes. Bastard, no.'

'Do you have to make jokes?'

'If I don't make jokes, I'm going to start crying.'

Behind Andrew, as Jinny had planned, she had a full view of the hotel reception. In the event that someone they knew might arrive she could take precautionary measures. She saw a couple enter the hotel, arm in arm. The man rang the reception bell with a flourish, gave over his credit card and signed a piece of paper. For this ritual he was presented with a key. He waved it playfully at his companion and still arm in arm, they moved away toward the lifts.

Jinny jumped to her feet, 'I'm sorry. I can't do this now. I've got to go.'

* * *

THIRTY-FOUR

Andy's place

A strong breeze puffed through the window and the net curtains shimmied violently. Suddenness brought her back to the moment and she saw the man she had ditched at the Hotel bar watching her. 'You're awake.'

'Well spotted.'

'Why didn't you say anything?'

'I like watching you.' He beckoned her to him but she refused to obey. 'Come here.'

'No.'

'Come here,' he insisted. 'Please.'

She shook her head, 'This is the new me. I'm no longer a doormat.'

He sat up and immediately regretted it. He held his head in hands until it cleared. Seeing his distress she sat beside and rubbed the back of his neck. 'How come you're drunk? That's not like you.'

'As it happens it was all for nothing,' he opened his hands and let her view a wicked grin.

'I was just about to leave…' He took her jaw in his hand and waited a time before kissing her. The ache in her groin fired fiercely and playtime was over. 'Are we?'

'Not tonight.'

'Why not?'

'I've got a headache.'

There was a ring of the front doorbell. 'I'd better go and see who that is. Somebody probably left something.' He got to his feet and wobbled precipitously.

'Never mind,' said Jinny, pushing him back onto the couch. 'I'll go.'

She found the light, managed the stairs, opened the door and came face to face with Gillian Finn. 'My car's broken down.'

* * *

Jinny studied the ceiling and wryly recollected her expert knowledge of anaglyptic papers. Her lifetime experience of bedroom architecture, including ceilings, had almost doubled in just two weeks.

They lay entwined, awake and content. Jinny propped herself on an elbow and with her free hand brushed his hair from his face even though it did not need brushing.

'Do you think she heard anything?'

'The whole bloody street heard.' She took him seriously and bit her lip but he was more surprised the 'bloody' went without a reprimand.

She surveyed the sand walls, assessing how soundproof they were. The moonlight glowed on the glass fronted paintings and puzzles were posed in every colour of the rainbow.

'Why do you keep so many secrets?' she asked.

'Why do you?'

'If I'm going to keep seeing you and there is no guarantee, you are to stop being hostile. If I ask a question it's supposed to get an answer not a hostile question back.'

'Point taken,' he said. 'Why do you?'

'You're impossible.'

'I'm impossible. You meet me in some cheap hotel and tell me you never want to see me again. Look very pleased with yourself while doing it I might add. Then you turn up here without any explanation and have your evil way with me and I'm impossible. You must think I'm some sort of easy lay.'

'I don't think anything of the kind.'

'I wouldn't worry about it. You only have to click your fingers and I'm yours.'

'Really.'

'Really. I fancy you, big time. Happy now?'

'Tell me I'm beautiful some more.'

'You cheeky cow.'

Once again wanting to express her feelings for him she kissed his forehead. In her mind it did not require a response but he misinterpreted her intentions and tried to kiss her back. If it had been Angus she would have offered to run a bath, iron a shirt or fetch his dry cleaning.

Pulling away she said, 'Stop that. Secrets.'

'I'm not sure what secret you're referring to.'

'Cambridge.'

'Oh that,' he tried to pull her to him but again she resisted. 'My mother says it's a family trait. A fault in the male line. All the first born for as far back as can be traced are males and they share many weird idiosyncrasies.'

'That doesn't explain the secrets.'

'One of which is that we have a tendency to be self-deprecating. I'm embarrassed by the kudos other people put on Cambridge. It's no big deal. My dad is similar.'

'Did he go to Cambridge?'

'L.S.E. My grandfather was also cool like that.'

'Cool?' Jinny was making fun of him for sounding like the students.

'Yeah, well wicked. Where we went to church their was an elder called Captain Bull…'

'That's my maiden name.'

'You're kidding. I hope this man is no relation. You have family in Enfield?'

'None that I know of.'

'Captain Bullshit we called him. The Captain wore a blazer with his regimental badge and spoke with gravity about the 'War'. My grandfather who barely spoke about another human being without respect, and could see the worthy side of the saddest cases, disliked this man with a passion. While he was alive I never took the trouble to ask and find out why. I was too young to understand.'

'What was there to understand?'

'My grandad didn't talk about the war much. Thought of it as a job he had to do. The Fascists had to be beaten.'

'What branch of the services was he?'

'Army. You know how so many of that generation went on about the war because it was the most significant experience of their lives. Grandad didn't have much good to say about the army. My abiding image of the man, nose in a book, smoking, with an endless stream of smoke billowing out of his nostrils. I asked him what book made the best reading of how the army truly was.'

'Who did he recommend?'

'Sword of Honour. He said that the Trimble character summed up the army to a T. That man Captain Bull from our church who went on about the 'War' was a quartermaster at Aldershot.'

'What rank was your grandfather?'

'Major.'

'Did he see action?'

'He spoke Italian fluently. Does that help?'

'Not really.'

'What am I going to do with you?' He caressed her face. 'Your turn. Chipping up here on a Saturday night without a note from your mother.'

'I can't...'

'What about Thursday. Running off suddenly without an explanation.'

'I can't tell you.'

'Yes you can. I'm not going to lie here judging you.'

'No but you will pity me and that's worse.'

He thought about that for a while. During these intense exchanges his judgement was poor. He expected her to be as positive about their new intimacy as he was. Every time she came he wanted to stand on the roof and yell 'yippee', something worthwhile just happened. He rarely saw the need for negativity but women have post-natal depression, men do not. Perhaps women get post-coital depression. No, that was more of a male province.

He could not pity her any more than he did already and his pity was not for her marriage.

Where he failed was to be sure that what he did and said was received with the intention in what was imparted. So many times his audience did not hear what he said. He assumed they were not listening, assured of a response they were expecting and not able to cope with a response they were not expecting. They ignored what they misheard. How facile life is in literature where misrepresentations are few.

He understood she was vulnerable and had warned himself to be on his guard and not be playful in ways that she did not understand. Joy got the better of him. He was carried away on a wave of exhilaration that was crashing all about them. He had lost her and now she was back. He was a spoiled child who had been given back his toy.

He pushed her on her back and expressed his feelings with tactile small talk. Soft fingers teasing her breasts until the nipples hardened. Licking them tantalisingly, resting his cheek on her stomach and nuzzling her pubic hair with his nose.

'What are you doing?'

'I'm smelling your secret self like a dog. Are you sure there aren't any skeletons in your cupboard?'

'What kind of skeletons?'

He flipped his body to face her, 'Your hair colour and down there,' he raised his eyebrows. 'Around the dirty bit. The colour is so un-English. So…'

'So what?'

'Unique.'

'Is it?'

He nodded, 'You have to tell me. Everything, or all this sex is pointless.'

'I don't see the connection.'

'If we share we're human. If we fuck we're animals.'

'You've kept things from me.'

'They're not pertinent to us. What is hurting you and driving you to me, here, now, in my bed, being indescribably beautiful is pertinent to me.'

She pretended to think about what he had said but this need to touch him, to return this physical affection swept over her. She noted his penis, within her reach but that was not a suitable place to express what she felt. It was too explicit and unsubtle.

'You're not going to tell are you?' He turned over, pressed his face into the pillow and pretended to cry. The duvet, caught in her legs, left part of his leg and the swell of his bum uncovered. Putting her hand on that part of his body felt so right and her fingers could discern a favourable reaction. She was inspired and greedy for more and stimulated by these responses. Her hand made out the shape of his back, caressed his neck and wended its way back down. If she really excited him, he might climax. Momentarily doubt returned and was quickly forgotten as she concentrated on what she was doing, surprised that giving was a pleasurable exercise.

He smelled so nice. So Andrew. She took his hand and placed it in her mouth and bit his palm softly. He turned to watch her and she dry kissed his fingers.

It was not he who had grown undeniably hot but she, and again she beat him to a climax.

They lay for a long time, neither moving or talking, each wondering in their different ways what was happening and why.

Jinny was in a new and unimaginable world. Why was she comfortable and happy in this strange man's bed? At the hairdresser's she read articles claiming the weird and wonderful with a pinch of salt. This was young persons' domain, a strange world of flight and fancy. Would it be as natural if he were in her bed? No fear, there her eyes would not be on the ceiling there but on the door. Was Angus wondering where she had got to?

Andy's thoughts were vacillating. Secrets, Jinny's new self and other phantoms. Was Karen's ghost watching him defile their bed?

Jinny had come a long way from the woman who clamped his hand and claimed, 'down there is dirty' to licking the fingers that touched. He did not want to know what had brought about such a reformation, the truth was too big a burden to be carrying at three in the morning.

What had been going on in that Wyford double fronted?

His arm was going to sleep and he shifted slightly. She moved her body to fit his new position and put his hand back where it had been. 'I like it there,' she announced, kissed his cheek and nuzzled into his neck.

'The night of the party at Margery's, Angus had a sort of breakdown...'

'I knew...'

'Please,' she clamped his mouth. 'No jokes. He's in love with his PA but she doesn't love him. Nothing was resolved before the American trip and when I got back nothing much had changed. On the Tuesday Angus' mother and his two aunts came to the house like some sort of delegation. His mother said that there will be no divorce and there was to be a reconciliation. Angus and I made up.'

'How…?' She put her hand back over his mouth.

'We met on Thursday. While I was talking to you I saw Angus and his PA come into the hotel and take a room.'

'What are you going to do?'

'I honestly don't know.'

'You can stay here if you like.'

'No,' she said flatly. 'We both know that's not a good idea. Odd emotions because of new sex. I'll find a flat or something.'

Light was breaking when they finally dropped off and she woke with a start, lost in the unfamiliar surroundings and unfamiliar noises coming from other parts of the flat.

Jinny put on Andrew's dressing gown and went to the bathroom. She searched the medicine cabinet but was unable to find a new toothbrush. She surveyed his brush and considered. His tongue had been in her mouth why not his toothbrush.

Gillian, dressed and ready to leave, sat on the couch watching television, a breakfast bowl balanced in her lap. Still sheepish, she looked guardedly at the older woman. 'What have you decided?'

'I could run you home and your father could deal with the car or…'

'Or what?'

'I don't know. Perhaps Andrew will have a bright idea.'

'I'm sorry about all this but I had nowhere else to go. I was stranded.'

'I believe you,' Jinny lied.

'Could I make you some breakfast?'

'I don't mean to be rude but I'd rather do my own. Having you do it for me makes me feel like I'm in my dotage.'

Gillian shrugged and returned to the screen.

Jinny made some coffee and toast, checked on Andrew who was fast asleep. Jinny felt disinclined to leave this girl alone with a man she had no hold over.

Images flashed on the screen and having nothing else to take her attention she followed the narrative. By the time she finished her breakfast she was totally engrossed. She sat next to Gillian on the settee and tucked her legs under her.

'I don't know where he finds these films.'

'What language is this?'

'Scandinavian?'

They spent a quiet hour or so. When it finished Gillian put the film back in its box and the box in its place on the shelf.

'You shouldn't worry about me,' Gillian confessed.

'How so.'

'Andrew and I didn't do it. He has to be emotionally involved to…you know. From what I heard you don't have to worry about me. I'm not a threat to you. You should be grateful for your good luck.'

'What else did you hear?'

'I won't tell anyone, I promise. Not even Margery.'

'Promise,' the young woman clasped her hands together. 'In that case I'll give you that lift.'

'Thanks.'

'I'll get dressed.'

Andrew was awake and watched her dress.

'I'm going to take Gillian home.'

'Will you come back later.'

'I don't see how I can.'

'I'm going away on Saturday morning for a long weekend. Coming back Tuesday.'

'Where?'

'France.'

'Oh,' she put her hand to her mouth. 'What am I to do?'

'Come with me.'

'Seriously?'

'Seriously.'

CHAPTER THIRTY-FIVE
Antibes outward bound

The airport was frenetic with passengers towing luggage. There was no structure to the mayhem. Jinny and Andy remained at ease, feigning the air of an established couple. On the same wave length, observing the foibles of their fellow travellers, amused at their anxieties and oblivion. They checked in without a hiccup and ate a breakfast of coffee and croissants, with every bite liberally spraying a snowstorm of flour.

Seating was in rows of three. They were near the back, fortunately no one occupied the aisle seat. As they took off she took his hand and he did not mind being cute. He was looking forward to a weekend of sunshine, good food and sex. Halfway through the flight the third of those was scuppered.

'I've started my period,' she whispered.

At Nice airport they were met by the car hire company and she was impressed with how easily he spoke the language. They drove smoothly along the coast road, blue sky and sea to the left and ribbons of building painted sparkling white, pink and yellow ochre capped with orange pantiles to the right.

'You speak French well.'

'I should,' said Andy. 'I did a French degree.'

'I thought you did English.'

'I know,' said Andy. 'Another secret. Teaching French would be too dull. I was lucky enough to be sent down here for my year abroad. I made a few friends and the flat we're staying in belongs to Jerome.'

As the sprawl of untidy towns grew denser the traffic made slower progress in an unbroken chain of stuttering cars. Andy pulled the car off the main road at a place called Biot, slipped under a railway bridge and headed inland. They negotiated a series of roundabouts, passed a stall selling giant tomatoes and a college for the study of olive produce.

Gradually the scenery grew prosperous. Landscaping grew thicker, houses less utility, there were flower beds separating the road lanes. Laurier rose bushes, birds of paradise and plumbago flourished in the clear air. Bougainvillea climbed fences and stair rails in clumps of strident red and mauve. They turned into a street with a garden centre dwarfed amongst apartment blocks. High on the top of the street Andy turned the car through 180 degrees to enter an automatic gate enclosed among a cluster of fir trees. The car crunched over a carpet of cones and he pulled into a car space in front of a four storey apartment block. They wheeled their luggage through a winding path with a cavalcade of olive trees, pyracanthus bushes thick with orange berries and lush grass speckled with daisies. Inside the flat block was cool and peaceful, the lift's progress spoiling the serenity. They alighted onto an unlit hallway with three doors feeding off. Their's was the middle flat.

Inside was dark and shadowy. Andy pressed a button and the rickety shutters clattered open flooding the room with light and colour. The walls were painted orangey yellow and the furnishings were Provencal. The bedroom had a blue and yellow duvet cover, the tablecloths were red and gold. Chinese sculptures sat inscrutably on antique furniture and impressionist posters pulsated on the walls. They went out onto a balcony that was the full width of the accommodation. To the right was a bell tower, all that was left of a once grand chateau, beyond the bell tower stretched the town of Antibes against a backdrop of Cap d'Antibes with its cedars and firs posing on the horizon. To the left was the coastline, the Baie des Anges and Nice sleeping in the afternoon haze. An aeroplane made its way across the bay to land at Nice Airport.

Below them, thick with vegetation were the gardens and a further crop of olive trees that were striving to outgrow the block. Birds fluttered and cried, cicadas croaked incessantly and not a car could be heard.

'It's beautiful,' she said.

'Yeah.' Andy, wistful for oats, was slightly irritable that he was not going to get any.

After stocking up at the supermarket, they showered, dressed and walked in to Antibes for dinner. It was a warm night and ordinarily Andy would have chosen to eat outside. Still wanting solitude he picked a restaurant in one of the alleys off the main square. It was decorated with olde worlde décor, fake beams, strings of garlic, hanging copper pots, marmites and Pavlova on the walls.

Andy asked for a table in the rear section, where the air conditioning was most effective. They sat directly under the fan, which stirred with a comfortable hum.

'What do you like to eat?'

'I like most things.'

'My friend Harry, he's just become a parent again so he wasn't at the party that night, is pro-English like you. He won't eat anything unless it's egg and chips, roast beef and Yorkshire pudding, stuff like that. He came down here for a holiday and he ate pommes frites for two weeks.'

'Did I do something to upset you?'

'No,' Andy pretended to be suitably mystified but they both knew she had. She just did not know what the problem was.

'Why are you attacking me?'

'I didn't realise you were taking it personally. You seem to take everything I say personally.'

'You're doing it again.'

'Sorry. What are you going to have?'

'I'd like the crevettes mayonnaise and faux filet.'

'Prawn cocktail, steak and chips,' he translated.

'What's wrong with that? Good wholesome food.'

The waiter made a timely arrival, 'Je vous ecoute.'

They gave their order, Jinny in perfect French with a better accent than his own. The waiter turned over their glasses and hurried off.

'Salop.'

'What does that mean?'

'Dearest darling.'

'I'll bet,' she said. 'Angus speaks French impeccably. He has a talent for languages. The twins are taking after their father.'

Andy, because sex was not on the menu, was teetering on the edge of irritation. This saccharine pose she adopted for her family caused a violent wave of annoyance. He took a drink and waited before speaking.

'Naturally,' he said with much more sarcasm than he intended. It would not do to fall out on the first day. She had not noticed anything untoward and carried blithely on. Angus this, the twins that.

They walked home through the empty streets in the warm night air reeking of pine, past the carousel, the sleeping shops and cafes with the cicadas still going full throttle. They sat on the balcony in the dark for a while and then went to bed early.

* * *

CHAPTER THIRTY-SIX

Jinny meets his parents

The gardens were a variety of shrubs with flowers, spiky mauve, orange yellow, pale blue. The streets sloped steeply down, punctuated with parasol pine and olive trees and in the distance was the harbour wall and sailing boats skittering along bright blue sea beneath cloudless sky.

The town was sleepy in the summer sun. It was hot, the local population lingered over lunch beneath awnings, umbrellas or cooled in air conditioned cafes.

They entered a square where fountains gurgled and the first miniature train of the afternoon serpentined its way to Juan.

Free seats in the cafes beside the bus station were hard to find and the cobbled street was sparse with occasional promenaders. They continued on to the car park square and stopped at the drinking fountain in the far corner. Andy guided her to a shaded seat and asked what she wanted to drink.

They sat silently soaking up the atmosphere, observing the other tables and infrequent passers by. Jinny got an odd feeling that Andrew was expecting someone but she had learned that questions were rarely supplied with answers. They sat dreamily quiet for almost half an hour. She was fascinated by the pigeons taking the waters. Her companion broke into a broad smile and stood to greet a middle aged couple.

The woman, she estimated was approaching sixty, she had blonde hair, dark glasses and a square face that had once been pretty. She wore a turquoise T-shirt which bulged with breasts and coffee coloured cargoes that bulged softly at the belt. The man was tall, head shaved virtually clean and blue eyes. He wore a soft blue shirt open at the collar with 'Antibes' on the breast pocket and white shorts. His midriff was also protruding in the belt region but he camouflaged his bulge by wearing his shirt outside his shorts. Their bare arms and legs were healthily tanned.

'Hi,' said Andy. 'I thought you might turn up here.'

There was a reorganisation of chairs and once they were comfortable, Andy introduced his mother and father. Neither parent showed surprise at his being there but both were glad to see him. His mother pumped him with questions about his new job and his father sat patiently enjoying their conversation. He also shyly checked her out, studying her with practiced eyes.

Without realising quite how Jinny had been made to feel comfortable. His parents percolated a warmth that infected her with a need to return their geniality. In a few minutes she felt as though she had known them years.

'I've been assigned to pastoral care. I've had to deal with all sorts of problems. Exclusions, that's the new word for expulsion. I've even had to cross swords with a barrister over a boy being excluded.'

'I'm glad to be away from it all,' said his father. 'I don't pretend to understand modern teenagers but I can't say I like them much. Your generation was selfish but this current one is off the chart.'

'Jeff,' said his mother. 'You make yourself sound old and crabby.'

'I'm not old and crabby,' he replied. 'I used to be young and crabby but I'm growing out of it.'

'The young have all the power and they don't know how to deal with it,' Andy summoned the waiter with a wave.

'It's because they have all the power they have nothing to rebel against. Their protests are silent, secret and sulky,' Dorothy Avecore stopped to read the menu while the waiter hovered. 'Orangina, s'il vous plait. Do you have children, Jinny?'

'Two boys, twins. Alex and James.'

'How old?'

'Seventeen. They've just taken their A levels.' She left it there and saw Andy smiling inscrutably.

'I've heard a lot of viewpoints on this topic of teenage angst some of which are clearly pertinent but there are no easy answers and no easy cure.'

'We as parents, at least a generation before, did the wrong thing. You can't be friends with your children.'

'True. You can't give them everything they want and then accuse them of being materialistic.'

'They are nevertheless.'

'I am not the least materialistic,' Andy interrupted his mother.

'No,' said his mother. 'That's true but your selfishness has left you with a poor sense of duty.'

Andy was obviously hurt by this rebuke and was about to defend himself but because of Jinny's presence and this being her first meeting with strangers he let it go. It was no time for a family spat.

'How d'you mean?' he asked. This was a new Andrew. He put his question in a tone that reminded her of Year 11 and the accused was clearly going to protest his innocence and blame another party.

'We contact our parents every week. When did you last contact your grandparents?'

'Since Karen...'

'Andrew,' his mother interrupted angrily. 'It was the same while Karen was alive. You only phone when it's convenient. If you visited them just once a month it would take the pressure off us but even that is too much trouble.'

There was a pregnant silence. Andy's complexion, already ruddier from a day in the sun deepened to cherry. His head bowed and he studied his hands, struggling not to respond with some petulant riposte. He was tongue tied because the accusation had some foundation.

Jinny, embarrassed for him, struggled to find a suitable question to lighten the moment. She looked to his father for inspiration, who merely smiled and raised his eyebrows.' So what are the official reasons for the suffering of the modern teenager?'

'Isn't it the times we live in,' suggested Jinny. 'It's hard to rebel in a period of prosperity.'

'You are totally right, a person cannot grow without adversity,' said Jeff. 'Andrew knows that better than most.'

Jinny felt inflamed by his father's approval. Andy shifted out of his hangdog slump and gave his mother and father a quick glance each.

'In our day we dissed our parents because they were uncool and, more essentially, old,' said Dorothy. 'Now we live in a youth culture where nobody wants to get old. Nobody admits or accepts they are getting old.'

'Like you calling me crabby.'

Dorothy ignored him, 'Adults and authority no longer command respect. Politicians, TV personalities, even the Royal Family are sleeping around.'

'They always were but now it gets into the news...'

Jeff was interrupted by a cheeky pigeon landing on the neighbouring table and pecking at the remains of a baguette and knocking over a glass. With remarkable reflexes Andy's father caught it before it hit the ground. Without comment he replaced it on the table.

'...Television portrays our politicians, our police as totally corrupt. Swearing has become commonplace because it is on television so often it has lost its impact.'

'There's a theory that England's flood of creativity started in the 60's was brought about by the need to rebel and as this rebellion has subsided the creativity has fallen away.' Jinny continued while Andy remained sullen.

'It's not so much rebellion anymore as bad behaviour.'

'Tantrums,' said Dorothy, lighting up a cigarette.

'There is another side to this,' Jeff leaned forward and momentarily touched his son's knee and sat back again. 'The parents don't develop. My generation carry on like teenagers.'

Andy waved away a plume of smoke.

'Society is shrinking,' said Jeff and coughed half-heartedly. 'Special interests are being marginalised.'

'Soap operas don't help,' Dorothy stopped to allow the waiter to serve their drinks. 'Merci. You have a character die in Monday's episode and by Thursday their fiance is engaged to someone else. I'm exaggerating but children will accept what is on the television as normal behaviour.'

Deciding that Andy was not going to contribute until he had had it out with his mother Jinny discreetly excused herself and reposed in the cubicle for longer than was necessary.

'Did you have to do that now?' Andy remonstrated.

'Yes,' said Dorothy. 'I did. It's needed saying for a long time.

If Jinny had not been with you I would of got the 'Oh for goodness sake' that I normally get. The time was right.'

'Now you've made me look foolish in front of my friend.'

'You'll get over it,' said his mother. 'You can't grow without adversity. Some silly prat told me that. Anyway if I know women, your friend will be thrilled to have seen the little boy in you.'

Jinny returned to find her ploy was paying off.

'Youngsters seem to give up too easily,' said Jeff. 'I don't mean just divorce. Friends of ours who live here have a daughter who has chucked her place at Cambridge at the end of the first year. We don't know all the details but the parents went along with her choice when she should have been made to persevere.'

'Perhaps it's because she's a girl and it doesn't matter so much.'

'It matters,' said Jeff. 'Her parents are nice decent people but they aren't doing the girl any favours.'

'We're becoming like America, the young are finding it hard to maintain a commitment.'

'What's all this counselling about?' asked Dorothy. 'We survived without mental breakdowns.'

'I don't know.'

'We had family.'

'Jack and Joy are a close knit caring family but Charley quit Cambridge and had a breakdown. You can't say they didn't care. Expectations were less than they are now. We simply got on with life because life was more straightforward.'

'I keep coming back to the marked difference between now and then. It's the power of television.'

'There were films.'

'Once or twice a week. TV is all day everyday.'

'Andy,' said Jeff. 'You haven't had much to say. What do you think?'

'I blame the teachers.'

* * *

There was a fond farewell and they agreed to meet for lunch the following day. As they retraced their steps back through the town, the sun had lost its strength and the town was thronging with shoppers and sightseers. They waited in the queue of a charcuterie and Andy ordered dinner.

As they made there way back up the hill to the apartment Andy apologised.

'What's there to be sorry for?'

'My mother,' he whinged. 'And me.'

'It's a funny thing,' she said, leaning forward and struggling to put one foot in front of the other. 'It's a shame. I never felt more like making love with you than I do now.'

Inwardly Andy's frustration flared higher. His mother had been right about Jinny's reaction to his ticking off. He did not want to concede that he was remiss in his diligence to his grandparents. Just to be on the safe side he would visit as soon as he got home.

CHAPTER THIRTY-SEVEN

Cap Ferrat

Never had she been so content. He lay sleeping quietly, so quietly that she checked that he was still breathing, the way she had done with the twins when they were first born, putting her ear to their mouths and resisting the temptation to prod. She touched his naked thigh and he shifted perceptibly.

It was good to be away. She could not remember a time when she was not constantly juggling. If it was not dexterity with time and management it was trying to keep everyone in her life happy. She bent over backwards to accommodate the three of them and more often than not her plans blew up in her face. All her efforts seemed to come to nothing. She only did these because she cared about them but all her good intentions rarely brought reward. She was a fool to herself.

They had watched a film that evening and the characters had transported her to a forgotten time. Eight years old and sitting in a theatre for the first time she was as happy as she had ever been. Sat deep in a red velvet seat waiting for the play to begin an air of expectancy murmuring all around. The dimmed lights, the cerise curtain with gold piping and tassels and the dusty smell of face powder. Puck's irresistible energy had captivated her and created a mood and an atmosphere in her memory that had not been matched until this evening.

They were still unable to make love because of her period and she had intended to go to bed early. Andy put the DVD on and somehow the plot had regenerated her. Not only did she see the film through but they went to bed, kissed, talked and fondled. She did not tire of his mouth pressed to hers or his gentle fingers tracing the shape of her breasts and hips or teasing her libido at the top of her bottom cheeks.

She had not experienced happiness like this with Angus, nor from her children. What was she thinking, placing her face in her hands and shivering with shame. How could she think such a thing? What would become of her. She fell into a troubled sleep and dreamed of crowds of people pointing her out.

* * *

The cafe was above the marina. Below, boats bobbed gently in the breeze, gleaming sails in the sunshine, stark white against the blue sea and sky. It was lunchtime and the walkways were empty.

The foursome sat quietly, soaking up the prosperity while a petulant waitress reeked havoc amongst the tables. Customers asking for salt and pepper received cruet with a crash. The adjacent table was cleared with clatter and was taken by four youngsters, who greeted them politely with raised eyebrows, friendly smile and a 'bonjour'.

'Young French adults are not as dismissive of old people as their British counterparts,' Andy's father whispered.

Andy also assumed they were French but their conversation proved otherwise and he listened wanting to establish their nationality. They were well educated and were showing off, talking alternately in French, German, Italian and English and had all studied abroad at one time or other.

The grouchy waitress took their order with a petulant scrawl and the boy nearest to them continued. He described his experiences in very good English with an unidentifiable accent. 'Italians are wonderful people. I love them and when I came here to France I was warned that the French are arrogant and generally unpleasant and that turned out to be untrue. They are as warm as the Italians, lovely people. When I was in England I found the people very nice…'

Andy felt Jinny's body stiffen. Her ears were pricked and she had also been eavesdropping. Andy caught his father's eye, smiled and received a nod.

'They're very good at queuing. Well behaved. If you ask directions they will show you so helpfully they almost go the whole way with you but you never know what they are thinking.

I found it very annoying after a time and when it came time to leave I was glad to get away. You need a bit of the hypocrite in your life.'

Jinny's body was prickling as well as her ears.

Andy's father, sitting opposite Jinny leaned forward and whispered, 'It's good to be young. Life is so simple.'

'Somebody should say something.'

'You do not agree with them, you feel you should put them in their place. It's only his opinion after all.'

'You agree with him don't you,' Jinny struggled to be polite.

'I think he has a point, but the word 'hypocrite' is not what he means.'

'What did he mean?'

'Twinkle,' said Andy's mother.

'Sorry.'

'You get it or you don't.'

* * *

The meal was simple and pleasant, the petulant waitress continued her selfish havoc and they had to wait an age to pay the bill. Andy suggested a walk around the village and they separated into pairs. The sky was still blue and cloudless, the concrete shimmered in the heat and warm currents swirled in the streets.

'Do you mind if I ask you a question?' said Jinny. She and his mother walked behind the two men. Jinny slowed her step, hoping to be out of Andy's earshot.

'Sure,' said Dorothy.

'I get the feeling that Andrew took his wife's death very hard.'

'Yes he did,' said Dorothy. 'Too hard. It took me a while to sort out why.'

There was a silence as the older woman considered whether she should tell a comparative stranger a truth about her son.

'It was guilt.'

'He was not responsible,' said Jinny. 'Why would he be guilty?'

'He was not responsible in any way but part of him, a small part, was relieved that she died and that was where the guilt comes from.'

'Relieved?' Jinny was shocked.

'Oh yes,' said Dorothy. 'She was pregnant and Andrew was terrified of the responsibility that comes with children. I suppose I should be satisfied that he's not one of those men that have children for a whim. You care for Andy?'

'Yes.'

'And your family?'

'They must come first.'

'I'm not going to say any more about it. I'm sure you will do the right thing but there is something I must warn you about Andy. Your relationship is doomed to fail.'

'Why are you so sure.'

'You are obviously a very sweet person and I don't want you to think I'm being rude but you don't know about twinkle.'

'What is twinkle?'

'You know or you don't know. It cannot be taught.'

Jinny was not worried about twinkle, She had love and that was more than she had had before.

* * *

'What's with this woman?' asked his father.

'Don't get the wrong idea, dad. She's married.'

'I don't have the wrong idea,' his father teased him.

'You certainly seem to.'

'You'll never change her.'

'You don't think.'

'No,' he said. 'She's got the look you like but she's too set in her ways. Is she first generation English.'

'I don't think so. Her maiden name is Bull.'

'When we were last in London I went for a Chinese take away. There was a Daily Mail on the counter and the proprietor was holding court in a thick oriental accent, complaining about asylum seekers.'

'I know what you mean but I don't think so.'

'Bull,' he mused. 'Too English. A good name to hide behind.'

'I asked if their were any skeletons in her cupboard.'

'It doesn't matter much. I've not often given you advice Andy...'

'Just the once I think.'

'I'll give you another bit. Don't compromise too much for this girl. If you both compromise too much, neither of you will be happy.'

* * *

Their walk ended at the car park and there was awkwardness about saying goodbye.

'Aren't there any casinos here?' Jinny asked.

'Only at Monte Carlo,' said his father. 'There is one in Juan and Cannes but that's all as far as I know.'

'Would you like to visit one?' His mother asked Jinny.

'I've always been curious about the glamour.'

'You will hear a lot of tales concerning casinos.'

'Words like buzz, rush, high but there is only one word that can be attributed to a casino, whether you are the owner or a customer, which ever side of the establishment you are on. Greed. Casinos are very unpleasant places and not the least bit glamorous.'

'One thing you can be sure of,' said Mrs Avecore with assurance. 'In the long run, gamblers never win.'

CHAPTER THIRTY-EIGHT

Antibes last day

In the late afternoons the sun circled to the side of the apartment block. With the shutters and the patio doors open, they lay on the bed letting the breezes cool their bodies.

Andy wanted to ask what conversation Jinny had shared with his mother but was reluctant to put the question. .

Jinny was running through that conversation. Her retaining ability allowed the action replay to be repeated verbatim, but she kept getting stuck on the precise inflections. This Karen was being portrayed as a remarkable person and it was only natural to paint a rosy picture of a dead person. It was unlikely that she was sainthood material but what was twinkle? It was such a silly word to carry all this kudos. She was sure Mrs Avecore was being helpful, there was nothing catty in her intimation that she may not be a suitable partner for her son. She needed to know more about his dead wife but was afraid to bring up the subject. The mood was not appropriate but then it never was. How was she to win him over? She wanted to do things for him but what. He had got in such a temper when she offered to run his bath that time.

'I'm going to have a quick shower,' he said.

He disappeared into the living room and music played softly. He slipped out of his shorts and stepped into the en suite.

Unfamiliar sounds filled her ears and generated energy while she watched him wash. Why was he more attractive to her than Angus? He did not have those severe folds at the base of his backside or the beginnings of a pot belly. The copper coloured body hair was preferable to dark brown. His penis was smaller than Angus' but was less metallic when it was erect. What was she supposed to think? What was she supposed to do? Should she do the things that those women were doing in the pornographic films she had found on Alex's computer? Here she surprised herself and found that what had once been revolting and unacceptable was not filling her with nausea but quite the opposite. Could she help him to climax? Was that the root of his problem?

The shower was shut off and Andrew began drying himself doing a comic dance to the rhythm of the music. When he finished this ungainly action he lay down beside her and pulled a face.

Suddenly inspired, she forced him to turn over on his face and touched his back with the same respect as he did to her. Unpractised, she teased as best she could, letting the back of her hand glide barely touching. His reaction emboldened her to continue without inhibition. She found herself tantalising and then kissing his backside in a fashion that excited her as much as it excited him. He remained passive and made no attempt to take the reins and she proceeded with more confidence. When she took his penis in her mouth, she was sure he was objecting but she held him tight and prevented escape. The feeling of power she experienced rushed inside her and the shock when his sperm shot into her mouth was outweighed by an overwhelming sense of victory.

Come at last.

The liquid was sickly and salty and she expirated into a tissue. Her need now was urgent and she slipped out of her underwear and directed his hand.

Andy was bewildered and confused by the self excitement her action had generated. The folds of skin had transformed themselves into a rosebud and he intended to caress each petal with gossamer but she again overruled his intention. She forced his hand firmly onto her and guided the pace of massage she wanted and almost instantly she was shuddering. He had always considered fellatio a male indulgence.

Once again they lay, each immersed in their own preoccupations. 'I don't know how things are going to turn out between us. I don't know that I could ever leave Angus and I certainly couldn't leave the twins but I need you to know that I love you. I know that scares you to death but you should understand that whatever happens doesn't matter. I am just grateful to have known what love feels like.'

'Sex…'

'Don't insult me, Andy. This isn't sex. What I just did was more than sex. I've had sex and that wasn't it.'

'I think all these orgasms are addling your brain.'

'I thought it made you short-sighted.'

'It does,' he smiled. 'Metaphorically.'

'I don't care what you say,' she sat up angrily and started dressing. 'And I don't care if my love is not returned.'

'You're like my wife in that respect,' he said. 'You never let a matter drop.'

She stopped dressing and turned to face him, 'Am I like her? In any way.'

'You most certainly are. You're a woman and you're beautiful and full of surprises and…'

'And what?'

'Full of shit.'

Jinny went red, so deep a red that Andy was ashamed for his joke. He had reached a dangerous stage in their relationship. A comfort zone where he dropped his guard, where he felt that he was superman and could get away with anything.

'I'm sorry,' he said bouncing across the bed and sitting beside her, ridiculously naked and humble. 'I didn't mean it how it sounded.'

She was hurt beyond repair. How had he thanked her for his release, for confessing to him her toughest secret, by spitting in her face. For the first time he had revealed his true self, the cavalier. He had been toying with her and now he had humiliated her. He knew what he had done and although he pretended to be distraught, he had enjoyed his joke.

Women have no sense of humour. She stood to zip her skirt and he clasped her about the legs acting out a pantomime prostration. 'I'm so sorry, I went too far. What do you expect, I'm only a man.' More jokes. His foolish male ego wanted to keep playing, even when it was making the situation worse. It was playing with fire and therefore all the more fun.

Jinny wanted to walk away and he allowed her a few steps still clinging on. 'Put it down to post-coital depression.' She put her hand in his face and pushed him away. He knew it was time to let go and released her. On top of all his other crimes he had belittled her. She had gone to unimaginable lengths to express her feelings for him and he had tossed it away like a spent condom. Soiled her grand moment and turned Beau Geste into Mr Pooter.

He would do whatever it took to make it up to her but the damage was done. In Jinny's eyes their relationship was no longer up in the clouds. For Andy that was a good thing. He wanted to proceed but on a more level-headed playing field.

In the living room she pretended to read and he let matters ride. Let her stew on it for a while, things will seem different after a good night's sleep. If only that sleep were not seven hours away.

He had always been the same. He knew what he wanted, that was a plus but, and it was a big plus, but once he got what he wanted he was not much bothered anymore. He might be being harsh with himself but losing Karen had not been his idea and might be at the root of his protracted melancholy. The baby had not been his idea either and he was scared as hell about bringing a child into the world. Especially this world. Was he guilty about being let off that particular hook. If he were really honest wasn't he happy to be off the hook, period. A free agent.

'Who knows,' he muttered. 'All us men want out of life is to be left alone. Watch a game of footy and drink a few beers.'

* * *

That night they ate in a dungeon and were served farcis and milo-melo chicken by the white rabbit. The damage was done. The spell was broken and would not be repaired. For the remaining hours of their weekend Andy tried hard to save the situation. He was on his best behaviour, holding her hand in the street on the way back to the apartment after late dinner. He cuddled her in the night and had her silhouette cut out in black paper by a Chinese as a memento of the holiday but the edge was lost.

* * *

They made love just the one more time before breaking up for the summer holidays. It lacked the intensity he had come to expect and fortunately for both of them his flood gates had opened. They used his premature climax as the excuse for unsatisfactory sex.

Once again, Jinny had decided that her duty lay with Angus and the twins and that she must make an attempt at reconciliation.

Andy only had himself to blame. Why had he done it? Was it some sort of death wish? He wanted to justify his actions as purposeful. He should not be responsible for their separation. As hard as he tried to make this fit his actions he was certain that there was another underlying motive. The chasm in their views and attitudes. Her lack of twinkle. But the inroads he had made in offering her an alternative lifestyle were remarkable in such a short time. She was thawing out. It might be for the best if it ended now.

CHAPTER THIRTY-NINE

Jinny alone

On the flight back from Nice the atmosphere between Jinny and Andy was muted. He dropped her off on his way home but she refused to make any definite arrangements.

Angus' attitude toward their marriage was as indeterminate as ever. He cross-examined her, wanted to know where she had disappeared to not because he missed her, but because he had had trouble organising his laundry. 'I needed time to think,' she kept it vague.

'You're not seeing someone?' Angus held her by the shoulders and checked her eyes for lies but thank goodness she managed not to flinch. 'Not you surely, Mrs Goody two shoes. It doesn't bear thinking about.'

He laughed horribly at his own poor wit. 'Jinny Parish, seductress.' He closed the study door still cackling with humourless mirth.

While she was away Angus had put Bobby in kennels. She let things calm down before confronting him about the dog.

'You weren't here, the boys weren't here and I was busy. What else was I supposed to do?'

'It's your dog. Bobby is your dog. You named Bobby after some footballer.'

'What's that got to do with anything,' Angus snarled. 'You're always bringing up things that are totally irrelevant. If it's my dog then I can do what I like. I wasn't here to take care of him. I'm a busy man. I got rid of him. Subject over.'

School broke up for the summer holiday and in the bustle of the final days of term Jinny was able to keep her head down. If she had taken leave of absence she would have drawn attention and then comment. As it was she was visible but not dwelling too long. She skittered in and out of the places she was expected to be. She did not relish this solitude but felt safer keeping her distance afraid of having to explain herself.

She received a single farewell card from a leaving student. On the front was a picture of geese parading in a farmyard and inside a note from a girl called Judith Steed who was not continuing into the sixth form, *Thank you for all you did.* She felt extraordinarily touched by this message. Judith had failed to complete her homework early on in the year and having been ticked off, announced she was going to be a hairdresser. At the open evening her mother confirmed this ambition. After that, Jinny had scarcely taken any notice of her.

Teaching was a wonderful vocation. You were not always aware that you were getting through. It was so nice to be respected by your students and fellow teachers.

The holidays began uneventfully, Angus came and went without comment. Jinny left Bobby at the kennels for the time being. She used her generous amounts of free time dreaming up plans for her escape but avoided implementing them. She was afraid of the consequences. She was like an underage girl discovering she was pregnant. What was the point of not confronting the fact immediately? Most of these unwanted pregnancies were not dealt with until they show. The lucky ones were the ones with morning sickness and parents were smart enough to put two and two together. If it was left too late there was no chance of an abortion. So many girls ruined their lives just by leaving it too long. A lifetime spoilt for the sake of a month.

This was her life, terrified knowing that the inevitable was coming, that there was no way back but procrastinating anyway. Maybe it would turn out fine tomorrow. The gestation of her marriage might be saved by a miscarriage. A miscarriage of justice?

He had told her that Karen had suffered severe morning sickness. She pictured the girl in the photograph making love with Andy, making a baby and she was inordinately jealous. She ran the bath to purge her dirty mind and body.

The perfumed water soothed her. For a lucid moment she saw that she must confide in someone, an outsider with some worldly intelligence. The trouble was she hardly knew anyone who was as intelligent as she was, let alone more intelligent.

She could speak to Reverend Fulsom. He would not be shocked by her confessions but would she be able to face the man again when he knew what she had done? Catholics' temperament left her at a loss. She knew that all was supposed to be anonymous in a Confessional but the clerics must get to know their congregants. How did the confessors have the nerve to reveal their most intimate sins to celibates?

She could try counselling. Doctor Tariq might recommend someone or she could try the Citizens Advice Bureau. Better still she could ring the Samaritans. She would prefer it was anonymous. Was her problem serious enough for the Samaritans? They dealt with depressives and suicides. It would not be right to waste their precious time on her and Angus' infidelities.

She could not call the Samaritans for another reason. Freda Gill might take the call. She was a member of the St Thomas' congregation. When they moved back to Wyford, Jinny rejoined the Church. Toddlers groups were held twice weekly in the John Dore Hall and Jinny had taken the twins along. This was how she met Freda, whose two children were roughly the same age. Freda's plans were unfulfilled, she bragged as to how she would leave her husband as soon as the children were off her hands. Her husband was not professional and she seemed to have nothing but disdain for the man. Even then Jinny had her fixation with brightness and Freda's husband was a very low wattage.

This side of her was inexplicable because Freda had a very good heart. When Ken Farlow's wife, Deidre, died of cervical cancer she cooked him dinner three times a week. People said that she was cooking her way into his trousers but Jinny knew for a fact that was not the case. Ken used to come round to them on Thursday nights for a drink and always complained of chronic indigestion.

Freda never did leave him but her son followed in his father's slipstream. He did not live up to expectations and became one of those acetic happy clappies that hang around the church for solace.

No, she could not ring the Samaritans. If Freda answered the call she might end up depressed and suicidal.

She knew she could not go on waiting for some outside source to trigger a denouement, as each day passed without a miracle, deepening her premonition of a bad ending.

She saw Andy on just the one occasion and was determined that nothing would happen but he kissed her so sweetly, she gave in to him. It was the nice thing to do.

To pass the empty days she wandered the streets of Wyford vigilantly watching for faces she knew and readying herself to avoid them by whatever means. Most of her acquaintance was away for the school holidays and she did not have to take evasive action.

One of her rambles took her past the Premier Hotel. She took to using the bar and drinking gin and tonics, hiding in a corner with a full view of reception, waiting for Angus and Jez to show up, getting sustenance from his continued infidelity. She returned home to the spare bedroom and wallowed in self-righteousness.

She ignored Andy's calls and messages. Their relationship had been wonderful for a time, now it was not the same. The magic, if you could call it such a thing, had gone and it was all his fault. He had been mean and disrespectful. If he loved her things might be different. She so wanted to be loved by someone other than the dog.

She woke up one night with her nightie around her neck, her panties nowhere to be found and perspiration pouring off her. She conjured moments of America and Antibes until a yearning ache gnawed at her so hard she groaned with pain. Eventually she slept and dreamed of catherine wheels and roman candles.

This was how it was to be. She saw her life stretching before her, lonely and bitter purposelessly wandering the streets. Reminiscing register lists, name by name, a litany of youthful faces passing before, providing her sole comfort. Hunched over and wrinkled, having pupils to tea,

Goodbye Mrs Chips.

This must not happen. She was still young. She had plenty of time to start over.

The day the A level results were to be posted on school notice boards was grey and overcast. Jinny lay in bed, staring at the gap in the curtains willing the sun to shine and waiting patiently for the sounds of Angus leaving. Then it would be safe to come out but all was deathly quiet. He might have decided to go in late today and pass by the school before setting off for work.

Desperate to use the en suite she barged into the bedroom which was empty and the bed made. She rechecked the time and found her watch had stopped. It was over an hour later than she thought. Angus had left no information on how she could contact him. There was a text from Andy which said, 'Good luck for today'. He was trying hard to get back in her good books.

She tried to have a leisurely breakfast but she was keyed up and checked the clock every few minutes. This merely protracted the wait. Just as she was to leave she was buttonholed on the telephone by Alfred Kent, the verger. Angus had promised to donate an old photocopier to the church and Alfred wanted to fix a time for delivery. She tried to explain that only Angus could make such an arrangement but Alfred did not listen. He was a cussed character was Alfred. He had called, dead set on finalising this delivery and was not hanging up until it was completed. She fetched her diary and chose a date at random and wrote Angus a note.

She set off late for school with her head full of fantasies. Visiting Oxford for picnics on the river, wandering among the colleges, sitting on a park bench enjoying the *dreaming spires*. For the first time in days her heart surged, a sunbeam of her own and the sun yawned through the clouds. She quickened her step with a skip and followed her fuzzy shadow along the path to the school.

At least the boys would be unaffected by her and Angus' separation. They were old enough now to stand on their own two feet.

She left the park at the gate by the tennis courts and could see the school entrance ahead of her. Parents who had got there before her, were already leaving, smiling, cuddling and patting the shoulders of their offspring. Those parents she knew caught sight of her, averted their eyes and her full heart shrivelled. She quickened her pace hurrying to her fate. There was a crowd of year 13's hugging and squawking and blocking the view. Patiently she wriggled her way to the front but when confronted with lists her eyes would not focus. She closed her eyes for a few seconds to let the panic subside and found their names. Parish, Alex, B.A.B. Parish, James, B.B.B.

In Pemberton Park there is a croquet court with a pavilion. At the weekend, an old gentleman gives lessons on how to play and this shed is left unguarded during the week. It is therefore wrecked by vandals. Countless times the doors have been ripped off and windows smashed. It is just a shell but those who know the park well know that if you are caught in a storm you can shelter there. Someone had written on the walls.

'Vandalism is the British way of expressing oneself. Destruction as art.'

Someone else had scrawled, 'Let's play count the condom.'

Jinny held her face in shame and humiliation. A single A between them. All that boastfulness about her brilliant boys and now this. Why hadn't the teachers warned her of the impending disaster. Anyone moderating the course work would have had an inkling. She could recall nothing abnormal about her last visit at the school. No doubts had been aired. No, she was wrong, Mr Turner did want to speak to her and they had been interrupted by the headmaster wanting to know what St Bryans' expectations were. He was worried that they might be overtaken in the results war and she enjoyed the kudos. If all the results were as below expectations as her own two then Wyford Grammar would easily be surpassed.

Her estimation was close. If the point system per pupil was implemented the gap between Wyford Grammar and St Bryans results in the previous year was just forty points. This year it was down to single figures.

Jinny knew that she should attend St Bryans and be with her fellow staff members. If she did not go, she might be the only member of staff not to attend. Andy had postponed going away until after the results were published.

* * *

Betsy March checked the scores thoroughly but St Bryans overall results remained behind her Wyford rivals. It was close but not quite there. Word had got around and the local press arrived to report their success but she remained disappointed and refused to see the journalists. She delegated Andrew to do that for her.

'I need to discuss something with you.'

'Yes,' agreed Betsy. 'It will be good to talk. We haven't really had a good chinwag since you arrived. Get rid of the reporters and the other hangers on and I'll be in my room.'

Several councillors were at the press conference feeding off the success of the saved school and there were rumours that the local MP was to make an appearance.

Andy answered the journalists' questions with one eye on them and the other eye on the door. All the other teachers had put in appearance and he guessed why Jinny might be the exception.

* * *

The sun's momentary flash was fleeting. The sky had got darker and darker and Jinny had dwelt too long. Rain fell down in sheets and Jinny watched the stair rods plummet for a while. She got out her mobile and pulled up Alex' number. Her finger hovered over the call button. It was eleven am here. Therefore four or five am where the boys were. Thankfully it was too early. She put the mobile back in her bag and it beeped just the once. There was a message, a text that read, 'well?, angus.' She punched in A,BAB & J,BBB and pressed send.

Her phone beeped again. 'all that money for tutors' read the message and it was not signed. All went quiet, there were no more calls.

She knew she should get to St Bryans but he would be there and she was in no mood for him or any confessions. There was no one she could share her disappointment with. Margery would be sympathetic but there would be that underlying humiliation. Everything in her life had reached a similar point. Her marriage, her children and herself. There was no denying it. She was a failure, a cuckold and a sex toy. Men! Fathers, sons and lover, none of them were worth a damn.

* * *

'Thank you for dealing with that rabble. How would you describe them?'

'Parasites?'

'That'll do,' said Betsy and sat behind her desk. She was dressed for the job. No mufti for her during the holidays. He had never seen her in jeans, so he was unable to establish whether the myth about her pretty bottom was true or false.

He needed permission for an unorthodox procedure and concerned because of his involvement with the parties, he was strangely reticent. Longing had grown like a cancer since Jinny had begun baulking him.

Face to face with the boss, the mixture of nerves and deprivation tortured his throat and words emerged as froggish croaks. Nor could he get comfortable in his chair.

Betsy carried on as though nothing was out of the ordinary, 'You deserve a thank you for your contribution last term.'

'I was just doing my job,' Andy croaked and wriggled.

'I knew you would fit in well. Everyone has a good word for you.' Betsy made an oddly male gesture, pinching her nose between thumb and forefinger then spreading her hand like a wing ran her hand down her face as though removing a mask. In an instant the charm was gone and as she leaned forward. Andy felt she was going to confide in him. If he did not know better he was sure she was going to be bitchy about someone, 'You failed me in one respect. Unwittingly, I hastened to add.'

Andy felt his mouth opening and shut it quickly.

'Part of my scheme. I do scheme,' she fluttered her eyelids in a girlish way but only succeeded in looking twee. Was she going to pass him a note under the desk? 'I rather thought that your appointment would scare off one of our few remaining pieces of dead wood.'

'Who?' Andy asked, have a strong inkling of who it was.

'I thought that bringing in an outsider over the head of the existing staff and especially a free spirit like yourself would shake up the apathy but I also expected one of our number to get indignant and leave. She did ask to see me shortly after you arrived but unfortunately she did not keep the appointment. You're a smart chap. Who am I talking about?'

'Jinny Parish.'

'You agree that I'm right.'

Horns of dilemma, thought Andy. Another fine mess you have got yourself into. 'I think that when I arrived Mrs Parish was both arrogant and...' He was going to say 'repressed' but felt it was too sexual an adjective... 'to put it bluntly, up herself. I think that has changed dramatically.'

'I've heard rumours...'

Here we go. Andy was suddenly on guard. Was she pulling his leg? Did she know everything and was getting it out of him with this masquerade. Sense stepped in and the butterflies in his stomach flew away. Betsy called a spade a spade. If she knew she would have come right out and said it. Now he had to quickly decide what he could and could not admit to knowing.

'I think I'd better stop you there,' said Andy with more righteousness than he should be allowed. 'I know more than I should but I prefer not to talk about it.'

'Of course, you were in America with her. You must have had a lot of time to talk.'

'I was a shoulder to cry on,' maintaining his best business like manner. 'When I first met the woman I thought she was dyed in the wool, a hopeless case. Since the book club and the America trip she has thawed out. With a bit more defrosting she could be all right.'

'Nice turn of phrase,' said Betsy. 'We'll see how it goes. What did you want to see me about?'

'Funnily enough, Mrs Parish.'

* * *

Jinny waited at the airport amongst the ever changing sea of expectant faces. Passengers trouped along a corridor demarked by railings. For security reasons, family and friends who were restricted to a designated area, watched and waved along one side. There was the occasional oblivious inconsiderate who stood blocking the corridor at the entrance, causing trolleys to veer to avoid them. Jinny decided these miscreants were of foreign extraction.

After a seven hour flight all you needed was to hang around while complete strangers embrace directly in your way. Jinny was also struck by how false and over the top some of these reunions appeared to be. Some embraces lasted for an eternity as though the arrivals had been detained at Guantanamo Bay for years rather than a couple of weeks' holiday.

She admonished herself for her cynicism but continued to watch the searching eyes rather than the arriving passengers. The boys saw her before she saw them and she heard a familiar call, 'mum'.

They looked unbelievably well, thick tans and they had grown into the new outfits she had bought for them. They rushed to where she stood and flung their arms around her neck and hugged and hugged. She thought they would never let go. When they released her they both spoke at once, two machine guns firing and she could only catch random words. The timbre of their accents had a discernible trans-atlantic twang. She briefly thought of complaining but was so overwhelmed with their enthusiastic greeting, nothing else mattered.

'Girlfriend…Awesome…Florida…Awesome…Disney Corporation…Awesome…being home…not so awesome.'

As she negotiated the car around the M25, on and on they talked like friends as well as brothers. It reminded her of when they first went to school and came charging out the school gates talking at one hundred to the dozen and non-stop all the way home.

'Is dad home?'

'I don't know.'

'Is he coming home to see us?'

'I honestly don't know. I should think he will be. He hasn't seen you for two months.'

'Yes he has.'

'He visited us in Orlando.'

'He was with that woman of his.'

'She's a right slapper.'

Slapper, thought Jinny, how come they know such words.

'Are you and dad getting divorced?'

'We haven't talked about it. I don't know anything that's going on. I certainly didn't know your father went to Florida to see you.'

'He didn't tell you?'

'No. It seems I'm the last to know.'

'We've bought a present. You just wait until you see it.'

* * *

'There's a Mr Avecore on the line.'

'Do we know him?'

'He says it's personal.'

'Give me two minutes, then put him through.'

Angus replaced the receiver and revolved his chair so that he was facing the window. The view stretched north towards the motorways. If he had stood on tiptoe he would see the rooftops of St Bryans. To the east a Virgin train sped northwards to Edinburgh. He swivelled his chair to face his new secretary.

'You'll get used to it all in time,' he promised. 'I like my e-mails re-typed with the irrelevancies edited out. You can assign one of the juniors to do the typing but I suggest that you check the accuracy before giving them to me. Some of these girls are barely literate.'

His telephone rang.

'That will do for the time being,' he said and waited for the woman to shut the door after her. Then he picked up the receiver. 'Yes, I'm Angus Parish…I don't understand, don't you work with Jinny? You're not my sons' teacher….I don't see how but if you insist. Where?…Hold on a minute.'

He triggered the intercom.

'Lucy, what time is Gottlieb this afternoon?'

'His flight is delayed, I just checked. He'll be at least an hour late and he's due at two pm.'

'Well done. Write Mr Avecore in for two pm.'

'Yes, sir.'

'Hello…You heard…I'll see you at two.'

* * *

'My life used to be teeming with people,' said Jinny. 'Now it keeps coming back to you.'

'Come and see me.'

'No, sex with you is not the answer.'

'Why did you answer the call,' he asked. 'Don't say you didn't know it was me.'

'My mobile was in my bag. It took a while for me to find it and in my hurry I didn't look.'

'If you had seen it was me?'

'I wouldn't have answered.'

'Let's meet,' said Andy. 'For coffee. Somewhere safe for you.'

'I'm going.'

'Agree to meet me, please. I need to see you.'
'I'll think about it,' she said and hung up.

* * *

Jinny felt like a dog with four owners each attached to a lead around her neck. Each owner was taking her 'walkies' and each pulling in a separate direction.

Angus did not come home on the night the twins returned from America and they spent a pleasant evening, the twins expanding on the details of their good time. Jinny had much to discuss with them but resisted stemming their flow. They went to bed that night buzzing with renewal, buoyed with a remembered warmth and love of previous times.

Once she was sure Angus was out for the night, for appearances sake, she slept in the master bedroom. Expecting the twins to sleep late she awoke to hear strange noises downstairs. The strict regime and regular discipline of their summer job was entrenched. Without any ill effects from the night flight, they were up before her, full of energy and brought her breakfast in bed. Basking in yesterday's good will and reminiscence, they would picnic by the lock at Cordwainers Cross. It was mid-week, there would be a few fisherman but it would be relatively quiet. Jinny made sandwiches and the boys went out to buy treats.

It was a beautiful summers day. Cloudless sky, men and birds sought a fish dinner. Herons petrified with patience and drowsy fisherman dozed at the waters edge. Kingfishers flashed tourquoise streaks and swans came begging for food. Dog owners, creatures of habit, used the towpath in the opposite direction towards the marina and there were few passers by.

Sunshine and food cooked the trio into a mood of satisfaction and sleepy well-being, even Bobby slumped onto his full stomach and dutifully dosed.

Lying stretched out on the fragrant grass, sleepily the twins revived memories of similar childhood outings in surprising detail. Argued and laughed of close calls with the water. The man who got entangled in the ropes when the lock was empty and nearly fell in. He had to lie still until the water level rose, the rope loosened and he could escape.

'If the water had gone any lower he would have been throttled.'

In unison they tired and fell silent in utter contentment. Alex petted his mother's hair and she dreamed of times gone by.

Two months ago they were all different people. The boys had not noticed what transformations she had undergone in those eight weeks. If only she could go back to the way things were.

It was clear to her now that she had been living a lie, so going back was futile. Realisation had done her no favours although it was much less hurtful coming face to face with your own truth. Somebody else's truth was much less digestible. God knowing the truth was of little comfort to Jinny either. Having been sinned against she had committed a sin of equal gravity. Having been driven to it was an excuse but it did not lessen the sin. In truth, she had lusted after Andy before she knew of Angus' adultery.

A wave of love swept through her and she gave thanks for being alive. Was it the nostalgia, being with the boys and being reminded of better times. It was that moment's thought of Andy. A man who did not love her but did everything a lover should. Thought of her well being first, made note of what pleased her and acted upon it. Cared for her and let her know that he cared. That was how lovers should be but he did not love her. It did not make sense.

Languidly, they cleared up their mess and walked contentedly home along the towpath and through the park. It was that hour when the sun lost its potency but the heat lingered. The boys craved ice cream but would not settle for anything other than Ben and Jerry's.

As they approached Gillian Finn's house, she could see Gill sitting on a wall talking to a young man. He made her laugh a lot but as they drew near the boy fell silent.

It was that Morrissey boy, who looked strangely adult out of uniform. He barely acknowledged knowing her, Gill smiled warmly and said, 'Hello.'

A rush of self pity filled her eyes. She needed to confide her troubles to a sympathetic ear and at least Gill had knowledge of one of those dog owners who were pulling at her. She thought of stopping on some pretext but her nerve failed her. She smiled back and continued on her way, relieved that the subject of A level results had not come up. She had been avoiding the subject with the twins. It could wait until their father was there. This was a matter for him to deal with.

Having been deprived of ice cream the twins were insistent on pizza for supper. While they set up the garden table, Jinny got two boxes out of the freezer and prepared a salad while the pizzas heated. In honour of their new found maturity she opened a bottle of rose wine.

They had virtually finished when Angus appeared in the french windows. He looked tired and gruff but managed to shake the boys hands in mock respect. 'You got home all right? No delays at Miami?'

'We had go back to Tampa to pick up extra passengers.'

'They were a few minutes late,' Jinny's voice boomed inside her head. She felt that she was entering into a conversation with strangers.

Angus ignored her, 'I'll have a quick shower and you can tell me all about it.'

His arrival did not spoil the mood but created a new atmosphere. Their party was on hold and it might or might not continue later. Jinny kept looking about her expecting a bomb to drop. Her intuition told her that this was not going to be a fun evening.

Angus reappeared in a Wyford Town football kit. It was the new design for the Premiership season. The shirt was a size too small and emphasised his growing pot. The shorts were a bad cut, wrinkled across his backside and tight against his thighs.

The boys were not concerned with these niceties and got him to show off his exclusive treasure. He paraded up and down like a model on a catwalk and despite her dread, Jinny giggled at his comic performance.

He sat at the garden table, rubbed his hands together in a false bonhomie and asked breezily 'What's for dinner?'

'What would you like?'

'You haven't made anything?'

'We had pizza.'

'That'll be fine.'

'There isn't any left.'

Angus got that sulky look that had been appearing more regularly of late. 'That's nice…'

'Who knew you were coming home? You didn't make an appearance yesterday.'

'I'll order some Chinese takeaway,' he offered without apology. 'Where's the number?'

'On the pin board by the dresser where it always is.'

In his ill-fitting costume Angus groaned out of his chair, his voluminous backside of the Parish tradition sashaying grossly back inside the house. The twins, curiously quiet, exchanged mutual glances and followed after. Sensing that this conspiracy affected her she joined them.

Jinny with her heart re-ignited expected to discuss A level results but the boys had other ideas. In a bizarre pantomime, obviously pre-planned, they led Angus by the hand and sat him in his favourite armchair. The pair of them had memorised speeches and presented him with the crimes of his infidelity. He listened to what they said with amused contempt. On the strength of their new confidence they gave him an ultimatum.

'If you do not stop seeing this woman we'll never speak to you again.'

He listened in silence until they had finished, his eyes turning toward her. 'I've already stopped seeing Miss Norris.'

'You've said that before. I saw you with her at the Premier Hotel two days after your mother was here.'

'Following me, were you?'

'It was an accident. I was meeting somebody.'

'You were meeting somebody,' he repeated knowingly. 'I'll come back to that in a minute. I have already stopped seeing Miss Norris. She is now Mrs Hanson.'

'She's married?'

'Isn't that what I just said?'

The boys congratulated each other as though claiming a victory but Angus was not paying attention. He was smirking at her and Jinny knew that look. I know something that is to my advantage. There was unmistakable evil in his eyes.

'Ask your mother when she's going to stop sleeping with her toy boy.'

Once again, Angus floored her. His streetwise know how

timed the bombshell perfectly. Daddy's peccadillo was a touch of the naughty boy and deserved his wrist to be slapped. Mummy in someone else's bed was a slut.

At that moment, having won them back for twenty four hours, they seemed lost forever.

CHAPTER FOURTY

Andy and Angus

Andy was ushered in to Angus' office, new, big and minimalist. Every footstep and movement resonated or squeaked on the wood floor. Angus had a big voice and it boomed around the room.

There was no move to make the usual pleasantries. Angus sat anchored in his big chair and offered no hand in friendship. Studying his guest intensely, a steely eye working out the visitor's motives.

'Are you fucking my wife?' he asked through half open eyes.

Andy laughed inwardly. The man's got balls, he just does not how to use them.

'I'm not much into sex. I have been…helping your wife out since the…' Andy continued the impotent pose he found he had adopted. It was simplest to go with the flow.

'Have you. How exactly?'

'Sympathetic ear, you know. Shoulder to cry on.'

'What are you here for? I'm a busy man.'

Andy almost lost patience with the 'busy man' but hid his annoyance and said, 'I'm only here to help.'

Andy explained how he had nipped into Wyford Grammar to check out the twins' results.

'I couldn't get hold of Jinny so I guessed she was upset. While I was there I met a Mr Turner.'

They had discussed the twins' results and Andy had come up with an idea. He showed Angus an envelope.

'I will need to interview your sons,' Andy dropped the weedy act. 'Alone. There is one condition. I do not want your wife to know about any of this. If she finds out the deal's off.'

Angus did not want to respond to Andy's ultimatum. He

neither liked or was used to having demands made of him and he sat silent without speaking.

'I'll take that as a yes, shall I? If you agree to my conditions I want to see the boys tomorrow at my office at St Bryans. Ten sharp.' He smiled in his best boyish fashion. 'I'm a busy man.'

He left with the sweet memory of his rival for the hand of Jinny Parish, stunned, with a bemused look on his face.

* * *

Alex had been completely compliant and Andy assumed his brother James would be more of the same. He guessed wrong.

'I don't want any part of it,' the boy said defiantly. 'You can stick your offer.'

Andy, taken aback, struggled to gain some equanimity. Why the hostility? What motive could be behind this? Andy searched his experience for what might be the boy's problem.

James' face gave nothing away. He looked well with a tan and was more poised than his brother. Alex was wearing a suit but no tie and was, the brother eager to please. James was more of a rebel and looked cool in a linen shirt and jeans.

'What's the problem?' Andy played for thinking time. 'I promise that whatever you tell me will go no further than these four walls.'

James narrowed his eyes in a familiar sardonic way and shook his head. 'I can't trust you. All teachers are liars.'

Cynical little bastard, thought Andy and plumped for the pressure syndrome. Lots of parents get a sniff that their children are capable of great things and put undue pressure on these children to achieve. Some children simply have to be born to be put to this sword.

Some rebelled, wanted a quiet life and some, anxious to please their parents, folded and cracked, to hide the ignominy of their failure. The majority of these pressurised kids like any combustion unit over filled with steam, exploded. They grew wild and lost control, some even commited suicide. Some of those that make it to where their parents wanted them to be, arrived at university and killed themselves. The meeker breed hid behind some unassailable rock, such as religion. It was hard to condemn a righteous child.

James, from what little he knew, did not fit any of these options.

Just for something to say, Andy said, 'Your brother seems happy enough with the idea.' and the well opened.

The mention of his brother was a spoonful of foul medicine. James' poise evaporated and his pallor turned sickly. Why exactly? Sibling rivalry, jealousy, hate. None of those applied because Alex was the meeker one of the two, James was the driving force.

'He would be,' said James with amused contempt. These boys were a chip off the old block. The one seated before him had more of his father than Alex. Was it possible for twins to have mixed genes?

'Mr Turner told me that your results were a bigger surprise than your brother's.'

James disdained to answer.

'Is he a liar like all teachers?' Andy started making up a detail or two trying to bring out the boy's problem. Flattery would be good. 'He says you're much smarter than your brother.' That lie went well. 'He said there was a noticeable dropping off in the standard of your course work in the last couple of terms.'

Andy could not interpret James' response to this lie but the boy was thinking about it. Andy felt that he was nearly there, on the brink, how to tip him over? Easy. Annoy him with his brother's prowess. Easier said than done.

He sat watching the boy prickling and fold into himself like a hedgehog, suffering his lonesome problems, his eyes writhing.

'Mr Turner had the notion that you're envious of your brother.' This was not what he was searching for in the way of a catalyst, but snap.

James sat upright, snorted like a dragon. 'Mr Turner is an arsehole. Envious of that prat, what a wanker. I've had that worm hanging around my neck from day one. I'm not carrying the little bastard any longer.' Exhausted he slumped back in his seat. He had none of his father's staying power.

'Do you mean to tell me that you failed your exams on purpose to avoid going to the same university as your brother.'

'And what happens,' James whined from his slouch. 'The fucking idiot fails and I'm lumbered all over again.'

Andy shook his head. This was a new one. He had never taught twins but had been at school with a pair called Pinn. Being an only child he often wondered how they dealt with the variation in their abilities. Daniel always did better than Louis and Andy wondered how Louis coped and if he minded.

'If you get a scholarship and I can't promise. It's pretty much up to you. What I can promise if you go to different colleges and do different subjects you'll never see each other.'

James, scrunched up in the chair, looked at him sideways.

'Not all teachers are liars,' said Andy. 'But that might be a lie in itself.'

'Why all the secrecy,' James unravelled and sat up straight. They were going to continue man to man. 'You my mum's toy boy?'

'Toy boy? Your mother and I are about the same age.'

'My dad called you her toy boy.'

'I see,' said Andy. 'Your father hurt your mother a lot. Who did she have to comfort her? You and your brother were away. You know you forgot her birthday. She checked her mobile a hundred times that day. So you see, I was there and nobody else was.'

CHAPTER FOURTY-ONE

Jinny in disgrace

Outnumbered, the vengeful atmosphere drove her from the house. She was being treated like a leper. Her sole ally, Bobby, happy for her attention, was company for her escape. She purposely set off in the direction of Gillian Finn's house but there were no signs of her. She walked the empty streets hoping to bump into somebody she knew, anybody. She allowed herself one final corner and saw a woman and a dog in the distance. As the woman drew nearer she saw that it was her ex-neighbour Mary Brooks and she prepared a greeting. Whether by accident or purpose, she would never know for sure, Mary crossed the road.

Because of the mood she was in, Jinny took the possible snub as affront. She was a pariah, a common tart and everybody could read her sins on her forehead.

She rushed home, let the dog into the house and drove around to Margery's house. The place was in darkness and there was no answer to her tentative knock. Desperate now, she drove to Marcia's but it was the same story. Being August, Parliament's break was Charles's break, they would be at their apartment in Alicante. Betsy March's house was in the next street and the lights were on but Jinny could not knock there. It did not feel right. She needed to talk and there was only one possible listener left available to her.

She turned off the engine and sat outside for twenty minutes, her heart racing, unable to make the decision. It had to be 'no'. She switched on the engine, put the car in gear and stalled the engine. She had needed a sign and this was it. It seemed an age before she heard footsteps on the stairs and the door opened.

He had not shaved for a couple of days, his usual neat appearance was tardy and his eyes seemed dull. On seeing her his face brightened. He sat opposite her without speaking, which was much appreciated, waiting quietly.

'Whatever happens this evening we are not going to fuck...'

'Pardon me.'

'You heard. My life is absolute rubbish. Ruined. Wasted. It's nothing to do with you, not directly. I don't really mean that. It's not your fault, is what I meant to say. You should not blame yourself for anything I'm going to tell you. Why is it when a man is unfaithful it's seen as a mild aberration when a woman is unfaithful it's the end of the world?'

'Life is unfair. Especially for women.'

'That doesn't help.'

'It wasn't meant to. The truth rarely does.'

'Truth, truth, truth. I've had more than my fair share of truth. I'm sick of truth. It's all...,' she struggled for another expletive. 'Bollocks. That's a word you like. It's therapeutic.'

'What is?'

'Swearing.' She told him of the ups and downs of the past two days. How in twenty four hours her sons had been her best friend and were now her fiercest enemies. 'There are no mitigating circumstances.'

'What are you going to do?'

'I don't know,' she shook her head. 'I don't know.'

'Move in here.' She glared at him. 'Until you've made up your mind.'

'What happens when the sex between us becomes routine. I'll be a year older and in exactly the same quandary as I am now.'

'I shouldn't think it will take that long.'

'What?'

'For the sex to wane. It will be more like six months.'

'Are you making jokes?'

'Sorry.'

Jinny snatched up her bag and made to leave. He barred her way and there was a silent scuffle. Inadvertently her forehead gave his nose a glancing blow and caused it to bleed. She switched into a motherly efficient Jinny and he let her administer to him.

'You'll live.'

He grabbed her around the waist and put his head in her stomach. 'Stay.'

She remained lifeless, like the twins had as children when they were being disobedient and would not do as they were told. She would pick them up and they would become as a rag doll.

Andy sighed and released her. He sat back, rested his elbows on his knees and put his head in his hands.

'Goodbye,' she said and he did not answer.

* * *

Jinny's morning lay ins in the spare room, grew more protracted and more reflective. She lay, hands behind her head, staring at the ceiling just like the old days, noting the cobwebs and cracks and occasional bluebottle or spider.

Twinkle? What was twinkle?

Other mornings she berated herself, enjoying bouts of self flagellation. There were mornings of daydreaming and fantasies always including Andy with bare arms. She was tempted to quote Henry V, but shut her eyes and squeezed them tight waiting for the temptation to pass. She was going to be a better person from now on. No more clever clogs. She was laid in bed but she felt so improved her head was held higher from a horizontal position.

The morning it occurred to her that she may not be as bright as she thought was the final cog in her turning points. In recent weeks she had learned so much. Like Angus' other life, things she had no idea existed.

That made her the fool.

She had forgotten about Toddlers' group until recalling Freda Gill. Women together talk in a candid way that made her uncomfortable. She had been too reserved to join in, and when called upon laughed shyly. The things they admitted to, but she was only half listening in case their revelations applied to her, using her double nurturing to immerse herself. Shirley Smith admitted that she had doubts at the altar and if it didn't work out, she would divorce. Shirley and her husband had been married a year and had two baby girls. Jinny had closed her ears to this openness. The twins were two years old and the Toddler group believed that Jinny had been married for three because that was what she had told them. Shirley's marriage, built on stronger foundations than her own, had not lasted.

No more lies. Be a better person. No more quotes. No more boasting. Be more positive. Do not settle for less. She repeated this mantra each morning. Life was going to be better from here on.

* * *

Tomorrow was Saturday, Angus' birthday and the obligatory Parish party. She had not given a thought to his present, nor did she feel inclined to. Do they do castration on the National Health? He might behave more acceptably if he was spayed. That went for a lot of men she knew.

The town centre was filled with parents and children and there was nowhere to consider in peace. She briefly flitted past the bookshops and men's stores but inspiration failed her. She decided the problem was too close. She would go for a quiet cup of coffee, let the problem wash over her and inspiration would strike.

Costa and Café Nero were heaving with short tempered mothers and squalling kids, hardly the backdrop to a quiet moment. On the first floor of the Arndale Centre was a Chinese restaurant. She would order some tea and eat a spring roll.

She caught sight of Margery and Hugh Mason having lunch, hidden in a gloomy corner of the restaurant. She took her tray and hurried over. Margery looked extremely guilty but Hugh Mason stood up to greet her with a big smile and said, 'Jinny. you just missed Marcia. It's been a regular staff meeting here this morning.'

Margery's eyes danced merrily and she took an inordinate time cleaning her mouth with her serviette.

'How's your summer been?' Hugh asked.

She looked at each of them in turn and tears began rolling down her face. They listened intently as she told them everything that happened. Wearing her heart so thoroughly on he sleeve her confession was unexpurgated but Hugh and Margery did not stir and waited patiently for her to finish.

'I'm at my wit's end because I don't understand anything that's going on.'

Hugh put his hand on her arm, 'I wish I could help you more. What goes on between husband and wife has too much history for glib responses from reprobates like me. I can admit that Andy's behaviour is right up my street.'

Jinny clutching for any clue put her hand over his and felt his surprise at her touching him. He laughed to himself and checked her face before continuing. 'It's called the fisherman phase.'

Hugh paused for effect, took a mouthful of coffee and wiped his moustache.

'He's got you caught on his rod line and he's reeling you in. The line gets tight and it's a matter of will and strength. If he wanted to he could complete the catch and bring you ashore but there's no fun in that. It's when that rod line is taut that he holds it there for a moment and considers.'

'We are talking about relationships.'

'Bear with me.'

'He lets the line go slack for a minute, giving you the opportunity to pull away and then he reels some more. Playing cat and mouse, fisherman and fish. The trick to this manifestation is understanding what is at the root of it.'

The women shared a quizzical look.

'In my experience there are three main reasons. Cold feet, that's simple enough to recognise. Uncertainty works both ways. Is he sure of himself and is he sure of you?'

'Conscience?'

'That comes under the cold feet heading.'

'You said there was a third possibility.'

'That doesn't apply in this case. It's for those who enjoy the chase and enjoy dragging out the kill.'

Margery gave him an old-fashioned look and he grinned back at her.

'I'm sorry to be thick but how do I fit into all these theories?'

'You don't directly,' Hugh played with the beard around his chin. 'Andy wants you right enough. He's just like any modern bloke. He's afraid to commit.'

CHAPTER FOURTY-TWO

Charlotte returns

Jinny was preparing the final bits and pieces for that evening's party still considering Angus' final offer of reconciliation. She was to make up her mind while he spent a week at the New York office. He was returning today for his birthday party.

Angus had conducted these discussions as though they were a business meeting. They had sat in his study, he at his desk, she as the interviewee. He had even minuted the proceedings. How could she have ever been attracted to this pompous man?

What were his motives? Free relationship. He was suggesting they lead separate lives but live under the same roof? He would pay all the bills, even give her a stipend so that she could maintain her independence. No questions to be asked by either side. 'For the children's sake', he pleaded and there were tears in his eyes.

Keep thy foot out of brothels
Thy hand out of plackets
Thy pen from the lenders' books
And defy the foul fiend

She was not to do that anymore, she had promised herself but old habits die hard. She attempted to compose a prayer. She needed guidance. Last Sunday, Reverend Fulsom had taken her to one side and offered to listen.

'What makes you think there's something to discuss?' she asked.

'You're not yourself, Jinny,' he stared hard. 'I see turmoil in your eyes.'

She could not open up to him. She could not expose her and Angus' dirty laundry to a priest. Shame, a new emotion, was spilling into every aspect of her life and leaving an irrevocable stain. What was she to do about Andy?

Their last meeting had touched her heart in a new way. Seeing him in pain and so wonderfully pathetic. That was her second action of power over a man, denying him sex. She felt as good about that as making him climax. Things could not continue as they were. Could she be part of a free relationship. A modern marriage. It was a simple choice, Andy or Angus, neither of whom seemed to love her enough. With Andy, sometimes the mere thought of him excited desire but shame quickly followed in its wake. Angus promised a life of security and that included the boys.

There was more truth to face up to. Her separation from Andy and the pain it brought helped her to know that she had never known love before. Her father was kindly, avuncular and his affection limited to a pat on the head, a pinch of the cheek. Her mother had little love to give and what morsels were on offer found their way to Charlotte. She imagined her father was deprived of sentiment but he inhabited a world where feelings were suppressed. Angus did not love her, probably never had. He had been press ganged into marriage. So wrapped up in themselves, the boys were a disappointment. Angus had prompted the situation and they had taken his side.

What had she done to alienate them? Her shame flared so thoroughly she again felt the need to run and hide, to run so fast that she might outrun her calumny and leave it behind forever. The pain would not subside and she searched the kitchen for relief. A half drunk bottle of wine she was saving for Sunday's casserole would not be strong enough.

James was sitting watching the big screen television, his chair blocking the drinks cabinet.

'Just stand up for a moment. Please,' she added like a servant asking for special permission. Sulkily he got to his feet but did not move to help her shift the heavy chair. She found a bottle of brandy and went back to the kitchen to drink in private. She poured a generous helping, gulped a mouthful, which burned and found its way down the wrong hole. Coughing and spluttering violently, the two boys came to her rescue. James clapping her on the back and Alex barking instructions.

In the middle of this uproar there was a ring at the doorbell and Alex was sent to answer. He returned with a couple following behind. Through her tear-filled eyes she could not see who they were. A tall man and a stocky woman who might have been Asians.

'Hello, Jinny,' said a distant haunting voice. 'It's been a long time.'

Without either knowing, Angus and Jinny's sister Charlotte had crossed together over the Atlantic.

* * *

The twins' curiosity about their aunt waned fast and using study as a pretext they disappeared. Charlotte had filled out, her complexion had become a shade of *yellow an' brown* and looked oddly unhealthy. She wore a low cut blouse, her *burned bosom* had grown and her midriff bulged. Recognizable mannerisms routed out long forgotten moments.

Michael, tall and cadaverous, hung on his wife's every word. He was kindly, avuncular and Jinny saw that Charlotte had married their father.

As soon as the boys were out of earshot, Charlotte asked, 'What's going on with you and Angus?'

'What do you mean, going on? He's on a business trip to the States. He's CEO of the European operation.'

Lack of communication with her sister had made Jinny forgot how clever Charlotte was. Her attempt to cover up was met with a condescending look. 'You've got problems, it's written all over your face.' Jinny's eyes flashed over her head to the beanpole above her. 'Mike, make yourself scarce for half an hour.' He smiled uncomfortably and loped from the room. Bobby sensing a kindred spirit loped after him.

Jinny told her everything, from the night of England's eviction from the World Cup, to New York and back. 'The saddest part of all this has been the twins. They've taken Angus' side.'

'Men stick together,' said Charlotte. 'It's all right for men to go tomcatting but a woman's place is in the home.'

'You never liked Angus.'

'He's not my type,' admitted Charlotte. 'How can you be surprised about his infidelities. He was like it when you met him.'

'You think you're changing them.'

'It's a woman's wildest dream, take my word for it. As time goes by, men and women for that matter just become more of what they are. I have.'

'Don't we learn from our mistakes?'

'I don't think so,' said Charlotte. 'I think we enjoy repeating them just so we can tweak at them, hoping they will work out next time. Then we can become bitter and twisted because things have gone against us.'

'You've become cynical.'

'You think so? I just described our mother. After dad died she had no one else to blame. She sat in a chair and churned up her insides over all the injustices she felt she had suffered.'

'It's the same for me. The boys taking Angus' side is so unjust,' Jinny complained. 'It's not as if I was the instigator like you were.'

'What are you talking about, you poor fool.'

'*Dost thou call me fool?*'

'Lear,' said Charlotte. 'I see you're quoting Shakespeare the same as daddy did. It can't endear you to your friends.'

You knew where the quote came from and had to let me know you knew, the same as you always did. 'How am I a fool?' Jinny asked resentfully.

'I only left Tom when he came out of the closet.'

'Closet?'

'What clues do you need. A son he insisted be named Truman after his hero. Goes to live in Morocco. Tom's gay.'

'No.'

'Yes,' said Charlotte getting up from the chair. 'He's not the only one in the family.' She went out into the hall and returned with a cardboard wallet labelled in large letters, SCHERTZ. She opened the flap, unfolded a sheet of paper and spread it across the table. It was a handwritten genealogy of the Schertz family with untidy arrows pointing every which way.

'Didn't you ever think it was odd how our very English parents had little family. There were mum's sisters and their husbands but that was it. No grandparents, nor did those missing grandparents have brothers or sisters. That never strike you as odd?'

Jinny shook her head, 'Why should it strike me as odd? I didn't know any different.'

'I've been curious about it for years,' said Charlotte searching deeper into the wallet. 'After mummy died, I went through the papers and kept anything that looked worth keeping. I didn't read them at the time. Of course, I forgot about them for months until last Christmas. I found this.' She opened a flimsy birth certificate written in French. 'It seems that our name is not Bull at all, it's Scherz…'

'German.'

'French. Alsace Lorraine. In the 30's our grandparents recognised the Nazi threat and thankfully for us, had the foresight to escape to England.'

'Why thankfully?'

'Let me finish. To cover their tracks they changed their name and became more English than the English.'

'Where did you get this information?'

'This is daddy's birth certificate and this a marriage certificate for our grandparents,' again she unfolded more delicate stained paper. 'The rest I got off the internet. After Hitler came to power the Scherz family moved to Lyon. The reason for this re-location from Alsace was there was a larger Jewish community.'

'Jewish!'

'I have located a relative who returned to Alsace after the war and she sent me this photograph. That's your grandmother and grandfather on their wedding day. The brothers and sisters in the picture are dead. They did not have foresight. Mum has a brother who is still alive and he lives in Antibes. His name is Alain and he's gay.'

'You're joking.'

'No, not at all. Funnily enough Schertz means joke in German but this is totally true. We are Jewish and French. We haven't got a drop of English blood.'

* * *

The party was in full swing and as usual the Parish's overwhelmed the other guests. Gottlieb could not be heard and that was a first for him. Jinny had been allowed a couple of friends, Marcia was still away, which was curious because when she bumped into Hugo and Margery at the Chinese café he said she had just missed her. Margery promised to come but there was no sign of her. She had been offered another guest but she could not invite Andy under any circumstances

She so wanted to tell about Charlotte's news, that her marriage was back on track, and the twins' change of fortune. Charlotte and Michael, lovers of intellectual exercises were pitting their wits against the Parish clan. She was too busy to watch but she hoped for a triumph for the Bulls or Shertz or Shertz's whatever the plural.

She was returning from the garden when she saw Margery looking timidly about her, intimidated as she had been at that impromptu party when Angus got promoted. Margery turned as though about to leave and Jinny had to charge through the throng to head her off.

'Margery,' she touched her shoulder for her to stop. They embraced like long lost friends. 'You look different.'

'I am,' said Margery. 'In more ways than you can imagine.'

'Have you had any more problems with, you know.' She glanced down at her chest.

'No,' said Margery. 'All clear.'

'So much has happened.'

Jinny got Margery a drink and they went to the study and closed the door behind them, the festive racket muffled they were both oddly silent as though silence was reverential.

'Tell me,' said Jinny.

'What?'

'Everything.'

Margery being given the chance she had been waiting for, to tell, was strangely disappointed that suddenly she had a need to save her news for a better and more appropriate time. It was like preparing your favourite meal and then finding you were not hungry after all.

'First you,' said Margery. 'Isn't it wonderful what Andy did for the boys.'

'Andy,' Jinny nodded without understanding but not wanting to look the fool yet again. 'Yes. How did he manage it? I've not been told the full story.'

'You're not seeing him anymore?'

'I had to put my marriage first.'

Margery told what she knew. How Andy used his influence and had explained to the powers that be that the boys results were affected by the possible marriage break up and got permission for them to take a State Scholarship examination to assess if they were Oxbridge material. They both did well enough to get offers dependent on their re-sits.

'I must go,' said Jinny. 'Please cover for me. I'll just speak to Charlotte. Let me introduce you.'

'Your sister Charlotte.'

'The very one.'

Jinny having arranged cover drove to Andy's flat. On the drive over her mind raced, so did the car and was flashed by a speed trap at the bottom of the motorway.

'Why hadn't she been told? What was all the secrecy for? She did not know any Jewish people other than Shylock.'

Let me give light, but let me not be light,
For a light wife doth make a heavy husband.

Arriving outside Andy's flat it occurred to her that his opinion was what she had been debating and Angus' prejudices were of no consequence. Apprehensively she rang the bell, afraid of what he would make of the change.

He was surprised to see her but invited her up. 'You're lucky to catch me.'

'Oh!' she replied. 'You're going away?'

'I'm in the bedroom,' he beckoned for her to follow. 'It's safe.'

There was an open suitcase on the bed and clothes and objects neatly piled ready for packing.

'I need a change of scenery. Can I get you something? Tea, coffee, pregnant.'

His attitude was not as normal. His jokes did not have bravura. He seemed lacklustre and under the weather and making light of it.

'I'm fine. Why do you need a change of scenery.'

'I'm not feeling too well. I've got this ache.'

'Have you seen a doctor?'

'Yes, he says it might be a grumbling appendix. Something's grumbling, he was not too sure what exactly.'

'Is it safe to be going away?'
'Entirely safe.'
'Where are you going?'
'To see my parents. I'm catching the last flight out, I should be leaving for the airport soon.'
'I want to thank you for what you did for Alex and James.'
'You're not supposed to know,' he said sulkily.
'I tricked Margery into telling me.'
'I could do it, so I did it.'
'It was kind...'
'Forget it,' he said laconically. 'I must get going.'
She took his face in her hands, 'You're losing your twinkle.'
'Am I?'
'I've got something more important to tell you. I didn't know who else to tell, so I came to see you. I had a visitor this morning. My sister Charlotte. She found some papers of my parents and not everything is at seems.'
'You're illegitimate.'
'Just one more,' she threatened. 'And I'm going home.'
'Sorry.'
'What would you say if I told you I was Jewish?'
His face remained serious but she could see from his eyes that his response was going to be facetious. In some ways it was a relief, those eyes also told her that it did not matter to him. She told him all that Charlotte had found out.
How the pieces of the puzzle fitted. That extraordinary beautiful colour hair of hers was so obviously continental. He was intrigued that her beauty was born out of this unlikely source.
'Well,' she asked. 'What is that evil mind of yours thinking?'
'So, you're English?'
'Yes.'
'And you're Jewish?'
'Yes.'
'I was wondering,' he said. 'How it feels to be the chosen race twice over.'

CHAPTER FOURTY-THREE

Angus' party

Jinny arrived back at the party without being missed. The sisters had taken charge of the cake and candles. The Parish's could always be relied on to hog the limelight. Angus was tipsy and performing to all and sundry.

On the drive to Andy, she had fluctuated between wonder of his reaction and closure on all that was new in her life. Angus had not had time to listen to Charlotte's news. He needed a nap after his red eye flight and the caterers had arrived just as he awoke.

'You never run my bath like you used to,' he noted.

Having been busy, she was about to make an excuse but said, 'Lots of things I used to do I shan't be doing anymore.' and felt good saying it. 'Our new relationship does not include skivvying.'

She smiled at the recollection.

On the way home after seeing Andy she felt a weird relief. It was like wearing a pair of beautiful new shoes and not taking the precaution of preventing a blister. Now the blister was lanced, the plaster was in place and she could walk with complete freedom. Gosh those shoes looked good and went well with her new dress, new jacket and new underwear. She would give all those old clothes she had thrown off to a worthy cause. The past.

She brushed off the bad things that had occurred in recent weeks and dwelled on all that was good. She cast her mind back to the flight to New York and Andy laying back against the headrest, turning toward her. Without any tangible reason the intimacy of that moment as they faced one another caused her heart to reach the heavens. How lucky she was to have shared such a moment. That wonderful aching want that came later. Desperate to be with someone, sharing intimacy in a real fashion, exerting unselfish pleasures and getting unrivalled pleasure from giving. If it had not been for Angus' lapses she might not have been so lucky.

Charlotte and her husband were the first to leave and Jinny threw her arms about her sister and hugged for all she was worth. 'Jinny, what's got into you?'

Jinny let go and kissed Charlotte lovingly on the cheek in the way that Andy had taught her, 'It is not what's got into me, it's what I have rid myself of.'

'Come and visit. I've put all our details in here.' She handed her an envelope. 'It includes our e-mail address.'

'When are you going home?'

'Wednesday.'

'I'll see you before you go.' Jinny hugged her again. 'Thanks. Thanks for everything.'

Guests dribbled away, Jinny even kissed her mother-in-law as she left but sidestepped her questioning eyes. As the last guest left and the caterers finished clearing away, the twins went to bed and Angus clasped her to him.

'Have we got a deal?' he asked, breathing whisky fumes into her face.

'I promise you an answer in the morning.'

'It's my birthday, you know.'

Jinny understood the implication. She was to vacate the spare room tonight and they were to re-consummate their marriage as they did on all anniversaries.

Jinny had a quick shower and got into bed, luxuriating on being naked amongst clean sheets. She was tired and struggled to stay awake pending Angus' turning in. She dreamed a troubled dream of Andy. He was chasing her and she was evading him at every turn. She kept an appointment at the doctor and he barged into the surgery.

'What are the symptoms,' the doctor asked.

'I ache,' said Andy.

The doctor applied his stethoscope to every part of his body. 'It's not your appendix.'

'I know. It's her.'

Jinny rushed from the surgery and ran all the way home, quickly locking the door behind her. She could hear Andy panting outside. She went upstairs to bed and peeked through the curtains and saw him sitting on the bench in the front garden, his head in his heads and the cat nuzzling his arm to be petted.

Jinny awoke with a start. She thought she had heard stones thrown against the window but assumed it must be part of the dream. The space beside her in the bed was empty. She put on a robe and went downstairs to investigate. Angus was asleep in front of the television snow, head back snoring, drool on his chin and shirt.

She left him to it and went back upstairs. She slipped off the robe and was about to turn out the light and climb back into bed when a foolish impulse made her stop. She peeked through the curtains and there was Andy sitting on the bench. He must have seen the light because he got to his feet and waved.

Jinny rushed down to meet him as naked as the day she was reborn.

* * *

She opened the door and he clasped her to him in a less indulgent way than Angus had earlier. His mouth smelt of spearmint and tasted the same.

'Christ you feel good.'
'How's your appendix?'
'You tell me,' he said.

Epilogue

Andy wandered through the Mall suspecting that he had missed their rendezvous. Nowhere could he see a Next for children. Shopping centres had become so homogenised that you had to struggle to recall your whereabouts and within this homogenisation, except for the name above the entrance, shops had become interchangeable. What was the difference between Vodaphone, O2 or Phones 4U, they all sold much the same products. The same could be said for clothes and shoe shops, all that varied was the price.

He was about to give up the search when he found an old familiar face smiling at him, 'Richard,' they shook hands. 'How long has it been?'

'Four years?'

'At least five.'

'Are you still at St Bryans?'

'Yes, it's changed a lot since you were there.'

So have you Andy decided. In a relatively short time the boy had become a man. Success had quickened the process in the same way that young sportsman mature at a faster rate than average. He expected it was something to do with surviving against the competition.

'I read about the school in the local rag. You've made quite a reputation for yourselves.'

'Not as big as yours. What you doing with all that money you're making.'

'I got married for one,' said Richard. There was something behind the reason for telling him but Andy could not imagine what. 'You're entirely responsible for the whole thing.'

Bemused, Andy could not figure out what was causing him so much amusement. He nodded toward a woman coming out of

Mothercare. The woman had a mass of blonde brown hair fastened up in a clip. Her once troubled face was bright and vibrant. She grasped Richard by the arm and kissed his cheek.

'Look who's here.'

'Andrew.'

'Gill,' said Andy. 'Or do they still call you Mickey?'

'Mrs Morrissey. How's St Bryans?'

'Much the same as ever.'

'What are you doing in Wyford on a Saturday?'

'Margery's wedding.'

'She's not marrying Mr Mason is she? I heard they had a thing.'

'No, she's marrying your successor.'

'Not an NQT, surely.'

'Sort of, a new teacher who was a mature student. He's a really nice man.'

They were interrupted by a small girl grabbing at Andy's trousers, 'Daddy, where have you been? You're not where you're supposed to be.'

'I'm not? Gill and Richard I'd like you to meet Octavia.'

'That's not my name.'

'It will be if you don't quit being so bossy. Tell these people your name.'

'Karen.'

Jinny, struggling to juggle her packages and handbag made slow progress joining them.

'You remember these two.'

'Richard Morrissey and Gill or is it Mickey?'

'Gill.'

'I saw your play. It was really good.'

'Thanks.'

'I love the title, it's so ironic,' Jinny smile disappeared behind uncertainty. 'It was meant to be ironic wasn't it?'

'Yes it was,' Richard was surprised by her query and his eyes lingered.

'I'm not just saying it. It was really good.'

'How's your grandad?'

'He's great. Pop in and see him.'

'I will.'

They separated into that boy, boy, girl, girl conversations that occur when couples meet. The men having exhausted their small talk kibitz or do asides as the women carry on.

'D'you know I was very jealous of you at one time,' admitted Jinny. 'I behaved out of character. I went completely crazy.'

'I can't believe that.'

'It's true.'

'You had nothing to be jealous of.'

'Really.'

'You had twin sons,' said Gill. 'How are they?'

'One's engaged.'

'To a one-legged African lesbian.'

'Andy, stick to your own conversation. I almost wish she was. She's the daughter of a Right Honourable. They met at University and seem to like each other. The other one did a round the world trip and hasn't come back yet.'

'We visited him in Sydney last year. This thing is three years old and has already been around the world.'

'We must go,' said Richard.

'Good to see you both.'

Jinny and Andy watched them leave.

'Well done.'

'For what?' Jinny asked.

'Not quoting, Shakespeare.'

'The title of his play.'

'You know what I mean. Mummy is developing some cool and she might even develop class.'

'Shut up, you silly ass.'

'Yes, silly daddy.'